Praise for

American Duchess

"Harper entices readers with this lively novel about wealthy American heiress Consuelo Vanderbilt. . . . Harper's story highlights how the wealth that prevented Consuelo from making her own decisions also enabled her to better the lives of those less fortunate. This immersive novel believably puts the reader in Consuelo's shoes." —*Publishers Weekly*

"A sweeping history of the Gilded Age, this novel is for fans of historical fiction, PBS's *Downton Abbey,* and the recent royal wedding." —*Library Journal*

"This tender, well-researched novel lets readers see the economic, social, and political highlights of the nineteenth-century Gilded Age brought to life through Consuelo Vanderbilt's eyes."

—*Booklist*

The It Girls

"*The It Girls* is a glorious romp through the lives and loves of the scintillating Sutherland sisters. Karen Harper does a wonderful job of bringing Lucile and Elinor to life in this richly imagined and impeccably researched novel. Readers who enjoy historical fiction are in for a treat!"

—Hazel Gaynor, *New York Times* bestselling
author of *The Girl Who Came Home*

"Fans of Kathleen Tessaro and Penny Vincenzi will enjoy the layers of intrigue and the sweeping plot. Harper's ability to shift between raw ambition and tender compromise makes this family-focused novel a genuine delight." —*Booklist*

The Royal Nanny

"From cozy firesides of country houses to glittering halls of ancestral estates, Karen Harper gives the reader unprecedented access to a world of monarchs. Told through the eyes of an endearing narrator, *The Royal Nanny* is a gem, revealing that those forgotten in history are often the true treasures."

—Erika Robuck, nationally bestselling
author of *Hemingway's Girl*

"Peels back the decades and pulls aside a protective veil of secrecy, helping us understand the forebears of Queen Elizabeth II, including her father, King George VI, of *The King's Speech* fame. A compulsive, page-turning read that reveals both the gilt and the tarnish of the British Royal Crown."

—Sandra Byrd, author of *Mist of Midnight*

"Fans of *Downton Abbey* will devour this vivid tale of one nanny's unwavering love and sacrifices endured for the sake of the royal children in her care. Full of emotion and heart, Lala redefines the meaning of motherhood while Harper gives us a behind-the-scenes look into the lives of the royals."

—Renée Rosen, author of *White Collar Girl*

"This is a beautifully told novel of a woman who was surrounded by all the glitz and glamour of royalty but remained unaffected. . . . Readers will greatly admire the protagonist while learning about the quirks of the royal family and the events that shook the world in the early 20th century."

—Historical Novel Society

The

QUEEN'S
SECRET

Also by Karen Harper

American Duchess
The It Girls
The Royal Nanny

The

QUEEN'S
SECRET

A NOVEL OF ENGLAND'S WORLD WAR II QUEEN

KAREN HARPER

WM

WILLIAM MORROW

An Imprint of HarperCollins*Publishers*

P.S.™ is a trademark of HarperCollins Publishers.

HarperCollins books may be purchased for educational, business, or sales promotional use. For information, please email the Special Markets Department at SPsales@harpercollins.com.

FIRST EDITION

Designed by Diahann Sturge

Library of Congress Cataloging-in-Publication Data has been applied for.

ISBN 978-0-06-288548-7
ISBN 978-0-06-297965-0 (library edition)
ISBN 978-0-06-302770-1 (international edition)

20 21 22 23 24 LSC 10 9 8 7 6 5 4 3 2 1

To Don for his part in all our research trips to England and Europe. Thanks for putting up with museums and stately homes. I couldn't have written my historical novels without you.

A Note on the Royals and Their Names

Although it can be confusing, the names given to the royal children of Queen Victoria, King Edward VII, King George V, and King George VI at their christenings were often different from the names used by their families. This was a family who loved nicknames. And to make things even more confusing, when ascending the throne, they could choose a new name. Hopefully, the following will make navigating the royal family tree a bit easier.

Queen Victoria, the matriarch, deceased before this story begins.

Edward, Prince of Wales, later King Edward VII, son of
    Queen Victoria. Edward, deceased before this story begins,
    was father of George, Duke of York.

Alexandra of Denmark, wife of Edward VII, Princess of
    Wales, mother of George, Duke of York, and grandmother
    of David, Prince of Wales, and Bertie, King George VI.
    Deceased before this story begins.

George, Duke of York, son of Edward and Alexandra, later King George V. Deceased before this story begins.

Mary of Teck, Queen Mary. Widowed in this story. Mother of six York children:

> Edward, called David by his family, popular Prince of Wales, briefly King Edward VIII, and later Duke of Windsor after he abdicated his throne.
>
> Bertie, second son of King George and Queen Mary. King during this story as King George VI. Wed to Queen Consort Elizabeth Bowes Lyon. See her family below.
>
> Mary, only daughter of George and Mary. Not in this story.
>
> Harry, son of George and Mary. Not in this story.
>
> George, son of George and Mary, Duke of Kent. RAF pilot in the war.
>
> John, deceased before this story begins.

Children of King George VI and Queen Elizabeth Bowes Lyon:

> Princess Elizabeth, later Queen Elizabeth II, born 1926.
>
> Princess Margaret Rose, born 1930.

The Bowes Lyon Family in this novel:

> Claude, 14th Earl of Strathmore and Kinghorne, father of Elizabeth Bowes Lyon.

Nina Cecilia Cavendish-Bentinck, recognized mother of Elizabeth and of nine other children, including these mentioned in this story:

Fergus
Rose
Michael
David

The

QUEEN'S
SECRET

Prologue

After all the grand celebrations leading to my one hundredth birthday, I had feared dreadfully that the calendar day itself would be a disappointment. But the streets were lined again with Britain's best, our loyal subjects who had ever loved and bolstered me. And my dear Charles, Prince of Wales, was with his granny once again, my escort, my gift to the future, for I had formed him with love and joy much more than his busy mother or strict father had. So hard to believe he was fifty-one years and single as I had been for so very long—why, nearly half a century.

"Look at the signature here," I told Charles, showing him the telegram that had just been delivered to me on a silver salver by my own footman. We stood at the iron gates of Clarence House ready to board the ceremonial landau for a parade through the park and then back to Buck House, as that old roué King Edward VII had dubbed Buckingham Palace. "Everyone in the kingdom who makes it to this lofty age," I said, "receives such a message from our queen, but not one signed *Lilibet.*"

"Even after seventy-five years in the public eye, you are always queen, mother of a queen—yet just my cheeky granny," he teased. "You know, the *Times* editorial had headlines simply screaming you saved the monarchy from both abdication and invasion. And don't tell me that's mere poppycock."

We had always had such fun together in good times and even bad. Diana had left him five years ago and had died three ago—or was it fifty, for it seemed like forever? But he was deeply in love with the woman I suppose he should have wed from the first, and we shall see how that goes. Ah, to long for one, yet wed another . . . I had done that, more fool me, yearning for the elder, but wedding the younger.

I snapped back to this day and mounted the carriage steps with little help. Bloody good for one born a Victorian, daughter of "only" a Scottish earl and the dearest woman, my real mother. Yes, I always thought of Cecilia that way despite what I knew, despite what that dreadful David and his lowest of the low paramour had ferreted out and said of me—*Cookie! Scottish kitchen Cookie!*

The staff had decorated the carriage with garlands of flowers in blue and buff, my racing colors. It would be a fine day to be at the track, reading the daily racing forms, cheering on my horses, mingling with the jockeys, considering a purchase of new horseflesh with a cocktail in my hand. "Queening," as Bertie used to call it, could be hard work, and the track was one of the places I really let down my hair—ha, short as I kept it now compared to my early days.

As we circled the Victoria Monument, the crowds were thick and loud, many waving little Union Jacks. The Coldstream Guards were mustering inside the palace gates, preparing to play "God Save the Queen" and "Happy Birthday" when we returned. Oh, yes, I'd made them show me the agenda for this day so I could be properly prepared. Always properly prepared . . .

I recognized a cluster of palace staff, ah, then some of my own fifty from Clarence House. Why, there was Bessie Miller, whom I simply could not do without to keep my English complexion absolute perfection during the war, and even now in my dotage.

I waved back, smiling, nodding as the cheering clusters of people blurred by. Many waved with that dreadful American wrist flap, so unlike what I had learned from Bertie's mama, Queen Mary. More elegant to simply lift one's arm and slightly rotate the hand, she had said—said that and so much more.

The thickest clumps of the crowd were no doubt waiting for my balcony appearance later with Elizabeth, Philip, and the rest of the family, even dear William and Harry, restless teenagers both, one to be king someday. But in my mind, I saw that day we knew we had won the war when I was queen and Bertie was there, Winston too—victory! "We want the king! We want the queen!" it seemed all of London had chanted eternally.

"They love you, Granny, and always will." Charles leaned close to shout in my ear.

"And I them. Through thick and thin, forever."

I smiled and waved more, always had. I meant it too, though some had said I merely put it on, that I was plastic, even conniving. Well, that hellhound Herr Hitler had not called me "the most dangerous woman in Europe" for nothing, for Bertie and I—Winston too—stood up to him. We won, though the fight was bloody and, partly thanks to that damned David and that common adventuress wife of his, it was near disaster for Bertie—for us.

I blinked back tears and kept smiling. As we made the trip round St. James's Park and back down the Mall, I saw youngsters throwing a shower of confetti. I nodded and lifted my hand to them, but suddenly I was seeing another day, one with tall buildings and those strong, shouting Americans when Bertie and I rode through that storm of ticker tape in New York City. In a way that trip to Canada and America was the beginning of our work in the war, but it was the making of us too.

Oh, yes, Bertie did his duty—did his brother David's duty too, the coward, the deserter. Why that partly caused my beloved husband's death! I am glad David went into exile with that woman. After all, though I came to all this the hard way, it was my destiny to marry Bertie; love came later—as did all of this, what was behind us and, for me, some remaining days to live, to love, and to remember.

CHAPTER ONE

The Making of Us

9 June 1939

The noise of the whooping crowd, which was estimated to be between three and four million, echoed off the New York skyscrapers, nearly deafening us that Friday. Out windows high above our motorcar, people threw ticker tape, even long spools of it. Riding backward with us were Herman Lehman, the governor of New York State, and the city's chatty mayor, Fiorello La Guardia, and we were heading for the World's Fair in Queens—rather an appropriate-sounding place for me to visit, I thought.

Though the weather was absolutely ghastly at 36 Celsius in the shade with stupendous humidity, I refused to wilt. At least Bertie had worn a conservative business suit and not his woolen, heavily medaled Navy dress uniform. I wore a plain blue crepe dress and cape with a hat sporting high ostrich plumes, which tended to snag ticker tape. How I wished I could shake off our problems as easily as I shrugged off all that paper.

We had already spent a day with President and Mrs. Roosevelt in Washington, a meeting of minds that had gone quite well with talk of possible war with Hitler and even with Italy. But we had relaxed on the presidential yacht on the Potomac to Mount Vernon, where Bertie had placed a wreath on Washington's grave. That grand man might have led his neophyte nation against us British, but we admired him—and to think he had turned down becoming king. And now, instead of a historical enemy, Franklin saw us and dear Britannia as a bulwark against Fascism and Hitler, and we were hoping, if worse came to worst, that America would be our ally.

The mayor, indeed, was quite a card. He was of obvious Italian heritage and evidently popular. Our briefing papers had noted that he had helped to end corruption, hated gangsters, and was not Catholic but Episcopalian. He had a round face and slicked-back dark hair. Each time he spoke with his high-pitched, squeaky voice, I had to be careful not to startle. My dear younger brother had talked like that to make people laugh when we played at charades or the two of us put on a bit of a play. At least this man's voice carried above the roar of the crowds.

"I must tell Your Majesties," he said, "I've been an early critic of that madman Hitler for five years at least—from the first, yes, from the very first. I had a Jewish mother who spoke mostly Yiddish, and Hitler can't hide what he's doing to her people. Locking them up, thieving from them at the very least."

"So we have learned," Bertie said. He was tired and looked it, so I kept smiling and waving for both of us at times.

Leaning a bit toward the mayor yet trying not to look as if I slumped, I raised my voice to say, "We have learned through French channels that you are quite right to be concerned. You see, when we were in Paris I—we—had a well-placed source who said the same, so we are not deceived on that point, Your Honor."

Oh, yes, I had met in the privacy of the couturier Lanvin's fitting room with Léon Blum, the former prime minister of France, when we were last there. I spoke excellent French and understood fully what that Jewish man had warned me about that was happening to the Jews in Europe within Nazi reach.

I had been horrified and outraged not only at the information I passed on to Bertie and our government, but by hearing later the rumor that I was having an affair with Blum. Quite ridiculous, though it was sadly common for some women to meet their lovers amidst the muslin cutouts during a fitting for their new gowns. Why, Blum was nearly thirty years my senior, and I would never be unfaithful to the king. But now I was upset to hear the mayor bring up another topic I had rather not hear on this day of days.

"Rather a setback, then, when the former king—your brother, sir," La Guardia said with a nervous nod Bertie's way, "went to visit Hitler in Germany two years ago with his new wife on an official visit. Rather well-received they were too."

"Not in Great Britain. Not to our liking," Bertie said.

That might be dismissive, but I was proud of how decisive he sounded, with hardly hesitations or stutters anymore unless he was terribly provoked.

"Dreadful and entirely counterproductive," I put in. "Sad to say, the former king wanted to give his wife a place to be treated like the royal she was most certainly not, and that was the double folly of it. Ghastly," I added under my breath and felt my stomach tighten as ever when talk or memories of that woman arose.

I returned to waving and smiling, hoping that was the end of that topic. It was a shame and a scandal that David, alias the former King Edward VIII, and that common adventuress he had married, had toadied up to Hitler, however thoroughly German Queen Victoria's family had been. They were once known as the Saxe-Coburgs and Gothas but had renamed themselves the Windsors during the Great War. Oh, indeed, I could grasp the sad ties to the Huns. But that was in the past. The Germans had made war on us in the "war to end all wars" and might well do so again, but not if I had any say in the matter, and I intended to. Those damned Huns had killed my dear brother Fergus in the "war to end all wars," and I'd do anything I could to avenge his horrible death.

And so I waved and smiled some more.

* * *

After all the public bustle, demands, and humid heat heat heat, Bertie and I greatly appreciated our visit to the Roosevelt home in Hyde Park, New York. It was cooler here, along the Hudson River, shaded, quiet, and private. It reminded me of many a middling-sized country home in Kent or even dear Scotland. We were to stay a night and a day here. Bertie and the president spent some time alone, and I could tell Bertie liked him.

"Advice like from a father," he whispered to me, though, thank the Lord, Franklin Roosevelt was night and day from Bertie's overbearing and critical father, King George V, who had caused so much of my husband's early physical and emotional distress. "Didn't make one feel nervous at all," he added as we joined the Roosevelts outside under huge trees for what they deemed a picnic lunch. It was after our attending the service at the nearby Episcopal church, where I had felt quite at home.

Just wait until I told Lilibet and Margot about this picnic, I thought. I couldn't wait for our reunion with our girls next week. But now, plates on laps, one plate with the entire meal except for drinks and dessert! And what the Yanks called "hot dogs," which I had to force myself to eat because they reminded me of one of David's passions when he was Prince of Wales. He craved anything American, however borderline barbaric, including fast, slim, cigarette-smoking, and mostly married women.

The president had invited his elderly mother, Sara, the family matriarch, to join us. Because of the president's paralyzed legs, his male attendant helped him from his wheelchair into a high-backed seat, then handed him his tray and drink. Despite our lack of goblets and champagne, the president led a toast to the health of Bertie's mother, the widowed Queen Mary, and then launched into a toast to his own mother.

"She has been a real mother to me all these years, and I love her dearly," he said, and went on at some length.

The glass in my hand began to tremble, nearly to slosh the white wine. *A real mother to me . . . all these years . . .* How desperately I missed my own mother, the light of my early life, who had died just last year before our trip to France. *A real mother to me . . . all these years . . .*

* * *

"Dearest, do come inside for a wee talk," my father, the Earl of Strathmore and Kinghorne, called to me that summer evening at Glamis Castle nearly on the eve of my seventeenth birthday.

Glamis was the grand ancestral seat of the hereditary Strathmore earls, and we were proud of it as the place where Shakespeare had set his tragedy *Macbeth*. Sir Walter Scott had visited and used it in his novels—more delightful reading than that murderous play where Lady Macbeth had blood on her hands.

"Is David coming too?" I asked, referring to my dear brother, two years younger than I. David and I were especially close, for our other eight siblings were older. A space of seven years stretched between them and us, such a long gap it seemed.

"No, just you for now. David later," he said with that distinctive Scottish burr he proudly flouted even when others of the Scottish aristocracy tried to sound as English as possible.

My mind spun back to what I could have done wrong, not that it fretted me. David and I were loved and coddled, corrected when need be but never really punished. Mother darling often referred to me as "Darling Elizabeth," so our love and respect was mutual. I knew we were cherished here on the extensive grounds or at our smaller, charming estate in Hertfordshire at St. Paul's Walden Bury. I had enjoyed a lovely, happy childhood, roaming the grounds, playing games and charades at night, spending warmhearted winters before the crackling fireplace.

But since we still had some wounded soldiers here at Glamis Castle recovering from shell shock and injuries, did he think I had flirted overmuch with them when I tried to make them feel at home? After all, when a fire broke out without Mother on the premises, I had helped get everyone out and oversaw the firemen when they arrived.

Oh, Mother was sitting in Papa's study too when I stepped in. I sat tight next to her on the velvet settee. Such a kindly, beautiful, and fun mother, and I longed to be just like her. She read to us, made certain we were not overtaxed by our governess or tutors, took us on walks in the park, applauded, laughed, and—

"Since you are old enough now, nearly quite the grown lady . . ." my father began, sitting across from us in his favorite horsehair chair, "and will attend your first ball soon—where, by the way, I hope they do not do that wretched foxtrot."

"Now, my dear Claude," Mother put in. "It's all the rage for the younger set."

"If you wish to take this over, my dearest," he said with a narrow look at her, but also a wink—for they were quite the love match—"I shall hold my peace."

"No, you start," she said.

The tension and suspense hovering in the room was so unfamiliar that I began to tremble. Mother must have seen that, for she reached over and covered my hands, clasped in my lap. How

I wished I looked exactly like her, with her oval face and light arched eyebrows. Yet I was too proud to pluck my heavy ones, and I did resemble her a bit, didn't I?

Father cleared his throat. "As you know, our darling daughter," he said, "we gave you the sobriquet 'our angel' because you are that to us. Dearly beloved, you and David both."

"Just as you love the others," I put in. "Even dearest Violet and Fergus, who are gone—gone to heaven."

"Yes. Yes, of course, lass. You see, we have loved having and rearing children."

"Of course," Mother said, "all of you, but I suppose one tends to cling to and cherish the last—the youngest ones the most."

Papa gave her another narrow look. "So we feel it is time to explain to you," he went on, clearing his throat, "and we will to David too—that after we could have no more children and wanted more, we decided something."

Mother said in the awkward silence, "Because there were complications with the last births, Rose and Mike, and I could bear no more children."

"So," Papa said, "it is not one whit untoward—that is, not done, that—ah—"

He looked as if he would have a winter coughing fit, when it was quite fine weather. Mother turned to me and said, "It is a done thing that if a happy couple—a solid family—would like more children, they can talk it over and decide to have the father go into a good woman who agrees to bear a child and then give that child—children—to the family to rear."

"I am adopted?" I gasped. "David too?"

My stomach fell to my knees. True, I was not the best of students, but had I been so dense not to know—to sense—this? Even tutored, I had failed an important exam the first time I took it—damn that beastly test! But I—this woman—I adored and . . .

I didn't cry but clamped my hand over my mouth and bent over as if I would be sick. But Mother—was she still my mother?—pulled me up and into her arms while Papa came to sit on my other side.

"You and David are more ours than the others, because we chose to have you!" Mother said with her mouth pressed against my mussed hair along my temple. "Have we ever given you one moment to feel you are not ours in head and heart?"

"So I am of Father's blood, but not yours?"

"You are of his blood and of my heart, and what could matter more than that?" she asked and squeezed me so tight I could barely breathe.

Finally, after a moment, I hugged her back, my arms tight around her waist, my face buried against her shoulder. Oh, I knew enough of the birds and bees to figure out what they meant.

"We love you, our angel, and always will," Papa said and patted me on the back.

I knew enough of my Bible to realize why I had overheard, more than once, some of our Bowes Lyon relations refer to David and me as "the Benjamins." After all, Benjamin was the dearly beloved and youngest of his father's and Rachel's children and had many older half brothers.

I amazed myself by not exploding into hysterics, though I did still hold hard to Mama as I asked, my voice quite calm, "Then was my birth mother, so to speak, one of the maids?"

But even as I asked that, I knew the answer. How often at Walden Bury had the French cook Marguerite Rodiere smiled at me and David and offered us a sweet or some sugary-topped Scottish shortbread when it seemed the others must wait for mealtime? How she had looked so longingly at me and smoothed my hair and once tenderly washed my scraped knee, then darted off when Mother came into the kitchen.

Mother said now, "We tell you all this, dearest daughter, before you begin to move in public and social circles beyond our family. There will be friends, dances, courtship, perhaps with highly respected and noble beaus. It is a secret we—and you—must guard because others might not understand that it was a mutual decision between your parents who love you very, very much and always will."

"And as you young people say," Papa put in with a hand on my shoulder, "ain't we got fun as a family—mutual love too? As Mama says, you and David are just as much ours—actually more—by choice—than any other child. And yes, your birth mother is Marguerite from Walden Bury."

I nodded, still feeling a bit shell-shocked. Yet I loved these people and wanted to make all this easier for them. "So, no wonder I took to speaking French—you said I did. I was glad to have a governess who taught me German, but isn't French so much prettier?"

Evidently grateful I was taking the news so well, they embraced me between the two of them. Papa said, "We wanted you, and, in a way, chose you, and that's that. Keep it close to your heart, guard that heart well, our dearest. You are Lady Elizabeth Bowes Lyon, daughter of the Earl of Strathmore and Cecilia Cavendish-Bentinck, your mother who sits right here, and never forget that. It changes nothing!"

But somehow, I knew it had changed—and could change—so much.

CHAPTER TWO

The Last Dance

"Can you pick out their launch amidst all this watercraft?" I asked Bertie. We leaned over the railing of the steamship *Empress of Britain* as we sailed into Yarmouth Bay on the Isle of Wight, nearly home. Lilibet and Margaret Rose, whom we called Margot, were to be brought out in a launch to travel the rest of the way with us, though that would only be the last two hours of our five-day homeward journey from our Canadian-American tour.

"Don't see them yet, but glorious weather. Reminds me of my best Royal Navy days. My dearest, we have missed a lovely holiday summer by going on our tour, but it was important business."

Bertie covered my hand with his on the rail. Despite the swarm of small boats close below, I kissed his cheek. Dear man, never really far or free from the burdens of the kingdom, even at sea. At luncheon today, he had admitted he loathed going home to all the talk of possible war and having to deal with powerful men like Churchill who refused to believe "peace in our time" with the Germans was possible.

"Damn, but I still like and trust Prime Minister Chamberlain," Bertie groused, picking up on his fretting even now. "I know rabble-rousers like Churchill expect war, but Der Führer signed the dratted Munich Agreement, didn't he?"

"I told you, I don't believe Hitler and his Huns are to be trusted."

"But did Churchill have to carry on with his usual loquacious, high-flying oration? He said something like, this is the first foretaste of a bitter cup which will be proffered to us year by year unless we arise again and take our stand for freedom as in the olden time. War! He means war after the devastation—albeit victory—of the war to end all wars, and with the bloody Germans again!"

"That is frightening, my dearest. The man does have a way with words, but then so do you these days. Your unease and hesitation problems with speaking are far behind you. Mark my words, the speech you have prepared for our people about our new bonds with Canada and the United States will smooth things over and warn the Germans."

"But the latest privy news I had is that our people are going to the beach with baskets of food and gas masks—*gas masks*—just in case!"

I put my arm around his waist and held him tight. "The thing is, Hitler knows we will fight. And as an island nation we have the sea to keep him off so he can't just march in like he did to his nearby nations. Yes, I detest him too—hate the Huns—but—"

I stopped and pointed. "There! There they are, waving, ready to come aboard! Oh, Bertie, look how much taller Lilibet is, however short for her thirteen years! And our little Margot, almost nine, and we shall have such a birthday for her. Lilibet! Margot! Darlings! Oh, look, Bertie, they have brought one of the corgis!"

I quite forgot the royal wave I had so cultivated. How I loved them, our precious princesses. I hated to leave them to go off on official duties like this, however important to the Empire. Why, I'd left our heir Elizabeth for six months when she was an infant, and had vowed never, never again to be away that long. I could not wait to hug our girls.

* * *

"Mummy, I have so much more to say than when we talked on the transatlantic telephone line," Lilibet told us, sounding terribly grown-up, when we finally got through our initial hugs and greetings. "Crawfie says we are both doing awfully well on our history reading."

"She is not working you too hard during the summer, is she?" I asked. I had had words with Marion Crawford, their nanny and governess, more than once about "all work and no play makes Jack a dull boy." I insisted my girls be brought up observing life, not just studying facts ad infinitum.

Margot said, "Sometimes on gardens walks, we go over almost everything we read and recited in the morning. A bloody lot of review."

"Margaret Rose, do not say 'bloody,'" her father insisted. "That's men's talk."

Our younger daughter was perched on his knee. As much as

he loved Lilibet, little Margot was much more demonstrative. Why didn't he see that Lilibet was more like him, dutiful and worried she'd get things wrong? At bedtime, she even lined up her shoes neatly for the next morning, whereas Margot was more devil-may-care, even tried wearing a favorite pair of shoes to bed to save time and fuss the next day. Ah, but we loved them both dearly and spoiled them as best we could—even as I had been spoiled and poor Bertie most certainly had not.

As much as I admired Queen Mary for her advice and help, she had hardly been a doting mother to him or her other children. Sometimes I thought the way Bertie described her when he was growing up reminded me of that dreadful, twice-wed American woman whom David, Prince of Wales, had so desperately fallen for. And as for Bertie's father—batten down the hatches for a hard, icy blow.

With our girls at our side and the corgi wrapping his leash around the king's legs, we sailed homeward bound, waving over the railing at yachts and other boats with our dear people cheering us on. Bertie began to sing "Under the Spreading Chestnut Tree" with all the silly motions that went with the lyrics until he had both girls aping him and laughing. We segued into the sprightly "The Lambeth Walk" with its strutting steps, slapping our thighs amidst a gale of giggles.

"I say," Bertie put in, out of breath, "if we just had a gramophone here, we could practice a bit more and take to the road on tour!"

Finally, Crawfie came out for the girls, and we sent them inside to spiff up and prepare to disembark with us.

"If they call for us to appear on the palace balcony later

today," Bertie told me, breathing hard with both hands on the rail, "we'll all four go out. I regret that we stood out there smiling with Chamberlain, touting 'peace in our time.' I fear now it was a dreadful mistake to align myself with him on that. And to think the crowds below kept singing '*For he's a jolly good fellow*,' whether they meant him or their king! But I do not want Churchill forming a government and calling at the palace all the time to urge we must get into another damned war!"

"We may have no choice," I told him, taking his arm and giving it a squeeze. "Bertie, if we have war—real war—God forbid—we will weather it together, all of us," I insisted and swept my hand as if to encompass the crowds waiting below and our many subjects far beyond these docks. I went on, my voice quiet, almost reverent, "Sometimes I wonder if we are not already fighting a war, one of love and right against the forces of evil. Come on, then, Your Majesty, let's take the train to Waterloo where your mama awaits and then take our girls home."

"I need you, my beloved, and always have," he said, turning to me with tears in his eyes and a trembling lower lip as we went inside together.

* * *

"Oh, ma'am," said Bessie Miller, one of my closest private servants, in her sprightly Cockney accent, "just see if your fair skin didn't bounce right back from all that heat we had in the States." She held up my silver-backed looking glass, so I could view my face more closely. "Over there, thought I'd took a bath before I took one, that Yankee humidity and all!"

Still red-haired and freckled and quite devoted to my service, Bessie had been with me nearly since I'd wed Bertie sixteen years ago. Then we were the Duke and Duchess of York and thought we would remain so, far from the crown. Though Bessie could trim my hair in a pinch if we were on tour, her greatest contribution these years had been her overseeing of my complexion and bathing. I never used soap on my face but rather Cold Cream of Roses mixed to perfection by Malcolm Macfarlane in his pharmacy in Forfar, near my beloved childhood home of Glamis Castle. He had sent me a jar of it for my wedding, and Bessie and I had never used aught else on my skin.

My dewy, youthful complexion had been remarked on far and wide. I must admit I was rather privately proud of it, even at age thirty-nine. Bessie always said it made my violet eyes stand out. As for my hands, the girl—well, now a woman of thirty-six—used a secret blending of warm rose water with crushed almonds followed by a hand cream of oatmeal, rose water, and lard. No matter, I always tried to tell myself, that women like David's adored Yankee were thin as boards and I was a bit more rounded. Bertie was keen on me just the way I was, however much his older brother mooned over the skinnier types. And could I help it if I had a healthy Scottish appetite and adored Scottish shortbread, lots of chocs, and drinkie poos?

"There, a touch of powder and perfume and you are ready for the dancing, ma'am," Bessie said, stepping back to survey her work as if I were a piece of art. She was a staff member with whom I was on more familiar terms than most. She was a dutiful daughter, one who had never wed but kept close to her siblings and parents, and I admired that.

"Awfully quick notice for Their Majesties to pop in like this, but I know everything will go right well," she told me as she gathered her tray of cosmetics, curtsied, then backed toward the door before turning away. "You never leave one detail unturned, not you."

I pondered that as I was decked out in my jewelry by Catherine Maclean, my dresser, a faithful Scottish friend from near Glamis. A bit anxious, I did not wait for Bertie to knock but stood in the carpeted corridor of the palace, since our bedrooms and sitting area were a good fifteen paces apart.

The Prince and Princess of Yugoslavia were our guests for a ball tonight, with nearly eight hundred accepting our hastily delivered invitations. It promised to be a lovely event, but I felt I could read the dire handwriting on the wall of old Europe. This might indeed be the last social hurrah, not only for the season, but for the season of peace. So as soon as this gala night was over, we were taking our daughters and heading for a last holiday on the royal yacht before . . . well, before dreaded difficulties could begin.

At first, I had pictured just sailing off into the sunset to escape the looming tough times and my own fears—Bertie's too, of course. But we were king and queen, and there was no escaping the battle to come. I feared Mr. Churchill was right and Chamberlain wrong. And as we prepared to enter the ballroom with our honored royal guests, every step mattered, for everyone was always watching.

* * *

Two days after the lovely ball—everyone stayed up till all hours as we danced the night away as if no storm clouds were looming—the king and I set out with our girls on the royal yacht *Victoria and Albert* for a short holiday. Bertie was in his element, for we visited the Royal Naval College at Dartmouth where he had studied, though when assigned to ships at sea, his digestive problems had led to surgery and long periods of convalescence.

The five hundred cadets gave us a rousing welcome and rolled with laughter when their king astounded and amused them all—me and the girls too—by reading from a mocked-up College Punishment Book of all the rules he'd broken while a cadet here. I was so happy that the king, whom so many saw as shy and serious, could show them the fun-loving side his family knew.

But where had Lilibet gone? I looked around again. Margot was chatting with two cadets who had been kind enough—or perhaps had been assigned—to entertain a young girl, but Lilibet?

Then I saw her behind us, off the rostrum, smiling at and chatting with a young, blond cadet who towered over her. At this distance, for one moment, it was almost as if I didn't know my serious daughter, as if I observed a much older lass. When Bertie and I left the dais, I whispered to him, "Whoever is that man Lilibet is speaking with?"

"Fear not, keeper of the keys," he said, taking my elbow and glancing over at our eldest. "Not simply some rogue or lay-about, I assure you. I spoke to him earlier. That's Prince Philip of Greece, a cadet here now. I dare say you remember hearing of all his family woes."

"Oh, yes, that's right. We met him at the Duke of Kent's wedding several years ago. A handsome lad."

"Hardly a lad anymore and quite older than Lilibet, but she seems to have taken to him today."

I wanted to work my way over to her, snag her back, but we were pulled away by our hosts again. Bertie had teased me about the short, secret list I kept of eligible young men of the English nobility, for I had privately vowed that I was never going to follow in Queen Victoria's footsteps, marrying my beloved children off to distant royalty, I don't care one whit if it abetted foreign relations. Besides, the kaiser of Germany had been a cousin to King George, and did that stop the war to end all wars? But I did recall that this Prince Philip of Greece had rather a patchy background.

I remembered now. He was the nephew of King Constantine of Greece, though he was also distantly related to the British royals through one of Queen Victoria's many granddaughters, who lived now in Kensington Palace. He had a spate of older sisters somewhere, and his parents had fled his homeland after Greek rebels had sentenced his father to death. Philip might be a prince, but he would inherit no throne and obviously had made England his home.

I also remembered that his parents had parted ways, and his mother had some sort of mental problems. Well, indeed, the Royal Navy could soon send Philip far away. After all,

Elizabeth—dear heavens, I could hear her giggle from here—was entirely too young and inexperienced for that—for him. Surely, nothing would come of it, though I could not claim the same confidence about the encroaching threats of war.

We had been informed that, back in London, the cabinet had met for a long session and Prime Minister Chamberlain had recalled Parliament, despite the summer hiatus. It had not been made public, but the king was going straightaway back to London while the girls and I were heading for a respite in Scotland. For once, I did not feel I would be at ease and content in the arms of my homeland. If worse came to worst, we would not stay long but hurry to be back with the king in London to face whatever might come our way.

"Oh, Mummy," Lilibet said when the cadets filed out and she finally came back to my side, "isn't it just lovely here?"

She was blushing. Her eyes were glowing. She bounced a bit when she walked.

"It's been a very nice visit," I managed and shooed her and Margot out ahead of me, following their father.

But why, oh, why, did I recall at that moment how I felt the night I had first danced twice with Bertie's brother, David, Prince of Wales, so long ago? I'd had to fight to keep from grinning that evening. As much as I loved to dance and was adept at it, I had almost stumbled over my own feet when he'd asked for that second foxtrot and then a third dance—a romantic waltz.

And then, as if to whet my silly, girlish passions and hopes, that dreadful London newspaper *The Daily Star* had dared to print the gossip that the unnamed daughter of a Scottish peer would soon wed the Prince of Wales. They meant me, and I was so shaken, not only because it was a lie, and some thought I or my family had released the news, but because I had actually wished it to be so. And then he had turned out to be the traitor of all time!

Holding both my daughters' hands as we walked toward where our yacht was moored, I felt myself blush at the mere memory. Although I'd been wretchedly embarrassed, Father had only been amused and Mother assured me it would not do my reputation one bit of harm. And later, Bertie, even when I'd already turned down his proposal of marriage twice, had never mentioned it. Nor, thank God, had it deterred his avid pursuit of me.

Lilibet broke into my thoughts, nearly skipping along at my side while Margot, for once, was so much more subdued. "Mummy, wasn't Prince Philip of Greece absolutely the most charming and handsome man there?"

"Come along then," I said and gave her hand a tug. "We're off straightaway to Scotland, far away from foreign cadets, even ones who have made England their home."

CHAPTER THREE

Ghosts and Monsters

One golden August afternoon at Glamis, I mounted my favorite mare Forfar, and Lilibet and Margot rode quite easily on their ponies. Four men from our mews rode behind, one the girls' Scottish riding master. After a lovely picnic at the edge of the forest, we cantered back on the long drive toward the turreted castle. Although we were having a fine time, my heart was with the king in London, for he had written that the international situation was deteriorating.

"Mummy, I've something serious to ask you," Lilibet said and, excellent rider that she was already, reined in her horse a bit so I pulled back too. Hoping it was not more about Prince Philip, I nodded my encouragement. Margot, a bit of a daredevil, went on ahead with her riding master hurrying to catch up with her.

"It's about the monster of Glamis," Lilibet said, her face and voice so serious. "I overheard some of the kitchen staff, a cook said—"

"You are not to bother any of the cooks, my dear. Those kitchens just breed gossip."

"I wasn't bothering them. They gave me some scones and milk for Margot and me. You said the cooks used to do that for you, but maybe that wasn't here but at Walden Bury, so—"

"What about the monster of Glamis?" I prompted before she could go off on that tangent. "You know all self-respecting, old estates—especially a castle—must have stories of ghosts and monsters. Most of them are mere poppycock only to please tourists and keep children up at night until their parents tell them that they are mostly mere fairy tales."

"But I must ask. Is it true that back years ago one of our ancestors here at Glamis bore a terribly disfigured child and the family hid him in a kind of a bricked-up room until he died years later, and the word got out it was a terribly deformed monster?"

"Perhaps there was some birth defect, but nothing dire like that. Dearest, electric lighting was only installed here ten years ago, so you can imagine how the shadows and darkness bred rumors—ghostly and ghastly, but untrue."

"But I overheard that, in later years, someone of the Bowes Lyon family had servants hang a towel or cloth in each window of the castle, but when they looked from the outside, there were spaces where certain windows had no cloth—and that area would be where the bricked-up monster rooms were, but no one could find them from inside," she said in one breathless rush.

"Lilibet—Elizabeth—people love stories like that, to dwell on the frightening and dreadful, even if untrue, and that is all. I thank you for asking this of me without your sister being all ears, for she is sometimes excitable as is."

"But in a family that had a former lady of the castle burned at the stake for witchcraft . . . I mean, someday, when I marry, I actually would not like my husband to know all that—such a terrible thing in the past of my family. Why, it might make him hesitate to propose."

I almost laughed. If anything would make a man hesitant to propose to our eldest someday, it would be that she would be queen and he not more than a prince, walking several steps behind her. Still, what she had said hit me hard, not so much that she was actually thinking of a future marriage at her age—and no doubt with that Greek prince again. But she had reminded me of how I'd hidden my birth mother from everyone, including Bertie, or at least that was my continual prayer despite David and that woman somehow uncovering that fact and taunting me with the nickname *Cookie*. I had no illusions that their intent was to shame and threaten me, for that gibe went deeper than referring again to my fondness for bakery goods and all sorts of sweets.

"This is not like you," I told Lilibet, trying to keep my temper in check. "Not a bit like our sensible, reasonable daughter and someday queen to be sorry for such things—rumors and legends. Royalty must rise above superstitions and curses with ghosts, monsters, and the like. The only monster we all need to worry about lives in Berlin and is named Adolf Hitler. And I must tell you I am planning to take the night train to London to be with your father in all this talk of war, so I will leave you two with Crawfie and the staff here—but that does not include the kitchen help from whom you might hear silly rumors, my dearest."

"Yes, Mummy. Well, you know, even with the electric in the castle, some parts of Glamis still seem very dark and frightening at night."

I reached over to pat her shoulder as we jogged into the massive shadow of the castle. "I understand, Lilibet, really I do. But Glamis, just like Buckingham Palace, is a place of light and warmth and love, because we are a strong family. I am happy you asked me about those rumors, really I am, and I am so grateful we can be honest with each other in all things."

Almost all things, I thought, as we jogged a bit faster to rejoin Margot. Because I had told no one—not even Bertie—that one of the major reasons I was rushing to London was because he had noted in a postscript to his last letter that there had been discussions amongst parliamentary leaders like Chamberlain and Churchill about David and that woman coming back to England in case there was a war, so the Germans would not get their hands on them in Europe.

I saw David as a dangerous deserter, one who might even have conspired with Hitler, during their trip to Germany, to replace my Bertie should the Germans bomb or invade Britain. I would bide my time for now about insisting that the Duke and Duchess of Windsor remain in permanent exile, but I must find a way to keep my hand in all those decisions. For to have that American adventuress even on English soil again, let alone queen . . . Never!

I tried to stem the flood of memory from the time I first saw her true, cruel colors, her disdain for Bertie and me. We were still the Duke and Duchess of York then and trying to keep up a relationship with the future king. We had gone to Fort Belvedere, David's refuge near Windsor Castle, where he entertained his sophisticated friends and more or less held social court with that woman as his hostess. Wallis in Wonderland, I had heard some courtiers had called her. His parents disapproved of it all, but what was that to him? The man was absolutely besotted.

Bertie loved his older brother, for they'd been through thick and thin together in their boyhood years. Their father had been sarcastic and brutally critical, and it had damaged them both, though in different ways. They had three other brothers who had been harangued with his insistence on perfection and taken his wrath too. The last son, John, had died young, and the other two had tried to cope in their own ways. The brother who was now Duke of Kent had rebelled with drinking, drugs, and wild affairs, so all had been damaged somehow. But, even if we were loved, weren't we all?

At any rate, I put up with that woman David adored and later married, but that night when we walked in, we clearly heard her entertaining some of their female, so-called steamer set with an imitation of how I walked, swaying a bit. She stuck her bum out and feigned to wear a fussy hat.

"Old-fashioned and dowdy—the dowdy duchess!" she laughingly dubbed me. "I swear, she might as well be wearing a fancy sofa cover most of the time. Dreadful clothes in an attempt to hide a too-full chassis," she crowed amongst peals of laughter from the group.

I was absolutely appalled at the public mockery, and Bertie was too, though we were quickly greeted by David, as if to block out the tittering, slender, supposedly fashionable women across the room. She did not have the decency to look one bit ashamed, though she avoided me the rest of that dreadful evening. My dear Bertie swept me away as soon as he could and said nothing of it all but "I love you just as you are, my d-dearest."

"And he loves her just as she is, evidently."

"He's b-bewitched, not himself."

"I fear he is very much himself. You know, it has nothing to do with that woman's spiteful statements, but I have been thinking of changing designers. Norman Hartnell has done some lovely day dresses and gowns lately."

"I'm s-sure you would look smashing in any of them."

"But perhaps not at the fort again. I'll not have her thinking she's won if I change designers."

"I f-fear—f-fear," he'd said, stuttering as he did if he was distressed or distraught. He swallowed hard and went on, "In our family war, Wallis, twice married as she is, believes she has won. But she'll n-n-never be accepted, never marry David and be queen."

"Never say never," I said, too late realizing I'd spoken aloud here at Glamis and that both Lilibet and Margot were staring at me.

"What was that, Mummy?" Lilibet asked as we dismounted.

"Just hoping we do not go to war, my darlings. Never."

* * *

I traveled back and forth between Buckingham Palace and Glamis, always taking the night train with our private car. I must admit I liked that timing, because the Scottish conductor knew I might be a bit tardy and always waited for me. Yes, I might move slowly and savor each moment and person, but was that so bad? Being late was a sad habit I had never tamed, but Bertie just smiled, and even his irascible father approved of my calming effect on my husband's nervous temperament enough to put up with me. Early in our marriage, when I made Bertie and myself slightly late for a luncheon at the palace, I had apologized to the family.

To everyone's amazement and Bertie's elation, rather than the usual lecture and scolding, King George said to me, "You are not too late, my dear. I believe we have sat down two minutes too early."

Bertie beamed with relief and joy. The rest of the family and our closest friends also credited me with a calming effect on my stuttering husband. Now Bertie tripped over his words only when he was completely distressed, and seldom in public.

I believed Bertie's father, His Majesty, also forgave my foible of being late because he credited me for seeking the professional help of a therapist for that speech impediment that had shamed Bertie since childhood. His stuttering brought his father's wrath down on his head more than once, which I felt only made the situation worse. I can recall the king shouting, shortly after we were married, "Speak up, boy! Get it out. Get it out right and right now!"

I had even accompanied Bertie to all his therapy sessions with our now dear friend Lionel Logue in 1926 and 1927, and was proud to see that Bertie did so well in public speaking on our Australian and Asian tour, as well as on our more recent visit to Canada and the United States.

But now in late August over ten years later, I felt I must stay longer in London, for war fever was in the air, and decisions were yet to be made on the David-Wallis situation.

* * *

Despite drowning in final preparations to deal with Hitler, Bertie met me at the station with two security men and held hard to my hand as we motored back to the palace. I had taken the night train again to have a lovely last day with our daughters and so that fewer people, including the newspapers, would know I felt the need to keep going back and forth. And because Bertie had said a very early-morning arrival was better: Evidently there were swarms of Londoners at train stations in the daytime, sending their children into rural shires or even to Canada for protection against possible bombing attacks. Panic, though yet controlled, hovered in the air.

On the darkened streets—no total blackouts imposed yet—I was horrified to see sandbags piled around public and government buildings, including the palace. All this in the week I had been away this time? My favorite poster I saw here and there as our headlights slashed against it read, *Keep Calm and Carry On.*

"Chamberlain has said the right moment is not yet here to write a desperate letter for peace to Hitler," Bertie told me suddenly when I took a breath after giving him a detailed report of how the girls were doing.

"I feel I must stay longer this time," I told him. "I have asked my sister Rose if she will become guardian of our girls if war comes here, or worse than that happens to the king and queen. After all, she trained as a nurse in the war, has a daughter herself, and has always loved the girls. We can hardly put that on your mother."

"Yes, fine, but we must think on the upside," he insisted, with more force than I had heard from him.

"Speaking of your mother, I have had a lovely letter from Queen Mary," I added as we motored through the palace gates and they were quickly closed behind us. "She said she is appalled that the world should be faced with another war because of the wickedness of the Nazis. Poor dear, she suffered so as queen in 1914 when that bloody German war began. Bertie, I want to help, to do what I can here."

We held hands even tighter. He hesitated before he said, "You might help to oversee the wrapping and stowing of the palace's precious paintings and other works of art, the nation's heritage. Churchill tells me the Nazis have, to put it nicely, 'a very acquisitive nature,' not to mention a possible Luftwaffe bombing attack could wreak havoc. He suggested too that there will be a time for both of us—you and me—to speak on the wireless to the nation, me in a general speech and you to the women of the Empire and beyond. Years ago, that would have bothered me, but—thanks to you and dear Logue's lessons—I shall rise to that occasion."

"Indeed you shall."

"Also, with your fine French, perhaps you might even address the women of France."

Foolish me, but I wondered if the long-retired Walden Bury cook Marguerite Rodiere back home in France would hear that speech—and remember me and be awestruck—for even I was that—at who I had become. But I only said, "A fine idea. Has Winston Churchill begun to advise you then?"

"The man is a force of nature and will be in our wartime government one way or the other. I fear Chamberlain cannot last as P.M., not after his misreading and misleading in the appeasement situation. I would favor Lord Halifax, a more peaceful man, like Chamberlain, of course."

"But there is a chance Churchill could become P.M.?"

"We shall see. We have signed a pact with Poland, that if the Nazis invade there, we are at war with Germany again. Hopes are fading, my darling," he said with a sigh and put his arm around me as the motorcar pulled up to our private entrance in the courtyard.

I leaned close and meant to kiss him on the cheek, but he turned his head, so our lips met before we realized one of our guards had opened the door.

"Maybe we can bring the girls back from Scotland and house them at Windsor, should Hitler attack us here," he whispered.

"Let's not even say that dread name," I said and scooted off the seat to get out. "Surely not that. Our RAF boys will shoot his Luftwaffe from the sky if he dares attack here."

"I'll explain more about the way of things later. For now, let's say a prayer we are back together."

* * *

But life soon turned to nightmare. Desperate, last-minute negotiations with Germany came to an end when Hitler's forces invaded Poland on 1 September 1939. Our government tried to mediate a peace between Germany and Poland, but that was a fool's game. Neville Chamberlain declared war with Germany, and France followed suit. Our summer season of peace was shattered. The prime minister made a wireless broadcast from Downing Street that Germany had ignored our peace overtures and we were at war.

Our Empire quickly declared war on Germany to bolster the mother country: Australia, New Zealand, Canada supported us, so it was almost a worldwide war already. I was shocked when the Republic of Ireland dared to declare themselves a neutral nation, as British-Irish bad feelings went back a long way.

Tears threatened as I paced our palace rooms that night, fearful of what was coming next. I came across my dear Bessie Miller, cleaning up my cosmetics table in my dressing room, perhaps because we had all been warned not to leave breakable objects about where they might be shattered and cut someone during an attack.

"Din't know you was still up, Your Majesty," she said, holding a tray of empty jars and brushes to wash as she bobbed a curtsy.

"Difficult to sleep in the silence, wondering if and when war might indeed come here. Have you had an opportunity to speak with your family?"

"Like all us East Enders, they're keen to get ready for a bad blow too. We're true Cockney, through and through. My Da and my brothers working the East End docks and all. Got a cousin who's a Pearly King, I do."

"I didn't know that, my dear. And, you see, you are all dear to me. If you feel you need time to help them out, I mean more than some regular time off or your wages that you have sent them all these years, you let me know. I feel my biggest job now, besides supporting His Majesty, is to bolster everyone's spirits, no matter what. And do keep me informed of how things are going with your people, for we are all Londoners working together through these tenuous times."

She curtsied and beamed as if I'd just given her the keys to the kingdom. Several of her glass pots clinked together as she went out. And what was that other piercing sound? I followed her out into the corridor, only to see Bertie running in a dressing robe from his suite, and household staff as well as guards appearing up and down the hall.

I thought for a moment someone was screaming, but then I knew. Not the roar of planes yet, thank heavens, but the rising and falling wail of an air-raid siren shrieking from the palace roof or courtyard.

"Not now, not yet!" I kept saying, as Bertie seized my arm and a guard hustled us downstairs to the newly built air-raid shelter. Some of our depleted staff were there too, Bessie still holding her tray, though she was shaking so hard the cosmetic jars rattled.

We heard no planes, no bombs, for I assumed we would be able to hear them even down here. Could it have been a mistake, or just a drill?

After what seemed an eternity but was just an hour and a half, according to Bertie's wristwatch, a guard lit an electric torch for us, then the wailing went deathly still. The walls seemed to close in. Were Londoners in their small corrugated iron Anderson shelters in their backyards or gardens? It had seemed wise to use the tube stations underground, but that was still frowned upon. Closed in like this, I thought of Lilibet's questions about the monster of Glamis being bricked up all those years. But even here, ghosts of the earlier war with the Germans hovered in my head.

"Either a drill, Your Majesties, or someone's nerves got the best of him, and he accidentally hit the air-raid switch," a palace guard finally informed us. "No enemy planes or bombs reported."

Despite that good news, disaster was on the doorstep, and Bertie and I could be trapped here and targeted as king and queen.

CHAPTER FOUR

Wire Netting and Glue

My extensive wardrobe aside, today, just within the palace walls, I wore jodhpurs as I oversaw the protections for the palace. The staff was completing the final boarding up of the windows that graced the larger rooms and chambers, now quite stripped of most of their historic grandeur.

Again, I thought of the rumors of the monster of Glamis having its chamber bricked up as we greatly closed ourselves in here at the palace. Our reduced staff—even our personal servants—were using glue and wire netting to cover the windows still in use, so if a bomb hit, the glass, supposedly, would not shatter.

At least we were in a period the newspapers called "The Phoney War," though Bessie had told me some were cheekily calling it the Bore War. Poland had been horribly bombed and had surrendered to the Nazis, but it seemed nothing was happening here, and all waited with baited breath. And prepared as best we could, like today.

"Your Majesty, is the height of the crystal chandeliers suitable then?" my supervisor asked as he stood beside me.

He gestured toward the huge cut-glass chandeliers that had been lowered to three feet above the floor lest a bomb blast shake them loose from their normal lofty height. Their fall would be much less this way, and pieces of old carpeting were piled under each.

"Yes, that looks to be the best we can do," I told him, and led the way into another room. But I glanced first out one of the newly netted windows. Diffused light entered, but it was like seeing the autumn trees outside through a scrim or blur of rain, even though it was a fine day—that is, a fine day to prepare for war to come to dear England.

Poland had been taken by bombs and starvation. Hitler's horrible Luftwaffe had struck from the air and his Panzers from the ground. Even here, Bertie had said, rationing would surely come. One more glance out the window showed me the last of the palace mews carriage horses being sent to Windsor. Come spring, they would be put to work on farms, for we must try to grow more of our own food. Starving Poles had made that warning clear enough.

I sighed and took yet another tour of the steel shelters outside being built for the palace sentries. Back inside from the brisk autumn air, I oversaw the final packing of the many precious collections of smaller treasures, mostly gifts to the crown, not to mention some of the little collector's pieces Queen Mary had managed to finagle as gifts.

I saw Bessie was helping to pack them away and put a hand

on her shoulder where she knelt, madly wrapping priceless treasures.

"Oh, ma'am," she said, startled, looking up a moment. "Well, I warrant we are all kneeling to our queen today," she said with a little smile.

How I admired her buoyant spirits. If my greatly reduced staff who were here for the duration with us—or wherever we ended up—could be stalwart and cheerful, so could I. I had heard some had been calling my Bessie "queen of the cosmetics"—Queen Elizabeth, at that, for my name was Bessie's given name too.

I bent my knees and whispered in her ear. "Do not let them tease you, for we Elizabeths shall stick together through thick and thin, shall we not?"

She nodded and broke into another smile. Although she was so much older than my girls, I thought of them at that moment. I needed to speak to Bertie again about bringing them back at least as far as Windsor, where protections and fortifications were also being erected. Perhaps Hitler knew we would fight, that our RAF boys would shoot down his Luftwaffe aircraft, so he dared not try an invasion. Surely, the ancient stone fortress of Windsor would be safe.

But this dreadful waiting for the Germans to strike was torment too.

* * *

I became exhausted from my many public visits that autumn as we prepared for real war. Bertie and I had visited the London

Air Raid Precaution Headquarters and done inspections of air-raid plans, including shelters. We took a launch down the Thames to the East End docks, which would be terribly vulnerable if we were bombed. I visited the regiments of which I had been made honorary colonel. I was appointed commandant-in-chief of the women's services, including the Royal Navy Wrens and the Women's Auxiliary Air Force.

Bertie and I had finally convinced seventy-two-year-old Queen Mary to move out of the city to Gloucestershire, where she would be safer from bombings. She stayed at the home of a niece, but her letters showed she was not happy to be "countrified." She had, she said, passed the time by trying to rid the Badminton estate of ivy that clung to absolutely everything!

Worse of all, David, the former king, popped back into London to discuss his future, but I made certain I was not about at that time, so he met only with Bertie. That day that David had darkened our palace doors, I was moved to happy tears by cheers from crowds for me both outside and within when I went to meet the leaders and workers of the Red Cross and the hospitals, and the ambulance drivers, so many of those people fine, brave women. Afterward, Bertie admitted David had still acted as if he were not only older brother, but king!

"He lorded it over m-me—well, tried to k-king it over me," he said, alarming me with his sudden return to stuttering.

I vow, it was as bad an attack of nerves as he'd had since just before his coronation, when he'd feared he would stammer during the crowning ceremony in the Abbey.

"David t-tried to give me orders, so I only listened, then did what I bloody damned knew was b-best after he left."

And that, I knew, meant figuring out where to stash the Duke and Duchess of Windsor in the immediate future so they didn't rush back to Germany to support Hitler, or so David didn't agree to be set up as a puppet British king in exile with promises of ruling the Empire again after the defeat of England!

And yet, thank the Lord, no attack on England yet, which, I suppose, helped Chamberlain cling to his office—and Bertie go back to his proper speech, as he used to call it, the very next day.

The prime minister had, however, accepted into his cabinet the "Conservative" Winston Churchill, though I had to laugh at the idea that that fierce bulldog Churchill, who insisted we prepare for a brutal war, was "conservative" in any way. Bertie agreed, though, that Churchill, whom he feared as a warmonger and a bit of a bully, could be next in line to lead the nation, and at such a perfectly beastly time.

* * *

Although Bertie remained tied to London, just after mid-September I went to Scotland again to see our girls. They were living at Balmoral now, and I felt a bit guilty to be reunited with my children when so many—the Scots too—were being separated from theirs. Lilibet had written that "we have hundreds of evacuee children from Glasgow living nearby," though I was also told some families were taking their children back into the cities, since nothing dangerous had happened. But what, I thought, if the so-called Phoney War became only too real?

I hugged both my girls as they met me at the front door of

our rural Scottish home of Balmoral Castle in Aberdeenshire. We walked inside arm in arm.

"Well," Margot declared after our greetings and hugs, "we had a big sewing party, knitting for our soldiers last week, and we are having another one today, and some members of the Black Watch are coming to say thanks awfully, aren't they, Lilibet? And wait until they get to meet the queen!"

"That will be lovely. You know your uncle Fergus who was . . . was lost in the earlier war with Germany belonged to the Black Watch. How handsome he looked in his uniform. I still miss him terribly."

"Lost as in died for sure?" Margot pursued. "You mean, not lost like he could be found again somewhere, only with shell shock or something like that?"

"Silly," Lilibet cut in, "lost meaning died. Don't you recall the painting of him, looking so fine at Glamis with the black wreath on it? I really would like to see how the Navy cadets look all spiffed up in their dress uniforms."

I had decided to ignore all blatant or veiled references to Prince Philip, so I said nothing to that. He was at sea, as far as I knew and, with the war, likely to remain there. Surely, the memory of his shining allure would soon fade in my eldest daughter's eyes.

* * *

"David's still demanding that his wife be given the HRH title," Bertie told me in October, when we both had hopes we were finally rid of the so-called Duke and Duchess of Windsor, who had lately been traveling like nomads between France and Spain. "But she'll not have the title Her Royal Highness from me or my government!" He huffed a bit and went back to reading the newspaper. How I wished I could sit in on some of his top-level meetings, at least the ones Bertie had with his prime minister each week here at the palace.

Yet I sighed in relief, something I had done little enough of since we began this dreadful waiting-for-war game. I could not abide David and that woman coming back to England. A Duke of Windsor solution must soon be found; the merest hint of a shadow king in exile could be disaster, almost as horrid as having him—and her—back here.

"You know," he went on from behind the paper, "I never told you this, but there was quite a scurrilous report explaining Wallis's hold on poor David years ago, when it became obvious she had her hooks in him, so to speak. David mentioned it again to me, still quite put out about it, for he blames it for turning many of the so-called movers and shakers against Wallis."

He crunched the paper down into his lap again and looked at me just as I jerked alert. "It came to be called the 'China Dossier' and was terribly titillating and sexual in nature—a smear from the days she lived in Hong Kong and toured China before her divorce from her second husband. No one knows the source of the dossier, but it was someone who had the inside, intimate story on Wallis, that was for certain."

My heartbeat kicked up so hard I could hear it. I looked away, down at the photos of our girls I had been sorting through. "Sexual in nature?" I said, hoping that would not bring up the fact that, since our honeymoon, we had lived an affectionate but chaste life as man and wife. Oh, a few knew that both of our girls were conceived through artificial insemination, but we were indeed their parents. After my own past with a double mother, I had made certain that their births were properly observed and registered.

Of course, my preference for affection with celibacy had meant turning a blind eye to Bertie's occasional short-lived liaisons, but I knew he loved me, and it was worth it to avoid what everyone called duties of the marriage bed. I had guilt attacks for this at times, but I had not realized I felt this way so strongly at first. Indeed, I did my duty on our wedding night and honeymoon, but I'd become ill for a while and after that it seemed easier to avoid sexual intercourse. We had a strong union in every way but that, indeed we did, but . . . why must he bring up the China Dossier now? Surely, in these terrible times where I supported and held him up every way I knew how—but one—he did not need to use something he had learned about the dossier to pressure me into deeper intimacy. I suddenly felt as if I were looking again through a window blurred by wire netting and glue.

"I never discussed it with you," he said, putting the paper completely aside and lighting another cigarette. Its smoke enveloped me, clung to my clothes, but I had long learned to ignore that. Yet I could not ignore the topic of the dossier. How much could he know about it, and why bring it up now?

"What sort of hold on David did she supposedly have?" I asked, for I must appear to be curious. "I always thought he was simply attracted to domineering, sometimes abusive women because your mother had been a hands-off mother, or else he needed someone strong to tell him what to do."

"Be that as it may, this scandal sheet suggested that Wallis's hold on David was that she'd learned some sort of sexual trick—some sort of hold—the Shanghai Grip or Squeeze, I believe it was called, from Chinese whores during her earlier days."

"How . . . outrageous!" I said, trying to look a bit outraged myself. Here our worry was bombs over Britain, and a bomb-shell had just exploded on me here!

I tried to calm myself and sound rational. "I mean, David would have been better off without her, but, well—but," I nearly stammered, "did people believe that, and did it get back to David and that woman?"

"It evidently did, though its source was never discovered, even though I warrant they had their suspicions." He blew out a perfect smoke ring that rose and then dissipated. "Rather a shocking claim, but people were rabid to know how she had such a hold over him. Darling, I knew you hated Wallis for her cruel mockery of you, so I didn't even mention the dossier to you at first. Besides, the content wasn't for a lady of your taste and standing. Believe me, if Winston couldn't find the source of it, it's not to be found."

"Winston Churchill tried to track down its source?" I was beginning to wish I had not concocted all that, but the woman needed to be stopped—not that it had stopped David from wanting her. I knew Bertie would be shocked if he knew what I had done, mostly because I had removed myself from the libido part of his life.

"Yes, Churchill told me so at a party a good while ago,"

he said. "The point is, David's original insistence on making Wallis HRH and, no doubt, queen has made him a lot of enemies. Unfortunately, Adolf Hitler is not one of them. Well, darling, I didn't mean to get off on that tack. Perhaps I'm just gearing myself up to deal with Winston should he become P.M. But, especially after Chamberlain, we need a strong hand at the tiller of our ship of state."

"Yes, but I know the thought of dealing with him upsets you." *Me too, especially now*, I almost said.

But what I didn't say—and I prayed Bertie didn't know and would never know—was that I had been the one behind the China Dossier.

CHAPTER FIVE

Remembrance Day

I was extremely nervous about speaking on the wireless to the Empire's women. As much as I loved talking to people, I could not simply turn on formal oration like a tap, at least not when my words and voice were going out into the vast unknown. But I had rehearsed. And if Bertie could overcome his stammering to speak publicly, I could surely reach out like this. I had often looked over his speeches before he gave them, and he had approved wholeheartedly of this one.

I glanced down at the bright red poppy I wore on the lapel of my suit, for this was Armistice Day, 11 November 1939, a day of remembrance honoring our losses in the war with Germany over twenty years ago, a war I remembered well. My brother Mike had been sorely wounded and shell-shocked, and the Huns had as good as murdered our dear Fergus. I had helped to entertain and befriend the nerve-wracked soldiers we took in at Glamis. And to face all that ruin, heartbreak, and death again staggered me.

"Are you ready, Your Majesty?" the BBC man said as I seated myself. I spread my typewritten pages out before me on the desk but held to the top page. "When I give the sign, ma'am, and after the announcer introduces you, you may begin."

A camera with a man behind it was trained on me, but I had no intention of smiling or waving today. Let them record a moving picture for later use while I concentrated on being serious, keeping calm, and caring. My hand began to tremble, and the paper shook. I wished I could fan myself with it, though it was not especially warm in here this early November day.

Oh, we were live and on the air, as Bertie always put it. The announcer's voice came from another microphone, "To the women of the Empire, Her Majesty the queen."

I began by mentioning our seven-week trip to Canada and the United States of America, thanking all for the kind reception we had received there. "I speak today in circumstances sadly different from then. Peace has been broken, and once again we have been forced into war. I speak for the women of the British Empire to offer our deep and abiding sympathy to the women of Poland, nor do we forget the gallant women of France who are called on again to share our burdens of war."

My voice quavered over that line. Was she out there, listening, the woman who gave me life, for sadly my beloved English mother, Cecilia, had died last year.

"To us women has been given the proud duty to serve our Empire in its hour of need. The tasks you are undertaking whether at home or in distant lands are vital." I tried to keep my voice steady, to sound as if I were sitting in someone's parlor.

"It is not so difficult to do the big things, the novelty, the excitement of new and interesting duties, but it is the thousand and one daily, smaller duties and irritations of family life that must be borne. Your husbands go off to allotted tasks. Your children may be evacuated to places of greater safety. The king and I know what it is to be parted from our children.

"We women, like men, have vital work to do to save our country. The king and I sympathize with your sacrifices. We all yearn for a new day with peace and goodwill. We all have a part to play in this struggle to build a new and better world.

"Meantime, to you in every corner of the Empire, I give a message of hope and encouragement. We all have a part to play, and I know you will not fail in yours. We put our trust in God, our refuge and strength in all kinds of trouble. I pray with all my heart that He will bless and guide and keep you always."

My words were followed by an orchestral rendition of "God Save the King." Suddenly the music seemed sonorous and sad, rather than martial and uplifting.

"Well done, Your Majesty," both men in the room said.

"As our current and future tasks must be," I told them with a nod and firm handshake. "We must work together, all of us."

* * *

The winter months stretched out in endless waiting while Hitler's onslaught continued on the Continent. One thing that lifted my spirits was posing for the famed photographer Cecil Beaton, for I thought his portraits of me were very regal and I hoped my serious and calm demeanor gave people strength and hope.

"I especially favor this one," I told Bertie, showing him the close-up where I wore a frothy rhinestone-studded Norman Hartnell gown with a bejeweled necklace, dangling earrings, and a diamond tiara.

Beaton had taken pictures of me in profile and looking straight into the camera. In neither did I appear as plump as I was, but could I help it if tenuous times made one crave food and sweets even more?

"Very stunning," Bertie said with a little smile. "Very you—always lovely inside and out to me from the very first. But," he said, clearing his throat, "that is only one reason why I persisted when the lady said no."

I did not like it when he went off on that tack, for indeed I had refused his proposal of marriage twice before accepting. I had not been in love with him and there was the embarrassment with David—including the fact that some of our friends knew I had set my cap for the so-called catch of the century, the Prince of Wales, and been roundly rebuffed. Well, at the time I could not fathom becoming Bertie's wife, paramour, and duchess. But he had been so doggedly determined.

"I was overwhelmed when you proposed," I told him now. I'd mentioned several excuses over the years, none of which seemed to fly quite right.

"The third time's the charm, they say," he said as he rose and came round his desk in his private library where I had popped in to show him the sample photographs. "That and the fact you had a bit of pressure from my mother, no doubt."

"The queen—Mama—did not pressure me."

"Not directly, but I think you did get the word she was going to cut you and the Strathmores from the approved invitation list because I was miserable mooning over you. And then, your acceptance put me over the moon, so there!"

He embraced me and began to move in the steps of a slow dance, pulling me ever closer. "I know it was my charm and charisma that made you say yes, my dearest," he said in my ear as he turned us a bit and chuckled.

"It was your bedrock character and honesty," I told him, looking up into his face.

For one moment, however much under duress we both were, it was like going back to those days of fun after the war—the earlier German war. How open he had been with me. How protective, gentlemanly, and kind. No mystery in the man then except when he might propose again. One thing that had convinced me—yes, in addition to the word that came to my mother that his mother thought I was leading her dear second son a merry chase—was how much Bertie loved my fun family. He had confided that his childhood had been difficult and strict and had vowed he wanted just the opposite for his own children someday.

He whispered as we still swayed a bit together, "Let's keep Christmas at least as we always have, this wretched waiting be damned. Sandringham with the girls, little gifts, walks outside, we four together. And maybe dancing close like this, maybe more."

He pulled me even tighter, and my breasts pressed against his chest. Our thighs shifted together, my nylons and silk slip and light wool skirt sliding between us. For a moment I felt the glimmer of sensual desire for him, which I had always needed to summon, though he could be so easily swept away in love-making. My hesitation at full intimacy and possession had been the only barrier between us.

"To be continued," he whispered. "Ah, now what did you come in to say and where was I in reading these wretched war dispatches from that ever-present red box?"

We laughed together uneasily as if we were awkward youths, meeting secretly. Something sweet—and sharp—sparked between us and flickered out as he turned back to his desk.

"Our going to Sandringham, yes," I said, but my voice did not sound like my own. "After all, it will be four months since you will have seen your girls then. War or not, a good time will be had by all!"

That crooked half smile of his lifted, and he winked at me. "You are more beautiful than Cecil Beaton has made you. I shall hang that one above my bed wherever I go, and you may come to see that I am telling you true if you choose to visit me privately—day or night."

I nodded and nearly forgot what I had come in for. We had not had a discussion or a row over my wish for a celibate marriage since before Margot was born. And now—when things were so busy and so tense?

I left the profile portrait leaning in a chair, staring at him as he bent over his desk, reading dispatches again. I fled the room and the well-aimed bombardment of thoughts and leashed passion he had just thrown my way.

* * *

"Whatever happens with—and in—the war, I want to remember this day," I told Bertie as we walked the wintry grounds of our Norfolk estate at Sandringham. It was where Bertie had been reared, and his memories of it were mixed: his formal mother, strict father, loving nanny, and his brothers and sisters, including David, of course.

It was good to see our own children enjoying themselves so. Both Lilibet and Margot had pink cheeks, had been laughing, and were out of breath from pretending to fight a duel with each other wielding two of Queen Mary's old walking sticks like sabers, whacking away.

"En garde!" Lilibet kept saying, though they were well into the duel.

"Touché!" Margot shouted back, though it came out more like *touchy*.

And then we all heard the roar and squinted up into the winter sun through the bare-limbed trees.

"Bertie, did you arrange some sort of an RAF flyover as a surprise?" I asked. He had given me several gifts beyond our usual exchange of Yuletide presents. However laden as he was with cares and fears about the coming war, he had tried to be lighthearted and attentive this holiday week.

"Girls, come here!" he commanded, looking back to see where his bodyguards and equerries were.

The four of us huddled together, looking up. "Are they friendly?" Margot asked when the planes screamed overhead.

"They may make another pass," he said, ignoring the question. He pulled the three of us close to the solid trunk of a chestnut and squinted up again at the sky as his bodyguards and others of our party ran closer and the roar became deafening as the planes passed overhead again. Yes, three bombers, flying low.

Lilibet shouted over the roar, "What if they have those horrid spider swastikas under their wings? What if they are heading for London?"

"Stay back!" Bertie shouted as his entourage came closer. "Let's not give them a clump of human targets—any targets at all!"

My heart thudded in my chest and, with Bertie, I held the girls against the rough tree bark. I reached for him, pressed shoulder to shoulder against him. *I should shelter him*, my mind screamed. *God save the king!*

"Sir! Sir! They're ours! They're our boys!" one of his equerries shouted. "Some sort of salute, I hope, and not reconnaissance or warning!"

"Not the time for a flyover, like on the Mall," Bertie muttered. "Not here at peaceful Sandringham."

Margot piped up, "So will the bad Nazis only drop their bombs in London, so that's why we have to stay in Scotland or maybe at Windsor someday like you said, Mummy?"

"We shall talk about it all later. Let's head back in. We are going to sing Christmas carols again tonight. Come on then, and best bring Granny's walking canes with you."

"In case we need to fight the Germans!" Margot said as she ran to retrieve her "sword." "Crawfie said they might be behind every tree!"

Bertie and I just looked at each other. Did the war—which was not on our sacred soil yet—have to hover over us even here?

* * *

Although I had met and knew Winston Churchill, I did not really *know* him, so I was looking forward to chatting with him at the dinner Bertie and I were giving at the palace for the war cabinet members and some other ministers and officials. It was possible that Winston could become prime minister should Chamberlain be forced to resign, so I was prepared, Bertie too, to work with him through the war if it came to that.

Since both of us still held some things against him—his early support for David staying on as king even if he wed that woman—I wanted to be certain he knew I would help the war effort in any way I could. I had even copied out for Churchill the William Wordsworth poem titled *The Excursion*, which I supposed the poet had written when Napoleon was trampling Europe.

As the poem goes, *At this day, when a Tartarean darkness overspreads the groaning nations* . . . and it ends with lines about fighting evil with good. Now if I could just corner Churchill for a moment in this shifting crowd of men where I was the only woman. He and I were both rather centers of attention with the voices getting louder, but I did manage to approach and offer the poem to him.

He skimmed it, and tears gilded his eyes. "Very thoughtful

and highly appropriate, Your Majesty, very much so," he said and bowed to me a second time. "I shall treasure it in coming days and all my days. I do remember this poem from my school years and am honored to have a copy of it in your own hand."

"If I can do anything to help—beyond my public talks and visits, I mean."

He glanced quickly around, evidently to see if anyone was in earshot. "Of course, His Majesty is torn about having to deal with the Duke of Windsor," he said, that often-stentorian voice quite muted now. I startled at his quick change of topic, and to one that bothered me greatly. Did this man read minds?

"I believe," he went on, speaking quietly but quickly, "you have seen, more clearly than the king, that the former king is—or could be—a liability in all this, especially the public perceptions of him. Anything you can do to convince and assure His Majesty that the duke and his wife be assigned somewhere harmless but safe—outside of England, if I have any say in it—will be most helpful."

"Good. Yes, I see."

"I'm sure you do. Ma'am, I never did support his marrying Mrs. Simpson, I assure you. I thought she could be his mistress *en-titre*, but it didn't do for her to be entertaining at Balmoral with him, nor to be the wife of a king, morganatic or not. Not only indiscreet of the Prince of Wales, later king, but dangerous. For whatever reason, I believe you felt the same."

"I did. Yes, that's exactly it."

"I am pleased we agree, and I have this opportunity to clear the air with you on that before events go further. We do not truly know what is coming, ma'am, yet I dare say some sort of trying times. I realize what a close and important advisor you are to His Majesty, and should I become such also, I would hope and pray that you and I could also work together."

I remembered then that Bertie had said Churchill had tried to discover who was behind the China Dossier. What if he had learned it was me and would hold it over me and—

"Ah, there you are," Bertie said to me, coming up behind. "Winston, we shall have to include your Clementine for dinner next time here and without all the dire war talk."

"Very kind of you, Your Majesty. I believe with our clever wives supporting us, we shall forge ahead in these dark days, and our ladies shall lighten our steps."

So good with words, so very clever, I thought. So had he guessed or learned how far I had gone, how much I had risked to sully David's paramour? And should this clever and powerful man become P.M., could I work with him as Bertie must do? I wondered in our current situation what Winston would think of the line in the Wordsworth poem, *The bad have fairly earned a victory o'er the weak*. And who was who?

CHAPTER SIX

Beloved Brothers

*C*aptain David Bowes Lyon, I presume," I told him with a smile, but tears blurred my vision as I hugged my youngest brother. "How are you, my dear?"

He hugged me back hard, then set me at stiff arm's length to look closely into my face.

"I see all these war threats and queenly duties have not aged you one bit. And I'm fine. Waiting to be called up. You look quite splendid, even without all the ermine, crowns, and that fur of an entire fox you like to wear that looks as if it might take a bite out of you. I shall have to start calling you Queen Foxy."

"Ever the tease. Well, perhaps I have put on a stone or so," I admitted to him as I never did to others. So however did he keep himself so trim?

He was so handsome with his classic good looks and wavy brown hair. I loved him dearly and always had, my childhood playmate, my friend—and fellow keeper of the secret of our heritage, though he had told his wife.

But David had another closely kept secret, for, despite his wife, for whom he cared deeply, he much preferred the intimate company of men. He was two years younger than I, but we had seemed almost like twins as we grew up, sharing our happy childhood days, even singing and acting together in amateur performances on the Glamis Castle stage to amuse everyone before he left for school at Eton. So in polite society and even at home, he was still playacting about his romantic preferences.

When Margaret Rose was born, I had asked him to be amongst her godparents, though that wretched David, Prince of Wales, became the second David to so serve. But rather than recall that, I asked about his family as we sat on the chintz sofa in my drawing room.

"How are Rachel and the divine Devina and Simon?"

He went on in some detail. Bertie would be joining us soon, for I had come up with an idea I was pleased he would champion. It was a way to keep David safe from serving in combat, yet he would do a very delicate, important service for our nation in wartime.

"The family keeps me hopping," he said with a smile. "And I'm still keen to garden, but there are rumors that, if we are attacked—even if we are not and there is a sea embargo of goods—we will be asked to ration food."

I sighed and poured tea from the service I'd ordered—with scones, his favorite blueberry ones—as I told him, "Yes, times are tense. I fear the masses are getting bored with war talk but nothing happening here yet, thank the good Lord. Here at the palace, we are waiting for the other shoe to drop—in the form of bombs. How can the Huns put up with that madman Hitler?"

"But I do recall," he said as I added just the amount of milk he had always liked in his tea, then handed it to him, "Kathe Kübler, that dear German friend and governess of yours, wrote to you that she quite liked Hitler."

"She was blind on that. Their entire country was—and is. So unfortunate, what happened to her. I'm sure it quite changed her earlier opinion of that madman. I am sorry you did not like her."

"I admit she taught you excellent German, but I warrant you'll not be using it in your next speeches to the nation or mentioning it to anyone. But she quite changed her tune about Der Führer, didn't she?"

I sighed again, a habit I was trying to break, at least with Bertie and the girls and most certainly in public. So many worries, including that it was looking dire for Chamberlain in Parliament. Bertie was still fearful he might have to work with Churchill, who seemed a warmonger and a bit of a bully, though we both had to admit he was terribly clever.

"Lizzie?" David said, using the long-ago pet name only he had ever called me. "An entire farthing for your thoughts. No, I did not like Kathe Kübler from that time she cooked and ate the first rabbit I had ever shot on my own. That was petty, I suppose, but she had no right. She seemed to me to be pushy and possessive—of you. Maybe the whole lot of the Huns are like that. But what did you mean by she changed her opinion of madman Hitler?"

"I knew you didn't like her as I did, so I must have not told you, though I suppose you would not have gloated. David, yes, she was more than a governess to me, a friend, a travel companion, and she taught me Deutsch well, though, as you say, I most certainly will not tell anyone that now, but stick with our mother tongue and French."

"The French are going to be overrun, I fear. Do you think about . . . about her? Our Marguerite? And did you ever tell Bertie?"

I shook my head. I could not even say the words, but went back to his earlier question about my onetime governess and friend. "When Frau Kübler returned to Germany before the Great War, she worked her way up to becoming headmistress of a large school in Munich. When Hitler came to power, she wrote me defending that demon. I recently destroyed the letter in which she said the British stories about him were not true, and he had some fine qualities."

"So you learned then that she was misguided at best, that she wasn't so wonderful after all."

"There is more. A terrible blow, such irony. You see, she is Jewish and when that was discovered, the Nazis had her sacked in one day from the position she loved and had worked so hard to attain. She became an outcast. I fear for her even now."

"Perhaps she was fortunate to be only sacked, for I've heard worse than that."

"Yes, I know. David, when the king and I were in France last time, I met with a formerly highly placed official who warned me, and I told Bertie that Hitler not only hates the Jews but plans to imprison and persecute them en masse. Of course, the entire world should have learned that in '38 when Hitler torched synagogues, vandalized Jewish homes and businesses, and so many Jews were killed. I pray not, but expect worse to come, and I do hope she is able to stay safe."

"And now that Hitler's going to stomp through Europe and try to come here—"

The door opened, and Bertie sailed in with a smile. David stood and bowed, and I quickly wiped tears from under my eyes. Bertie shook hands with David and gave him a little slap on the back.

"Good to see you, even in these wretched times," Bertie told him. "And despite all the water under the milldam, you make me wish I could see my own brother David again too."

I said naught to that as I poured Bertie tea with the lump of sugar he favored.

"So, did my lovely wife explain that she and I have been thinking about a very important assignment for you to help with the war effort?" Bertie asked, sitting in the armchair across from David.

"I am eager to help any way I can, sir. But we . . . we were catching up on old times."

"Call me Bertie when we are here like this. You can forget the bow and the 'sir's when it's just family like this, even for a serious talk."

My, I thought, but Bertie was in a good mood today, with a little wordplay and absolutely no stammering. Lately, when he spoke his fears that the rabble-rouser Winston might actually be the next P.M., he became terribly nervous.

"She hasn't so much as given me a hint of the offer of some post," David told him.

"Elizabeth—go ahead, for it was your idea," Bertie prompted and took a sip of tea.

"When we were in America, we made friends with President Roosevelt," I explained. "We thought he took to us personally quite well, and Bertie trusts and likes him. But the Americans have become, if not isolationists, at least pacifists after their dire losses in the Great War."

Bertie put in, "Which, of course, we fully understand and sympathize with. But Roosevelt seemed open and honest with me and wanted to weigh in against Hitler, even though his people and his Congress do not see the need even now."

"You are wanting a wartime ambassador to America?" David asked.

"Actually," I said, "it would appear to be just a friendly outreach from the royal family, but your purpose would be to convince him to convince his country that we are going to need more shipments of food and armaments, probably much more help. The times are coming when . . . when we fear the Satan that rules the Germans and is tearing up Europe will very soon turn his invasion sights by sky and sea to England."

David breathed out hard. "I see. A mission with the touch of the personal and the covert, at least for now. So this is not an offer but a . . . a prediction, and you have to speak to Chamberlain first? But isn't he going down? I read and hear there is such unrest against him that some in the Commons are insisting he resign."

I looked at Bertie, then at David. "And, if so," I said, "we would favor someone like Lord Halifax, someone who's been wary of war, not warning we must wage war, for that is Winston Churchill."

"I see," David said again.

But he did not see everything I did. Though he and I knew the secret of our real mother, he knew nothing of my other secret, and I feared Winston did. I had been behind that damned China Dossier, which Winston could hold over my head to make me convince and assure Bertie that he was the man to lead our nation and we'd best sanction his plans for war.

* * *

"I cannot believe the man is late," Bertie exploded after pacing and muttering. "Newly elected prime minister and late to his second visit to his sovereign!"

Winston Churchill had been elected in a contentious Parliament, where some of the members had actually shouted at poor Neville Chamberlain, "Resign! Resign! Resign!" So we were resigned to dealing with Churchill now, and he had been charged with making a war cabinet.

"It just isn't done, to keep the king waiting!" Bertie went on, still pacing with his trail of cigarette smoke swirling behind.

"There must be a good reason." I tried to soothe him, for I knew if it had been Chamberlain or Halifax calling on us,

Bertie would not have been so distraught. We needed to get off to a good start with this man, for the times demanded it.

I could not allow this sovereign–prime minister relationship to be like oil and water, not in wartime. Besides, I had personal reasons beyond the great national ones for wanting us to get along well with this man, who had once championed Bertie's brother as king but now, I hoped, saw the man and his wife for what they were. More than an embarrassment. Trouble. Danger. If Hitler seized or colluded with David to make him king in exile or here—disaster.

"I can hardly scold him for tardiness, as burdened as he suddenly finds himself," Bertie muttered, more quietly now. "But it is not a time for laxity or slipshod manners, and we have decided to meet weekly."

I almost asked, "Who gives a hoot for manners when the Germans are killing innocents and stealing entire countries?" but I hit on another tack: "Here, my dear," I told him, scooping up yesterday's *London Times* from the side table. "When a man can orate like this—tell the truth and challenge us all to action . . ."

I began to read from the very meat of the address Winston had given recently in the House of Commons, a short but stirring and brutally honest speech. It was a rallying cry, not glossing things over as, no doubt, Chamberlain had done, and swept the king along with him. When threatened, it was not my way to sit back and take it, and I knew Britain must not either.

"Here, Bertie, let's credit the man for this much and give

him some time and help to work things out. Listen to these stirring words: 'I have nothing to offer but blood, toil, tears, and sweat. . . . You ask, what is our aim? I answer in one word: It is victory, victory at all costs, victory in spite of all terrors, victory, however long and hard the road may be, for without victory, there is no survival.'"

He stopped pacing and ground out his cigarette butt in one of the numerous ashtrays. He leaned stiff-armed on the back of a chair as if to brace himself.

"I greatly admire his oratorical skills," he said, his voice calm now. He looked past me, not at me, and I wondered what he was thinking. That he had feared for years to open his own mouth to speak in public? "And if he wrote that as well as delivered it, more power to him."

"Now here's an idea," I said, putting the paper down. "I will walk down to meet him while you wait here. Perhaps he is tardy because of war business."

"Can you believe he not only created the new position of minister of war, but named himself to that? He hardly needed extra duties."

It was as if he had not heard me, while I expected to be not only heard but heeded. And I relished a moment or two with our new prime minister not only to befriend him, but to see if he was still of the opinion—so I had heard—that the Duke and Duchess of Windsor were not to be brought back to England during the war. It was rumored that the Duke was making such demands, and I feared Bertie, loving his big brother yet as he did, might agree to that.

"I'll be right back, dear—with Mr. Churchill, so you just have another smoke and calm down. We have to make this work."

He sighed, came around the chair, and sank into it. "Don't know what I would ever do without you," he said.

"I think I shall propose to our new—of necessity—friend Winston that he come for luncheon next time," I added and darted out before Bertie could yea—or especially nay—that.

I hurried down the carpeted corridor and marble stairs just as I saw a black motorcar followed by another, no doubt security, pull up at the courtyard entrance. Now I was nervous. I cleared my throat and straightened my dress jacket as I waited near the door where some palace staff stood. When they noticed me it was bows and curtsies and a bit of surprise to see me, but I said nothing about the shift in protocol.

Yes, there he was, puffing on a cigar he handed half-smoked to his chauffeur as he emerged from the backseat. His round face made him look younger and jolly, but when he spoke . . .

His blue eyes widened in surprise as he saw me waiting a few yards inside the door. "Your Majesty, such an honor. I regret business about embargoes made me late, so is His Majesty boycotting me now?" he said with a grin that crinkled his face. He bowed, and I offered him my hand, which he kissed.

"I wanted to greet you and welcome you to what will, I am certain, be many a meeting here," I told him as I gestured him toward the stairs. "And I wanted to suggest we—you and His Majesty—I mean, meet for luncheon hereafter, not so rushed in these busy, dangerous times. 'You ask what is our aim?'" I quoted his own words from his Victory speech. "It is to get on with each other well and win this war!"

"I shall consult you on my next oration. And I believe you will be happy to hear—please, you must sit in on this visit and attend the luncheons, ma'am—to hear my thoughts on 'handling' the Duke and Duchess of Windsor in the chaos of this war, which he and his wife have made a bit worse."

"Then I will be honored to stay and hear—and help, if I can."

"I wager, ma'am, you can. And that you will."

CHAPTER SEVEN

Trapped on the Beach

$\mathcal{I}$ stood quietly while Winston greeted the king and apologized for being late. All I could think of was at least Bertie wasn't quite the stickler his father had been on promptness or this new P.M. might have been thrown in the Tower.

I thought neither man looked his age, Bertie at forty-four—though a bit thin in body and gaunt in the face, and Winston at age sixty-five, rather portly—physically more of a match for me, truth be told.

It was their second formal meeting, for the king had officially sent for the new prime minister and charged him to form a government the evening he was elected. This was our first change of P.M. in the three years of Bertie's reign. We had begun in the chaos of the abdication, the marriage of David and that woman in France, and now this dreadful, looming war.

When we were seated, I in a side chair while the two men sat more face-to-face, the two of them spoke of many issues, domestic and foreign. I kept still, mourning the fact that Winston vowed that dire times were ahead. I had several points I could have added, questions to ask, but did not, now at least. Finally, Bertie brought up my idea of meeting for luncheon in the future. I hoped this wasn't the end of the meeting, for I—we—needed a decision on the current fate of the Windsors.

"The luncheon suggestion is brilliant, Your Majesty, and I greatly appreciate the hospitality as well as the advice and counsel," Churchill said. "And I shall try to be prompt."

"I must tell you, Winston, my father would have had a stroke if you were late—unless you were my wife, who seemed to get past him on that score while my older brother and I used to catch the very dickens from him. And I must admit the luncheon idea was the queen's. She is one of my closest advisors, you see."

"I do see, sir. As my dear wife, Clementine, is to me. Then I am doubly grateful to both of you," he added with a little nod. "And one more topic before I take my leave, and that a rather sensitive one, namely the former king's situation during these hostilities."

Bertie frowned, and I sat forward a bit. "Yes," Bertie said. "I hear that the Duke of Windsor and his—his wife—have been at times indiscreet."

"Let me lay it out for you, sir. And ma'am," he said with a nod my way. He pulled a paper from his sheaf of them in his flat black leather case, adjusted his small wire glasses, and said, "The former king phoned me from Nice, France, insisting a British destroyer be sent to pick them up and bring them to London."

A destroyer, I thought. How appropriate a request.

"However, I told him there was but one British ship in Bordeaux's harbor and that was a scow transporting filthy, black coal."

I actually fought to stifle a laugh, though I immediately scolded myself, for the Windsors' not falling into enemy hands was of great import. I just didn't want them here, making demands, trying to horn in, especially that woman. And David would not prop Bertie up but would make him the little brother again, when I had worked so very hard to shore him up, and he was doing so well.

"I suggested that they drive to Spain," Winston went on, "which they did, and they are staying with the British ambassador in Madrid. The ambassador then telegraphed me with the duke's demands."

"Demands?" Bertie said, sitting up even straighter.

My heart began to beat harder. I had much to say but forced myself to keep silent. I was starting to trust Churchill. Is this really why he wanted me here, to deal with Bertie on his yet-beloved brother?

"In a nutshell, here it is, Your Majesties," Churchill said, reading now from the paper he held. "The duke insisted they be formally received by both of you, saying that he and the duchess were fed up with being marooned abroad. But there is more."

I tried to remain immobile, but shifted in my chair, holding tightly to the carved arms.

"He demands that the news of that royal welcome and meeting appear in the Court Circular, the official record, and be publicized in the newspapers so that everyone knows."

"Impossible," Bertie voiced my thoughts. "Absolutely out of the question. We've heard that his wife has said publicly that she expects bombs to fall on Britain and that she and her husband would accept a German victory. Treason! Outrageous!"

"Indeed, sir!" Winston said, and I nodded madly. "Unfortunately, I have all that on good authority. For all we know, the former Mrs. Simpson has been stirring up anti-British interests, being soured on not becoming queen or at least not being given the HRH title."

I gripped the arms of the chair harder, fighting to keep my anger and angst in check. I did not want to burst out with my feelings, for it might endanger any later advice I could give, nor did I want to let either the king or his new P.M. think I could not be logical and calm if I were to be in their future luncheon meetings. And, I thought, if I showed Churchill my anger, he might indeed believe I could have been behind the so-called China Dossier to ruin Wallis Simpson.

"So I have a proposal, Your Majesties." I was deeply grateful that he included me with his words and a look and a nod my way, and it was at that very moment that he truly became Winston to me instead of Churchill. "Quite frankly, I believe we all agree that the Windsors should be somewhere safe, somewhere distant from Hitler's grasp but somewhere harmless, for what they might say or do. Therefore, I propose that we name the duke as governor and commander-in-chief of the Bahamas. That has been bandied about before, but I say we act on that and now."

"The Bahamas?" Bertie repeated. "A place of little power or importance but of great distance from here and Germany. Well, I warrant they can't get into trouble or danger there."

"Exactly," Winston said.

"But do you think he will take it?" Bertie asked.

"He'd better, because he simply cannot come back here, not now," Winston said so strongly that I almost imagined him addressing the Commons. He stood and bowed to us both again as we stood also. "I shall also inform the duke that this assignment requires that he stay out of the U.S., so he doesn't meddle with our requests for further aid or get his or the duchess's misguided comments in the rabid newspapers there. We shall send to America a more trustworthy man named David, yes, your brother, ma'am."

I breathed easier. I pictured the Windsors trapped on a distant beach like castaways. Fighting back an urge to smile, I squeezed Winston's hand in silent thanks when he took his leave.

* * *

Dreadful news soon wracked us all. England might have had a new, strong prime minister at the helm, but it seemed not to stop that hellhound Hitler. Not only had his forces rampaged through the Sudetenland and chopped up Czechoslovakia, but, of course, Poland had been swallowed between him and his ally Stalin. Hitler's Panzer forces on the ground and Luftwaffe in the air had invaded Denmark and Norway as if it was a mere walk in the park.

We were already sheltering Dutch royalty who had fled their homeland and were now living in Eaton Square, soon followed by the Norwegian king and crown prince, both of whom I was very fond of. We had even gone down to Euston Station to greet them, and they were currently living here in the palace.

France had then been open ground to Der Führer's greedy reach, so Britain had sent men and war machinery to help stem the tide on the Continent. But now as the lovely month of May blended into the June of a nervous 1940, the British and Allied fighting forces and their armaments had been trapped on the French beaches of Dunkerque, which we British spelled Dunkirk.

Fearful our men would be captured or annihilated there, and that could mean an early end to the war, our government put out a hue and cry for even small watercraft to rescue our soldiers and equipment by bringing them across the Channel to our shores. The entire nation was terribly on edge.

We had sent our daughters to live at Windsor Castle, a bit over twenty miles away from London, and I visited them often. Today I did my best to both listen to the radio, which, of course, could not say much of the evacuation, and also listen to our children's questions.

"So couldn't some of them just swim away off the beach there?" Margot asked as we walked in the gardens, trailed by corgis, four family dogs now.

"Of course not," Lilibet cut in, "because soldiers are not to abandon their rifles, and they would be ruined if they were wet. Mummy, remember you said we could take pistol shooting lessons either here or at the palace."

"Yes, I intend to, and you can too. My dears, not only is the water at Dunkirk almost instantly deep, but the last report I had was that there is not enough room on the smaller vessels, so those are acting as ferries to get the men, who are in long queues, even up to their necks in water, onto the larger ships."

"We are up to our necks in this war, and they'd best not come here, the Jerries!" Margot insisted in a most unladylike voice. "So then their rifles would get wet and not work while they are in line in the water!"

"Hush. We do not need our Army and Navy secrets broadcast over a megaphone clear to France or even here at Windsor. There are posters in London that warn *Loose Lips Sink Ships*, so think about that. But yes, a valiant effort is being made to rescue our forces, so they can fight again."

"But what about French fighters being trapped there too?" Lilibet asked.

"I hear our transports are going back to try to save them too. From now on, we shall remember the Dunkirk spirit and not give up in this war," I said, trying to sound upbeat and hopeful.

"Maybe it will never come here," Lilibet said. "After all, we are an island, and they'd best stay off our beaches, or we will trap them there. And one thing more, Mummy."

"Yes, dear," I said, hoping it would not be something about the thankfully distant Prince Philip again.

"Papa says I'm becoming too much of a woman now to be called Lilibet, just because I never could pronounce my name when I was small. He's begun to call me Betts."

"And you like that, or you do not?"

Margot put in, "I don't like it. It sounds like going to the racetrack and betting on horses, or on who will win the war or something like that. But I do think when he calls me Margaret Rose it sounds more grown-up than Margot, but when he's put out with me, he says both names."

Lilibet subtly elbowed Margot back a step and said, "I was asking Mummy first, and I am the eldest."

"Poor you, queen someday," Margot shot back. "It isn't really that much fun to be queen, is it, Mummy? I mean, it's a lot of hard work and worry, especially if wars come along."

"Both of you just take your turns talking. Now Lilibet had asked me a question. My dear, you were named after me, but we thought it would be confusing if we were both called by the same first name. So Lilibet worked well, but if your father insists on Betts, do you mind?"

"I love him and want to help him, especially now when he's always worried about our boys fighting—and bombs coming here on aeroplanes too, so it's all right, but very different. I still like Lilibet better. I want to grow up, but not sometimes."

I hugged them both to me. "I know exactly what you mean. And I understand your feelings about being the younger daughter, Margot. After all, I have many more older siblings than you do. And believe me, when one grows up and doesn't see them much anymore, one misses them terribly. So despite this wretched war playing havoc with our lives, enjoy your time together now, promise me, my dear Elizabeth and Margaret Rose."

* * *

Little family tiffs whilst waiting for real war to come soon seemed nothing. Nor did our forces' skin-of-our-teeth escape from Dunkirk. Nor the grousing of Londoners who hated the blackouts and stumbling about in the dark and motorcar and pedestrian accidents when no bombs had fallen. And it wasn't just changes in the city everyone talked about. Citizens complained about the repositioning of street and road signs on the eastern coast, so if there was an invasion, the enemy forces might become confused.

I had to admit the huge barrage balloons tethered over our parks in case of dive bombers were a terrible sight day and night, like hovering doom. The king and I had been attending a meeting with several charity groups including the Red Cross. We motored back to the palace in the afternoon on Saturday, 7 September 1940, while Londoners partied in curtained pubs and restaurants as if they had not a worry in the world.

I thought too that the silent ack-ack guns in the parks were a scar on the early-autumn beauty. Even at the meeting with rousing speeches today, I had overheard people complain about the required limit of five inches of bathwater in tubs, a rule we also followed. Some upset citizens during this so-called Bore War had put up crude signs reading *Snore War* and scribbled out the words bravely claiming, *London Can Take It!* to write instead *Take What? Our Own Govt's Bloody Blackout?*

"That 'London Can Take It' is a brave sign," I told Bertie. "But when the bombs fall and the Nazis come, we've seen our fellow royals in European countries cannot sometimes take it."

"We've had a rash of royal visitors, have we not, my dear?

Poor Queen Wilhelmina having to flee the Netherlands in May when Hitler's forces came calling."

"So sad. She had only the clothes on her back and that too-big tin hat for protection when we met her at the Liverpool station and took her in. I think it was a great comfort to her when her daughter and grandchildren arrived here safely too."

"And a good move on your part to find them a house in Eaton Square and then suggest they go to Canada for the rest of the war to be completely safe." He sighed. "If any of us royals are completely safe in this chaos in our homelands."

"My two favorite royal Norwegians seem to have made the best of it, but then they are men."

"I would argue the females of the species are more hardy than the males—at least around here," he said and patted my knee. "But of course we had to take in my uncle King Haakon and Prince Olav."

"I hope to find a place for them to stay outside the palace, for it would be dreadful if they were hurt here. Bertie, they both try to cope by sleeping all the time, and that hardly helps!"

"But we, at least, are a help to other royals who need us. I know, I know—I swear you would take everyone in at Buck House if you could, including your entire staff's families in case our land is bombed too."

I did not argue that for, when we were barely back at Buck House, I thought I heard thunder in the distance on this sunny day. But it wasn't the sounds of a storm I heard but rather a *boom-crump-boom*.

Once we were inside, Bertie took a phone call from Winston that London was at last under attack.

Before running down to the shelter, we opened a window casement and stood there, his arm clamped tight around me as we both gaped at the sight and shuddered with fear and anger.

The eastern sky over the Thames and East End was black with a swarm of planes like mad, diving bats. Bertie said, "They bombed our RAF bases on the way in, but we still scrambled some fighters. Yet there seem to be hordes of the hellhounds."

"Smoke and fire too," I told him, my voice quavering. Tears ran down my face. Bombs killing our people. Fires burning London, just as in the capital cities and nations of the European royals who had fled here.

"They're hitting the East End, the docks, the factories, but that doesn't mean they won't come here," I said. "Let's go downstairs."

But I didn't budge for another moment, horrified, mesmerized. Bertie didn't either but began to recite from memory part of the radio speech he'd given in early September to the nation and Empire. "For the second time in the lives of most of us we are at war. Over and over again we have tried to find a peaceful way out of the differences between ourselves and those who are now our enemies. But it has been in vain. We have been forced into a conflict."

I gripped his hand tighter and added, "Life, sadly, publicly and personally has too many conflicts. God forbid any are hurt and God bless our beloved people."

"Let's go down, darling," he repeated as several of the staff knocked and rushed into his sitting room to escort us, one holding the single corgi our daughters did not have. "At least the girls are at Windsor," I said, choking back a sob.

I worried about all the Londoners who must be surprised tonight to know that real war was here. I thought of Bessie's family, of anyone who lived or worked down by the East End along the Thames. At least it was a Saturday, but some of the factories had been pushing round-the-clock shifts with overtime pay.

Bertie tugged me away from the dreadful display of color and noise and those damned diving planes peppering the sky. No more Phoney War, no more Bore War. The battle had come at last to England.

CHAPTER EIGHT

Target Practice

That monster Hitler's Blitzkrieg besieged our beloved island home and city. We huddled in the palace shelter that afternoon, though Bertie was told none of the bombs were falling near us. Not true, I thought. They fell on us and in us as we mourned for our dear people and our land.

With our diminished staff in the shelter next door to ours, we sat for hours in our dimly lit one, yet probably the most unusual, posh one in Britain, truth be told. It appeared to be a shapeless catacomb with a conglomeration of furniture, gilt chairs, a velvet settee, and a huge Victorian mahogany dinner table. On the walls were oil paintings that could not be stored elsewhere, most of charming landscapes to make us wish we were in the country in the sunlight. I sometimes moved about, speaking to all who were huddled here to buck them up.

But besides sitting by the king in our shelter, I also went next door to comfort poor Bessie, whose family and friends were East Enders where the bombs were falling. The staff had an old piano stored here, but no one was attempting to play it, and the furnishings were a far cry from those in our shelter.

"Will you give me leave to go home, Your Majesty?" she'd asked me more than once. I had been holding her hand just as I would have held my girls' hands had they been here, which, thank the Lord, they were not. No bombs at Windsor, Bertie had been told.

"You mustn't go into the area if there are still fires," I told her. "You would just get in the way of the firefighters. You tell me the street, and I'll find out how things fared. There are shelters they surely went to, your people."

"Everyone says they should be allowed to use the tube stations underground, ma'am," she said with a sniffle, which was at least better than another flood of tears. The handkerchief I had given her was a wet wad. "But the 'guv'nors and powers that be'—that's the way my da said it—claim folks will just get underfoot with their blankets and all in the tube stops, even along the rails. And crowd the loos besides making do with their own necessary pots."

I decided to talk to Bertie and Winston about using the Underground stations. I'd heard people did anyway and balked at being moved out to newly dug shelters. And weren't our people's lives worth crowded tube stops?

Eventually, after what seemed an eternity, we were told the all clear was sounding. Out we all went like a little flock of sheep, timid, wary to see the dusk before the coming darkness through the netted windows. One of Bertie's staff took him aside, whispering, nodding. Meanwhile, not only was my body screaming from exhaustion, but the trembling that began during the first of the bombing was back again.

Bertie came over and took my elbow. I leaned into him as we headed up two flights of stairs and down the corridor toward our suites.

"Our planes scrambled, but much damage done," he told me. "Darling, you are shaking."

"Nerves. Outrage that it is finally here. Winston promised the nation blood, sweat, and tears, and I fear that it has all come calling. Damnation, I could use a drink!"

"You need sleep, and I need to get to work."

"I couldn't sleep right now. I told Bessie I'd let her know about her home area. And do ask whomever you must to see if the Underground stations can be used for shelters."

"So far, no."

"You advise and consent, so why not suggest? Tell them yes."

He hugged me at the door to my rooms and turned the knob for me.

"Bertie, I know you have so much to do but come in for just a minute and hold me. Hold me!"

He looked surprised but hustled in behind me and closed and locked the door. He sat on the chintz lounge chair where I sometimes put my legs up and pulled me onto his lap.

"I don't mean to delay our king from his duties," I said and wrapped my arms around his neck. The square of medals on his midnight blue naval uniform was hard and cold against my cheek.

"You are my most precious duty—you and the girls—and this beleaguered nation."

I held hard to him and he to me. He lifted my chin and kissed me with a strange combination of desperation and desire, and I kissed him back, opening my lips to his. Such sensual passion had been so long put away between us, and at my behest—my fault. This terrible attack had shaken me when I must be strong. No excuse, here protected in the palace with a shelter to run to, far from the fires.

But I felt better now, safer, a bit saner, sheltered in my husband's arms with a fire in me I'd forbidden for years between us.

* * *

I pointed my Enfield .38-caliber revolver at the wooden target of the man with the bushy black mustache and pulled the trigger. I was out in the depths of the palace gardens alone but for a guard, plugging away at what I thought of as Hitler. If I ever had a chance to shoot him like this, I would. Bombs had fallen on London and our seaports for weeks now. France was overrun, and, I swear, even if it meant my own death, I would not tremble as I tended to do during air raids, though none had come to this area of the West End and—*bang, bang!* Ah, got him in the crotch that time, so I hope he felt that.

But I was aiming for his heart and head. More practice needed. I had, however, greatly disturbed and been scolded by the greylag geese near the copper beeches on the lake.

A voice behind me made me jump. "I pray, Your Majesty," came Winston's now familiar ringing tones, "that is who I think it is and not your own prime minister who you think has been stalling on opening up the Underground stations. We have done so now."

I lowered the pistol and shook his hand. Behind him, in the shadows of a chestnut tree, stood his security man, called a detective, who always wore a bowler hat.

"Then I approve of our prime minister wholeheartedly," I told him. "You did know the king was out this morning?"

"I did, but some of this can't wait, and I plan to tour the newly bombed areas, so I will be quite busy this afternoon."

"I would like to go with you."

"Excellent public relations that would be too, but I hear Your Majesties plan to tour the East End again soon. As I have told the king, however, there is some bad feeling from the tough and sturdy people there that they are taking the brunt of it all, while the 'toffs and royals' are unscathed."

"I can understand that. So one of my staff has been telling me. Her family home was burned the first night of the Blitz, and her parents are living with one of their sons."

I gestured to a bench surrounded by plane and hornbeam trees. He seemed to be quite out of breath. Winston's girth always made me feel petite by comparison. We sat comfortably side by side. Both of our security men kept their distance but shifted their positions to keep us in sight.

"What news then, that I might relay to the king?" I asked. "Something about the Windsors on the beach in scenic Nassau, Bahamas?"

"Aha," he said. "I must tell you that the Duke of Windsor

himself once warned me you were a marshmallow with a bit of arsenic hidden inside."

I gasped, then laughed. "Did he then? And I thank you for being so honest to share that with me. So, on to the arsenic—what news of them?"

"More of the same, yet worse. Thank God His Majesty rules here, not his elder brother, whom I was much misguided to champion for a while, though I never would have let him share the throne with Mrs. Simpson. I helped him write his now famous abdication speech, you know."

"I did not know, but tell me what you have learned now."

He cleared his throat and produced a piece of paper from his coat pocket. "I wanted to be sure I repeated it all correctly, ma'am. This is from, let us say, someone who serves in their abbreviated household there."

I must remember this man was not above using spies, domestic ones at that. I nodded and gripped my hands in my lap around my pistol.

"The duchess has called the Bahamas 'a sweltering dump and a hellhole hotter than the hinges of Hades.' And upon first seeing the shores there, as beautiful as I hear they are, she said loudly, 'We have been sent to the island of Elba and you, my darling, are far better than Napoleon.'"

"At least she knows some European history."

He stifled a grin. His jowls hardened as he frowned. "But more seriously, and you may tell the king this if you do not think it will hurt or anger him overmuch, the duke has been heard to say that if Britain can be heavily bombed, at least peace will come sooner. To which his wife added, 'I feel I've already been bombed by Buckingham Palace. Yes, I've suffered worse than their Blitzkrieg bombings.'"

"What traitors they have become. I will tell the king that—in time, at the right time."

"So there they are for the duration, partying with the rich if not the famous. But I have another bit of intelligence I must share with you, a quote about you not by the exiles but from the mustached mouth of our enemy, Herr Hitler," he said, pointing at my target, which was riddled with bullet holes.

"Really? He said something about me?"

"Indeed, and I would take it as the highest order of compliment if I were you. Perhaps he even meant it that way."

I realized I was holding my breath as he said, "I have it on the best authority that he has said you are propping up the king, perhaps something he got from the Duke of Windsor or even his wife. I have decided not to tell the king that, but, of course, you may if you must."

"Perhaps someday. It's not true, of course—propping up—although we comfort each other and are a team. The king has come a long way in the three-plus years he has had the burden of the throne thrust upon him, then the war—and he will see it through."

"I agree. I see he and I have a great deal in common and I value the partnership we are building. But that is not all from Herr Hitler. My sources tell me that after viewing film footage of your and the king's successful Canada–United States tour, he said—more than once, I believe—that you are the most dangerous woman in Europe, making allies, rallying others to England's cause. And, again I say, I would take that as the highest compliment."

"I hope that is true and will be more true—and not just because I would shoot him with my revolver—as soon as I can control it."

We shared a smile. I thought he might take his leave, but he went on, "Now to other news I am sure you will share with His Majesty. I believe I have heard that you do not care for my friend and ally Lord Beaverbrook, nor does the king. Ma'am, it is essential for the war effort that I place Beaverbrook in charge of aircraft production, which must be accelerated, obviously, even though our RAF boys are becoming more skilled at knocking the damned Messerschmitts out of the sky. If I were to present to you a dossier on Beaverbrook, I am certain you would determine he is the best man for that essential task and would share that with the king."

However had he learned I, as well as the king, did not favor "The Beaver," as his rivals called him? I had not trusted that man since I'd heard he was the one who had ferreted out that I was behind the China Dossier—and had, no doubt, shared that with Winston. I had tried to move beyond that, but had this man, the only one in the kingdom more powerful than my own husband, done so? I was no fool and I'd picked up on Winston's smooth sliding in of the word *dossier*.

"If you judge him necessary for the war effort, I would certainly understand, and I am sure the king would second that," I managed, fighting to keep my voice steady.

"Ah, then, after we rise and I bow and back away, I will not fear that a stray shot will hit me in the posterior," he said with an impish grin.

Despite how this man could rattle me—and perhaps control me—I had to smile. "As you can see, I am not the best of shots yet, but I will be. And I'm going to see that the princess Elizabeth learns to shoot too. The king says he'll not have his eldest daughter in uniform whether she is serving the wounded or bucking up spirits, but I say she should learn to shoot and to serve."

"Then I would wager, Your Majesty," he said as he bowed and took several steps backing away, "that the princess Elizabeth will in due time be a boon and a boost to our war effort."

"Winston, one more thing," I said as I stood and went a few steps closer. "These bad feelings of the East Enders toward those of us who have not been bombed these weeks of the Blitz—these social class difficulties—do you think another visit by their king and queen could patch that over or make the feelings worse? Bessie, my East End staffer, and indeed my friend, has told me the people there feel as if day-trippers come in to gape at their ruined homes, rather like visitors to a zoo, then go back to their nice, comfy homes. She says the gawkers often eat up what foods the restaurants there have to offer, when food is scarce in bombed-out areas."

"I think you and His Majesty should go yet again—and again, everywhere and anywhere in the kingdom. Eyes and feet on the devastation, hands pressing the flesh there. Forgive me for being so blunt, ma'am, but I have seen your presence alone, your smile, your kind words, work wonders and, God knows, we need wonders here—and there—if we are to survive as a city and a nation. Only a united citizenship and victory will do."

I nodded and waved to him as he disappeared with his faithful watchdog right behind him.

For a moment a shaft of fear shot through me, that if Hitler thought all that of me, I might be somehow targeted.

Then I steadied my hands and went back to shooting my pistol at the target of the man who thought I was the most dangerous woman in Europe. I vowed that, somehow, I would show him that was true.

CHAPTER NINE

More Bombs

*F*ear not only of bombing but of invasion ran rampant. Churchill had told us in private that there was classified information about a German Operation Sea Lion to take our beaches whilst pounding us with more bombs, concentrated on port cities, some of which had already been hit, and, of course, London, home to nine million people, nearly one-fifth of Britain's population.

Our prime minister had broadcast to the nation in his usual ringing, defiant tones. We had agreed with him that one large contribution the king and I could make was to see and be seen, so we were endeavoring to make trips out to other cities and the countryside, together or separately, to boost morale. But today we were heading for the second time to survey the devastated East End of London, to the neighborhood called West Ham, from which Bessie hailed. It had been pounded especially hard last night so I had let her go there today ahead of us with the promise that, unless her family really needed her, she would be back at the palace by dark.

I told Bertie in the motorcar, "I actually pondered possibly dressing down today, but Winston said they want to see their queen, not another gawker, so I'm dressed to the nines again. I fear I shall stand out like a sore thumb."

"More like a lovely entire hand reaching out to everyone. Wouldn't do to go down there any other way. I approve that you look every inch a queen, for it will lift spirits."

"And I look every kilogram of weight, I fear."

"My dearest," he said, reaching his hand over to cover my knee, "you are beautiful to me—ravishing—and ever will be."

Ravishing? An interesting word since we had been more physically affectionate than usual lately. But with the military discipline that governed his entire life, he kept holding back from taking the lead or pushing for more. Oh, of course, my wanting a platonic marriage had wounded his pride and self-esteem, but I had built him up in other ways.

I sensed he wanted me to make more of the first steps, but who had time for that in this chaos? Besides, a royal marriage and lovely honeymoon aside, I did not find physical love exalting but . . . a bit messy. Yet one thing this war had done, was that Bertie had no time for or interest in the few women I had tolerated as his "special friends" off and on over the years.

The closer we drove to the East End this time, the more we both grasped the extent and impact of German bombs. Barricades and detours had kept our earlier tours out of the most heavily bombed area. I saw clearly the single hit we had suffered at Buck House in the garden three days ago, which caved in a few walls and landed in the garden—thank heavens—was nothing next to this, even though what the police thought was a dud had detonated hours later and terrified us all. But we had been assured by the local bomb mechanics that this area was safe with all ordnance exploded.

We saw such large craters in some of the streets that our driver had to take a most circuitous route. We might not be gawkers but we both gawked. Even poor Bessie's dramatic descriptions and the newspapers' photographs could not convey this. At least we had to smile at the black humor of some people when we saw a man on the sidewalk holding a hand-printed sign as if he were picketing: *At least Jack's safe in the Army!!!!*

Everywhere in West Ham we saw dust, mounds of yellow rubble, and collapsed walls. A clock without hands reminded me of the daily statistics of human injuries and death. A filling station had been completely gutted by fire and explosions from petrol reserves that had blown out nearby buildings. I pointed at a storefront that was devastated, yet sported the crudely printed, cheeky words on a poster: *More Open Than Usual.* Ah, our beloved Londoners did have backbone and wit.

As we pulled up to our disembarkation point, I saw crowds had gathered. Oh my, but we would be walking round and through piles of rubble here too. Should I not have worn pumps and this light-colored suit and big brimmed hat? And Bertie wore his dark blue dress uniform, which would show every hint of dust. But, I prayed, getting dirty might show them we were with them, of them.

The moment we stepped from the motorcar, we scented a rank odor, coal gas and ash, I expect. And too, the smell of wet plaster from all the fire hoses that had shot water for hours on the flames of burning buildings.

We were greeted with curtsies and bows by the local aldermen and their wives. As we turned to walk with them, the king remarked on the devastation, but, for one moment, I startled as my feet crunched through a glitter of shattered glass. Nor did it help that at that very moment, several newspaper cameramen appeared and popped those bright lights in our faces—but then, at least, those who could get a paper would know we cared and dared.

A three-story house—I wondered if it could belong to Bessie's family—looked every bit like a dollhouse I had once, that is, with open fronts to all the rooms. Pictures and a calendar hung askew on walls, some furniture tottered there, and curtains fluttered as if some giant had ripped off the front of the place to expose its people to prying eyes—and to utter devastation. Saddest of all, on the second story was a bathtub and lavatory with a roll of toilet paper blowing in the breeze as if waving forlornly down at us. It hit me then with stunning force as it had not before: Not only people's homes, but their intimate lives and bodies had been ripped open.

"Everyone salvages what they can, Your Majesty," an alderman told us, seeing where I was looking.

"Salvage what the savages don't destroy," I said and everyone in earshot, even the king, nodded or murmured agreement.

We continued to pick our way through and around the rubble. The king made observations. I spoke to people in the crowd and shook hand after hand. I was tempted to take off my beige gloves, not to save them but to, as Winston had said, press the flesh of our people.

"You are all being so very brave," I told a cluster of women. "I admire your courage greatly."

"Will you be leavin' London, then, ma'am?" a woman asked.

"Except for visiting our daughters who are at Windsor, we are staying in London. The king won't leave his people, and I won't leave the king. And I was born in London, you know, so I consider myself a Londoner too."

Actually, I knew that was not quite true, but my "mother" Cecilia had been in London when I was born in St. Paul's Walden Bury in Hertfordshire, so I had never changed her story of a London birth. My parents' claim I was delivered here was to avoid any questions about where—and to whom—I was actually born. And once, when questioned closely, I did say that my mother delivered me here in our city home, then went immediately to our English country home to convalesce.

A few people applauded my comments that "the king won't leave" and "I am a Londoner." A man back in the crowd called out, "The Jerries, they don't like the blackout, at least. Do their dirty business daytime, so you's brave to come here now. And thankee for the gov'ment opening up the tube stops, gov'nor— Your Majesty, I mean," he called to the king.

"We hope to have even more RAF planes in the sky soon to help protect all of you, and we will rebuild when victory is ours," the king told them, raising his voice. "The queen and I deeply regret that you, the backbone of our city and nation, have taken the brunt of these attacks so far."

"They come here, we'll fight them in the streets!" a man called out.

"And I with you!" the king shouted.

Tears filled my eyes as the crowd did a hip-hip-hooray for us, and someone started to sing "For He's a Jolly Good Fellow," though that soon petered out.

As we headed back to the motorcade, still stopping to encourage and praise individual East Enders, I saw Bessie in the crowd near our escort vehicle. When I walked nearer, I motioned her over. She came, leading a bent-over, grey-haired woman by the hand. Could her mother look that old?

Bessie curtsied, and the woman nearly went off balance trying the same, but Bessie held her up.

"Your Majesty, this is my gran, because my mum's having more trouble today. Bombs hurt her ears something awful, and she's having nightmares, even in daytime like this."

"I am so sorry to hear that but very pleased to meet your gran," I said and exchanged a few words, asking about her life.

"Been through worse, Majesty, lost two sons in the Great War. But this one's just turned bloomin' bad too."

"With strong women like you and your neighbors, we will make do and make it through. I am sure everyone will do their bit. Bessie, are you planning to stay here longer? Do you need more time with your mother? I worry about your going back across town alone in this chaos. Some of the omnibuses have been lost and had their routes changed or halted, you know, and you mustn't be out in the blackout."

"Just got to get Gran back to my cousins in the crowd," she said, craning her neck. "Then I'll be setting out on foot."

"Not walking. And there are many potholes and roundabout ways. You take care of your dear gran and meet me at the motorcar straightaway. I insist," I added, when I sensed she would dare to argue.

She did as I said and stood nervously by the big Rolls Royce when I had said my farewells and the door was held open for me.

"Bessie's going too," I told Bertie under my breath. "I will not leave her here to walk home alone. Get in with us," I told her, "because the detective needs to sit in front with the driver."

Blushing madly, she did as I said. Bertie climbed in after me so I sat in the middle.

"Put her over here, so you can wave on our way out," he told me.

And so, my dear East End girl rode away with us, sitting between her king and queen. She and I had a good laugh the next day and Bertie just rolled his eyes when one of the newspapers reported that Princess Elizabeth was seen with her royal parents in their motorcar returning from the East End.

Indeed, we needed things to smile at and laugh over, and I had that snippet of newspaper framed for Bessie. It made me miss my own girls again, though I believed they were safe, so that was the very least of my worries.

* * *

One of my arranged trips into the countryside to see and be seen, while the king went elsewhere to assure our people, was to St. Paul's Walden Bury, which had been my English country home whilst I grew up, when I was not in Scotland. Distant relatives lived there now but were away. I was happy to see the big, old house again, yet nervous too, since I was a jumble of emotions about the place.

Such happy memories. Yet as I walked through the familiar rooms preparing to mingle with the crowd outside, I could not but help think that this was where my real—that is, my biological—mother had worked and lived for many years. And conceived and bore a girl child, and then my dear brother David shortly after.

How I loved the large, redbrick house with its grey slate roof and gardens stretching to woodlands. It was where I had finally accepted Bertie's proposal to be his wife. It seemed so lovely here, so peaceful compared to bustling, beleaguered London.

Outside, through windows blessedly not covered with wire netting and glue and beyond walls that had not been bombed to oblivion, I saw the clusters of waiting townsfolk had been augmented by farmers from the nearby town of Welwyn and surrounding areas. I was deeply moved as I went out to a lovely welcome with applause and gave my usual speech about all of us British hanging on in perilous times. I then moved through the crowd to speak to people individually.

"So special you are here," one rosy-cheeked woman said. She bobbed me a curtsy, and I took her hand. "You being born here and all, I mean."

"Actually, I was often here as a child, but born in London," I told her with a smile. "My nickname in my toddling days was 'Merry Mischief.'"

"Well, ma'am," she said, "I did bookkeeping work for the baby doctor Dr. Thomas in Welwyn, and he claimed to be present here at your birth, he did. Got paid his fees for the delivery too."

My stomach fell to my feet. I knew the doctor's name. And had he said who the woman in labor and delivery was? Yes, he had probably brought me into the world by tending to the house's pretty French cook.

"I believe he tended to my mother, Lady Strathmore, and me when we arrived here shortly after my birth in London," I told her.

"Oh, if you say so, Your Majesty. I guess you would know even though there's a real nice plaque nearby says you was born here."

I forced another smile. Several years ago, I had been part of that dedication day, having accepted the invitation to attend before I realized several local folk knew I had been born here—and had arranged a ceremony and plaque to commemorate and celebrate that.

Rather than dig myself in deeper—for I had seen in the crowd a reporter from the *London Times* who was tagging along, I moved on, smiling, chatting, waving.

Again, midday though it was, I wished I had a drink, a strong mixed one, as a matter of fact, my can't-do-without Dubonnet and gin. I often had it packed to travel with me but had overlooked that today. I had no intention of turning into a sot, but lately it helped me to cope, to cling to the good things and times before this bloody war. Because the temporary oblivion the most dangerous woman in Europe, the queen of England with the stiff upper lip and stiff drink, sometimes sought was hard to come by lately.

And there it was lurking in the sunny beauty of this place, one of the several bombs in my past life I feared could yet explode. That I was the daughter of a foreign cook. That I kept the king of England from my bed, so that our two princesses were conceived through artificial insemination, though surely borne by their loving mother. That all of those bombshells made me a fraud of the highest order who both had adored and now hated the man who had once been king, and the horrible, lower-than-low woman whom he adored and had given up his throne to marry. And what he had so cruelly done to me.

* * *

Almost all of our family's rooms were on the north side of Buck House, the girls' bedrooms two stories above ours. We had no central heating, but tried to make the rooms as cozy as possible with radiators as autumn set in. We had mostly adapted to what was already in that living section of the palace, except for Bertie's having ordered a squash court and swimming bath built for the girls and him to enjoy, though I went in too upon occasion when no one but the family was about. How the girls loved splashing and swimming. And a glass roof covered the pool and court so whenever the London sun was out, we enjoyed the warmth.

So it seemed more than the roof, squash court, and pool were shattered when a bomb hit that area in 1940. I dreaded telling Lilibet and Margot when I saw them at Windsor next.

The morning after the bomb, the tenth of September, the king and I walked amongst the ruins. Even he blinked back tears. It was as if something had been taken from us again, the early family joy of being together, learning things, splashing each other when there was no war, no sad separations.

A newspaperman in our little entourage remarked, "Your Majesties, this is a dreadful loss."

I turned to him. "Since this is the royal palace, the enemy means it as an assault on our nation, not just on us. We do make rather a large, obvious target. But compared to the loss of entire homes—of lives of our dear people—this is a small thing. Just glass and stones, not blood and bones. Our hearts are with those of our nation who have lost dear ones in battle or on the home front. We will endure and win."

Bertie took my arm and faced the little crowd of staff, security, and newsmen.

"The queen and I stand in solidarity with our bold people. As our prime minister says so eloquently, only victory will do."

Once inside, we held hands, almost had to hold each other up.

Bertie said, "Winston has nothing on you, my love. Do you think we shall ever have a woman P.M.? I would say tally-ho for one, if she was as bold and bright as you. I think I have said this before but don't know how the bloody hell I'd manage without you."

"I don't mind talking to the nation about this loss, but I will hate telling Lilibet and Margot. And if we can have queens who rule like Elizabeth the first and Victoria, why not a female P.M. someday?"

"And we are rearing Queen Elizabeth the second, are we not?"

"I pray she won't be queen for many, many years. But Bertie, our world is being bombed to bits, so when we rebuild, perhaps some things will change, a new, modern Georgian era under my beloved King George VI."

Though we never showed affection to each other in the public places in the palace, he put his arm around my waist as we climbed the dusty, rubble-strewn north staircase together.

CHAPTER TEN

To See Clearly

Sadly, I became used to the wasplike buzzing of planes over the Thames and East End. Except for one day, London had been repeatedly bombed for weeks—long, terrible weeks. At least our Spitfires had taken down German planes, some of which had bombed the West End.

Our enemy did not realize it, but that actually helped our home front, our cause. Just when the East Enders were turning against the West Enders because we had not been hit, we were. That made Londoners more united, though I felt our bomb damage here at the palace—especially a mere luxurious swimming bath and squash court—hardly let us look the poor East End in the eye. As tragic as it was to have one dead and two injured on our palace grounds, there were thousands of injuries and deaths in London, mortality statistics that, despite the bomb shelters, were staggering.

Today was Friday, 13 September—ha, Friday the Thirteenth.

The king and I had established the routine of spending our days in London but our nights with our girls at Windsor. We could see that was the best strategy for now.

I took yet another sip of my drink, frowning, remembering how the Prince of Wales, damn him for a traitor, used to tease me that Dubonnet was not a real "cocktail" even mixed with gin. Every slang word, everything American, fast, and modern—and svelte—that's what he liked. He'd used such crude slang he'd picked up in the United States, such as "hit me again," meaning his butler should pour him another drink.

I took a second swallow. It went down well. How stupid I had been to once imagine I would be his queen, and here I was, queen anyway, and at war with him as well as Germany.

I drained the glass and decided to nip down the hall to see how Bertie was doing. He had been working hard to memorize a coming speech and study the war papers, as we called them, that Winston had left for him to read. "Just leave the documents, and I'll study them tonight and discuss them soon," he usually told Winston at what the three of us jokingly called our weekly "picnics."

At the luncheons we kept the food simple and simply served, for each of us selected from the side table what we wanted, to avoid having servants hovering. I almost always sat in so far, letting Bertie mostly do the talking and deciding, at least in front of Winston. But I was honored they included me and listened to me. I believe Winston knew it not only bolstered Bertie, but that I would support the P.M.'s point of view and not just the king's.

I went down the hall, careful to walk a straight line and wishing I could see out the netted windows. Some of the aeroplanes sounded close. From the motor sounds, Bertie could even tell whether the plane was ours or theirs. I hoped they were RAF Hurricanes and Spitfires in the sky and not just the damned Luftwaffe.

I knocked and went into his study, which always smelled like leather and cigarette smoke. It had a marvelous view down the Mall, and I saw he had the tall, main windows open to enjoy the September air, despite the battles in the distant sky. I hated to say it, but we were getting used to that and sometimes, unless our security men dragged us there, had decided to forgo the daily wasted time in the palace air-raid shelter.

He was alone, for once. No aides, no secretary.

"Darling," he said, looking up, wreathed in a haze of cigarette smoke before the crisp breeze blew it away. "Just reading dispatches. Our aeroplane production will soon be up under Lord Beaverbrook's aegis, both fighters and big bombers, so we can strike at Berlin. Hitler has promised his nation and capital that will never happen, so it is high on our list."

"I know. Any other news of the day?"

"The forces of Herr Hitler's evil twin Mussolini are invading Egypt. We must fight them both, and Japan's making noises it wants to be allied with them."

"At least Japan is far away," I said, walking behind his desk and putting my hand on his shoulder. He covered my hand there with his.

"I'm glad you came in for several reasons," he told me, sliding his chair back. "Listen to a part from my speech I go rather haltingly over, will you? I fear I'll catch my breath—hesitate a bit. It's the impact of the words, I think, that is rattling me."

"Of course," I said.

"I should kiss you like a Brit would do to a Brit he loved," he said with a little laugh, bending over my hand to kiss the back of it. "But I shall also say, '*Enchanté, madame*'—like a Brit would to a Frenchwoman," he said and kissed my palm, even darting his tongue briefly out to lick my skin there.

Feeling that surprise move down to the pit of my stomach, I froze for a moment. Was he alluding to—could he have an inkling I was part French? Could his brother or his brother's duchess have told him to get back at me? But he'd never said a word, never even hinted at it.

"Elizabeth? Just teasing. Sit over there, and I'll sit here, since that's the way it will be when I speak into the microphone."

I smiled and nodded and did as he said. He began in mid-speech with the section that was evidently bothering him: "Let no one be mistaken. It is no mere territorial c-c-conquest that our enemies are seeking. It is the overthrow, complete and final, of this Empire and of everything for which it stands, and after that the c-c-conquest of the world.

"You see!" he went on, smacking his hand on the desk. "There is something in that section that bothers me, frightens me!"

I stood and went around his desk again. "Bertie, this whole war is frightening and you are doing yeoman's work—a fine job of leadership and inspiration."

"Perhaps I am afraid I will make some colossal mistake—'Let no one be mistaken.' And that last line seems like predicting doom, Armageddon, the end of the world. Drat, now I've got an eyelash in my eye," he muttered, blinking madly.

"Here, don't rub it. Let me see. Look up," I said, bending over him.

"Sit on my lap to get closer and not hurt your back, twisting like that. And do I scent you have been having a drink without me?"

"And do I scent," I shot back, feeling suddenly defensive, "that you are smoking mad and smoking too much?"

"Compared to Winston's cigar smell, who cares?"

"I see it. Hold steady, and I'll get it."

"Must I have an eyelash in my eye to get you onto my lap, my love? Since that day London was first bombed, you haven't repeated that request."

"Don't blink so much. Here, let me help to hold your eye open."

He slid his arm that was around my waist downward and stroked my bum.

"Bertie, you are distracting me."

"I'd like to. But whatever is that—that louder sound? That buzz, that droning *whir-whir* growing louder? Bloody hell, it can't be!"

He gripped me hard and stood so fast I almost slid to the floor, bumping my hip into his desk as he set me back.

"It is just the constant hum of those Luftwaffe planes, of course," I told him as if I were one of Winston's military advisors. "Bertie, let's go into the lavatory so we can have better light than from the window and see the eyelash in the mirror. Bertie, what?"

He moved to the window. He even leaned out a bit, staring with his jaw dropped open. I joined him there and saw what he meant. Out of the cloudy sky dropped a German plane, close, heading right for the palace down the Mall.

"Damn!" he said, sounding more awestruck than afraid. "It sounded like one of them, and it's coming straight at us!"

I gasped and tried to drag him away, but he stood as if bolted to the floor. Indeed it barreled straight at us with a Spitfire right behind, with our plane perhaps afraid to shoot in our direction.

The *whir* became a roar. The Messerschmitt passed low overhead, and, for the first time, I heard the scream of the bomb descending, which so many people had described.

The shriek of it seemed endless. I may have screamed too. Then came an earth-shaking blast, close, too close. We both went off our feet to the carpeted floor, clinging together. My ears hurt. My soul hurt.

We clung hard, then Bertie rolled us against the wall, shielding me from the open window as the entire palace seemed to shake. Despite our efforts at netting, we heard glass shatter near and distant. If the tall window next to us had been closed, we would have been cut to pieces, for its daggers of glass exploded into the room, clattering onto his desk and beyond.

"Downstairs," he said. "Downstairs to the shelter. A closer hit, and we would be gone."

We stumbled to our feet and ran across his study, crunching glass. My knees were suddenly so weak I almost fell. Before we reached the door, it opened, and an aide started in, saw us, and held the door open as we rushed past.

"It hit in the quadrangle, Your Majesty," he said, quite out of breath. "Several hurt, I fear, men repairing the chapel."

"Damned Huns!" Bertie muttered. "We will strike Berlin."

As we hurried down the corridor—thank God, it looked quite normal except for missing windows—we heard cries from outside of "Bandages! Bandages here! Ambulance. Send for an ambulance!"

When we reached the ground floor, we saw the palace's first-aid members—selected staff—were busy with the wounded. I gaped at the devastation of the quadrangle with broken flagstones and soil thrown everywhere from the huge hole where the bomb had landed. I glimpsed one man on the ground, bloodied. I instinctively started over to see how he was, to comfort him if I could, but Bertie pulled me on.

"There may be another attack," he told me. "The bastards have changed tactics and may again. Winston's big fear is night bombings, but not this."

As we passed the kitchen toward the shelter—I could not wait to be sure the housemaids and Bessie were all right—Bertie stopped to question one of the workers who had not been injured. I darted several steps into the kitchen, for it had a glass roof, and I could just imagine it would be devastated.

It was one of the ironies here at Buck House that Queen Mary had asked me to keep on the French cook, a man. But he was excellent and of good spirits, even now when food was scarcer, and menus greatly abbreviated. Thank heavens, the glass roof had not rained down on him and his assistants, for it was quite intact overhead, one of the vagaries of bombing where one thing stood perfectly intact next to a collapsed building.

"I am so happy to see you well, monsieur," I told him in French. He was a bit of an ally and conspirator, for he knew well my sweet tooth and my love for what I called chocs, which were becoming rather hard to find these days.

He bowed and greeted me. "Just a little problem outside, yes, so tea and scones may be a bit late, Your Majesty. But have no fear, for Britain and France shall rise again, no matter what, yes?"

"Yes!" I told him and felt calmer for the first time since we had seen the plane roaring toward us. "I believe you will have to order that served in the shelter, for we shall truly sit there this time."

"When it is one's time to go—we go," he told me with a shrug. "And I believe, madam, it is your time to go from here at least, for the king is like an invading force in the doorway."

"Come now!" Bertie commanded.

I joined him, and after we checked to see our staff was in their adjacent shelter, we sat alone in ours. We always counted heads and listened to stories. Bessie had several new ones from her devastated neighborhood, but we didn't have time to hear all that.

After things quieted down, I told Bertie, "Now we can really look the East End in the face. I just pray those poor construction workers will pull through."

"Them and all of us and dear England," he whispered, gripping his hands together so hard his fingers went white. "Winston's so distraught about our losses, so perhaps we should not tell him how close that plane came to dispatching us. If that pilot dropped his bomb a second earlier, if we'd had the windows closed and caught all that glass . . ."

"Yes, I know. But Winston will hear the palace was hit."

He nodded fiercely. And if we were killed, I thought, would Winston have convinced Parliament to crown fourteen-year-old Elizabeth as queen and named someone to rule for her until her majority? Or God forbid, would he have decided to bring the Duke of Windsor back to rule until she was of age—with that German conspirator wife of his?

"I think it might be best," I said, "if we just let Winston, bright and perceptive as he is, realize we could have been hurt or worse, then see how he counsels us to handle it."

"Yes, yes, all right. You may be able to look the East Enders eye to eye now, but perhaps we should not advertise our vulnerability here—that the Huns could have k-killed us."

"Do you still have that eyelash in your eye?"

"Strange to talk of such again when we could be gone for good. I think it's washed out now—with my tears."

"You are not crying. You are ever brave through all this, and a great comfort to me, our staff here, and your people."

He gripped my hands hard in his as I went on, "We are a team in this, through this, my darling. You ever help me to see things clearly."

We sat in the dim corner of our shelter until the all-clear siren screamed. We went outside.

"Three workmen injured and one of them deceased, Your Majesty," an aide told him.

"See that his full wages for this entire chapel rebuilding

project are sent to his family," Bertie said. The man nodded, bowed, and backed away.

"Would that we could do that for all those being lost," I whispered as we went wearily upstairs. "One thing, though. I don't want Lilibet and Margot to know how close we came to—to the blast."

"Righto, my love. Onward and upward, as my father used to say, but then he used to say a lot of things, most not inspiring but brutal, like bomb blasts to David and me. To our dear brother George too. No wonder he turned to drink and drugs, not to mention other—others."

"But you survived, and here we are. Everyone has tough times in his or her childhood."

"Yes, you lost a brother in the first war and a sister to disease. At least everything else was rosy for you with your loving parents, and I always admired that. If it wasn't for this bloody war, maybe our girls would have the same charmed childhood as you did."

There it was again, not only his comparison of his strict parents with my affectionate, indulgent ones, but the suggestion he knew nothing of my true heritage. Again, I tried to tell myself it didn't matter who my mother was or that my worst enemies knew that my dear husband did not know. Or did he?

"Let's telephone the girls, for they are bound to hear" was all I said when I could have blurted out so much more, but now was not the time.

"And we certainly won't tell them how close we came," he insisted.

I intended to convince him to tell Winston or I would tell him secretly myself. No need to rile the man who knew at least my dossier secret.

"Yes," I said. "But it is best that children and sometimes even adults don't know certain sad or frightening things at all."

CHAPTER ELEVEN

Playacting

I almost felt guilty, taking time to visit my dress designer in such difficult times, but I was to be fitted for what were called "austerity clothes." After all, people expected me to look good—queenly—as one London paper had put it. Yet I needed to tone down my attire to emphasize the government's new clothing regulations.

"Welcome, Your Majesty," Norman Hartnell greeted me at the door to his Bruton Street townhouse in Mayfair. "I was telling everyone that you are fashion's North Star we steer by in these trying times."

I shook his hand as his staff curtsied behind him. I smiled at them before, with a wave of his hand, he sent them back to their duties. Norman was such a handsome man and still unmarried, an eternal bachelor, he called himself, dedicated to his art. We were much the same age. I had recently put all my fashion decisions in his capable hands, though Bertie had much to do with my finally leaving my longtime designer Madame Handley-Seymour.

I had stayed loyal to her and asked her to design my wedding dress, but I'd heard the murmurings it was old-fashioned, even . . . well, dowdy. So when Norman had designed gowns for Lilibet and Margot to be young bridesmaids for a family wedding, I saw his designs firsthand. And when I had come for the girls' fittings, I had been quite won over by the man's charm and designs for me to wear. I had hesitated at first because I knew that Mrs. Simpson had patronized his shop, but she, thank heavens, had moved on swiftly to Mainbocher, trying to enhance her thin, austere body and persona.

Even Bertie had chimed in with ideas of how I should be gowned, but now you might know, this war was ruining Norman's career too.

He escorted me toward his office through his lovely first-floor salon with its tasteful mix of Regency and very modern furniture. The lady-in-waiting who had accompanied me stayed in the salon, chatting with the shop's hostess. Beyond lay the spacious, mirrored fitting room with the seamstresses' spaces mostly upstairs.

The hallway was lined with photographs of women in Hartnell designs, though, out of respect, none of the royal family, only a copy of the Royal Warrant we had recently awarded him. It was always exciting to be here, for his clientele went beyond royalty to film royalty: Framed photographs of stars like Merle Oberon, Marlene Dietrich, and Vivien Leigh smiled at me from the dove grey walls.

Gone with the Wind was the hit movie of the year in the

States, and we had viewed an early run of it. The romance of the fashions had made Bertie decide that when we returned to entertaining again, I should wear full skirts—with crinolines, no less. Before the abdication, when I was so upset about that woman calling me the "dowdy duchess," Bertie had even showed Norman the Winterhalter portraits that hung at the palace, telling him he thought I would look lovely in that style, and so Norman had designed such gowns for me. Although that artist was German, which had made me want to disagree because of the so-called Great War, Bertie and Norman were convinced that the full skirt and feminine look with lace, satin, and pearls would be right for me during formal occasions—which we had so few of now.

I removed my gloves as we sat to tea in upholstered chairs across a small table with tea service laid out. I was charmed that he always poured for us himself while we reviewed my past and present fashions.

Norman told me, "I can remake any day dresses or gowns you need to fit the blasted rules, ma'am, but I cannot believe we've come to this. Rules on the amount of fabric in a garment? Specifics on the number of buttons, fastenings, and embroideries? By the way, I will have some of the entrancing beadwork, crystals, and pearls on your dresses and gowns removed for now, but I shall simply have the lavish embroidery dyed to hide it. It would be a sin to ruin some of those dresses. You know that I despise simplicity in design—in life. Your garments are works of art, and you so perfectly present them."

I took the teacup from him. "You've advised me so well, even to wear light colors, so people can pick me out better in these dark days—no mourning black, for that would be like giving in. I do think the three-quarter-length coats over the slimmer skirts for daywear and large hats give me more height. And I will ever be grateful for how quickly you managed to put together the mourning wardrobe for me when you had just completed everything for our trip to France before the war. You and your clever staff shifted so quickly from colors to French mourning white, when my—my mother Cecilia, Countess of Strathmore, died."

"I know how dear she was to you, but you rose to the occasion to be so deeply grieved yet carry on with steady aplomb. The French visit and North American tours went off fabulously—fashionably—well."

We shared a little laugh as he proffered a plate with scones and tarts. I could not resist trying several.

"And, of all people, you have helped me to be . . . well, to enhance my form and shape these last years, even now," I said, turning toward him more in my chair.

"We have adapted more than once, have we not? Colors just slightly muted now, dusty pink, blue, and lilac. Ah, that reminds me, I have a gift for you," he said with a broad smile as he popped up to take a hatbox from the shelves behind his desk. He had not touched his tea nor the pastries. I supposed that, and hard work, was how he stayed so trim.

"Every important woman," he said, "and you are the best of them—has her own style." He gave me time to put aside my teacup and sweets while he waited to put the box on my knees.

You might know, though it was not tied shut with a ribbon, it was covered with satin with a lace border.

I lifted the lid. "Whatever . . . ?" I asked and looked in at the items.

He leaned against the edge of his desk, hovering over me. "The mauve items are a gown and nightcap for you to don quickly should there be another air raid at the palace and you in bed, though, thank God, there has been no nighttime bombing yet. And that black velvet case is for your gas mask."

I had to laugh. "I'd best not let the East End know of that. But it's all delightful in these dreadful times. It lifts one's spirits. But for my other clothing, I'll trust you to stick to the austerity and utility rules. We must all do our bit for the cause. And I was proud to hear that you joined the Home Guard," I added as I put the items back in the box and perched it on his desk and he went back to his chair.

"I did, ma'am. We Home Guards are proudly augmenting professional security here in London, often at night—factories, the docks, main thoroughfares. Our duty is to be a secondary defense force and, if need be, to slow the advance of the enemy should they come here, to allow regular troops to regroup and deploy. We all must do our part—and my part is also designing for our dear queen."

* * *

In the dressing room, I stood on the small dais, surrounded by tall looking glasses, while Norman and his assistant Thelma draped canvas and cotton on me to find the correct proportions for my austerity clothes. Small seams and no lapels. Narrow belts. Skimpy lining.

"I sometimes feel as if I'm on a stage, playacting with everyone watching, but it is only these looking glasses that make me feel so here," I told him after he had recited measurements to a secretary, who wrote everything down. I was sadly certain that, despite cutting back on some foods at the palace per regulations—for the king and I were determined to keep the rules and suffer with our nation through all this—my measurements had gone up a bit.

"I can imagine, with eyes on you at all times, it is a bit like playacting," he said. "Now this day dress will be perfect with just a touch of pearls at the neckline."

"A pearl necklace, not sewn on—rules!" I told him.

"The queen may wear her jewelry to draw attention to the neckline rather than farther down. I cannot wait for the photographs in the newspapers."

* * *

Strange, but I knew women told their clothiers and hairdressers things they did not even tell their husbands. Norman understood I was sometimes playacting at being queen, and a queen in wartime at that. I told myself it was more like a history play and not a tragedy—and definitely not a comedy, though we tried to be lighthearted at times.

Actually, British citizens we spoke to were newly solicitous of us, as if the bombing of the palace had united us with them even more. Winston had absolutely insisted the attack on us be broadcast far and wide, though he didn't want it to get back to the Germans that the king and queen came close to being harmed or even killed in the apparently rogue attack, so that was not released at this time. Still, one woman even asked me if my "pretty things been blown to bits" like hers had been.

The very first day I wore a new austerity outfit with my trademark triple string of pearls, I had just leaned over to talk to a young woman in a wheelchair with a baby in her lap when the little boy reached up a hand to seize my necklace.

"Oh, no, Jackie! No!" the woman cried and made a grab for him.

"Quite all right," I assured her, putting my hand on the child's. "I have two of my own who used to act like that."

With a smile, I managed to disengage the little hand, nod at the relieved young mother, and move on, when a voice behind me said, "Oh, Your Majesty, I would have shot that picture of him with your necklace, so touching, so . . . real."

I turned to see a young woman when I was expecting a cameraman, but weren't they all in the service? "I understand," I said. "Let's stage it then."

"Oh, I'd be ever so grateful. I been trying to listen and learn, filling in like this at the newspaper, my big chance. Everyone's feeling you are one of us now, ma'am, since the palace been bombed and all."

"We have been bombed but we haven't lost all that these dear people have," I told her as I turned back to the surprised woman in the wheelchair and leaned over to hand my strings of pearls to little Jackie.

With a pop of her flashbulb, the young woman snapped the picture, thanked me effusively, then stopped to talk to Jackie's dazed-looking mother as I moved on. No doubt the photographer was taking the position of a man who had been called to duty—or like Norman, was serving with the Home Guard.

The photograph appeared in the *London Times* the next day with the photographer's name, so I snipped it out to keep. I wished I had my lady-in-waiting who had been with me that day get her name, but there it was, farther down in the article rather than under the photo since she had the presence of mind to also interview the crippled mother. I hoped I would see the brave lady photographer, Rowena Fitzgerald, again someday. And even perhaps Penelope Brown and her little Jackie. Not really playacting in public, but being myself, and with an avid, dear, and important audience.

* * *

That weekend at Windsor, Lilibet and Margot, with their governess Crawfie's help, had arranged two short drama scenes for us to see. How this reminded me of gay days growing up at Glamis when David and I would put on "plays" for everyone, some we wrote ourselves. Ah, such happy, peaceful times.

The town of Windsor had been bombed but not the sturdy, old castle itself. I was happy to see we were to be treated to scenes that could not possibly have any allusion to Philip of Greece, whom I was amazed to find Lilibet still pining for and reminiscing about as if they had spent hours, days, weeks together. Meanwhile, I kept my notes updated on possible future matches for her from British nobility.

Still, our eldest's care for others came through, which I told myself would stand her in good stead in the future. She had even asked me to say hello to her favorite police constable, Stephen Robertson, who guarded her at times when she, sometimes with Crawfie and Margot, walked our corgis on the palace grounds. He was a kind, conscientious man, one of our most loyal P.C.s, one who had even volunteered for night duty during these terrible times. I was glad our armed services let us keep some of our staff who would surely have been called to duty otherwise.

"The first scene is one Margot chose," Lilibet announced, standing at the front of the small stage recently erected for them here in the Queen's Ballroom, now stripped of its huge paintings, though the blue wallpaper made a lovely background.

They both wore white blouses with my old skirts belted about their little waists, knee-length skirts that looked quite long on them. Lilibet wore a cardboard crown. They had drawn and cut out a March Hare that Margot carried. A grinning Cheshire Cat, which looked to be crayoned instead of painted, smiled at us from the front of the stage, though the effect was a bit ruined by two of their corgis sitting there too.

"Margot's choice is from *Alice in Wonderland*," Lilibet went on. "She is Alice, and I am the Queen of Hearts. The second will be a short selection from *Romeo and Juliet*, where I speak most of the lines because she doesn't like that old-fashioned talk."

Their father applauded that little introduction, so I did too.

They disappeared behind the makeshift, old velvet curtain, then entered again. I must say, Alice ended up being chased by the Queen of Hearts, who kept shouting "Off with her head!" I mean, an English king had once been beheaded and two of Henry VIII's queens too.

Bertie shook his head at that, and I rolled my eyes but we applauded heartily again to their numerous bows as Margot beamed and Lilibet, quite out of breath, kept up a solemn expression.

And then to the romantic tragedy. Bertie reached over to take my hand and squeezed it once, in obvious pride for his daughters. Ah, I thought, Will Shakespeare should have written a drama about the lady who once longed to wed one royal brother, then wed the other and became queen anyway. A history play, no doubt, but would that also be a comedy or a tragedy? But I had the best of the bargain with the hero, not the villain, I thought, putting my other hand on top of Bertie's and forcing myself to focus on Lilibet's first attempt at the Bard's challenging, old-fashioned language.

> "I am yet a stranger in the world—
> I have not seen the change of fourteen years . . .
> Yet my bounty is as boundless as the sea,
> My love as deep; the more I give to thee."

On she went with the love words of Juliet to her young Romeo. Why had she chosen these passages, words of longing, of missing someone so beloved?

I sat up even straighter. She had even included a line about the sea, when Philip was at sea. Bertie would never believe me, so I would not bring it up and certainly not accuse her of pining for her own Romeo, whom she had spent so little time with—and look what happened to Juliet!

I fought to calm myself. *Storm in a teacup*, I told myself. Of course, both of our daughters were strong-minded, and was that not part of my heritage to them?

CHAPTER TWELVE

Locked Up

$\mathcal{D}$espite the shriek of the air-raid siren, we stood on the balcony where we had happily waved to the crowds after Neville Chamberlain promised "peace in our time," but now we were horrified and mesmerized. If we thought the Blitzkrieg bombing of London could not get worse, we were so wrong. Because Hitler's plan for daylight superiority in the skies did not achieve its end, thanks to our brave RAF pilots in their Hurricanes and Spitfires, October 1940 began a new terror: nighttime bombing. And, you might know, the very first night of it, we had decided to stay in London instead of motoring to Windsor to be with the girls.

"We must go get locked up in that damned shelter again," Bertie said, but he did not budge either. It was like seeing a moving picture or a huge kaleidoscope with vibrant colors on the black screen of the sky.

"What are those blasts of color that look like fireworks?" I asked, raising my voice to be heard over the distant booming. "It's like the sky on Guy Fawkes Day."

"Those huge sparklers are called incendiaries. They don't show up like that in the light of day. They fall and start fires."

"And so much more terrifying at night. People—at least they used to be able to sleep."

"Which we won't do one whit tonight, as good as locked up in that shelter. Let's go down. This is too awful—Winston's worst fear. And mine is that I'm terrified to the very depths of my soul whether, as the brave posters across the city say, 'London can take it.'"

I hugged him hard as we went inside and hurried down to our royal prison. And as we rushed into that solid cell of a room in the dim light, I nearly stumbled over a body—no, two!—on the floor.

Bertie grabbed my hand and righted me. Oh, our royal Norwegian guests, Bertie's uncle by marriage and his son, asleep—indeed, both snoring!

Prince Olav stirred and sat up. A handsome man in his late thirties, he was here in London with his father and their government in exile. He was the king's heir and only child and, had he been much younger, would have been a good prospect for Lilibet, however much I wanted her to marry British nobility.

"Oh, sorry, Uncle and Aunt Windsor," Olav said, obviously shaking himself awake and scrambling to his feet with a slight bow as his father snored on. "Best, we thought, to sleep down here once the noise began."

"A blessing you can sleep," I said, "but perhaps not so near the door. And I have very good news for you both, especially since the palace is an obvious target. I've arranged for both of you to move into Lord Harewood's house in Green Street,

Mayfair, where I hope things will be cozier and quieter. Better for sleeping."

"We are so grateful for your hospitality, Aunt Elizabeth, so grateful, and I'll tell Father right now when I wake him to move him."

"No—later will be fine, if we all make it till dawn in this jail cell," Bertie said. "We'll know to step over you next time—and step harder on those damned Nazis, yes?"

* * *

Christmas 1940 and New Year's 1941 were quite bleak, not only for the continued night bombing and bitter weather. We now faced the second year England must stand alone on our island under fierce air attack. Of course, our allies across the Channel were in enemy hands; German aeroplanes launched the night attacks from French bases. Yet we tried to make the holidays as cheery as we could for our daughters and our people.

We were heartened by our continued closer partnership with Winston. In January he wrote the king, *Your Majesty's treatment of me has been intimate and generous to a degree that I had never deemed possible.* And when I had walked him to the palace door after one of our "picnics," he had repeated the same words to me, adding, "It is a truth that neither the king nor I could do without you, ma'am." I cherished that moment.

February brought a bit of sun, but no real hope of American help. At least their Congress was debating a Lend-Lease Act that would give Britain extended credit so we could afford to purchase equipment, oil, and other goods and not have to pay for them until the end of the war. Perhaps even more good could come from a meeting Winston hoped to have with President Roosevelt somewhere neutral this coming summer—if summer even came. There were, however, new fears of invasion.

Yet I managed to keep my chin up, at least in public. Our nights and weekends at Windsor Castle gave me some respite in a weather thaw that February.

I walked into my bedroom at the castle, ready to ring for Bessie for my facial cream routine, when from behind a curtain a man I did not know appeared and grabbed me by the ankles and toppled me to the floor.

His expression was distorted by rage. He looked quite insane, distracted and unkempt, and kept mumbling something that made no sense. My first instinct was to scream, but he set me free and sat back on his heels, glancing around the room while I righted myself as far as getting to my knees. Though he seemed to have no weapon, I had the feeling that if I screamed he might do more.

God forbid, but he did look mad, with his eyes darting about the room. I calmed myself, biding my time to get to my feet and flee, or at least to be able to ring the bell for Bessie. Strangely, I felt I had seen that wretched, distracted look on some of the wounded I had visited recently, or even years ago on some of the soldiers we tended at Glamis in the first war, including two of my own brothers, Jock and Mike.

"Tell me about it," I said, quietly, recalling how I had calmed those others. "Tell me what happened."

"My family was killed by the Blitz. I deserted from the

Army, had to see for myself. Nothing left, them in unmarked graves. I . . . I been hired here to fix the lights, but there's no lights where my wife and two sons been buried."

"I am so sorry," I told him, getting carefully to my feet and edging away toward the bell to ring for help. "And you've been hired here as an electrician?"

He nodded, seeming to look through me rather than at me. He muttered, "Was repairing Spitfire motors at the aerodrome if they got shot up. I'm good as shot up."

My pulse pounded harder as he produced a pistol. He held it loosely, but his finger was on the trigger. Would he shoot himself or me? At Glamis years ago one shell-shocked soldier had killed himself with a gun.

I stopped shuffling toward the pull cord that rang for Bessie and my dresser Catherine. I prayed neither Lilibet nor Margot would come bouncing through the door right now, but they must be in bed. I did not believe Bertie would come in, for he had made it clear he wanted me to come to him for comfort. He was even wooing me for more, but with the war . . .

"I know how to shoot a pistol too," I told the man. "May I hold it to see if it is like mine?"

"Not a war weapon. It was my father's and made it through the bombs," he said and started to sob.

Rather than rushing for the pull cord, I approached him and took the pistol from his trembling hand. I sensed he was not going to harm me but shoot himself, perhaps here with the king and queen nearby in some sort of warped protest.

I walked as calmly as I could manage to the bell cord and pulled it.

"I'm locked up with them in the grave," he muttered so low with sobbing that I could barely make out his words.

I understood. How I missed my darling mother Cecilia and my dear, dear brother Fergus who had met a terrible fate.

When Bessie came in and I whispered for her to bring guards, wide-eyed she darted out to seek help.

Our guards took the limp and sobbing man away with his pistol. Bertie ran in, quite incensed, but I calmed him down. It turned out that the man had been hired through the Ministry of Labour and his background had not been thoroughly checked, so we had a bit of a mess over that. I blamed bureaucracy and men overly busy with the war for that security slip.

We tried to keep that news private, but Winston and the cabinet knew of the breach. Even, somehow, the Australian prime minister who visited London that next week knew. According to Winston, Robert Menzies had pronounced me "as wise and shrewder than all in the cabinet." Winston said if he meant that as a slam on our war cabinet, so be it, but he happened to agree.

And that comment, I felt, despite the fact I had visions of that poor man locked up in some sort of institution for mental defectives, almost made the frightening encounter worthwhile.

*   *   *

That night, when I finally fell asleep, I dreamed of the monster of Glamis, locked up in a windowless, airless room, or was it a shelter from the bombs, or even a room in an institution for the mentally ill?

But the monster had a face—two faces—not that of the man who had invaded my rooms at Windsor, but of my own nieces, daughters of my brother Jock. I had not seen Nerissa and Katherine Bowes Lyon for several years, for they suffered from a mental disease that was rumored to have run in our family for generations, and they were kept close at home. But their faces and fate were locked in my mind.

Even though I was lost in heavy sleep, I knew Nerissa would be about twenty-one years now and Katherine fourteen or so, near Lilibet's age. I dreamed of playing with them again, tending them during family reunions, trying to ignore their halting, jerking movements. They made strange faces over nothing—or was it over the bombing of their brains, their fear of the man with the pistol?

I pulled myself from sodden sleep and sat bolt upright in bed and looked around my dim bedroom at Windsor. Had bombs awakened me? No, a thunderstorm with lightning, but how unusual in February, how strange.

I was perspiring and yet felt wracked with cold. I pulled my knees up nearly to my chest and huddled under my down comforter but found no comfort. I turned over, wishing Bertie were here, but that was my own fault. Was I somehow a mental defective too? How that fear had haunted me, especially because I knew my nieces' parents were considering placing them in the Royal Earlswood Institution for Mental Defectives in Surrey. Nerissa, Jock had told me, had been legally declared an imbecile.

I tossed and turned, finally sitting up in bed and wrapping myself in my comforter like a cocoon. I would simply die if

Lilibet or Margot were ill like that. And was that curse on our family truly passed down from the monster of Glamis? But did Bertie's family too have a tinge of mental disease? His youngest brother, Prince John, had some epilepsy and other problems, so the family had partly hidden him away on the Sandringham estate, and the boy had died quite young.

I was haunted by another thought. Bessie had told me of a man cut in half by one of the night bombs, before she apologized for telling me. But I told her I had heard such things in my hospital visits, and I was glad she shared that, for she looked ashen and haunted. Weren't we all now?

But it wasn't that I had merely heard of some stranger being so horribly murdered by the Germans. It was my keen memory of what had happened to my dear brother Fergus that truly tortured me.

With the coverlet wrapped around me, I hugged my knees hard, seeing him again in my head and heart. How I had loved him, even above my other, older brothers, even more than Mike who had been shell-shocked. Fergus used to ride me on his shoulders. He would tickle-wrestle little David until the child laughed so hard he could not breathe.

So handsome in his Black Watch uniform was Fergus at his quickly arranged wedding to dear Christina before he left for the war. And those happy five days he had at home on leave at Glamis were the last time I ever saw him. He was twenty-six, and I fifteen.

But we had dreadful news from the front that not only was Fergus declared dead but his body was missing. It was reported that a comrade said that Fergus had been leading an attack on the German lines in the Battle of Loos when his leg was blown off.

I jolted now at the mere memory of first hearing that. I stretched my legs out, for my left calf muscles had cramped, so I scrambled out of bed onto the cold floor to try to walk it off. I could not fathom it then and still could not now: handsome, laughing, teasing Fergus blown apart then hit with bullets in his chest and shoulders, those strong shoulders.

Even after the war, his body was not found and that obsessed me too. He had a daughter I tried to spoil with birthday and holiday gifts. But since there was no body, I sometimes pictured Fergus walking the vast halls and lawns of Glamis at night—or maybe even up in the hidden rooms we could never quite find.

"Stop it!" I told myself as I paced madly, even stomping about a bit in my bare feet, trying to ease the leg cramp.

Finally, I collapsed back in bed and drew a pillow to my chest in a hard hug. How I wished someone was here, but I would not ring for anyone. And say what, that I had a bad dream? That this current war with its maimed and dead made my thoughts turn to my long-lost brother? That the Prince of Wales, my husband's brother, had so resembled dear Fergus that I suppose that's why I once loved him from afar, and then up close?

Perhaps if not for that last wayward thought, I would have gone down the hall to Bertie's bed. I needed comforting, but I just grasped my pillow to me until my tears made it too wet to hold.

CHAPTER THIRTEEN

Ghosts

March began as a blustery month, and we wondered if the stiff winds ever made a Luftwaffe bomb miss its target or helped one of our little Spitfires or Hurricanes to catch up with the Messerschmitts. Winston had given one of his energizing speeches last year thanking the RAF: "Never was so much owed by so many to so few." But the bombing went on.

Yet my heart had been temporarily soothed, not so much by those stirring words as by a short poem sent to me by a lady in the United States, from Chicago, no less.

Bertie laughed at it and Winston—despite his usual gloom in private lately—chortled when I read it to them. Both men were short-tempered but weren't we all? I thought Winston might even have lost weight. I wished the war had that effect on me for I tended to eat more, especially sweets to keep my energy up and as a reward for getting through another dreadful day—that is, when I didn't have a Dubonnet and gin nearby.

The little poem made it into a newspaper. Now I wonder who released that to them through a new contact, the young woman photographer and reporter Rowena Fitzgerald. Perhaps someone, I thought, who had once released a certain dossier amongst the ruling classes of the Empire. The poem read,

> *Be it said to your renown*
> *That you wore your gayest gown,*
> *Your bravest smile, and stayed in Town*
> *When London Bridge was burning down,*
> *My fair lady.*

"That's a good one," Winston had said behind his wreath of cigar smoke, which quite outdid Bertie's constant puffs of cigarette clouds. "But what I really like, as well as a correct reading of our bold, bright queen, is that it indicates the American populace are quite aware of our troubles and our willingness to face them, but it is utter rubbish if they think we don't desperately need their help."

Bertie said, "I think more Yanks are keen to help us than before. I say, I understand the fear of getting in with both feet after the so-called war to end all wars we've been through when they helped us over here. Surely, your summer meeting with President Roosevelt will help, Winston. We need troops as well as supplies. The thing is, with Roosevelt's physical condition, it will be difficult for him to fly here, though he wants to. Actually, his crippled legs are mostly kept from the people there, and the press goes along with it. Elizabeth, go ahead and tell him your suggestion."

"Of course," I said, turning toward Winston, "it would not be quite like having the president here, but what do you think about our—all three of us—inviting Mrs. Roosevelt to visit? It is well known that she is a strong, well-informed, and opinionated woman and has a say in things with her husband. And perhaps it would not annoy the Germans as much as if he were here himself, so that, during her visit, they might not go bomb crazy on the palace again."

"Humph," Winston said, and I thought he would dismiss the idea, but he added, "Bomb crazy—that's a good one. The blasted, bloody, bomb-blasting Germans are just plain crazy to follow that madman. Yes, let's pursue that idea through royal and governmental channels. Perhaps your brother David, ma'am, who is serving us so well but low key in Washington, would be the best liaison for this invitation."

"A bully idea," Bertie said, but Winston winked at me.

"Of course, ma'am," Winston went on, "you would think of that. Eleanor Roosevelt—a woman who has her powerful husband's ear—is well informed and has ideas of her own. A lady who is, I hear, popular with the citizens there. Yes, Your Majesty," he said, turning toward Bertie, "it takes one to know one, does it not?"

* * *

One evening at dusk, I walked through the rooms of the palace that we had made our living quarters, especially the ones that had rung with our girls' laughter, for I was missing them awfully during the weeks we were in London. Lilibet and

Margot had been very upset that the palace mews had been hit by a bomb, but at least we had long ago sent the horses into the countryside. Several state carriages and the girls' pony carts were harmed, though.

Just three days before that, Lilibet had given a talk on the BBC *Children's Hour* radio program to the nation's children. She had ended her short talk with words that now echoed in my mind: "We know, everyone of us, that in the end, all will be well."

But did we know that? Did Lilibet and Margot believe that now since the "home for their ponies" had been hit and our northside rooms, where we had lived here, had been thoroughly shaken?

Lighting my way by electric torch, I strolled past the girls' bedrooms, opening the doors and peeking in each as I passed. The bombing of the north façade had interrupted lighting here, though slashes of dying daylight still filtered through the curtains. The wind moaned in the chimneys like human voices, and the smell of dust snagged in my nose, so I sneezed.

How warm, light, and lively these rooms had seemed before the war. I could picture my dear ones snuggled up under their covers as I read them a story before they went to their own rooms to be tucked in. As soon as the war ended, when we had the funds, we must install central heating, for this winter had been cold, and this month of March had not improved things. *If winter comes, can spring be far behind?* This year it was far behind.

Bertie had given me such a compliment when we had moved into this vast palace, reluctantly leaving our cozy London home. "Elizabeth could make a home anywhere!" he had boasted to our friends. But was this vast building really home when our girls were away? And when bombs ravaged its history and beauty?

Again, I almost felt as if I heard high, childish voices and those of the nannies and governess. Years ago, Lilibet: "Mummy, Papa, look at what I drew on this paper, but Margot drew on the wall when Crawfie wasn't looking!" More recently, Margot: "I don't care if people say she will be queen, she's not queen now, and she's always telling me what to do!" And Lilibet, just before the girls had to leave London: "Be sure to tell Constable Robertson I will still walk the corgis after dinner at Windsor, even if he has to stay here to guard the palace. But when I come back, he can help again."

Dear, loyal Crawfie had once said living here was like camping in a museum. I jumped and squealed as a mouse skittered across the floor and disappeared under Margot's bed frame, now stripped of linens.

I moved on to the dark study above the Balcony Room. Poor Bertie and David had faced harsh lessons here, so Bertie had decreed it would only be a room to practice piano for our children. We both wanted their studies to be enjoyable, not grueling.

I returned to my own rooms, which seemed so dim and cold now. How I had surprised the decorating staff before we moved in so quickly after David's abdication when I said I wanted light floral wallpaper and peach-colored paint on the walls. No more dark hues and Edwardian flocked paper, yet my little retreat was now suddenly dark and dreary too. Would this war, this waiting for safety and peace, never end?

* * *

Despite the wax plugs in my ears I had taken to wearing to get some sleep, I heard the *crump, boom* of a bomb nearby. The sirens began to sound. I yanked out the plugs and pulled on the robe and warm nightcap Norman had designed for me and made ready to head for the shelter. If I did not see Bertie in the corridor I would fetch him first, no matter what befell. My thoughts unscrambled. It was the eighth of March, and that blast had evidently come from the gardens, not the palace.

A second, worse blast followed along with a show of light so bright it leapt through the slit in the draperies of my room as I rushed for the door, scolding myself for stopping to don my new shelter fashions.

Bertie met me in the hall. "It hit back in the gardens!" he shouted over the noise of something falling. "Maybe the forecourt too!"

What could be turned to rubble out in the vast gardens, I wondered. Trees falling into the old North Lodge or Wellington Barracks? At least it hadn't hit the palace this time. And at least Lilibet's friend Police Constable Robertson was not on duty in the gardens tonight, because I had seen the rotation sheet for plane spotters and security men.

An aide rushed up to Bertie as we made it downstairs. "Incendiaries, Your Majesties! Direct hit on the North Lodge and then the barracks!"

We waited in the shelter for the all clear. Bertie sent someone over to be sure the staff was all safe in their shelter. We could hear the muted tune of someone playing the piano over there. I recognized it as "Let Me Call You Sweetheart," which seemed so terrible. Sweethearts parted; sweethearts lost to terrible weapons of war forever.

One of the security men rushed in. "Your Majesty, the second hit toppled the North Lodge masonry! P.C. Robertson was working to put out fires near there and is evidently buried in the rubble, but we're trying to dig him out."

"He's not on duty tonight," I spoke up. "It must be someone else."

"No, Your Majesty. You know how kind he is. He switched duty, took the night garden beat for a friend of his tonight, a man who had a wedding anniversary today. Talked to him a while ago. It's P.C. Robertson under the debris, for a certain."

"Bertie," I said, gripping his arm when the man ran back outside, "he's the one who walks the corgis with Lilibet, and she adores him."

"I know. I know. I swear, if I could dig him out with my own hands . . ."

"I think we have the girls safe at Windsor, but they're not really safe from . . . from all this destruction—the ruination of their innocence and childhoods too. It haunts me and will them forever."

"Everyone will have apoplexy if I go out to watch—to oversee the rescue efforts, but I'll stand far back. You must stay here. I'll be right back."

But he did not come right back. I heard the shriek of an ambulance, many men's voices that came and went outside.

I wanted to rush there myself to see what was happening, but I could hardly argue with or defy him, though I wanted to—and in these nightclothes? Instead, I sat nearly alone in the "royal shelter" and prayed that Lilibet's favorite P.C. would be rescued and recover.

But, after an hour or so, Bertie's long face when he came back in—the shake of his head, then a helpless shrug—told me it was hopeless.

He sat beside me. "They heard a tapping or scratching sound beneath the debris, so they dug all the harder, thinking it was him, that he was alive. They . . . they dug him out, partly crushed, quite gone, though they rushed him to Charing Cross Hospital anyway. But no good."

I sucked in a sob. He put his arm around me, and I cried silently against his shoulder. Someone dead I knew, a loss that would bring the war home even harder to Lilibet and Margot.

"Something else," Bertie said. "Even when he was laid on the ground, then taken away, the sound beneath the rubble they had heard continued. I told them it was broken stones, rolling rubble, even a waterspout dripping. It stopped, but then it began again. As if his spirit was still there, saying thanks for trying or—or something like that."

"Or just everyone is going barmy, going mad," I said with a hiccough from my crying.

But the next day, when I insisted Bertie take me out to the site, I heard it too, more, I thought, like an unexplained tap-tapping. I overheard one of the workers clearing the masonry rubble say, "It's his fighting spirit, like all of us leave something behind."

"Blimey, his ghost from a violent, sudden death, that's what it is," said another worker, this one with a shovel.

Bertie whispered as we walked away, "This growing ruin-ation of our world haunts us all."

"When we can, we shall put a plaque to his memory there," I said. "Lilibet and I will dedicate it. Bertie, he was taking his friend's place tonight or he would not have died. 'Greater love hath no man than to lay down his life for his friend.'"

"And, if I must, I—Winston too—will lay down ours for this nation and Empire."

I took his arm and held it close for support as we walked through the ravaged March gardens, bombed and barely show-ing signs of spring.

CHAPTER FOURTEEN

Full Moon

$\mathcal{I}$ used to love it when the moon was full and bright," I told Bessie as she cleared my cosmetic jars from my dressing table in my bedroom at Windsor. "But not now, because it only gives the bloody Germans clearer bombing targets."

"Yes, ma'am. Don't we East Enders know. Heard a saying the other day that shows we still have backbone, though. Went a bit like this. *The night bombs keep us up, but they won't get us down.*"

"I like that! I shall tell the king and Prime Minister Churchill too. We all need a pick-me-up, don't we?"

"That we do! A good night to you then."

As she went out into my sitting room and then the hall beyond, I was certain I heard Bertie's raised voice coming from the corridor. Could he have received bad news about the nightly London bombings? Surely they had begun by now, especially with a bright moon. Was he talking to Winston on the telephone, for they had both raised their voices lately?

No—it sounded—though it could not be—that he was arguing with Lilibet.

I wrapped and belted my robe tighter and went out into the draughty corridor. It was the evening of the tenth of May, but the old stone façades and vast, high-ceilinged rooms kept this castle so chilly. I now heard both their voices raised and hurried down the hall to Bertie's study.

"If I am old enough for you to call me Betts, instead of Lilibet, I am old enough for that, Papa."

"My dearest girl, you only turned fifteen a few weeks ago! I'll not have a princess of the realm, my heir, volunteering for more than your Girl Guide service. Granted you have visited some bombed-out areas, but—"

"Oh, Mummy," she cried as I opened the door to his suite. "I heard I could have an honorary appointment as a colonel in the Grenadier Guards, but Papa thinks I'm too young to serve. I want to help! Granted, Margot is too young, but it is different for me. He said I shouldn't correspond with Philip too, but I'm just trying to keep up spirits for someone in the Royal Navy, and Papa is a Navy man, so why doesn't he understand?"

I forced myself to slow my steps and keep calm. *Keep Calm and Carry On*, my favorite London poster said.

"Well, fifteen is a bit young for private letters to and from Philip or any other male friend."

She pouted, but I could sense her backbone stiffen. Bertie lit another cigarette and paced. He, like Churchill, more than all of us, had been under terrible pressure lately with all the brutal bombing. To boot, the stubborn Americans still stood firm on not declaring war when we were increasingly desperate for fighting men and supplies.

I put my arm around Lilibet and snagged Bertie's as he went by. "Let's sit and talk. Where is Margot?"

Lilibet said, "Playing her grammy and listening to who knows what records. She wants to learn not only the waltz and foxtrot but the tango and the latest dance craze too. We read in a newspaper that line dances like the Palais Glide and Oomps-a-Daisy are all the rage."

Bertie and I exchanged glances. Two nights ago, the popular restaurant Café de Paris had been hit by a bomb just as "Snakehips" Johnson was leading his band in the popular tune "Oh, Johnny." All of the band except one had been killed, and a second bomb had landed on the dance floor. We had heard through private channels—not Winston this time—that the blast in such a closed space sent body parts flying and exploded lungs. Sadly too, since the patrons were quite well-to-do, looters of the worst sort soon arrived, an ugly aspect of the war.

Amazingly, we had also been told that dance halls and restaurants were still packed the next night. Devil-may-care bravery, I wondered, or callous disregard for the lost and their own lives? At any rate, at no time on God's green earth were my daughters going to learn the tango and dance crazes or go to such clubs, not even in peacetime!

As Bertie started to sputter again, I raised my hand. I sat Lilibet down on one end of the sofa, Bertie on the other, and I perched between them.

"I know everyone is on edge and rightly so," I began, shifting my thigh against Bertie's. He nodded and blew out a little puff of smoke.

I resisted the urge to wave it away. I was worried about him, for he had become increasingly short-tempered and even a bit gaunt. His hands sometimes shook.

Facing him, I went on, "I do think it is marvelous and shows Lilibet's maturity, doesn't it, Bertie? I mean that our eldest and heir wants to serve in a traditional and supportive way. Her wireless broadcast was excellent and so are the Grenadier Guards. She is hardly going out to go into battle with their vaunted infantry. I believe she can make a fine contribution to our fighting spirit without, of course, fighting, nor should there be any fighting within our family. Bertie, it would occupy her mind over other things she may indeed be too young for," I added, with another subtle bump of my thigh against his.

As preoccupied as he was—and rightly so—he would surely get my hint about giving her a focus other than mooning over Philip.

"I know she would do a spiffing job at whatever she puts her time and hand to," he said, leaning over me to pat Lilibet's knee. "I just have a hard time of it, realizing you are as old and as eager as you are to serve, my dear. Of course, the honorary appointment to the guards would be an honor indeed."

"Oh, thank you, Papa!" she cried and bounced up to lean over to hug him. "And Mummy! And I hope to volunteer to help with the land girls who will bring in the harvest at San-dringham next autumn—so short of men!"

She ran out, then came back and gave us a little, unneces-sary curtsy. With a smile, she was off down the hall, evidently to tell her sister or governess.

"Barely fifteen, going on twenty-one," he muttered, taking my hand.

"Remember that A. E. Housman poem?" I asked. *"But I was one-and-twenty, no use to talk to me. . . .* But we all have learned things in our own way, the hard way, have we not?"

"You too, my dear love?" he asked and kissed the back of my hand. "Such a happy family life, you Bowes Lyons, and you be-ing so admired, courted, and, dare I say, well-wed."

I nodded and managed to match his intense, serious expres-sion. How foolish I had been to love his brother, to think I could win the dashing playboy Prince of Wales who was always, as David himself used to say of himself, "raising tallywhack." And how blessed I was to have Bertie, despite how dangerous our lives were now. I saw Lilibet's obsession with the charming Greek who looked like a Norse god as being just as dangerous and harmful as my early passion for David had been. Never was she going to become entranced or entrapped by Philip, not if I could help it.

"Despite it all, my dearest," I told him and kissed his cheek, "we will find our way together through all this. Victory, just as Winston says!"

We stood, still hand in hand, when Bertie's night equerry appeared in the hall door Lilibet had left open.

"Your Majesty, Mr. Churchill is on the phone! Terrible

bombings in London! Westminster—Parliament! Everything afire!"

Bertie squeezed my hand so hard I flinched, then sprinted out into the hall toward his office, which had the secure phone to the P.M. wherever he was in the country. I hustled right behind him, quickly out of breath.

"I think he's at Ditchley, so they must have phoned him from London!" Bertie said over his shoulder.

Ditchley was the historic home and estate that the Tree family, Winston's friends and supporters, let him use as a weekend getaway. It had been discussed and decided that his own country home of Chartwell and the traditional prime minister's country getaway of Chequers, just south of London, were targets too easy to spot from the air, whereas Ditchley was quite hidden without a long drive leading to it like an arrow. And it was close to Winston's birthplace and beloved family home at Blenheim Palace, though he would never be Duke of Marlborough there.

Bertie made a dive for the receiver of the telephone lying on his desk and ordered the equerry out with a wave of his hand. I made it inside and closed the door.

He began to pace again until he realized the telephone cord would not let him. He sank into his leather desk chair, urging Winston to talk slower. I leaned against the edge of the desk next to the red documents box that went everywhere with us. When Winston slowed his speech, I was close enough to hear his words.

"Worst night of bombing . . . full moon. Westminster roof aflame . . . Parliament hit, House of Commons—damn them!

Big Ben took a bomb . . . fires all along the Thames. And we thought our RAF was taking such a toll on them they might back off. Hitler's still furious over our hitting Berlin and . . ."

I sucked in a sob. Bertie reached out to grasp my wrist. I leaned forward and braced his shoulder with my free hand.

"Something good—some sign—has to c-come along," Bertie said into the phone. "Call me again, Winston. Let us know what we can do besides curse the enemy and pray we endure."

* * *

Neither of us slept that night. We curled up together on the large leather sofa in Bertie's office near the phone, buried in blankets and grief. The quiet of Windsor seemed so wrong when London was being blasted. I tried to close my eyes but, lying in front of Bertie, I just stared at the block of moonlight coming in through the window. It moved slowly across the floor, so lovely and yet that was what was allowing the Germans to bomb tonight. I remembered a story Fergus had teased David and me with once about the full moon turning people into flesh-eating vampires. Yes, Hitler was that.

I jolted in Bertie's arms when he suddenly spoke. "I've been thinking about my brother George as an RAF captain, so daring and handsome, now air vice-marshal, though, of course, he earned that. But I still can't believe he left the Royal Navy with his passion to fly. Of course, the RAF seems much more daring and romantic, especially now, than the Navy."

"I know he's visiting RAF bases to boost morale, but you do that and so much more," I said, careful to walk the line between praising the gregarious George but upholding Bertie. I always thought too that their royal father's bullying of Bertie and David had made him resent his younger sibling a bit.

"It's easy to worry about younger brothers," I went on, when Bertie just nodded, his chin bumping my shoulder. "My dear David is safe in Washington across the ocean from all this, but I still worry about him. So I can see why you would think of George in these trying times—especially with the RAF, as successful as they've been, no doubt in great danger during this massive attack."

"Mmm. I swear, if anything happens to George, Mother will absolutely die. Her favorite of us boys—David too—you know. How she manages to turn a deaf ear to—well, she is quite deaf—George's carousing and flagrant sexual liaisons, I will never know. Yet I love him despite his waywardness—even his pursuit of other men."

"No, I don't know," I said, thinking of my own homosexual brother, David. I stirred a bit in Bertie's strong embrace, which had just become a grip.

Yes, I knew that Queen Mary favored handsome George, Duke of Kent, her youngest living son, for her last child, little Johnnie, had died young, and she had seemed to cling to George even more after that tragic loss. But I also knew that, though the Duke of Windsor would never be forgiven by his mother for not standing by his duty to the crown and family, she loved and missed him too.

I understood Bertie's feelings of resentment, for I couldn't help but feel jealousy when his brother George had wed Princess Marina of Greece and Denmark. The people were fascinated by her, and she was pretty and slender to boot. Drat—there was that intrusive Greek nobility again, so I must be doubly sure that Philip wed elsewhere. The Greek royal family had skeletons abounding in its closet, though I realized I had no right to openly criticize with all the Windsors and Bowes Lyons were keeping the lid on.

But how I understood wanting one's mother's favor! As king, it was a bitter pill for Bertie that, as supportive as the widowed Queen Mary was—and I worked hard to cultivate her affections for us both—she still favored George and David. What else could I say to comfort my dear husband about that or about the horrors happening now in our beloved London?

When the secure phone rang, I startled, and Bertie stumbled up to answer it. At least it was daylight outside, a sunny Sunday morning here at Windsor.

"What possible good news, except the bastards are gone?" I heard him ask, evidently speaking to Winston. "You think it might have been so brutal because it was their last hurrah, at least in the night skies? You had said you thought the German Satan was turning his greed and might toward 'Mother Russia.'"

I got up slowly, watching Bertie's expression because I could not hear the other end of the conversation this time.

"What? In Scotland?" Bertie shouted, then dropped his voice and nearly dropped the phone. "Rudolf Hess, Hitler's deputy Führer, flew there himself and parachuted in? Is that what you said? And we have him prisoner?"

My attention had snagged on the mention of Scotland. Surely, the Germans with their deadly Luftwaffe were not going to surprise us by invading my beloved Scotland!

CHAPTER FIFTEEN

The Fixer

I'll wager Winston wishes he were in his London bunker instead of at Ditchley," I told Bertie. "Safe but close to the seat of power—which may have been pounded to bits in these terrible attacks."

He kept his hand on the telephone receiver in its cradle, leaning stiff-armed on it, as if it were holding him up or would ring straightaway again.

He told me, "Winston says the House of Commons—so dear to him over the years—is . . . is rubble. He— I think, despite this good news about Rudolf Hess supposedly defecting, he was c-crying."

I blinked back tears and brushed a single one from Bertie's cheek. He looked devastated, weak and hollow just for one moment before he stood erect again. But he said nothing more, staring into space. I feared for him, for London, for us all.

"Tell me what this is about the high-and-mighty Hess landing in Scotland," I said. "Where and why? And Winston thought that was good news? But did Hess drop bombs there or will there be an invasion? Bertie, I fear for Scotland too!"

His knees shaking, he tugged me over to the sofa with our mussed blankets still there, shoved them onto the floor, and pulled me down to sit beside him. I remembered his tales of how his father had called him knock-kneed and forced him to wear painful leg braces, and he'd told me his knees had always trembled back then.

"If it's not a trick and Hess is not some sort of Trojan horse, it is a break for us. It seems Hess has deserted Hitler in some demented attempt to negotiate a private peace treaty. They must think they've beaten us so we'll at least bargain if not surrender. He is alone, parachuted out over the Duke of Hamilton's estate, whom he'd met at the Olympics in '36, and thought would help him—get him to Winston and me to plead his case."

"Oh, Douglas-Hamilton. So Hess bailed out south of Glasgow," I said with a huge sigh, grateful it was not near Glamis. "And alone? But it must be a trap."

"No, it's too daft, the number-three Nazi defecting or thinking he can broker a surrender. He was taken into custody by one of the duke's farmers with a pitchfork, no less, and his Messerschmitt crashed in a field. He was spouting something to the duke about the astrological signs being right for him to act."

"He sounds demented. Remember Winston said that Hitler consulted astrologers? And he told us not to pass on that he himself had consulted one too, just to try to learn what Hitler might be hearing and planning. Poppycock astrologers, Winston said."

"I'd forgotten that. What would I do without you?"

"I shall answer that another time, my love."

He threw an arm—then both arms—around me so fast and hard I gasped. He held me tight to him, and I hugged him back.

"I need you, Elizabeth, my queen, my best self, my comforter and strength. By the way, Winston said he will send an armored vehicle for me today so that on the way back into the city I can see the damage for myself and meet briefly with him in his Cabinet War Room bunker in Whitehall. I've never seen his lair built under the Treasury building. He's sending his minister of information, that clever Irish aide, Brendan Bracken, as a guide."

"The behind-the-scenes man people whisper is his 'fixer' for things that go wrong, whatever befalls."

"Exactly. I did not realize you knew that. Bracken makes many people nervous, but if Winston says he's the man for the job, I warrant he is indeed. But it is your decision whether to stay here with the children or come with me, take that terrible tour of the devastation, then head back to Buck House."

"The girls will be safe here," I told him, turning my lips against his cheek and kissing him. "I will go with you. Besides, I understand Clementine has actually decorated the bunker, so perhaps little me—the little woman—can learn some style tips from her, another little woman in this big war."

He set me back and forced a tight-lipped smile at my sardonic tone. "Ha! You two 'little women'—I imagine quite like Eleanor Roosevelt in the States—are more than the powers behind your thrones. I swear, you all prop up the men on them."

Although Winston and a few other men I admired had said somewhat the same, those words from Bertie, king and husband, made me want to soar.

* * *

Brendan Bracken even had a bit of a brogue, which, I knew, most up-and-coming Irish moving in powerful British governmental circles would try to subdue or erase. He had a good head of reddish hair he parted in the middle and wore wire-rimmed spectacles that made him look like a pedant.

"Yes, Your Majesty," Bracken was telling Bertie when I walked into the room, ready to leave with them, "I have had a snifter or two of that old Napoleon brandy with the P.M., and even been given a goose or two to get going with that gold-topped walking stick he uses."

Given a goose or two by Winston? I thought until I realized what he meant. He looked quite nonplussed when he saw me and bowed as Bertie made introductions.

"Quite brave of you to go with us, ma'am," Bracken said. "The sights are soul-shaking, considering how the enemy struck at the very heart of the Empire last night. But then, let's away, if you are ready."

As we went out and saw the vehicle—not a tank but a heavily armored automobile with a two-vehicle escort—I was glad I had decided to ask Crawfie to keep the girls away from the windows. I did not want them to think we were in dire danger or that their mother was going off to war.

The late-Sunday-afternoon countryside looked peaceful

and even charming, but then we headed into the city. A pall of smoke still rose above it; lorries and omnibuses clogged the motorways. We were stopped at a checkpoint before driving in, taking a roundabout way because of potholes and rubble. Here and there, firemen were still fighting flames by pouring water and foam onto smoking ruins.

"Brace yourselves, Your Majesties," Bracken warned, "though I'll bet you don't curse the way the P.M. did when I accompanied him into town earlier."

Bertie said, "Was Downing Street hit?"

"Number 10 had taken some close hits, sir, but the place he calls 'The Hole' in Whitehall is still accessible. The slab— five feet of protective concrete for a roof—has let us expand the rooms and staff there. Ah, but here we go for a quick view of the worst of the damage. Stephen," he called up to our Army driver, "be sure that sign's propped up in the windscreen, so we can get through the barriers."

As we drove up Millbank and crossed Horseferry Road, Bertie and I gasped and craned our necks to look out. Ahead lay the heart of London: Westminster Abbey, the Houses of Parliament, Westminster Hall, and Big Ben. All had been bombed last night.

If this man was Winston's so-called fixer, I thought, would that he could fix the devastation we saw here. He began to point out landmarks as if we were tourists first seeing the town, but the details he shared were as dreadful as the horrid scenes.

"Sadly, hundreds of citizens are still missing. No gas and water for those buildings standing. But the word is that Hess's capture will lift morale. Perhaps the only other good news is that St. Paul's was threatened by fires, but still stands intact, a symbol, the P.M. says, for us all. By the way, the Tower of London was hit with incendiaries but still stands strong—but here . . ."

His voice trailed off. If even a stoic, businesslike man could barely speak, I feared what was coming.

"We won't pass near it, but venerable old St. Clement Danes has burned," he began his dreadful recital again. "Even the ghosts of the Danish Vikings and the spirit of Sir Christopher Wren could not save it if they were still here." He sniffed hard and went on, pointing now.

"As for this area, the firemen tried desperately to save the structures. They say the Thames looked orange from the flames. It was low tide and that choked some of the fire hoses. The House of Lords escaped with but a hole in the roof and melted lead gutters from the heat. The Commons members just moved back into their chamber in Parliament a few days ago, thinking it was safe to meet here in the day when the bombing was at night. It took a terrible, direct hit. That shook the P.M. more than if Number 10 had been blasted."

"If St. Clement Danes was hit," I spoke up, surprised I still had a voice, "does that mean the newspapers on Fleet Street were also bombed? At least it was at night when few of their staff would be at work."

"Bad hit, ma'am. Lincoln's Inn and Gray's Inn too."

I thought of the young woman, Rowena Fitzgerald, who was striving to do a good job taking war photographs and writing heartfelt stories. Her face and voice stayed with me—that is, until we went way round on Great Smith Street to avoid the fire hoses and vehicles still fighting smoky blazes at Westminster Abbey.

I gasped, and Bertie swore under his breath as Bracken began his narrative again: "Yes, as you can perhaps see, the sanctuary of the Abbey was hit by incendiary bombs."

"That's where we were married," I cried—and did begin to cry again. "Even the altar?"

"Regretfully so," Bracken said. "Not only was your wedding there but, of course, the coronation of kings and queens for centuries. The last time I was there was to pay homage to your father, King George, as his coffin lay there, sir."

"Yes," Bertie choked out, then added quietly, "I t-t-too."

"As you can see, this entire area was beaten to bits. At three a.m., the shelter in Westminster took the direct hit of two bombs, and the Westminster mayor died instantly, we heard. We will have a tally of fatalities in time."

"We must remember," I said, my voice choked with emotion, "that the grand buildings are not all that was lost, but our dear people, human lives."

"Well said, ma'am," Bracken added after a little silence. "As for the sanctuary, about two-thirds of the contents were damaged by fire, and most of the roof is gone. In the palace per se, the Ministry of Works was hit. Major roof damage also. In the Royal Court, heat and smoke and water damage . . ."

His voice droned on. I tried to listen but my mind just stopped until Bertie interrupted to ask, "And Big Ben?"

"A blast on the south façade rained down giant shards of glass, sir, but the old mechanism kept on, chiming bravely until they turned it off for later repairs."

"And, despite all this, we will keep on, we will fight and win," Bertie insisted, his voice strong now, nor had he stumbled over one word.

I gripped his hand hard. He did not flinch. Bracken, perhaps at a loss for words for once, just nodded.

"Well," said my dear, beleaguered husband, king of England, "onward to Whitehall to call on my friend and cohort in all this, Winston Spencer Churchill. If we all have to move underground for the duration, to keep fighting the Nazi bastards, we shall do just that."

Bracken nodded. "You know, Your Majesties, the newspapers like to call me the P.M.'s fixer, but I believe both of you are the nation's fixers too."

From that moment on, I trusted Brendan Bracken. After all, it took one fixer to recognize another, and if anyone could pick up the pieces when Bertie took hard hits, it was I.

CHAPTER SIXTEEN

Night Radar

When we emerged from our vehicle at the doorway to the Treasury building, the air was sharp with a strange smell and I coughed. I raised my hand to my nose, and my eyes watered.

Ever observant and attentive, Bracken said, "A strange brew of odors, ma'am. Even here, it hangs over the city, dust, of course, ash and wet stone, but that unique smell is cordite, an explosive used in ammunition."

"And," Bertie put in, "I dare say, raw sewage from broken pipes."

Bracken indicated our direction into the building, down a hall, down two flights of stairs. We entered past a sign that read, *Mind Your Head.*

I was surprised to see the so-called Churchill War Rooms were quite extensive. Bracken said there were many tunnels and offices we would not see, so even some of it was restricted from the king, I thought.

Winston greeted us, his face solemn, and I noted he slid a

half-finished glass of what was, no doubt, his usual whiskey and soda, behind a typewriter.

"Such as it is on a dire day, I wanted you to know we are all here at work," he said, and led us on a tour with Bracken bringing up the rear.

I had expected a single secretary crammed in, perhaps a few guards and desks for Winston and Bracken. Instead I saw a huge Map Room, manned around the clock, we were told, by officers of the three armed services and their support staff. Everywhere we went, deeper in, surprised people popped up when they recognized us to bow and curtsy, but Winston just nodded as if that were his due and herded us and Bracken on, farther into the labyrinth.

I also quickly learned that this bunker was all business, without any touches of décor from Clementine Churchill or anyone else. It must be the Annex to Number 10 Downing Street, their other bunker, that I had heard she had decorated to make people more at ease. So Winston's "Clemmie" was a female fixer too, and quite the woman if she could put up with his eccentricities and outbursts.

"The moment I saw this cabinet room Neville Chamberlain had hardly used," Winston told us, "I said, 'This is the room from which I will direct the war.' I won't show you my Spartan office-bedroom, but I have a code-scrambling encrypted telephone that will replace the transatlantic one I have now, so I can call President Roosevelt. There's even BBC broadcasting equipment there in case I need that.

"Come, sit down here, if you don't mind," he said gesturing to a corner of a large, cluttered table where an area had been cleared off. Some sweets on a tray, a pot of tea and three cups, saucers, and some dearly rationed sugar cubes were waiting. "Brendan, I thank you for escorting Their Majesties, and I'll have you back to get them to the palace shortly," he told the hovering man.

The king nodded at Bracken, and I said, "Thank you for the tour, however terrible the viewing."

With a nod and a snap of his heels, Bracken backed a few steps away and disappeared.

"Good man, can make anything better, except this damned war, pardon my French, ma'am," Winston told me. "But I realize you speak beautiful French. Your addresses to the women of Britain and France were powerful, and I have in mind a speech you might make to the women of America, if you are willing."

"Yes, of course. Anything to help in all this tragedy."

"We must jolt their citizenry and Congress to back us in this war. As for your war efforts, ma'am, the hand that rocks the cradle rocks the world—and rocks its stubborn men, eh, Your Majesty?"

"Just so."

"Now, let me say," Winston went on while I took off my gloves and poured three cups of tea, "that we have hopes that Hitler cannot sustain attacks on our isle and on Russia at the same time. With his German Wehrmacht troops, he seems to be heading for combat with Stalin. The brutality and scope of last night's attack on London could have been what the German Satan thinks is the coup de grâce for us, the final blow, by air, at least."

"A blessing in disguise," Bertie said, "if the night bombings stop. It would do wonders for morale—almost as good as the Americans getting in. Do you think our captive guest, Herr Hess, can give us any answers to Hitler's demented thinking?"

"Perhaps so, but let me give you another piece of hopeful news in all this grief and mayhem. We now have very serviceable airborne radar, day or night, entirely classified information. You have heard we have been bringing down more Luftwaffe planes even at night, even last night, and the enemy can't figure out why. When asked by our press, our RAF boys just say they are eating more carrots, so they can see in the dark."

Bertie simply nodded at that, and I bit back a grin. Humor in this horror took bravado.

"I tell you," Winston went on in lecture mode while he took his cup and saucer from me, "that Luftwaffe commander-in-chief Reichsmarschall Hermann Göring made a big mistake not to destroy our war industry factories, but to turn on our people to destroy their resolve. Can't be done. Cannot be done!"

"Here! Here!" Bertie said, as if he were supporting Churchill in the Commons.

Lowering his voice, Winston said, "Bracken is working now on propaganda we shall simply call 'information' to assure and rally our people and those stubborn, isolationist Americans. Patriotic, inspiring movies, newspaper stories—you'll see."

"Winston," I said as the idea hit me, "I know a woman who has just the eye and brain for that sort of thing. She brings out the emotions, the best in people." I explained to him about how Rowena had staged the baby in the lap of his crippled mother reaching for my pearls.

"Bully. I'll tell Bracken and you might too, as he's building a staff he can trust. Aren't we all? Like night radar, I feel we can see into the darkness of this war, bring down the enemy, fly yet with courage. But as for building a trustworthy staff, ma'am, that reminds me that your brother David appears to be getting on well with President Roosevelt, just as I intend to when we meet secretly soon in Newfoundland. I hope our Anglo-American partnership will be forged soon and include men and arms. Roosevelt's been bucking his Congress, you know. I cannot wait to meet him, especially since you have both said how well you all got on. And, oh, yes, Eleanor Roosevelt has accepted our invitation, but the timing is yet to be decided."

That bucked me up. I raised my teacup, and Bertie and Winston clinked our china rims together in a solemn toast. Yet despite that and our enclosed area, Winston soon lit a cigar, and Bertie followed with a cigarette. I swear, if things weren't so dire, I would have protested. I would have become a fixer by putting both of those smoking sticks out in the ashtray sitting right next to some scones that were surely hard to get with sugar rations.

I was aching to ask Winston in private how the Duke and Duchess of Windsor were getting on in exile in Nassau, Bahamas. I hoped I could get him alone soon to ask if he had been told by them or someone else that I had tried to ruin Wallis Simpson's status in Britain with that dossier. And, since he often alluded to my speaking excellent French, had the duke or duchess even told him of my French mother, for I recalled all too well that they had both delighted in tormenting me by calling me "Cookie" in private.

But for now, it was best I fly with my own night radar and

pray others—like Bertie—never knew my secrets. So I bit my tongue, as they say, and did bite into one of those lovely looking scones.

* * *

My broadcast to the women of America was scheduled for the tenth of August in that fateful year of 1941. I explained that "hardship has only steeled our hearts and strengthened our resolution." I ended with my fervent hope that there would be a "day when we shall go forward hand in hand to build a better, a kinder, and a happier world for our children. May God bless you all."

Granted, Winston had helped me write the speech, but those final words were mine and from the heart. That same, momentous month, Churchill met with Roosevelt as they had planned, ironically with the P.M. going to Newfoundland on a battleship named *Prince of Wales*, for there was no such prince since David had deserted his kingship and his country. I was tempted to ask Bertie to change the name of the ship, but there were many things more important. Yes, much more important than my continued resentment of David, the onetime prince and king, for deserting his country for a twice-wed divorcée with a cruel, selfish heart. She would have made a dreadful queen.

* * *

Also that August, I turned forty-one years of age and took the girls to beautiful Balmoral Castle for a—hopefully—happy getaway. Bertie did not join us at first, for it was easier for him to keep in touch with Winston in Newfoundland from London.

"Mummy, wait until you play this new game called Monopoly!" Lilibet told me, bringing a box with rattling game pieces outside and plopping it onto our lunch table. "You can pretend to own houses and motels and make lots of money of your own."

Trailing her, Margot rolled her eyes. "I'd rather have some sort of game about parties, though I wouldn't mind the money to have one—besides your birthday party when Papa gets here, I mean." Lilibet just shook her head at such silliness. The imp crossed her eyes again and made a face.

"Margot! Both your father and I have told you not to do that because your eyes can get stuck, and where would you be then?"

"But they come unstuck—see? We have to have some silly fun here, don't we? In that game, it takes a lot of time just sitting still and counting money and paying fines, and one can go broke!"

We played for a while anyway, then took a walk round the grounds. Not so much because of the war, but because even Margot was sounding too adult sometimes, I recalled the tearful scene this morning when Bessie had helped me dress and do my ablutions. I had brought her along to Balmoral just to get her out of London, for when she went home on day trips to visit her family—who no longer had a family home—she always came back morose and depressed. I had so loved her inherent buoyant personality and hoped to restore it.

"Did something else come up when you saw your family last week, Bessie?" I had asked before she could leave my bedroom.

She hesitated. "Don't like to tell sad things when you have so much on your mind, ma'am, for the whole country, I mean, and not just one little family."

I turned toward her on my seat in front of the dressing table and looking glass. Since Winston had mentioned night radar, I now thought of my ability to read other's dark emotions like that. "If you can, tell me," I said gently.

She nodded, opened her mouth, then burst into tears. I stood, pushed away my seat, took her tray from her, and put my arm around her. She stood stiffly in my embrace, her shoulders heaving. I steered her over to the divan and sat beside her.

When she had quieted a bit and used the handkerchief I gave her, I said again, "If you can, tell me. If not, that is fine too, but sometimes it helps to share."

"To share. Yes," she said with a hiccough. "Thanks to you, I have money to share with them. But my sister Prudence—she's preggers, and her boyfriend is dead. She only found out when she wrote him and had the letter returned and stamped *deceased*. I mean, she didn't know him long, and they weren't wed. I met him once, so handsome and a lot of fun in these times."

"Preggers—pregnant? So she wrote to him, now she's mourning him, poor girl."

She nodded wildly and finally gripped my hand that I had put over hers clenched in her lap. I thought of Lilibet writing to Philip.

"It means shame on my family, though it's a sign of the times," she went on in a rush of words and emotion. "I mean, fast romances, broken betrothals, blackouts at night so it's easy to sneak off together, fathers off to war and all and women left behind. You know, people sleeping and meeting in the shelters what might never see each other again. Came upon a couple huddled in a bombed-out doorway—you know, down the servants' entrance. Oh, ma'am, didn't mean to say all that and not to you."

"It's all right that you tell me. Wartime makes everything topsy-turvy, doesn't it?"

"Mum says higgledy-piggledy morals, and I better not get caught up in it all."

"Of course you won't. You'll be here, serving with me, helping me to keep my chin up too."

I insisted she take a ten-pound bill to give to her sister to save for when the baby came. It shamed me that she evidently thought ten pounds was a fortune. But she was wrong, so wrong about something: I did understand falling hard for someone handsome who was a lot of fun. For I had been through an earlier war of my own, that terrible so-called war to end all wars. And I had made a foolish decision to love someone who was to me as good as dead.

CHAPTER SEVENTEEN

Tossed Salad

We had a lovely birthday dinner at Balmoral when Bertie joined us. But life was still pleasure mingled with business. A few days later we hosted Canadian prime minister Mackenzie King, a handsome but solemn man in his upper sixties, a Victorian by birth with a receding hairline topped by silver hair. He had never married and was somewhat stiff with us, or with me, I wasn't sure. But I could tell he was of a serious bent, even when Bertie teased him about being another "king."

After that, Bertie—with his own talents for being a fixer and flying with night radar—quickly changed his tone.

"Britain and our other allies are so grateful for your leadership to bring so much of Canada's strength to our struggles," he told King. "The funding, supplies, and volunteers for the cause—as well as keeping up home front morale—has been invaluable for our mutual cause."

"We shall stand with you all the way, sir. Same as I told

Prime Minister Churchill in London, same as I shall tell my Parliament and people."

He spoke quite plainly and bluntly. When one was tuned to Winston's high-flying rhetoric, it was a change. Too late, I realized I'd told Lilibet and Margot to join us to give our guest a tour of the Victory Garden here that they had been tending lately. But perhaps their energy, charm, and even high jinks would lift the solemn mood when they joined us for luncheon too. I was worried now their presence would not suit—but here they came.

Bertie introduced the girls and that went well, so I began to relax. Lilibet and Margot led the three of us out into the gardens where a late-summer array of vegetables clung to neatly placed wooden poles. A wire fence kept out rabbits, though we'd seen deer vault it with no problem. Lettuce, chard, and other greens had been replanted numerous times. Carrots and beets still displayed their tops, and potatoes grew in neat rows.

"We adore salads," Margot said. "The French chef at the palace in London likes to toss them all together, so we do too."

"But neatly," Lilibet put in. "More or less arranged too, with a mix of greens and color. We have already picked greens for our luncheon today with you."

"Very good, young ladies. But it is rather getting on in the growing season for northern climes like Canada and Scotland, is it not?" our guest asked, eyeing the past-prime garden.

Lilibet said, "That may be so, sir, but we are very honored you have visited us here, and very grateful for all you and your nation do to help us in these difficult times."

I saw Bertie startle, and my eyes widened too. It was as if our eldest, our heir, had suddenly grown into womanhood—and international tact.

"I thank you very much for that, Princess Elizabeth," he replied with a little bow.

It wasn't like lunching with witty Winston, but Lilibet helped out and Margot managed to behave. And before our time together was ended, Mackenzie King was telling the girls that his boyhood motto had been "We must help those who cannot help themselves."

"I like that very much indeed," Lilibet said, sitting at his right hand while Margot fidgeted on my left side. "Of course, as terrible as times are—and we do so appreciate your help and wish the Americans would get in too—we Brits certainly plan on still helping ourselves."

* * *

Winston, I could tell, was running himself ragged. He was disappointed that the capture of Rudolf Hess had given us no solid information. He had decided Hess was a mental mess, though he had ordered him safely stowed, guarded, and further interrogated in the Tower of London.

"The only good I can see out of that," Winston said and coughed into his handkerchief again at our weekly meeting, "is that Hitler will go even crazier wondering what his once third-in-command is telling us. I'm letting our newspapers have a good run with that. By the way," he added, his eyes watering, "our mutual friend Brendan Bracken has hired the young woman you mentioned as an aide. You were right, ma'am, as she's quite good with ideas for photographs for the cause."

Bertie and I looked at each other as Winston coughed into his handkerchief again.

"Winston," Bertie said, "you simply must get more rest. We—this nation and this war effort—cannot afford to have you ill."

He shrugged. "I ignore the health challenges and call it my 'black dog of despair' that follows me about, depresses me and makes me ill at times. Ever hear of psychosomatics, Your Majesties? That is, that the worries of the mind and heart can make the body ill? Now, I suppose my enemies here and abroad would say all sorts of Freudian claptrap such as old Winston has too big an ego, eh? I just pray the Americans get in somehow soon, and that's nothing to ah . . . ah . . . sneeze at."

He exploded in a handkerchief-covered sneeze to punctuate that, then added, "The best medicine I've had lately is our RAF boys bombing Berlin! Talk about giving that madman Hitler a taste of his own medicine!"

"Winston," I said, rising, "you simply must go home and go to bed. I shall call Clementine to be certain you do!"

"Ah, wives, eh, Your Majesty?" he said to Bertie. "Especially wives in wartime. Dear heavens, what would we do without them? Yes, ma'am, I shall hightail myself home to Number 10 and off to bed with a good stiff shot of medicine."

"I hope," I said, "you do not mean whiskey and soda."

"For a cold? Certainly not. Just straight whiskey, and if we didn't have this dratted rationing of everything—which I am being blamed for—I'd recommend that for all my generals. And with that, I shall take my leave."

I held Bertie's arm as we watched him toddle out, leaning a bit on his gold-headed cane. What, I thought, were we to do with this stubborn man? But, of course, what would we ever do without him?

* * *

Besides Winston's bout with pneumonia, which was kept strictly out of the newspapers, more bad news was soon on my doorstep. My favorite footman, Mervin Weaver, who had asked permission to join the RAF, went missing in his Wellington aeroplane. I cried for him and sent condolences to his widow, for he had been happily married. I also sent his grieving wife the rest of his salary for that year.

But even worse, even closer to home and family, my nephew John, the master of Glamis Castle now, the son of my eldest brother Patrick, was killed in action on the nineteenth of September this terrible year of 1941. He had been serving with the Scots Guards in Egypt, a country so important to the cause of fighting Hitler and his ally Mussolini.

"I'm so sorry, my darling," Bertie comforted me when we were preparing to head back to London after our quick run to Scotland for John's memorial service.

I hugged him back hard. We were in the suite they had given us at Glamis, once my parents', though Bertie had slept in his dressing room near the phone.

"Losing him just brought back all the other losses—being

here," I told him, my face pressed to his coat lapel as we prepared to go out to our motorcar, then take the train back to London. "I can almost hear my mother's voice here, Papa's laughter. And, of course, see Fergus, as if he is still young, chasing David and me through the halls for a romp or tickle game."

"All these losses, people we don't know and ones we do. It all just makes me worry about George more."

I nodded. I knew he fretted so about his younger brother, the Duke of Kent, however much it hurt him that his mother had favored George. Nor had I ever felt close to George, perhaps because his pretty, vivacious Greek princess Marina had, for a time, supplanted me in the public eye when she came into the family.

"My mother would never get over his loss," he added and heaved a sigh that I felt too. "She supports me, of course, does her duty. David's let her down awfully, and she'll never forgive him, though she yet adores him."

I said, "We'd best go out, my dear, as the motorcar and train will be waiting."

But I wanted to say, *David has let all of us—me too—down awfully, and I'll never forgive him either.*

* * *

I was listening to the wireless in my sitting room at Windsor on the evening of Sunday, 7 December, nearly at the end of that tumultuous year. I was glad to see 1941 go but feared what lay ahead. I knew full well what Winston meant when he talked about being followed round by the black dog of despair. Things were still not going well for the Empire and her allies.

"And now a bulletin from New York City," the announcer's voice intoned. "We have just received a report that the American fleet anchored in Pearl Harbor in Honolulu, Hawaii, has been wantonly attacked by Japanese planes. Many ships are burning, and the number of casualties is reported to be high."

The announcer's voice droned on, but his words became a blur. The Japanese had attacked the Americans! And the Japanese were in league with the evil empires that were doing us harm.

I rushed out into the hall, nearly colliding with a maid with a tea tray, evidently heading for Bertie's room. "Not now, Emily," I told her and sprinted past.

I was quickly out of breath. All the walkabouts I'd done to visit stricken citizens . . . too many sweets and chocs . . . I knew that . . . but this . . .

I flung open his door. Bertie was sitting at the small desk he kept here, frowning at some report.

His head jerked up. "My dearest, what—"

"I've just heard the most amazing thing on the wireless! Can it be true that the Japanese have bombed the American fleet at Pearl Harbor in Hawaii?"

"If they have, the Japanese have made a stupid move to bring them in. Roosevelt will declare war straightaway!" he cried, leaping up to come around his desk. "And war on their ally Germany too! Surely, Winston has heard, so why doesn't he call?"

Alan Lascelles, Bertie's assistant private secretary, popped his head in the door. He was a veteran round here, for Bertie was the third king he had served after Bertie's father and, briefly, his brother too. "Oh, sorry. Didn't know the queen was here, Your Majesty."

"Have you heard the news about Pearl Harbor?" Bertie demanded.

"Let me just say, sir, that the prime minister is on your secure phone line with some sort of momentous news."

He disappeared as fast as he had come in. Bertie had kept Lascelles on for his vast knowledge and the fact he had turned against David when he went so haywire, wed that woman, and deserted his country. I liked him for that too.

Bertie seized the receiver from its cradle. "Winston? Yes. Yes!"

A long pause. Winston speaking. I began to pace, but then shamelessly leaned over Bertie's shoulder so I could hear Winston, who must be nearly shouting into the telephone.

"Yes, the queen heard it on the wireless," Bertie was saying. "Surely they will get in now. Will you call President Roosevelt? I am certain he will contact you."

"I've already talked to him and am going over to see him," I heard Winston say.

"To the States now? To Washington?"

"Immediately. He tried to talk me out of that, but now is our time, Your Majesty! I will offer him our help in all regards."

"And pray that he will return that promise."

"Exactly. By the way, I know you will send him our condolences for their losses. Surely, he and his stubborn Congress will declare war on Germany now too, and then we'll have the Yanks over here again, thank God."

"But is there something else?" Bertie asked as I moved away, both stunned and yet relieved.

I saw Bertie suddenly wilt against the edge of his desk when he had seemed so energetic and animated. Surely this tragic but good news was not to be mingled with the tragic or the bad, like some—well, like some tossed salad the girls had been complaining just today they had not seen in their rations since late autumn.

"B-b-both of them lost?" Bertie asked. "Those damned Japs, as Roosevelt calls them! Pearl Harbor for them, these horrible losses for us. Now it's full-out war with Japan for us too!"

"What?" I demanded when he slammed the receiver down. "Both of what? What losses?"

"Our battle cruiser *Repulse* and the ship Churchill went to Newfoundland on—"

"The *Prince of Wales*?"

"Yes. Both sunk by Japanese warplanes off the coast of Thailand."

"One moment of hope—and then this."

"They were lost. . . . Lost, hundreds of crew, our fine, b-brave British ships . . ."

I broke into tears, and he held me to him. Even, finally, in the hope of help from the Americans, the king was crying too.

CHAPTER EIGHTEEN

Tangled Ivy

In the spring of 1942, I went without Bertie or the girls to visit Queen Mary, in exile, as she called it. Leaving London was not the thing to do, she'd argued, but she had agreed to be kept safe from the bombing by "camping out" in rural Gloucestershire.

Hardly a campout spot, I thought, as my motorcar driver took me up the lane toward the massive, beige Cotswold-stone building called Badminton. It overlooked a placid lake that reflected its lofty cupolas. Sheep grazed on the green, and swans swam perfectly in the glassy lake. The estate sat in the frame of the Forest of Dean with its ancient oaks, beech, and ash trees. I felt myself unwind a bit and regretted that my mother-in-law had evidently not relaxed here one bit but always had some project at hand.

I was greeted by Mary, Duchess of Beaufort, Queen Mary's host with her husband the duke, Bertie's nephew. They had been kind enough to take in Queen Mary and her sizable household for the duration of the war. The duchess was a lovely brunette and had been a bridesmaid at our wedding. We kissed in the French way, touching both sides of our cheeks. We walked in together past the grand, curving staircase with huge paintings of Beaufort ancestors and their beloved racing steeds hanging on most of the walls.

"Is she all right?" I asked straightaway when I didn't see Queen Mary.

"Oh, quite. A bit of a head cold is all. She actually slept in, anxious for your arrival, though, so she could show you her latest passion."

"Oh, dear. She hasn't been pottering about and asking for any of your collectibles?"

"I knew to put them away for now where they would not collect dust," the duchess said with a little smile.

I nodded with a smile in return. It had been common knowledge for years that the former queen had an acquisitive nature. Some had said that she pilfered things for her nest like a magpie, such as Fabergé pieces she liked. She was often wont to hint she would adore owning such and such an item, that she had not been able to find that particular bibelot, and how it would enhance her collection. And what were her hostesses to do but offer that as a gift to the king's wife even after he had died?

"So where in the house are her rooms?" I asked as we entered the drawing room where a lovely tea service had been laid out before an ornate fireplace.

The duchess smiled—or was that a grimace? "Everywhere, anywhere," she said with a little shrug.

"I must tell you how indebted the king and I are to you for your . . . your sacrifice in these trying times."

"We all must do our bit. Speaking of which, do you see that lovely painted Chinese screen over there? She has had a private commode installed behind it and uses it whenever—whoever—is about."

"Oh, dear. And what is this she writes me about landscaping outside? Mary, I am sorry, but best tell me, and I'll tell the king."

"No, that's the least of things, quite all right," she assured me. "You see, she is on a mission to oversee our woodcutters—especially that they stack the wood in a certain, precise way. But it is truly the tangled ivy on walls, tree trunks, and fences that she is—well, is at war with. I'm sure she will show you when she comes down shortly."

"Dear friend, you and the duke deserve a medal for service."

"We are honored to help, and she is a dear—under it all. She showed me your last letter, entitled *Mama darling*. You honor her too."

And so, before the former queen even joined us, Mary and I sat, drinking tea and eating tea sandwiches and tarts in the very room at Badminton where a former duke's children in the 1860s had been allowed to use light rackets to hit featherweight shuttlecocks in a game from India that had taken on the name of this grand house. With that game, they would not harm the paintings of the famous horses reared and raced here.

Too bad that my mother-in-law, "Mama darling," had made another game for herself here, one I decided to call "Tangled Ivy."

* * *

"Dear Elizabeth, I simply must show you my out-of-door project," Queen Mary told me after she joined us for high tea. I had shared what I could about the progress of the war, especially now that the Americans were in it too. The duke was at his post in London, but would be back soon, I was told, so I decided I might tell him a bit more than I had the ladies.

"I hear you are getting healthful, fresh air here, Mama."

"It keeps me young. Why, would you believe that I am in my middle seventh decade, if you did not know so?"

What to say? But I did not need to say anything, for she went on, "I worry so for my dear sons. Little Johnnie gone, of course, lost much too early. Dear David, far away on that tropical island. George flying too much here and there in those aeroplanes he adores. And your Bertie, of course, king and having to oversee it all. After this dreadful war is over, we must have a reunion of them all, get David back for at least a visit, even if he brings that woman."

And what to say to that? So I changed the topic. "Would you both consider briefly entertaining the American president's wife, Eleanor Roosevelt, when she visits here this autumn, in October, I believe? I would love for her to see our lovely countryside as we saw hers. A day or two here at Badminton, some time with the Churchills in the country, I think, then of course, a short stay at the palace. Beyond that, she will have her own agenda. I regret what dreadful shape Buck House is in, having been bombed and repairs quite neglected during all this."

"Why, we'd be honored, would we not, Mary?" the queen asked the younger woman as if Badminton were hers, just as the bibelots and ivy and woodpiles.

"I shall have to ask the duke, but we would indeed be honored," the duchess agreed.

"Thank you both," I said. "Now, Mama, why don't I change into some out-of-door clothes and you can show me your project? It won't take me long to freshen up."

"Well, there is a lovely, newfangled commode in this room if you don't want to go to yours. Yes, let's head out so you can see how things are coming along."

How things are coming along . . . kept revolving in my head as I went up to my room where a maid had unpacked and hung my clothes. I changed into jodhpurs and a flannel jacket over a blouse. I felt Bertie's mother looked and sounded good despite her cold, but she obviously thought Badminton House, perhaps her immediate world, still revolved around her.

Worse, the idea of a reunion with David and that woman worried me. At least, I hoped, the war was an excuse to keep them where they were.

* * *

"Sorry I missed your birthday celebration at Balmoral," Mama told me when I joined her downstairs. "Frankly, I was afraid I'd see an aeroplane on my way there and have an allergic reaction."

I almost broke out laughing. An allergic reaction was the least of anyone's worries if they saw a German plane coming over or at them.

"So, here's where my project began," she told me as she marched me outside and around the corner of the massive building. She held in her hands a short-handled claw-shaped rake as if it were a weapon and had handed me a pair of hedge clippers. If our hostess thought I had not seen her roll her eyes as we headed out, she was quite mistaken. But I was so grateful to her and the duke for taking on this task—this formidable, if slightly dotty, woman who had never quite given up being queen. Would it be someday that way for me too?

But why had Queen Mary not been more affectionate to her children, why had she not defended Bertie—even David—when their strict father had scolded and shamed them? She had been a wonderful grandmother to Lilibet and Margot when we were away on trips like the one before the war to Canada and America. Lilibet, especially, adored her, and I suspected her grandmother was giving her advice on being queen someday, which made me uneasy, as if Bertie would not be here long. Perhaps that is why our eldest had become so skilled and tactful with powerful, political men like the Canadian prime minister or even with Winston.

I recalled when I first knew my mother-in-law when she was queen. She had once indirectly threatened me and my family with social banishment when I turned Bertie's marriage proposal down a second time. But she had been kind to me since, and I had assiduously cultivated her friendship and opinions.

"Oh, you can see where the ivy had climbed here and clung

to this stone," I said, looking at the blank beige wall where she pointed. A ghostlike form of a climbing vine seemed etched upon the stone.

"Exactly. I pulled it all off, here, there, anywhere. Why, it was an eyesore, hiding so much. Cleaner this way. I just cannot abide anything clinging like that. I joke with the gardeners that before, one could not see the forest trees and house for the ivy!"

She dragged me here and there, even to the stone sign she had ripped ivy from to expose the Latin motto for Badminton House carved in it: *Prorsum semper.* Ever forward.

I thought of Bertie's latest saying when he was glum and exhausted, which was too much of the time. "Onward and upward!" he had said. Well, I was tired too from our constant visits to lift people's spirits at factories, hospitals, schools, service groups, and first-aid posts, sometimes with Rowena in tow, taking photographs and notes for Brendan Bracken's war "information" as Winston had called it. But as for the king, it was as if he had caught Winston's recent up-and-down health problems, but, thank heavens, Bertie did not disdain doctors and had not treated his head colds and sore throats with Winston's treatments of whiskey and snuff!

At least, around here, on this visit, as we plodded on to view numerous de-ivied trees and fences, it was onward if not upward.

* * *

One thing that cheered me greatly was when Cosmo Lang, archbishop of Canterbury, preached from his pulpit that I was a modern-day biblical Queen Esther. I had greatly admired the man who had conducted our wedding ceremony, overseen our coronation, and christened both of our daughters. He had written me in a letter much the same about Queen Esther once, claiming that my role of support and inspiration in the war was best compared to the Bible quote: *Who knoweth whether thou art come to the Kingdom for such a time as this.*

So he had dared to preach that I had the strength and courage and patriotism of that Old Testament queen, who saved her people from annihilation by the enemy. I must admit that I much preferred that reference to Hitler's declaring me "the most dangerous woman in Europe."

"Rather high-flying rhetoric," I told Bertie when he read it aloud to me from a newspaper after I had returned exhausted from Badminton. "But, of course, a great honor. Actually, as different as you and Winston are—our true leaders in such a time as this—I see many similarities between you."

"Neither of us will ever give up," he said, crumpling the newspaper in his lap and looking down the length of the sofa at me. I had perched on the other end to take advantage of the lighted floor lamp there. "And, you know, Queen Esther's power with the king came partly from the fact she coerced him in their royal bed."

That set me back a moment. We had been affectionate lately—more than usual—but still not fully intimate. Was this a rebuke or a challenge? But we were both terribly fatigued, falling asleep sitting up, nodding off in church, having to go to our beds to ward off debilitating illness.

"All right," I said, rising to at least the comparison challenge, yet changing the topic. "But there is more. Winston has a tough constitution and you do too. Both of you arrange problems from greatest to least and attack them in that order."

Obviously listening raptly, turning toward me by putting one knee up on the sofa, he nodded, so I plunged on. "At least you trust doctors when Winston does not, but this war is taking a toll on both of you."

"I have to trust my doctors for the kingdom's sake. Yes, this war takes its toll. Go on."

"Both of you speak beautifully and forcefully when you have planned ahead."

"A great compliment to your once lisping, nervous husband. So far, so good."

I wet my lips with my tongue. Why had I started this? "And dare I say, you both adored your beautiful but busy mothers, who remained rather distant. You know he adored Jennie Jerome and—"

"And I—all of us—Queen Mary—who ever acted the part of queen over that of mother. Yes, her reserved nature with us even affected David," he admitted, frowning. "I swear, I wonder sometimes if he took to Wallis Simpson so much because she treated him coldly—him, the playboy, like a matinee idol, the handsome catch of the century—and she insulted and turned him down at first. Maybe, though he didn't even know it, winning Wallis Simpson over would prove something to him after . . . after our mother."

"Yes, I—yes, perhaps," I agreed, anxious to get this comparison back to Winston, not David. "And if you want to get absolutely Freudian about it, as Winston says, both you and he had fathers you loved who, to put it nicely, barely had time for you and when they did . . . well."

I blinked back tears. I should not have started this tangle of . . . of resentments and aggravations. It was true both David and Bertie seemed to have personality problems that their younger brother George, the apple of his father's eye, had apparently never had, but at least I had tried to throw Winston into the mix too. Was there some fault in English fathers and mothers of the rich and famous? How blessed I and my brothers had been with mine—perhaps an aberration.

"Our other two siblings," Bertie went on, not looking at me now but off into space, "did not suffer quite that much, not Mary, of course, not the only girl."

I thought of the other two Marys I had been with recently, Mary, Duchess of Beaufort, and the dowager Queen Mary. All of these lives, noble, powerful, were just as open to heartbreak as poor Bessie's pregnant sister who had jumped off Tower Bridge and drowned herself, so Bessie had used the ten pounds I had given to bury her.

"I love you, my queen," Bertie whispered to bring me back to the here and now. "And always will, no matter what befalls."

"I love you too," I told him, blinking back tears as I scooted over to sit beside him. "War or peace, I too."

CHAPTER NINETEEN

Walkie-Talkie

Of all the many visits to troops we continued to make, perhaps the most interesting one, at least in 1942 so far, was to a United States Army camp near Ballykinler, County Down, in Northern Ireland. Thank heavens, Winston's presiding over the "marriage" of our country with the U.S. had gone well. Despite our terrible losses to German U-boats, Americans were being shipped over in droves.

What a raucous cheer went up when we visited Wolff's shipyard near the camp, where many of the Americans worked or were stationed. We were absolutely engulfed by well-fed, healthy-looking young men. How well outfitted they looked too, as we smiled and waved through another round of "hip-hip-hooray!"

What straight, white teeth the two officers had who guided us on our tour. "We are honored by your visit, Your Majesties," a Lieutenant Kettering told us. He was a redhead who could have passed for Brendan Bracken's brother or even his son.

"And we are indeed grateful *you* are here," Bertie told him.

"We know you have been busy to keep spirits up amongst your own soldiers and sailors and your brave airmen," Kettering said. He had a most unusual-looking instrument or weapon in his hand, which I noted Bertie kept eyeing. "More of us are coming, and I'll bet we work together well. As Benjamin Franklin said, 'We'd best hang together or we'll hang separately.' Sorry to hear of the setbacks in North Africa, Your Majesty."

"We have a new commander there, General Montgomery, whom I and our P.M. trust implicitly," Bertie told him. "We shall turn the tide, especially now that we are all in the same boat, so to speak. But, I say, whatever is that wireless item you are holding?"

"Quite newfangled, sir. It's called a walkie-talkie. For sure, it's wireless, but I can talk to someone far afield and he can talk back. Quite a handy-dandy article. Here, let me demonstrate, as my aide is on the other end right now."

Bertie watched, wide-eyed. I did too, thinking what a clever item it would be not only in battle, but on the home front. Why, I could keep in contact with Lilibet and Margot or easily summon Bessie when I needed her and not have to use the old Victorian wire-and-bell system. If there were any earth-shaking news—which it seemed now was our daily bread and butter—I could call Bertie.

"Smashing," Bertie said as the lieutenant demonstrated the instrument by talking, while we were walking, to his aide.

"I didn't realize this would be new to you, sir, and I shall see if we can give you two of them with the instructions," Kettering offered.

After a review of the troops and a conference with the other officers in charge—their generals were evidently on their way across the ocean if a U-boat didn't sink them first—we were driven away in our short motorcade.

"Well," Bertie said glancing at the pair of walkie-talkies he'd insisted not ride in the boot, but by his boots, on the floor, right here. "I wonder what else we'll get and learn from the Yankee troops. But I was thinking too, I've always had a walkie-talkie since I've had you, my darling. And what would I ever do without you?"

* * *

Not only Northern Ireland but our dear London was being invaded, but not, thank heavens, by the damn Germans. Rather, the Americans were here in the thousands with yet more to come. In late June, their commander, General Eisenhower, had arrived but we were yet to meet him. For now, Churchill's information minister Brendan Bracken was giving us a tour of the "American takeover" of Central London. We were in our motorcar with our chauffeur but with Brendan's narration as if we were tourists or newly arrived Americans. He sat on the jump seat across from us, riding backward as we gazed agape out our windows at the transformation of Grosvenor Square.

"So," he said, gesturing toward the window on Bertie's side, "only about fifty-five thousand Americans right now, but probably more than two million more to come, though not all to London. We already have, of course, the troops you've visited in Northern Ireland. The massive Eighth Air Force is getting settled in eastern England and is quite taking over there."

"I've read the private papers on that," Bertie put in, lighting a cigarette. I was tempted to help him with his new automatic lighter, but I didn't want Brendan to think he needed help because his hands were shaking. He inhaled and blew out a long breath of smoke. "They've brought troops and supplies with them for runways, airfields, depots, and bases. Winston is grateful, and I am too. What a beehive of activity there and here!"

Our motorcar, of necessity, slowed in the thick traffic. Officers in sharp navy blue, dark brown, or green uniforms strode back and forth across the square between the American headquarters at 20 Grosvenor Square and the American embassy. We were soon in a line of drab green Army vehicles taking officers here and there, no doubt to the British War Office a few miles away. Messenger riders on motorcycles careened through clogged traffic.

"Needless to say," Brendan put in when we started to inch along again, "our guests are keeping the once devastated stores and hotels in the area hopping. Never so many happy laundries, shoeshine boys, and tailors since the war began, at least around here."

"We are to meet and host Commander General Eisenhower soon," I said.

"I cannot wait to meet him," Bertie added. "He's done a fine job settling in with that initial press conference about teamwork and making himself available to reporters—ours and the internationals."

"He may call himself a farm boy, but he handles the press like a city mayor," Brendan said. "Besides, he looks and talks the part, and the P.M. loves that. Six feet tall, straight, broad shoulders. He looks people right in the eye."

"I have a young photographer, a female friend, who is quite taken with his kindness," I said, "so there are some women working for the press too."

"So many women have stepped forward here on the home front, part of the team. And, oh, yes, General Eisenhower calls the reporters part of his team, and they eat that up. Some have started to copy his American slang with things like *knowing the score*, his superiors being *big shots*, and the like. And what's amazing is that the P.M. says he's socially shy."

"Really?" I asked. "In what way?"

"To tell true, ma'am, he is what he says, a small-town farm boy, though he's worked in Washington for years. I read a dossier on him that his childhood home had no running water or indoor sanitary ah—arrangements. Our society mavens here have asked him to dinners, but he's not keen on that, told the P.M. he's not here to run a brutal war over teacups. And when he spent a weekend at Chequers, the P.M. noted that 'Ike,' as he asked the P.M. to call him, smokes heavily, ah—four packs of Camel cigarettes a day."

Brendan cleared his throat as Bertie flicked a silver snake of ash off the end of his cigarette into the ashtray he'd had installed in all our vehicles except the carriages.

"So, the general told the P.M.," Brendan went on, "that he is most uncomfortable when he cannot have a smoke until the 'To the king!' toasts at the end of banquets. He's even turned down a few invitations and put some noble noses out of joint, but of course, the P.M. loves him."

"When we invite him to the palace, he will come," I declared, "and we will have the toast early and put him at ease. A little sherry before the meal, then the toast, which Bertie will appreciate also."

"Or skip the toast or at least include Roosevelt and Eisenhower in it too," Bertie added. "It's classified but he's flying to Gibraltar soon to get a bit closer to the efforts in North Africa, but when he returns, we shall host him and help him in any way we can. We need this man."

* * *

We were entertaining family and friends at the Balmoral dinner table in late August in wretched Scottish weather. It was raining outside and from time to time, thunder rumbled. I was annoyed that Bertie was called to the phone during dessert, for I feared it could be bad news about our troops in North Africa again. Mussolini, Hitler's dreadful Italian ally, was pouring in troops to bolster the Germans there, and we needed to keep control of Egypt and the Suez Canal to ensure shipments of oil.

Besides, sometimes I felt I had a sixth sense about when a call would be about something dire. My goddaughter had joined the Wrens, our Women's Royal Naval Service, the first of our three services to recruit women so that the men could serve at sea. We had all thought she would be safe, out of harm's way in battle. But after a short stint, she died, not of war wounds but of meningitis. And I had a premonition it was to be terrible news when my secretary had come in to say I had an important telephone call.

Bertie might still tease me about being his favorite walkie-talkie, but I dreaded any sort of further tragedy. What if that call was from Winston with bad news?

While he was away, I nodded and responded, but I hardly listened. I nearly jumped from my seat when I saw Bertie return to the dining room. He was white as a ghost. A frown crunched his forehead and seemed to make his entire body slump. The chatter at the table faded even more. I saw only him. To my amazement, before he sat across from me, he handed me a note and looked away, but I saw grief and disaster written on him—and then the note.

I thought at first that Queen Mary must have died. In shaky cursive handwriting that did not seem his own, the note read,

Dearest, we must end dinner. I am afraid George has been killed flying to Iceland. He left Invergordon at 1.30 p.m. & hit a mountain near Wick.

I nearly cried aloud as I felt a punch to my belly. And to die here in my beloved Scotland . . . and in this weather!

At the table, the rustle of whispers began. Heads turned my way, then back toward Bertie.

I caught the eye of the Duchess of Gloucester and nodded toward the door, then stood. The ladies, then everyone, rose.

"Shall we adjourn to the drawing room?" I said, but did not budge as first the ladies, then the men filed out.

Bertie left the room immediately, heading into the back hall where the footmen had come in to serve. I found him there, leaning against the wall, his head down, his thumb and index finger pressed into the bridge of his nose.

"Is it solid information?" I asked. "Perhaps it is wrong. Perhaps there are survivors."

"They were on a Sunderland flying boat," he said quietly, his voice not his own. "It should not have taken off in this damned Scottish weather. It hit a hill on the Duke of Portland's Langwell estate. Perhaps—probably—pilot error, but they say George wasn't flying it this time."

"Oh, my dearest," I cried and embraced him. He stood stiffly in my arms for a moment then hugged me back, heaving huge sobs. A footman started down the hall with a tray, then spun back and hurried away.

"I'll have to telephone Mama," he choked out. "It will do her in, her dear George—and my dear George too. David will have to be told, but I'll try to keep him from coming for the funeral."

"Poor Marina and the children. And my poor Bertie, one of your worst fears. I must notify our guests what has happened and see them on their way, then break the news to Lilibet and Margot."

I hugged him again and took a step away. He snatched me back.

"Elizabeth," he said, his voice raspy, his lips against my forehead. "I don't think I can get through this. Lost battles, yes.

Bombings. But not losing George and seeing Mama suffer through it."

"Yes, you—and we—will get through this. We must, just as others have. This terrible family loss. The war. Now, you go telephone Marina our condolences and I'm afraid we must begin to discuss her wishes for the funeral. I'll be certain our guests get away despite this . . . this dreadful storm."

* * *

We buried our dear George, RAF hero, Duke of Kent, four days later in the royal burial grounds at Frogmore near Windsor after his funeral in St. George's Chapel. The burial site was not far from where Queen Victoria and her beloved Prince Albert lay in a round mausoleum encircled by a colonnade. It was beautiful on that day, no more brutal Scottish weather, but summer in the hushed gardens with the serpentine lake reflecting puffy clouds.

George's widow Princess Marina was holding up well, if I may say so, beautiful, even in her stunned grief. I deeply regretted that I had resented her at first, so stylish and slender, for she had reminded me of Mrs. Simpson when my wounds were still raw. And I admired Marina for being a good wife to George, through thick and thin. And were his use of drugs and flagrant sexual liaisons the thick or the thin of their difficult marriage? Marina seemed to linger now, not wanting to leave the still-open grave.

"Marina, dearest," I said to her when she finally walked a bit away, "did Bertie tell you of our suggestion that we bring your sister here to live with you for a while, just to have more family about?"

Her beautiful eyes looked flat, red-rimmed. "No, but he said he had an idea to help. It must have been that. I know he cared deeply for George—Mama too, of course," she added with a glance over at Queen Mary, who, stoic though she was, had taken to dabbing under her eyes again with a black handkerchief. We were all in mourning black.

"Tell me then," she said as the two of us walked a few steps away. I supposed we would never be really close because of our rocky beginning, but how much I wanted to comfort her now. "If you mean a visit from my sister Princess Olga, you do know that she has fled Yugoslavia for exile in South Africa with her husband Prince Paul—and that some regard him as a traitor who has collaborated with the Germans, which is most unfair."

"Be that as it may, the king believes he can arrange for them to live with you and the children for a while, if you wish."

"Oh, I do. And thank you both for arranging that." She reached out her gloved hand to squeeze mine. Our eyes met and held. One problem from the past patched up a bit, I thought, glad I could be a walkie-talkie for Bertie today to reach out to her.

* * *

In the weeks after, with trips to Badminton, I tried to comfort Queen Mary in her loss, even though it hurt me to realize she had favored George, not Bertie. And then the day she produced a letter from David and told me much of what it said, it hurt me even more to try to buck her up. It was Bertie who needed her love and support now, not David, who had his wife and was well out of the way of our war effort.

Mama said to me, "Shortly after George died, I wrote David an eight-page letter to comfort him as he has me. And I ended the letter with 'I send a kind message to your wife who will help you to bear your sorrow in George's loss.'"

I actually bit my tongue to keep from saying something sharp. Now with George gone, was David her favorite son, not Bertie, who had tried so hard to keep the country and his mother well?

She said, "In the letter he sent me back, he said that but for dear Wallis's love and comfort he would have felt very lost."

I hadn't spoken that woman's name—even in my own thoughts—for so long, I startled.

Mama went on, "David goes on to say he believes this entire dreadful war could have been avoided. He has missed me terribly these six years since the abdication and longs to see me again, to bring Wallis here, of course, to visit or to live. He says their great love for each other has intensified in the five years they have been wed. I'm so happy for him—yes, for them."

For once Bertie's wife and queen, his "walkie-talkie" who could supposedly solve any family problem, was speechless, but obviously my feelings mattered not as she went on, clutching the letter, "I must tell you, dear Elizabeth, that David feels the king, our Bertie, has been rather harsh toward him. He wants me—and especially you, he writes here, for I have this letter nearly memorized—to know that Wallis is a most courageous and noble person and her not getting the Her Royal Highness title is but another bitter blow for her to bear. But now that George is gone and Bertie busy with the war, he asks me to tell Prime Minister Churchill that the HRH must be given to his wife."

I felt as if I had sand in my throat. "But that has been all decided upon, by the P.M. and by the king—for the good of the country, and in these wretched times—George's death—that . . . that is all settled and would cause upheaval to revisit it."

"But you are speaking for the P.M. and the king, dear Elizabeth, and we queens must learn not to do that. Oh, I have no reason to want Wallis to have the HRH except to please and comfort David. You knew him well. You know how he is."

"I did. I do, Mama. If you'll excuse me now, I think I had best head back to Windsor, for Lilibet and Margot have been a bit restless lately."

"Oh, dear, yes. You just send them over here to me if they need tending, especially Lilibet."

I nodded and walked away in the beauty of the colorful autumn Badminton gardens, which had just become cold and dry. I suddenly felt sick, as if I had a throat so sore I could not speak. Each step exhausted me.

The next time Bertie teased me by saying I was his walkie-talkie queen, I would ask him never to say that again, for I had never been able to tell this woman that her son David, alias once King Edward, was not one bit lovable, only . . . well, flashy. I suddenly longed to hide away in my bed, hide away from the war of nations and the war in my heart.

CHAPTER TWENTY

We're Not in Kansas Anymore

After the Duke of Kent's funeral, Bertie insisted I go to rest at Balmoral before coming back into the stress and debris of London. I would rather have gone to be with the girls at Windsor, but I quickly developed a cold, and my exhaustion nearly did me in.

With a minimal staff of two maids, my dresser, my private secretary Gladys, and, of course, Bessie, I hunkered down to rest. I did not want to chance a recurrence of the tonsillitis or the other physical problems that had occasionally laid me low over the years, especially when my spirits were down. Oh, yes, I knew my head and heart affected my body at times—and once, a terrible incident with David. I must admit, this was the first respite I'd had, the first peaceful, undemanding rest, since this war began.

In the past, personal, internal battles had put me down: Whether to marry Bertie when I had still loved his horrid brother who had led me on and mistreated me so. Fear that the

Simpson woman would become queen or even Her Royal Highness. Tensions between me and Bertie when I left the marriage bed. And, as ever, like a monster that stalked me no matter how hard I tried to keep it locked behind walls and doors, the fact that my birth mother had been a French cook.

"Here it is, Your Majesty," Bessie told me, knocking on my door and pushing a wheeled cart with the moving picture projector into my bedroom. "And the film *Wizard of Oz*. Had to send to London for it, Gladys did. I think you've watched it before, ma'am."

I rolled over in bed and plumped up my pillow. I coughed into one of the several handkerchiefs I had at the ready. "I've seen it with the girls twice before," I told her, sounding stuffed up. "My P. G. Wodehouse books cheer me, but I need more of a pick-me-up, and this should do it. I'm off to see the Wizard, even if he did turn out to be a sham."

"You let the staff see it once, remember? But that song 'Over the Rainbow' is really sad, I mean, longing for things we can't quite have."

I sneezed, covering my mouth and nose. This would never do, so I must heal fast. Americans from generals to privates were already in London, and Bertie and I needed to have their commander, General Eisenhower—with a German last name, no less—to the palace for a welcome dinner, with toasts to the Americans.

Eleanor Roosevelt's visit was finally coming up this month. All our important guests would simply have to understand that we went by strict food rations in the palace just as did our citizenry. It was one well-known way to support and unite with them, and Brendan Bracken and Rowena made certain the press knew.

My secretary Gladys came in. "Your Majesty, I know you said to hold all calls unless it was the king, but just wanted to tell you that your art advisor, Sir Kenneth Clark, rang up and said he'd call back. Said he'd understand if you can't come to the telephone, but he wanted you to know he's insisting the paintings at Hampton Court need to be protected too."

"Oh, yes. Well, his advice is important—and I shall take his call if he rings again. People safe first, but the heritage of England, including its art, second. Meanwhile, let's run this movie. And do inform me straightaway if he calls again."

It would be like Kenneth to do that, I thought, with a little thrill that was not a chill from my cold. He was both persistent and protective. He had guided me through my selection of art, my commission of artists, even the very modern John Piper, to do watercolor war paintings of Windsor Castle. How appropriate it was that the first ones he had done were dark and moody. Kenneth had praised me for my desire to support living London artists, even ones working in other mediums besides oil.

How kind he had been to take me hither and yon and instruct me in the heritage of England's art and artists. From a wealthy family, he had an education and talents that had taken him to the heights as director of the National Gallery and Surveyor of the King's Pictures. I had praised him to Bertie, who had knighted him as Commander of the Bath in 1938 at the age of thirty-five!

And to me, Kenneth had been especially solicitous, beyond

the standard courtesy to one's queen. Sometimes, I almost felt he were courting me as a gentleman would a desirable lady, had I not been married, had I not been queen. I knew that, though he was wed, he had rather the reputation of a lady's man, and I could see why. He was quite handsome, masculine, muscular, and engaging, a brilliant conversationalist and speaker with a fine sense of humor.

I tried to thrust him from my thoughts and watch the movie I had almost memorized. I laughed again when wide-eyed Dorothy told her little dog, Toto—and I reached out to pet my corgi cuddled next to my hip—that "I've a feeling we're not in Kansas anymore."

Indeed, my life had been like that. I would have told my pet dog, "This isn't St. Paul's Walden Bury or even not Glamis Castle anymore." Sometimes, despite it all, I could not believe that I was queen of England, queen of the Empire. Mother of two princesses, one of whom would someday—far off, I prayed—take the throne. And, once again, we were at war with Germany, and I still foolishly clung to little wars in my heart about choices I had made.

"Your Majesty, sorry to pop in again, but Sir Kenneth has rung a second time," Gladys said, coming back in, "though I don't think the phone cord will stretch to your bed."

"I shall get up, of course, and take it at my desk. Ask him to wait a moment," I said and arose quickly, disturbing my little corgi friend.

I saw the quick look that passed between the two as Bessie turned off the projector and Gladys turned on the lamp and snatched my warm robe and slippers from the chair to help me don them, since my dresser had been given the day off. I blew my nose hard, so I would not sound as if I were inside of a barrel.

"Hello, dear friend Kenneth," I said when I sat at my desk and lifted the receiver. "I hope there is no problem."

"Your Majesty, nothing we can't handle together in this era of problems. So sorry to hear you are under the weather, and my deepest condolences on the loss of the Duke of Kent."

We chatted about the funeral. He told me we had an amiable American soldier invasion in London, and that a few officers and soldiers had taken advantage of the free concerts at the gallery, though most Yanks were keeping the shops, restaurants, and bars around Grosvenor Square hopping instead of attending free orchestral presentations.

"How kind and generous of you to extend that offer," I told him. "I had a wonderful time at the one we attended together."

I had to stifle a sigh. It *had* been a lovely day and event, and the publicity had helped to promote the concerts, available to all to keep spirits up, even though the entire gallery was stripped of its artwork. Brendan Bracken's up-and-coming protégé Rowena Fitzgerald had taken a lovely photograph of Kenneth and me sitting together, and Brendan Bracken had used the picture for what he called "the best sort of propaganda."

It didn't take much time for Kenneth to convince me that the art from Hampton Court should also be secreted, even though it was in the countryside. "A target, a magnet for bombs or invasion," he said, his rich voice strong. "As you know, that vandal Hitler and his hordes are known to steal art, my dear Q.E."

I smiled at his little nickname for me. He had first used it when he had shown me one of his favorite portraits of the first Queen Elizabeth, the famous Ditchley portrait of her with her three long strands of pearls. He said he had noticed how often I wore three graceful strands, and somehow, that intimate compliment, observation, and the private nickname had so endeared him. Once, he had even dared to reach out to straighten my signature pearls when they became tangled.

"I will bow, sir, so to speak," I told him, "to your expertise on this. Shall we store the Hampton Court art in the same place as the others?"

We had decided not to mention on the phone where we had stashed the nation's priceless valuables, even if we thought it a secure line. Very few knew that, though I had suggested sending art as far as Canada, Kenneth had won the day to use the basements of Windsor Castle. Also, just this year, priceless collections of art, miniatures, and manuscripts from the Royal Library had gone to an old, unused mine in North Wales. Both of us were dedicated to protecting our secrets, I thought with another unbidden thrill.

"One more thing," he told me. "My dear Q.E., I have it on the best authority that the Duke of Wellington is, shall we say, very hesitant to let his important art collection out of Apsley House to be stored. Of course, he's lately busy in North Africa, but he is briefly home on leave. I was hoping you might have a way to suggest to him that a mansion on Hyde Park Corner is hardly the place to guard such treasures in his care. I thought if you and I took a trip there, we might convince him before he heads back to service."

"I see. I— Yes, I know him, a fine young man, one I would consider for Princess Elizabeth if he were nearer her age."

I tried to get hold of myself. I was stalling for time. If Kenneth and I went together, surely we could convince the duke. I knew there was room to store the extensive Wellington collection at Frogmore. Surely such a royal venue would please the duke. Then there would be time alone with Kenneth again, a common cause, a little day trip, perhaps lunch or tea before or after. We had an affair that was not a real affair at all, perhaps only the possibility in my head and heart.

But then I thought of Bertie without me now, how he had insisted I get away so that I could have a bit of rest, even though I know he was exhausted and missed me desperately. Surely, he had more important things to do besides convincing a young duke to allow us to store his collection in case the city was bombed further or even—God forbid—invaded. Kenneth was right that Hitler was a thief as well as a mass murderer and destroyer.

I bit my lower lip hard, then said, "I will be returning to London soon. My days of reading Damon Runyon here are over, and Alan Lascelles lent me *Epitaph for a Spy*. I shall snag Bertie, however busy and distracted he is, and visit the duke straightaway whilst he is home. And I will let you know how that goes."

He sounded surprised. I half-regretted my decision, but there would be other times, hopefully, times of peace and not the big war overriding the little ones inside me. Oh, I knew Bertie had enjoyed an amour after I had requested a separate bed. But he had put up with that and loved and championed me. And didn't all that count for something?

After we rang off, I curled up in bed again, half wanting to call Kenneth back and set up a date. But no, and so I watched Dorothy with her Scarecrow and Tin Man friends, missing a brain and a heart, skip off toward the Emerald City, singing. Ah, but she had no idea there were some shocks and terrible times to come.

* * *

Despite my sour mood, I had to smile with pride when Bertie called that evening to tell me he needed my help to plan a banquet for General Eisenhower and some of his top brass staff.

"Dearest," he said, "as you know, we'll need your skills for the planning. If General Eisenhower is ill at ease because of his country upbringing, once we move that toast earlier so he—and I—can smoke, I could read him the statistics I have recently received about our citizens' London homes in ruins. Talk about difficult living conditions."

"I know. The numbers must be staggering."

"Listen to this list from my recent red box papers. Over seven hundred British homes destroyed since 1940, one in eight here in London. Water lines smashed. Six million of our citizens with no operating sewage systems. We have sunk so low that the basements of ruined buildings are being converted to rainwater catch basins—after the bodies are removed, that is."

I shuddered. "It is terrifying. We need all our strength and resolve—and we need the Americans. We must invite General Eisenhower as soon as we can. Then we can also invite him when we entertain Eleanor Roosevelt. And we could ask him to go with us to greet her at the train station when she arrives from her countryside stays with Queen Mary and the Churchills."

"I know you will smooth everything out, my darling, with the president's wife and the president's general. Both are essential to our cause, and Eisenhower is all for good old American teamwork with us, thank God. By the way, I hear he tells anyone who will listen that he's from someplace I've never heard of—Abilene, Kansas, a rough-and-tumble cow town, one of my aides said."

"Then, I dare say, set-in-her-class-conscious-ways, bombed-out London is a bit of a jolt after Washington and his early days. I promise you, dear Bertie, I shall greet him warmly and convince him that this just isn't Kansas anymore—and how to cope with us anyway."

CHAPTER TWENTY-ONE

If You Ask Me

*D*espite these dire days and food rationing even at noble and royal tables, life turned to a whirl of dinners and receptions. I cannot say a whirl of parties, for the war events were much too dire for that. Even Winston, who always liked a good time with conversation, was quite in the dumps, fearing we would lose in North Africa and on the Continent. He had not really recovered his aplomb after escaping a Parliamentary no-confidence vote this summer, although he had weathered it with a tally of 475 for to 25 against.

So here we were, greeting guests at the palace, which had been spiffed up as much as could be in these tough times. In a way, I was proud and defiant about our grand old lady, for, like all of us, she was still standing despite the ravages of war.

General Eisenhower arrived with John Gilbert Winant, called Gil, the American ambassador to the Court of St. James's. Our information was that they worked well together, although Winant was a bit of a loner, whereas the general had a very public persona, at least with his troops, though he was not one who enjoyed high-society persons. Oh, dear, for we were loaded with them here to meet the man of the hour—of the year!

The general wore a sharp, dark brown uniform with medals and three gold stars on his epaulets. He carried his billed hat under his arm. Yes, the newspapers had been right that he was tall and stood so erect, though he nodded his head slightly when he greeted the king, before he turned his blue eyes on me.

"So very pleased to meet you, Your Majesty," he said with the mere hint of a bow but a big smile as I offered my hand and we shook in that American way. "Very kind of you to invite us here in these trying times. My wife, Mamie, would give her eyeteeth to see all this."

"Oh—yes. Perhaps when these terrible days are over."

"And they will be, ma'am. There are big-deal difficulties ahead, but we will win in the end."

He did not sugarcoat the situation, but I believed him, and I was sure our people and his troops must too.

* * *

I rather thought the dinner was a success. Early toasts to the king allowed the men to smoke, though I could see some of the twelve ladies present were surprised at that. After the rousing, traditional "To the king!" toasts, the king himself led one to President Roosevelt. I saw General Eisenhower and his several aides snap to stiff attention for that. The next formal dinner we had planned here, the following week, was for their First Lady, Eleanor Roosevelt. Should I invite the military elites to that too?

My dear protégé Rowena and her camera—well, she wasn't really under my tutelage, but I had more or less discovered her—were everywhere snapping photographs, though the pop of her flashbulb was distracting. I motioned for her and the hovering Brendan to leave the room for now. Rowena had said one thing she "adored" about General Eisenhower was that he always looked into the camera when he was talking, though she liked to catch him off guard too. And she had noted that every time he mentioned Hitler or the Nazis, he went red in the face and clenched his fists.

"I warrant," I had told her, "it's very hard to catch that man off guard at all. And I hope Mussolini and Hitler learn that far too late."

Everyone had been talking to the general, but he sat now between Bertie and me at the head of the table, so I had his ear at last. "I believe you and I are of an age, General."

"Actually, ma'am, I'm fifty-one to your forty-one. I try to do my homework. I must tell you how key your amazing country is to our endeavor here that we—all of us—must become a team, a trusting and trustworthy team."

Bertie leaned toward us from his side and said, "I hear you even handled our General Montgomery, our vaunted commander of the Eighth Army, when he scolded you, General."

Eisenhower grimaced then grinned. "I believe we have come to an understanding, sir. He was appalled I smoked and drank."

"He's lectured Churchill on that too, but not me yet."

I could tell that Eisenhower, who seemed to smile broadly and easily, wasn't certain if he should laugh at that comment or not.

"But your 'Monty' is a strong leader, sir. It reminds me of the story when someone scolded Abraham Lincoln for trusting his very successful General Grant, who used to drink more than he should. Lincoln told the newspaper reporter, 'Actually, I'm going to find out what he drinks and buy it for all my generals.'"

We all shared a laugh. "But," Bertie told him, picking up his goblet with the same hand that held his cigarette as though he would toast Eisenhower, "in Montgomery's case, we would all have to become teetotalers and ban tobacco."

I finally managed to steer the conversation back to what I had intended. "General, would you join us for dinner when Mrs. Roosevelt is here next week? I know how busy you are, and we are so grateful you could be with us this evening."

"Oh, sure. I'd be honored. After all, the president is our mutual friend, and Mrs. Roosevelt is an important part of his life. She reaches out to all classes of people and speaks up. Quite the activist, as some call her. Her strong temperament would have fit right in for the old days in my home state of Kansas.

"Why, she even writes several newspaper columns which really reach our people," he went on. "Her 'My Day' articles touch on race relations, women's rights, and key events. She also writes a weekly newspaper column called 'If You Ask Me,' answering all sorts of off-the-wall to major political questions, not domestic namby-pamby at all. Some say that's as impressive as the president's Fireside Chats to our country. For sure, Mrs. Roosevelt will arrive with the say-so of the president and be able to speak for him too. If you ask me, to use her words, I think the two of you must have a lot in common."

I appreciated the comment and took that all in. Of course, if I went solo to the States, I would seem to have more authority too. When I had met her there, she had been more hostess than political spokesperson. It seemed to me that I had some of her attributes—at least, being in on the top political decisions in this war—yet my smiling visits to our citizens in war and peace, my bucking Bertie up and sometimes even guiding his decisions—still the so-called First Lady of the United States was evidently more important and powerful than that.

Suddenly, I was very worried about having her here at the palace, our official home that was, at least for now, shabby and, in some places, in shambles. I decided, for once, especially since the bombings had stopped for now, to bring Lilibet and Margot here for her visit, a family affair. If I could not match her in influence, lest she thought I was all smiles and nods and royal fluff, I would show her that was not true. Somehow.

My mind snapped back to Bertie's conversation with Eisenhower that had left me out for a moment. I heard the general tell Bertie, "I am willing to attend important functions like this and certainly any one you would choose when Eleanor Roosevelt is here. But I'll tell you man to man, Your Majesty, I have instigated a seven-day workweek for our staff and troops, and I don't intend to fight this war over fancy tables and teacups."

"Not only understood but agreed and applauded, General," Bertie said with a nod and a rap of his knuckles on the table-cloth.

They both lit another cigarette before the main course came. I scolded myself for feeling left out. And for fretting that Eleanor Roosevelt would think me all smiles and a provider of teacups, royal or not.

It was wretchedly dark and dreary in this half-ruined palace after the bombs. No way to impress her with the rations we held to here at the palace. Why, Winston had said that when President Roosevelt hosted him aboard the American ship in Newfoundland, they had dined on everything from smoked salmon to chocolate ice cream, cookies and cupcakes topped off with wines and champagne toasts, not just a spot of sherry. And we'd been wined and dined on our U.S. visit, though, of course, it was not wartime.

I was planning to give Mrs. Roosevelt—she had said to call her Eleanor, but I was beginning to have trouble thinking of her that way—my suite in the palace, but was that enough to impress her and let her know I was making a great welcoming gesture? Why, my bathtub was marked with the five-inches-of-water limit for bathing! So my hands were tied to keep me from being the hostess and equal I would like to be.

But, I vowed, I would keep control of the situation, entertain and inspire her, do as best I could. I had more than once admitted my favorite buck-up-London sign was *Keep Calm and Carry On*, but I, the first lady of our land, needed to carry my load and carry the day, win over and influence the president's powerful First Lady. All that, if you asked me.

CHAPTER TWENTY-TWO

We Two E.R.s

As you can see," I told Bertie when we walked from our motorcar toward the platform at Paddington Station, "I ordered a red carpet laid out for her, even though she's not a head of state."

"She'll be in the train's royal coach too. Besides," he added, nodding and smiling, but speaking quietly as people began to recognize us, "she is probably the unofficial head of state, just as you are. Winston and I were saying that we now have three days in London with two E.R.s, namely, my dear queen Elizabeth *Regina* and Eleanor Roosevelt, queen of the United States."

Ordinarily I would have laughed, but I was too nervous. "Best you not let anyone else hear that joke between the two of you," I whispered as we saw the locomotive pull the short train into the roofed station.

While waiting, we waved to the growing crowd that was kept back behind the ropes. We greeted General Eisenhower as well as the American ambassador, Gil Winant, and their entourage, whom we'd asked to greet Mrs. Roosevelt too.

Eisenhower told me, "I know she will help to lift spirits here as she does at home. As you always do, Your Majesty."

My first thought when Eleanor emerged from the royal car was that she looked every bit as broad-shouldered as the general, for she wore a huge fox stole draped about her shoulders with the head and feet of the beast hanging over her dark suit. It made her look so much larger than she was, though she was not—well, as generously proportioned as I. Perhaps I should give up my big, fashionable fur pieces.

"So good to have you here," I greeted her after the king did, with a smile and gloved handshake, "though, under the circumstances, we cannot hope to repay your lovely hospitality from our stay with you and the president."

After greetings by the general—I thought they talked a bit long—the ambassador, and others, the American E.R. introduced us to the two women she was traveling with, her secretary, Malvina "Tommy" Thompson, and a female colonel, Oveta Hobby, both of whom would ride to the palace in a separate motorcar.

In the vehicle, we spoke of her brief visit to see Queen Mary at Badminton. Yes, she had "enjoyed" the torn-down-ivy tour and was looking forward to her stay with the Churchills at the P.M.'s retreat at Chequers, not to mention her tour of our hinterlands: Canterbury, Bristol, Surrey, Liverpool, even Glasgow and Edinburgh.

"Of course, I am also looking forward," she told us, "to visiting with your people, especially women's service organizations, one of my important causes at home. I greatly benefit from talks with Mr. and Mrs. Everyman, as I think of them. I've already heard from some American Red Cross workers here that the thin cotton socks they have been issued are giving them blisters since they are on their feet so much, and I just now put a bug in Ike Eisenhower's ear on that, lest you were thinking I was whispering top secrets to him."

Evidently trying to hide his surprise at all that, Bertie told her, "Attention to detail is one thing that will win this war. That and a solid victory at El Alamein, where our General Montgomery's forces are in a fierce, pitched battle today. It's obsessing Prime Minister Churchill, as indeed it should."

"I can understand. You are greatly fighting that front on your own—Operation Torch, I believe it is called. But we hope to stand shoulder to shoulder, ship to ship, and airplane to airplane with you from here on."

Bertie and I both expressed gratitude and hope. The rest of the way back to the palace, the king concentrated on pointing out famous spots in London and the destruction of some of them. I concentrated on keeping calm with the plans I'd made for this three-day visit: time with our daughters this afternoon and a dinner tonight with some guests, sadly all in a vast, draughty, barely-hanging-together palace. Barely hanging on, just as I.

* * *

I quickly saw I had been right to have Lilibet and Margot here for the afternoon, if not the formal dinner, and it was so wonderful to have them "home." Rowena was the only photographer we allowed in to take formal photographs of us with the First Lady in the beautiful Bow Room with its circular array of full-length windows and marble columns. I had asked that the fireplace be lit in the vast, chilly room, and the flames from the hearth helped to warm us somewhat.

After posing, we had tea and time to talk. Margot was a bit fidgety, but Lilibet certainly rose to the occasion.

"Would you mind, Mrs. Roosevelt, telling me a bit about Americans of my age?" Lilibet asked. "You see, I hope not only to visit them someday, but to make friends with them too. You know, my uncle David married an American, though I really do not know her at all. She was from Baltimore, and I saw on a map that it is not too far from the capital where you live."

A moment of silence. There it was, I thought. Lilibet asking a perfectly normal question but bringing up my past archrival and eternal bugaboo.

"No, I do not know her, my dear, but I hope your uncle David and she are enjoying their relatively peaceful time governing Nassau. You have heard, I suppose, that pirates used to come from there."

She and Lilibet talked about ships and pirates from the old days—and Margot actually listened too—but I had a feeling the American E.R. had just smoothly guided the conversation away from what would have been a sticky wicket.

I might know, David and his wife would intrude here where Bertie was king, despite how we tried to keep them at arm's—

that is, at ocean's—length. David had tried to ruin me too, for in the old days, it would have been said he had ruined me. Damn David.

* * *

At our dinner for twenty that evening—I did not think our wartime budget and food rationing could handle more—I was put out at Winston for not being his usual charming and conversational self. Clementine knew it too. I'd seen her elbow him to get in the conversation, and she glared at him when he popped up more than once to go call Downing Street to see if there was any war news. Bertie explained to the table guests that they were at sixes and sevens waiting for word on the raging battle our troops were fighting in North Africa.

Winston had also mentioned privately that on his most recent visit to Washington, Eleanor had taken him to task for supporting the dictator Franco and she had urged him to integrate white and Negro troops, one of her big causes at home, not that the U.S. had done that yet. In short, when we needed Winston's charm right now, he was being a grump, though, I supposed, understandably so. After German general Erwin Rommel had taken Tobruk in April of last year, our troops and citizens desperately needed a victory of some sort.

At least "Dickie" Mountbatten and his wife, Edwina, were making an effort to be ingratiating and conversational, but then, that was Dickie. Who else could have survived with laud and even advancements but the charmer who had overseen the bloody fiasco of an attempt to take the French port of Dieppe only two months ago? That was a disaster after he had already lost his ship and many men under German air attack earlier in the war. Bertie said at least the huge loss of our men and many Canadians at Dieppe showed we were not yet ready for a beach invasion of France.

If I were Winston, I would have tossed Mountbatten in the rubbish bin, but they were fast friends yet, and I'd heard Dickie worked well with the Americans, which was the name of the game right now. As with the persnickety General "Monty" Montgomery, Winston had his favorites. I must admit that Dickie did remind me of David with his slippery charm, good looks, and air of noblesse oblige.

But what annoyed me too about Dickie was that he was Philip's uncle and now mentor. Worse, Dickie was also second cousin to Lilibet, which made it harder for me to cut ties. At least Philip was currently at sea, but I was chagrined that "Uncle Dickie" had brought a letter and photograph from Philip to Lilibet, and I had not caught that in time. Edwina had told me in the reception line that our eldest was quite over the moon with the picture, as they had requested to see her when they came in. So what could I do but smile and nod, at least for now?

"I must tell you," I said to Eleanor where she sat at the table between Bertie and me, "if you and the president visit us sometime after these terrible trials are over, the dinner fare will be quite different. We thought it important to greatly conform to the rationing imposed on our people, though we have bent a few rules this evening."

"I do understand," she told me. "As many hardships as have

fallen on Americans for this war, we are still in the land of plenty, and I hope my countrymen realize that."

We chatted about other things. She was much impressed with Lilibet and thought Margot was a dear. I did not tell her that our younger girl was more like a "deer," darting here and there, easily startled however darling she was.

But I did so want to get back to the topic of how strict our rules for food were. Perhaps, with Eleanor's influence and connections, it could lead to more shipments of American vegetables or even meat. And sugar—why I'd be glad to import sugar beets, not even the fine cane sugar we were used to. Our poor people stood for hours in line for gumdrops, the only affordable sweet widely available lately.

"We try to make do," I told her, "but no fresh salmon or cod for two years." I felt a bit silly since we were eating off of gold-edged china and drinking our meager sherry from Baccarat crystal goblets. "Ordinarily, we would not have plain chicken with such an important guest as you, but meat rationing came in during March of 1940, and it has been downhill from then. Actually, even here, we serve food on a par with our war canteens. Very few eggs, little bacon, butter, milk, but for nursing mothers, even cheese. Why, there were signs here and there of *Cheese, Not Churchill!* until we had them taken down. Not good for morale, I dare say."

"I can imagine," she said, cutting her piece of chicken. She had eaten her salad and seemed to like even the crude "war bread," perhaps because of the strawberry preserves we'd brought in from Scotland. At least, I thought, I had told the chef not to fix potatoes two different ways, as the War Office was touting and

Brendan Bracken was urging through his Ministry of Information, which was just a name for Ministry of Propaganda.

"And I do understand," Eleanor added, "that war rationing or not, what an honor it is to be here with you and the king at the palace. Oh, dear, there goes Winston out again. Tell me, do you know that 'Farmer in the Dell' song and game? Perhaps your girls used to play and sing that, ending with 'The cheese stands alone.' I was just thinking of that sign you mentioned, *Cheese, Not Churchill.*" She speared a small piece of cheese on her plate. "Whatever mood he is in, Franklin says we all need Winston and must stand with him and the king."

We smiled and clinked our sherry glasses together, even as the king joined us, reaching out with his glass. And here came Winston so quickly back into the room but not glowering this time, rather with a smile on his ruddy face. On his way in, he clapped General Eisenhower on the back, then broke loudly into the rollicking song—and the man could not sing one whit—"Roll Out the Barrel."

"What in the name of heaven?" I heard Bertie mutter. "Has Winston lost his mind?"

"A victory for Monty and for our forces at El Alamein!" Winston cried, flourishing his cigar and lifting his empty sherry glass off the table while everyone gaped at him. "Our first British victory of many, I vow! We will handle the rest of North Africa, then on to Sicily, Italy, France, and rotten Germany. And with the help of our comrade Americans! Many more victories to come, right, General?" he asked, turning to Eisenhower, who was on his feet too, with a huge grin. Others stood hastily, scraping back their chairs.

"And what an honor," Winston went on with a half bow toward Eleanor, "to have America's First Lady with us at this momentous time. To the king! To General Montgomery and our fighting men! To Mrs. Roosevelt and our dear friend and ally, President Roosevelt! To arms! And down with that damned devil Hitler!"

"Here, here!" resounded in the room. Some tapped silver utensils on their goblets. Someone shouted, "Tally-ho!" Mrs. Roosevelt's secretary, down the table, called out, "Yea! Give it to them!"

We two E.R.s clinked our glasses and smiled at each other like excited young girls. For one moment, it was almost like having a new best friend at a happy party.

CHAPTER TWENTY-THREE

The Big Picture

Everyone finally calmed down after dinner, so the men decided they would still like to see the film we had scheduled for entertainment, especially since it had a patriotic theme. We sat in comfortable furniture in the library to watch the well-regarded movie *In Which We Serve*.

I was chagrined, for Bertie had switched the choice at the last minute, evidently at Churchill's request. Worse, the film was actually about the tragic loss of a ship Dickie had commanded, the destroyer HMS *Kelly*, which was sunk during the Battle of Crete.

"A film recommended by our Ministry of Information," Bertie told Eleanor, who sat between us on a long sofa. "It was a favorite in the States too, I hear, co-directed by David Lean and Noël Coward. Much lauded for its imagery of national unity. That and international unity is what we need now going forward."

What could I say? How was it that some commanders would have been drummed out of service and court-martialed for two military disasters, but Louis "Dickie" Mountbatten had landed on his feet again after the losses at Dieppe? Never, never was Lilibet going to become more involved with Philip!

In the film the name of the ship the Germans had sunk had been changed to the HMS *Torrin*, the captain's name changed also, but it was clearly Mountbatten's story. When the ship went down, some sailors had jumped off and clung together on floating wreckage as the German planes returned to try to strafe them in the water. The main characters flashed back to stories of their loved ones. Some survivors of the attack died, some lived. I admit the portrayals were heartrending and the music rousing.

But I kept thinking that *In Which We Serve* could be the story of my struggles and battles too. I was working hard to serve the king, the British people, and the Empire, even the leaders of ally countries like Eleanor. And I would fight to keep Philip Mountbatten away from our heir.

* * *

After Bessie put my face cream on, then wiped it off that night, I told her of the important victory at El Alamein.

"Oh," she said, clearing things from my dressing table, "that will cheer Mrs. Roosevelt. Her maid Nancy said she was a bit down in the dumps when she arrived."

"I did not notice that. Perhaps just tired. Or," I said, turning toward Bessie, "do you know more?"

She rolled her eyes and gave a little shrug. "Nancy thinks she was a bit embarrassed."

"Why ever?" I asked. "Tell me if you know."

"Ma'am, Nancy says she thinks Mrs. Roosevelt felt a bit taken aback to be in a huge dressing room with closets all round when she had one suitcase. Because she flew the ocean in tight quarters, she said. Nancy only unpacked one evening dress, one afternoon dress, several extra blouses, and one skirt. Two pairs of shoes."

"Oh, I'm sorry for her," I said, thinking perhaps I should not have given her the entire queen's suite. I recalled being told that General Eisenhower had felt embarrassed at grand homes because he traveled light. And I knew he'd been so uncomfortable in his original posh quarters at Claridge's that he had quickly moved to the Dorchester.

I said, "You know, Bessie, I can tell you were very sad today, even when I told you about the toasts at dinner and our wonderful victory at El Alamein."

"A little sad."

"Still missing your poor sister, of course, and—"

Bessie took the tray, curtsied, backed away, then burst into tears. As I leapt up from the dressing table, she started away, then stopped and stood, shoulders shaking. From behind I put my hands on them, but the items on the tray were rattling, so I took that from her, put it down, and went back to pull her over to the divan where I had comforted her once before.

There, despite her age, I put my arms around her and held her as I would Lilibet or Margot after a nightmare.

Finally, she quieted, hiccoughing a bit. "Sorry, ma'am," she managed. "Got a few tears on your silk robe, I did."

"We've been through this before, my dear. It's all right. You are missing your sister, and that's quite all right. I understand about missing loved ones, really I do."

"Two things," she choked out, sitting back and swiping at her wet cheeks with her hands until I handed her my handkerchief. She patted her cheeks with it, then shrugged and blew her nose. "One," she said, sounding as if she were in a barrel, "the last time I saw her we had a bit of a tiff. Didn't know I'd never see her again, that she'd—jump into the river like that. I partly blame myself."

"Of course that would trouble you, but it surely isn't why she . . . she took her life. And I'm certain she knew how much you looked up to her and loved her."

"She lost her unborn baby too. Wasn't his—or her—fault—the baby's, that is. But the thing is, the man she trusted and loved, well, she wanted to wait till he came home to make love, if you know what I mean."

"Yes, I know what you mean. So she said no to him, then he went off and was killed—but if she felt regretful she had turned him down that last night they had been together . . ."

"She told me she loved him but told him not to do it. But he did—to her. Pushed her into it. Got rough, a bit crazy. He was—well, drinking. He was born higher than her, better off, so she owed him, he said, spending time and money on her before he was shipped out. Oh, ma'am, so sorry to spill all this and you not a part of it and forgive me for sharing that he—he forced her—even if she did love and want him when he came back home, then said no to his wishes for a . . . an intimate farewell, and then she caught the baby that one time. . . ."

She rushed on with more details I did not want to hear. But

I knew now what she meant and how tragically her poor sister had handled it. Violated, even if it was by someone she had loved and wanted and trusted. And was that not worse than being forced by a stranger? Yes, even with no baby involved, I knew well that terrible, tragic truth of being shamed, forced, though not exactly like that. And most certainly I would never jump off a bridge. Not yet.

* * *

The next two days, I felt as if I were Eleanor's lady-in-waiting, not that the places we visited did not cheer me too. But she had an unrestrained—yes, authentic—way of plunging right into a crowd and shaking hands, urging stories and almost confessions. She had a talent for, as she put it, "bucking people up." I thought I did too, but, in her American way, she went at it more robustly. Perhaps the aura of royalty kept people formal and back a bit, but not with an American First Lady.

"I have found," she told me at our stops between crowds at St. Paul's and a canteen in the East End, "that work is the best antidote for depression. And the war—such tragedy and loss—can lead to depression."

"I agree with you wholeheartedly. There have been times in my life—even not wartime—when I have thought it would all get me down and keep me down, but we women fight on, do we not?"

"Indeed. How very open and honest of you. We women, the ones bombed out of their homes, those of us cast in lofty positions, have so much in common. And besides," she added with her toothy, rare smile, "we all fight our own domestic and private battles too, beyond our public ones. You know, I'd best change the subject and just share with you that I have admired the way the leadership here gets on, for I tire of the way our Congress must always pick fights with my dear president and husband. You and I are sisters under the skin—under the pearls and fur pieces—are we not?"

We smiled and nodded at each other. Both wearing our fox stoles and large hats, we headed back to the palace together.

* * *

I finally had time to tuck my daughters in the second night of Eleanor's visit. A bit earlier I had felt we had become close enough that I could share with her what Bertie had said about our in common "E.R." names. She had laughed heartily.

But I was not laughing now when I saw the in-Navy-uniform, handsome photograph of Philip on Lilibet's bedside table, turned toward her.

Since the palace was so draughty, she wore a flannel nightgown, which actually seemed to deflate with her heavy sigh.

"Isn't he the most handsome ever?" she asked me, smiling at the photograph. "Though, of course, Daddy was that for you. When you first saw and met him," she said, looking at me, "was he the only one for you too?"

I clenched my teeth, though I managed a smile. "Well, there were other young men about before he and I became . . . serious. And, of course, we were much older than you. It takes time and several beaus to know who is the best, my dear."

"Not for me. But is it true that Uncle David was your beau first?"

My heartbeat kicked up. "Your uncle David was quite a lady's man, and I was one of his friends before I really knew your father well."

"Uncle David—talk about handsome!"

"Yes. But people say beauty is only skin deep, and that's true of handsome faces too," I said with a tilt of my head toward the photograph. God forgive me, I was so tempted to toss it in the dustbin, but that was unthinkable. I had to keep telling myself that, despite their similar looks, Philip was not David. Still, I had no doubt the young officer was angling for her and could be a big problem.

"Do you mean Uncle David wasn't a nice person?" she went on. "I think Daddy still misses and thinks of him. Like with Philip, I'm hoping that absence makes the heart grow fonder."

"For some people," I said, trying not to sound cold or bitter, "it is 'out of sight, out of mind.'"

She sighed again. "Perhaps not, for I am out of my mind, over the moon for Philip, and he is sadly out of sight except for this so wonderful photo his uncle brought for me."

Of course, I thought as I kissed her good night and turned out her bedside light, I must keep calm, not overreact but go at this carefully. What was that Eleanor had said about little domestic battles that could be as frightening as the big war ones?

CHAPTER TWENTY-FOUR

Queen In Deed

*T*he good news—the Allies were finally making progress in some theatres of war. The bad news—Hitler began bombing us again, quite randomly but quite terribly.

Horribly too, it became common knowledge that Hitler had clear intentions to wipe out European Jews, something I had told Bertie and others in power since I had talked extensively about that to the former prime minister of France Léon Blum before the war, but few had believed me.

Perhaps now they would. Once we defeated the Germans, they could stop such insanity and hold men and that nation accountable. And one state secret I cherished: We had broken the German secret code, called the Enigma system, so we knew more of their evil plans—and what our cryptologists read there was dreadful too.

But, despite the terrors of reality, once a month in the new year of 1943, I brought the girls into London for whatever cultural concerts or programs were available to broaden their horizons and lend the royal family's support to the arts.

"Mummy," Margot said as we entered the Aeolian Hall on New Bond Street for a poetry reading by some of our finest writers, "I've written some poems too, but nothing I'd read for six minutes and nothing I'd share with really smart people."

As mild applause greeted us, Lilibet put in from my other side, "Margaret Rose! At least act like you are smart. You are a princess, after all."

"Let's keep our remarks focused on the people here today, learning from them, greeting them," I said. Besides the honored poets, I was pleased to see a decent-sized crowd, no doubt of local literati. I nodded and smiled at the kind greetings. I waved a bit too, and the girls followed my lead.

Our host Osbert Sitwell introduced us to the poets present, several of whom I had met, all of whom bobbed us a bow or a curtsy. I thanked each one for helping to keep the arts alive in such trying times. I had borrowed Rowena from her usual duties at the Ministry of Information today, so she began to take photographs from the back of the room. And then I saw who else waited in the distance: Sir Kenneth was here and not a piece of art in sight.

He smiled and nodded when his gaze snagged mine. I was glad he stood at a distance, for I felt myself blush. I admit I had been putting off another day trip or even meeting with him at the palace lately. Of course, I had the excuse of wartime duties. He seemed to lurk here, biding his time, looking as handsome and determined as ever. Ah, so different these days to be pursued royalty instead of being the pursuer of royalty as I had been years ago.

I pulled my stare from his. I knew that my daughters recognized none of the people to whom they were being introduced, so I made a mental note to have their governess pay a bit more attention to modern British literature. The poets who would each read for six minutes were Vita Sackville-West; Walter de la Mare; Osbert's eccentric sister, Edith Sitwell; and T. S. Eliot.

During the program, I thought the readings or recitations went rather well, as they had each been informed the girls would be here today to avoid what Bertie sometimes called "adult material."

And Kenneth had dared to sit in the second row directly behind us, so, of course, I had introduced him to the girls. Neither of them recalled meeting him before, so perhaps that settled him down. But I felt his sharp eyes burning my back. I tried to listen to the poets, but I kept wondering if he would have favored some "adult material." He seemed suddenly overconfident, rather like Dickie Mountbatten or worse, like the man I tried to forget forever who was rightfully stuck on a tropical island right now.

Things went smoothly until Tom Eliot went far over his allotted time, reading from his rather challenging poem *The Waste Land.* Every ten or so lines he repeated in an almost frenzied voice the key phrase, *"Hurry up, please. It's time."*

Kenneth behind me more than once cleared his throat as if that were a message for me. People began to shift in their seats at Tom's carrying on. When he repeated the line a fifth time, Margot asked in a stage whisper, "Time for what, Mummy?"

I put my finger to my lips as the reading ended with "Good night, ladies, good night, sweet ladies, good night, good night."

Lilibet was trying to stifle the giggles. Margot was muttering that it wasn't even night. And when everyone sighed, applauded, and stood to leave, Kenneth said to me, "I was glad to hear, Your Majesty, that you and the king convinced the Duke of Wellington to store his art. I've examined it and would love you to see where we have secured it, if I could escort you there."

I knew that was in a deserted area of a rural castle. "Thank you, Kenneth," I told him, trying to keep my voice from wavering, for in another time—another lifetime—I might have agreed on that and more. "But I know you understand how things are now. Actually, I'm preparing another speech to our nation's hardworking women who are dedicated to taking over jobs for their men and staying true to them too in these tough times."

"If Papa goes to the front lines, Mummy will be Counsellor of State," Margot piped up. "Almost like a queen on her own."

"Well," Kenneth said, "she is a queen on her own, always. Your Majesty, I will look forward to our next meeting with pleasure." He bowed his way out of the aisle.

* * *

I worked hard on my second address to the nation's women. I didn't mind giving speeches into microphones, even at the BBC, but I did mind writing them. Both Bertie's private secretary Alan Lascelles and Winston helped me with it. But I put my heart into the delivery of the words, not worrying about a six-minute time limit or other queens listening in the way the poets had their own ilk critiquing them.

"I assure you the time will come when our men return to their hearth and home from war and take their jobs" was one line I wrote myself.

But I wondered, had times and people changed so much that women would not simply go back to their homes and want careers of their own? They knew they could do so much more now than manage a house and children.

"I tell you," I went on in the speech, "what is called 'women's work' is just as valuable, just as much 'war work' as that done by the bravest soldier, sailor, or airman who actually meets the enemy in battle. The king and I and our daughters thank all of you for your prayers. And we also pray that God will bless and guide our people in this country and throughout the Empire, and will lead us forward, united and strong, into the paths of victory and peace."

* * *

In March, Bertie fulfilled his steadfast wish to see our troops in the field with a visit to Tripoli, then on to Malta, where he mixed with our men and was fervently received. He sent me frequent wireless messages, for he knew I was concerned not only for his safety, but for his health. He had lost weight lately and developed a cough, but he was—as I overheard him tell Winston—hell-bent to do his bit in the field.

While he was away, I fulfilled ceremonial duties under the title Counsellor of State, rather than Queen Regent, as some of my predecessors had done. I lunched with Winston to hear the latest news on all fronts and gave him my opinion—what I reckoned Bertie would say, and Winston agreed.

I signed *ER*, not *GR*, on papers requiring the king's signature. My hand trembled at first when I did that. I do not suppose many of our citizens knew I was standing in his stead, but the magnitude of it suddenly shook me. Little Elizabeth from Scotland, once on the outside looking in at the royals, wanting to be a part, but then—then the mistake of my life to fall in love with one of them and be burned by that. At least Bertie had been the salve, so I signed the next document with a much more steady hand.

I also presided over an investiture at the palace, with several hundred people present, to award military honors. As I presented the nation's highest award for gallantry facing the enemy, the Victoria Cross, to some of our heroes, I thought of those who served in quieter ways, yet deserved such accolades too. For example, Rowena Fitzgerald behind the flash of her camera and my staff members, such as Bessie, clear on up to those who served our generals, even served the king.

My Bertie was coming home tonight, so I would lay aside such burdens and honors. I did not realize I had made the service go too long, because I had spent so much time talking to each honoree and their families. Well, I always talked more than Bertie anyway.

* * *

When the king came home that night, he looked ill—was ill. The doctor examined him, and I put him to bed. I let him sleep for six hours, then tiptoed in and sat in the chair nearby. Shortly, he yawned, rolled over, saw me, and stretched out his hand, so I went to sit on the side of his bed.

"Don't worry, my darling," he whispered. "I may have dropped a stone in weight, but my heart is lighter than when I went. You understand. You always do."

"I do indeed. More so now that I have taken your burdens and duties for a while. But you must get better now."

I bent to kiss his cheek, but he held hard to my hand when I tried to move away, so I sat again on the bed.

"And do not coddle me," he said, his voice more like his own, not so wan and quiet now.

"Just a bit perhaps, but you will snap back fast. Remember we are giving Lilibet a party. You remember, one she asked for. We've both been so busy with war work, but I have it all set at Windsor in a fortnight, and the guest list is going out tomorrow."

He nodded, and his eyes teared up. "Dangerous too how old she is. Just think how we felt when we were her age or even a bit older. We thought we knew everything." He sighed. "I can't say I made the best of decisions then."

"I neither," I admitted. "I didn't have much judgment then sometimes, but I pray Lilibet will."

"Levelheaded, that's our girl and our heiress."

"Then perhaps it's time for her to also serve as Counsellor of State when you are away or buried in work."

"Ha, my love. Do not bury me yet! And I could tell you were

fretting over inviting Philip for her dinner and dance, but she's determined. I say, give it a go, or she might resent us. Besides, who knows that she might not change her mind if she's actually around him more, sees him mix with other people, sees him dance with other girls. It will give us time to take a good look at him ourselves."

"Has she put you up to this plea?"

"She has not. I truly do not think she has much of the manipulator in her—yet. She wears her heart on her sleeve, when she must learn to be more guarded and wily."

He looked steadily at me, and I wondered if he meant something beneath his words. Did he imply I was those things? Could he have guessed or been told some of the secrets I carried? Coward that I was, I changed the subject and circled back.

"But you do agree she could serve as Counsellor with me, especially if we go together to our duties?"

"A smashing idea. And now, I'd best get some more sleep so I can be all dewy-eyed and eagle-eyed for that party you've been planning for her," he said with a huge yawn.

I kissed his cheek and hurried out. I would keep Philip on the guest list during his short leave from the Navy but keep an eagle eye on him myself. I'd seen a young, naïve girl make a fool of herself and hurt her heart over a man, and I refused to let my Lilibet make the same mistake.

CHAPTER TWENTY-FIVE

A Wing and a Prayer

At Lilibet's belated birthday party, everyone, of course, called her Elizabeth. That we shared a name made me see myself in her even more.

As during the Great War when I was young, this was a beastly time to be a young woman. I hoped this all went well. How many times had I thought of the young, wounded soldiers whom my parents had sheltered and entertained at Glamis. How many soldiers had my Elizabeth met and spoken to who were now dead or maimed? But at least she had some young friends here for a party at Windsor this evening, some, of course, briefly home from service.

"A penny for your thoughts," Bertie said. "Darling, this is quite a turnout."

As his words brought me back to the present, I turned to him and smiled. Philip was not here yet, and I could tell Lilibet was watching for him. Yes, she reminded me of myself, watching the door to see if the idol of the civilized world of my day, the dashing, playboy Prince of Wales, had entered a room yet. That still galled me, but I was angry at myself more than at my girl. Yet I wanted to protect her too.

"Sad to say, Bertie, but I preferred her reciting poems or putting on pantomimes. She and Margot did a beautiful job with the characters of *Aladdin* last Christmas holiday for us, even if their costumes were old curtains and blackout drapes. But tonight, those remade gowns from Queen Mary's closet came out beautifully."

I hated to admit that I had gowns that were much too large in the bust, waist, and hips to cut down, but these did not look old-fashioned, not on them. Margot still seemed a bit out of place, but then she was only twelve going on twenty-two, as we liked to joke. She had, however, matured enough to mention whether a boy was good-looking or not.

"Oh, Mummy, isn't it lovely?" Lilibet said, popping over to the corner where we sat. "The decorations, I mean. And the musicians are going to do several line dances, so don't worry that it will be all waltzes in hold, as my dancing instructor says. I just hope Margot doesn't spill more punch, but they covered it up with napkins. Oh, excuse me, please. There he—there he is! I must greet him. I'll bring him over."

I had told myself more than once that just because she called Philip "him" or "he" and didn't need a name, so what? It was to please Bertie, let alone Elizabeth, that I had agreed to have "him" here. After all, I had lectured myself, "he" was the nephew of King Constantine of Greece and somewhat related to the Windsors.

Our blushing "she" was bringing "him" over.

My covert detective work all came back to me in a flash and made me feel rather—was it silly or guilty? I had contacted several people in a judicious way to make inquiries about Philip's past and character. From a friend of his family we had entertained before the war, I had learned that his mother had psychological problems but then so did two of my cousins. From the headmaster of Philip's strict school, Gordonstoun in northeastern Scotland, I had gleaned that Philip was adventurous and athletic and had set high standards for himself. He had been called "a born leader" with strong opinions for whom only the best of everything would do.

So was that why he evidently had his sights set on our heiress, someday in the far future, the next queen of England and the Empire, however beleaguered it was now?

He bowed most properly and shook Bertie's hand when it was extended. "I am so grateful to have been invited to Princess Elizabeth's belated birthday celebration," he told us with a charming smile. "Since my family is rather broken now, I greatly appreciate being included amongst family and friends of Your Highnesses. It means more to me than I can express, and I'm afraid I'm incapable of showing you the gratitude I feel."

He spoke a bit more, answered a few questions, then they capered off to dance a waltz—in hold, as she had said, twirling about, both looking breathlessly rapt. At least it then devolved into some line dance called the Lindy Hop to a rather jazzy melody I barely recognized as "In the Mood." At first I was relieved to see that Lilibet and Philip sat that dance out with its kicks and gyrations—whoever gave the musicians permission for that?—but it was only because they huddled off in a corner, talking.

Margot came over, looking rather bouncy and hoppy herself.

"I have to learn that dance, but there's no one here I want to learn it from, if you know what I mean," she said rolling her eyes. "And the boys my age I have met are just too, well, jumpy. Boring. But I thought we'd best play something in style, so these guests think we're not a lot of tiresome stodgies here at the castle."

"You ordered that music and dance?" her father asked. "Isn't a foxtrot modern enough?"

"Papa . . . really," she said and flounced off.

"I'd hate to see Margot's seventeenth birthday party," Bertie muttered. "In war or peace. When was it Lilibet began to like young men her age?"

"When she first laid eyes on Philip, and he's not her age. He's a good five years older, but look at them."

"I thought he spoke well and was most appreciative. My darling, he's heading back to sea soon, and who knows what may happen."

"I don't want her to get her heart broken one way or the other."

He turned his entire body to look at me. "It happens, but, I think, never for you. And I can understand how much a young man from a broken, distant family enjoys our family and home. I know that was what first attracted me to you and your family despite the fact David said you would never like me."

"Did he? How . . . how unfair and how wrong of him!"

I realized I had almost shouted. Several other chaperones nearby turned our way.

"Shall we dance, now that the hopscotch is over?" Bertie asked.

I had to smile at his butchering of the name of the dance, but I looked over his shoulder each time we turned to keep a good eye on the hostess of the party and her beau.

* * *

I ran myself ragged, visiting troops, especially bomber commands, that spring. With Lilibet, I toured South Wales. The family managed a week at Sandringham, the royal estate on which Bertie had grown up, though to my chagrin, he talked too much of memories of his early days there with David.

Although it was top secret, we knew our soldiers and the Allies, under General Eisenhower, were preparing a massive assault on the German-held lands across the Channel. But somehow, life went on.

Both Bertie and Winston had wished to accompany our troops into battle in the huge but dangerous assault being planned. Winston had, evidently, easily been discouraged and realized the danger of that, but at first Bertie would not budge from the idea. I rather thought, if Bertie stayed back of the initial attacks, it would hearten our men and him. So I was upset that Alan Lascelles, his secretary, had somehow changed Bertie's mind.

"Alan!" I said as I cornered him in Bertie's office when I

knew Bertie was elsewhere, "did you talk the king out of being a part of this attack—at least at the rear of it?"

"Oh, Your Majesty," he said, looking up, quite startled. "Yes. Yes, I did. This nation and international alliance cannot allow our king and—or—our prime minister to put themselves in such danger. Both of them admit the casualties will be high. The Germans are dug in over there and will fight back like bloody he— Well, that is my opinion, ma'am, and I could not bear to lose the king."

"Neither could I, but some of his happiest days inspiring our troops and countrymen have been with our fighting forces. Granted, he would stay far back."

"He asked me to speak my piece, ma'am, and I did. He and the P.M. have time to reconsider, though I am certain now Mr. Churchill is not going. Besides, we must keep a close secret when the attack will be launched. Let that hellhound Hitler wonder, especially if the P.M. and the king do not budge from here."

"Do you know, Alan," I said, calming down a bit, "that Adolf Hitler once called me the most dangerous woman in Europe?"

"I had heard so. I may just be an aide and secretary to His Majesty, but, for once, I agree with Hitler—and thank the Lord he believes you are a danger to him."

"So if I am dangerous to Hitler, His Majesty should be encouraged to go in at least behind his troops, for he would be far more of a danger than I ever could be. At Malta, he was an inspiration to the common people. They pelted him with flowers, and he cherishes that."

"I too have seen that flower-stained uniform more than once, ma'am."

"I'm sorry I took you to task, Alan. The king will do what he will do. Of course, I would rather keep him out of harm's way, but I have seen how much being with our fighting men has invigorated him."

"I believe you would go in with your troops, if you were queen in deed, ma'am. As the first Queen Elizabeth said of herself facing battle against the Spanish Armada, 'I have the heart and stomach of a king, and a king of England, too.'"

"Thank you, Alan," I told him as I headed for the door. I turned back with my hand on the knob. "You serve us both well, and you may be right. You have persuaded me. If either of them consult me, I shall counsel His Majesty and Winst—the P.M.—not to rush in where angels fear to tread."

* * *

In early July of 1943, with no invasion of Europe yet, though the forces and armaments were piling up on our soil, I took our daughters and went to visit my elderly father at Glamis. He had been ailing off and on, missing my dear mother as did I. He insisted we have some friends in to lighten the mood for the girls, and one of our guests, Lady Cranborne, brought with her a new gramophone, now called a record player, and still all the craze, war or not.

Both Lilibet and Margot hung over the machine as it played one popular song after the other. "But it is wartime, and you must listen to this one," Lady Cranborne insisted. She put the needle down on the record. The song, she said, was "Coming in on a Wing and a Prayer."

Its lyrics were supposedly from some of our pilots trying to make it back to their bases after being in battle, hoping, praying they would make it down safely with a full crew aboard and their trust in the Lord despite a damaged aeroplane.

Lilibet came over to where I sat near my father and linked her arm through mine and put her other hand on her grandfather's shoulder.

"I'm keen for that song," she said as Margot played it over and over. "Not for the tune or how scary it is for our boys to fly into danger. It's because it's true for all of us: When we've been hurt or wounded, we pray like the very dickens we will make it safely home to try another day, even if we are only flying with one wing."

"I am proud of you, my dear," her grandfather told her, his voice raspy. "Remember that when times are tough, yes, Elizabeth?" he said, turning his eyes slowly to me. "Sometimes we hear things that set us back, but we go on. We go on to greatness and beyond."

I knew he was thinking of the time he and Mother—the mother of my heart—had told me about my French heritage. Had that made me desperate to earn approval from others? Even the elite, the royals? And so, had I overstepped with David?

"Yes, Papa" was all I could manage as my eyes filled with tears, and Lilibet made it even harder by dropping a quick kiss on my cheek before dashing back to the gramophone. "Yes, Papa," I repeated, "in all our wars, little ones and big, we must find a way to carry on to greatness and beyond."

* * *

Shortly thereafter, I was summoned from our little gathering to take a call from Bertie. I did not worry, for he had phoned every night. But I could tell he was on edge—no, nearly panicked when he spoke my name and asked if I was alone to hear some news.

"Yes, dearest, go ahead. Whatever is it?"

I thought Queen Mary might have died, but his rush of words showed it wasn't that.

"It's David. He's made another mess—a scandal. Catastrophe!"

"In little Nassau? He hasn't gone to the States? And don't invite him back here!"

"In Nassau, but he's making it go international, a scandal. Murder, maybe worse?"

"Murder? Of whom?" I cried and pressed the earpiece harder to my ear.

"No one we know. Details later. We must squelch all this. Can you come back directly, at least on the morrow early? Have someone else take the girls to Windsor and return first thing, because Winston's coming to the palace with all the details right after noon. I'm afraid David and the duchess will be demanding things of us, may say some things."

Was David dunning us for money again as he had before? And did Bertie know of what things David could possibly say to coerce things from us? And who was dead on Nassau?

"Send the aeroplane to the nearest airfield, and I'll be there," I promised as he rang off.

I put the receiver back on the hook and stared at it. I prayed I would not go down, that I would not crash in Bertie's affections if a desperate David started to demand help or funds. Yes, as Lilibet had said, I was coming in on a wing and a prayer.

CHAPTER TWENTY-SIX

Red Stains

The next afternoon in Bertie's office, Churchill arrived and an elite, emergency gathering took place to discuss the latest upheaval involving the Duke and Duchess of Windsor. It was four of us, for Bertie had wanted Alan Lascelles there to take notes.

"You might know," Winston began, "even distant, quiet Nassau could not keep him—them!—out of trouble."

I perched on the edge of my chair, gripping my hands in my lap. I was terrified what might come out, considering how desperate David must be to have royal support. We knew he wanted it for his finances and his marriage—that is, to have his wife recognized as Her Royal Highness instead of her title of duchess.

"I'll try to start at the beginning," Winston went on, his voice tense and his fingers nearly crushing his cigar. "Obviously, the Windsors have not been happy there. A hellhole, she called it and urged him to desert his post as governor and go to the States for the cooler temperatures and nightlife. She insisted a beauty parlor be built near the governor's residence—a building she hates, calling it a dump, on and on. They hobnob with both the social elite and the wealthy, though, of course, that was his lifestyle here."

Winston expelled a strong breath then sucked one in. No one dared question him yet, for it was obvious more was coming.

"The duke spends hours on the golf course, often in the company of a gold mine billionaire named Sir Harry Oakes and a Swedish-born German sympathizer, Axel Wenner-Gren, who evidently has a real talent for money laundering in Mexico. Wenner-Gren has worked for the German armament Krupp family and, according to J. Edgar Hoover of the American Federal Bureau of Investigation, may well be a Nazi spy."

"Bloody hell!" Bertie exploded. "The Americans are in on this investigation? Can't David steer clear of Hitler's bedfellow Germans? He's always asking for more funds. Money laundering? Perhaps he decided to get wealth his own way."

After Winston took another breath and then a puff of the cigar, he said, "Actually, the duke's money grubbing may be the least of the scandal erupting since this Sir Harry Oakes has been brutally murdered."

I had meant to keep silent, but I had to know if David had tried to blackmail his way out of this mess. I asked, "So David has been demanding help with this investigation, pulling our government or his—his royal family—into this mess?"

Winston shook his head so hard his jowls bounced. "Damn the man. He took it upon himself to solve the murder—which made some wonder what he was covering up—and he is making a sordid muddle into an international scandal. Fortunately, the king and I had agreed to secretly plant someone with him who would keep us informed, in this case, his aide, Major Gray Phillips. So I'm reading from Major Phillips's latest communiqué to me." He flourished a wrinkled piece of paper.

"Phillips informs me that the Duke of Windsor has imposed press censorship about Sir Harry's death. A blackout of news is supposed to be in effect. But it came too late. The people who discovered the body had already notified authorities.

"Ah, let's see what else is pertinent here. I skip a few details, ma'am, for the murder scene was gruesome—bullet wounds, private parts of the body burned."

Wide-eyed, I nodded. How strange that in wartime, such a simple description seemed so dreadful. And yet the mention of private parts brought back such terrible, vivid images, ones tied to David too.

While Bertie leaned intently forward and Lascelles scribbled notes, Winston read on, "The duke called two Miami policemen he evidently knew or who had been recommended. They flew over quickly and managed to botch the investigation. Major Gray notes that the native police force was not trusted and only assigned to scrub blood off the walls. The Miami detectives did not have a camera and made a mess of whatever bloody fingerprints were there in Sir Harry's bedroom."

I was starting to feel nauseous, but I knew I had to stay, not only to hear what happened but to be certain there was no hint of David trying to pressure us for help. Surely, he would not use his knowledge of his and my—our—skirmish to blackmail or force me or Bertie to help. And he could threaten to use the damning information about my French cook mother, for Bertie had never indicated he knew of that either. Oh, how did it ever happen that I had kept so many momentous secrets from my husband, now king?

Bertie said, "Winston, you mentioned the Federal Bureau of Investigation in the States. So are they in on the case now?"

"That's where things get sticky," Winston said, looking up from glaring at the paper. "It seems the FBI—and their man in charge is a real bulldog—has had a file. A dossier," he added with a pointed glance at me, "on the duke's activities, dating from his and the duchess's rather cozy visit to Hitler in Germany. Also the assistant secretary of state in the U.S. believes the Windsors are Nazi collaborators and has been keeping an eye on them. I have been informed that the duke could be charged with something called the Trading with the Enemy Act."

Bertie gasped and looked at me. "But that sounds like traitorous activity," he said. "Could he be dragged into a public U.S. or British court?"

As if I were assuring him—or, despite how I hated David, was indulging in wishful thinking—I bit my lip and shook my head, but I wanted to burst into tears. Whatever came from this awful situation, David had shamed himself and his country as he had once shamed me. Thank God he had abdicated and left the Empire in the hands of a good man.

"It seems, Major Phillips reports," Winston went on, "that the duke has deposited two million American dollars in a Banco Continental in Mexico where the funds will be what they call 'laundered'—that is, the ownership and trail obscured by this shady Wenner-Gren who could blow all this sky high."

"Or if David is somehow in with the Nazis," Bertie said, lighting another cigarette with shaking hands, "could he be blackmailed to cooperate with them—perhaps more than he has already?"

I decided I would dare to ask another question, hoping my voice did not tremble. "So the duke has undertaken this murder investigation but botched it somehow and that makes him look, if not guilty, as if he's hiding something related to Sir Harry?"

"Exactly," Winston said, glowering at the paper. "Yes to all your questions. Let me see here. Besides hauling in two Miami detectives who made a mess of the murder scene, he has dared to suggest the death might have been suicide."

Lascelles spoke for the first time. "After a man puts multiple bullets in himself, then sets himself on fire? Blood all over. A suicide?"

Winston frowned even more deeply. "Frankly, I believe the duke is hiding something, hopefully that he is just strapped for money, but who knows what else. And I wonder if he thinks we'll not cause an uproar over this because of . . . of a sort of blackmail he holds over someone. But what can he know that would come up to that level?"

I was certain I would be sick to my stomach.

"Such as what?" Bertie demanded. "I didn't give him those funds he's hiding. He dare not try to smear the throne in all this."

It would look bad if I fled the room to vomit. How I had tried to convey a brave front in the war, and if I crumpled at this, surely Bertie and Winston would wonder why. They knew I had been at odds with David, spoken bitterly against his ever coming back to England again, especially with that woman. But I was certain they thought it was Wallis Simpson's sins I was appalled at, not my own stupidity, however young and naïve I was then.

"So here's the worst of it," Winston said with a sigh as he crumpled the paper in his lap. "There was an almost immediate arrest of Sir Harry's son-in-law for the murder, and on flimsy evidence. The American newspapers and beyond have picked up this story. I've heard from Hoover that this scandal has knocked the war off the front newspaper page in New York City and other places, so there is no way of squelching it here, though I've pulled a few strings so our reporters would tone it down. And, you might know, the duke and duchess have fled to New York City, evidently to avoid questioning in this mess he's made of the investigation."

Reaching over to take my hand, Bertie said, "Here we are, making military progress in this bloody war, and now we have this! Sorry you sat in to hear it all, darling."

My fingers ached from gripping them together so hard. I clung to him. But would he cling to me if David became so distressed he tried to blackmail us—me? If so, my reputation, my position, perhaps my marriage, my whole life might as well be shot up and its private parts burned.

* * *

I hardly slept that night, but near morning I must have slipped into the exhaustion of nightmare. I was a soldier in the tall-tree forest, fighting with a blond German man, shooting at him.

Oh, not a German, but David, looking young as when we were briefly an item, long before that other woman.

"Help me, Fergus!" I cried until I remembered my brother was dead. I heard the shrill scream of the bagpipes from his Black Watch regiment as they marched to save me.

But no, it was my scream. Fergus could not help me, maybe no one could. And I remembered it all then in terrible detail: David pushed me down on the sofa where we had been sitting and kissing, and I had leaned my breasts into his upper arm. He had teased me, laughed with me. He had called me "my Scottish lass," and I thought he cared.

"This is your fault, you know, what you've wanted," he said suddenly, as if turning into another person. He yanked my skirt up.

"It isn't, not like this," I cried. "I haven't before . . . done this. You're hurting me."

He clapped his hand over my mouth and jammed a knee between my legs. "You have more extra flesh to offer than I usually favor," he said with a sharp laugh. His eyes were glassy. I smelled liquor on his breath, but we all drank at his parties. I had been wrong to linger when the others trooped out, but I was staying upstairs as a guest, and—

"Mmph," I cried and tried to bite his hand.

"You damn tease! You've been angling for me just like the hordes of hungry females, so pay up! You don't want me, you want what I am, what I have, the hand that will hold the scepter, so I'll give that to you right now! Bloody hell, I'm supposed to chase you, tart, not the other way round!"

I gasped when he yanked my underpants down, ripping the

cotton away. He raised his knee between my legs and thrust himself against me, though his trousers were still closed. "Fat, stupid pig, after me like the others, slopping from a trough of my future, my power and greatness! Give way! Pay up for the dances, the smiles, the attention you have demanded and flaunted!"

He grabbed at my crotch, shaming me, hurting me. I gasped in double shame for it was my time of the month and I had a sanitary pad there, one stained. Panicked, I kneed him, and he screeched in shock and fell back, then to his knees beside the couch, doubled over. Horrified at what he—and I—had done, I scrambled up, stumbling to my hands and knees, then to my feet, and fleeing for the door like a drunken sot, dizzy and ill, leaving my underwear behind on the floor. I felt sick too with the crashing down of all I had hoped and believed.

I looked back. He was bent over, retching, but he managed to look up and continue his verbal assault. "All show and no go! And if you tell anyone this—ever!—it will be the ruination of you, for I will claim you are as crazy as those two cousins your family hides or that phony monster of Glamis! Since I have learned incognito that your mother was a French cook, dear 'Cookie,' I swear if I hear one word of this, I will cook up such a story, you will never survive it!

"And if you ever tell anyone about this," he raged on, "I'll ruin not only you but your whole damn family!"

I feared at the time that those final words had silenced me, ruined me.

I sat up in bed now, hugging myself hard. Best to do what he said, even now, never tell anyone, even if he had destroyed my trust and joy of the love act forever. More than once he had leered and laughed at me when I must be in his presence. Once when I had another beau—though I was trying to steer clear of David—he had taunted me by flashing a photograph at me of my stained menstrual pad and panties.

I had never told Bertie nor anyone of what I knew now was a cruel assault, for I could never quite use that other word for it, for it hadn't gone as far as rape, though it was the rape of my dignity, my sense of self, the love I'd thought I had for him. After all, I had pursued him, wanted him, but not like that. Like so many other stupid girls, I had wanted to be his Princess of Wales.

I was certain David had not told Bertie. As brothers they, at least, still cared for each other, but I had hated David henceforth and had planned to steer clear of his family too. Until Bertie fell in love with me and pursued me, and look at me now: higher than mere Princess of Wales. I told myself I was doing well as queen, but was I not a miserable specimen of a wife?

Had David joked about me to that slender, mocking woman he loved and gave up his kingdom for? What if Bertie ever learned David had tried to take me like that? Or what if David tried to use that to make me pay somehow, pay him now since he was evidently hard-pressed for funds?

I curled up into a ball and, at least almost, wished I could trade places with someone like Bessie or Rowena with their simple, straightforward tasks and no man.

* * *

The day after Winston told us about the murder in Nassau, Bertie, evidently trying to buck himself up, proudly hauled out the dress uniform that had been ruined by the stains of geraniums the people in Malta had thrown at him in thanks and triumph during his visit there. He carried it into my sitting room, although he'd showed it to me twice before.

"You still have that?" I asked, rising. "I would think the laundry could get those stains out."

"I shall wear them like a badge in my old age," he insisted. "I was being pelted with their trust, gratitude, and love. I wish my father could have seen that. And who knew geraniums would stain like this? I don't think that flower is special as a war memorial, not like poppies are to us."

"But you felt their love. Albert Frederick Arthur George Windsor, King George the sixth of England, if I had a geranium, I would throw it at you too for that very reason."

He pulled me to him, crushing the uniform between us. I embraced him with my chin resting on the shoulder of his day uniform. He could not see my tears. I so wanted to tell him all the secrets that plagued me, my French mother, how I had created and circulated the dossier to discredit that Simpson woman, even how I had hidden David's attack on me years ago when I was but eighteen. How I hated him and his duchess yet.

I should have told Bertie about all that when he proposed the first time, but I could not bear to ruin his affection for his older brother—and I was afraid of David's threat, for a prince, powerful, beloved, would somehow cast the blame on me.

But, again, I stopped myself from sharing such anger, those confessions. I saw again the red flower marks on this uniform and remembered the blood on my lingerie that day, the photo of it that he flaunted later. Surely that had been proof I had not meant to seduce him that night. Yet how the shame and horror of it had stained my life so that I barely got through lovemaking on my honeymoon before I had claimed a sore throat and managed to ask for separate bedrooms, even later conceiving Lilibet and Margot without the marriage act.

But again, I did not tell him. How awful with his burdens this one would be, so I would continue to bear it alone and pray it did not fester and torment me more than it had—and that David would not dare to bring it to light.

I told him instead, "We have a lot of public appearances coming up, and I agree with Winston that you should address the nation whenever the continental invasion occurs. I now believe it is the better choice that you not go in with or behind our troops. It would not be flowers the Nazis will be greeting our troops with."

"I admit, though I'd like to be with them, it's best I hold back, but for how long? I shall pray about that in church."

And how long, I thought, would it be before I stepped forward to face my fears and admit—like in some church confessional booth—all my sins?

CHAPTER TWENTY-SEVEN

Happy Christmas?

Before our little family left London for our holiday retreat, Winston gave us some good news and bad about the recently completed murder trial in Nassau. The duke and duchess had managed to be out of town during the event, and it turned out the accused, Sir Harry Oakes's son-in-law Alfred de Marigny, was acquitted, thanks in part to the shoddy, botched investigation the duke had hastily overseen.

"I tell only the two of you this," Winston said as we sat at our final business luncheon until the new year of 1944. "Thank God the former king abdicated. His part in this sordid murder situation stinks to high heaven."

Bertie jolted visibly. "You don't think he could have had a part in the murder?"

"Only indirectly, getting in with the wrong investment bedfellows, trying to cover things up—and then there are his German friends, even there. But it's evidently over, no more investigation. My main thought is that, for more than one reason, he—and she—would never have brought us through this war as the two of you have, at least so far, and I pray that Hitler doesn't start bombing us again in desperation. We shall see how General Eisenhower's so-called D-Day invasion goes, when he deems the time right. Lord knows, we have a big buildup of troops and machines to go in when he gives the word."

"I'd still like to go in with them!" Bertie said.

I gasped. "But you know it will be a slog at first—hard going," I protested. "As Winston says, your place has been and is here, inspiring and leading from here—with me."

Bertie reached over to take my hand, but I was not to be coddled or deterred. "Winston, talk some sense into the king of England, please."

"I must admit, ma'am, that I too would like to be there on that day."

* * *

"I still think I should have worn my uniform," Lilibet said for the third time today as we neared our Christmas retreat in snowy, windy Norfolk. "Going to Sandringham for the holidays is a formal occasion, however much Papa shoots and we ride and walk about. Wearing my uniform makes me feel I'm truly doing something for the war effort, and I would like to do more."

In a three-car caravan with a protective vehicle ahead and behind, we were motoring to the traditional royal estate for a much-needed escape from the capital. I was looking forward to it tremendously and hoping the change of scene and relative privacy might give me an opportunity to "keep calm and carry on" as numerous London signs urged, though another motto actually upset me: *Loose Lips Sink Ships*. I wanted to share my secrets with Bertie about my birth mother and David's cruelty to me but kept telling myself it could destabilize our marriage and draw him from his necessary tasks. At least, thank God, he and Winston had been talked out of going in initially in the invasion of Europe, whenever that was.

"Really, 'Miss Colonel of the Grenadier Guards,'" Margot put in saucily, still staring out the motorcar window, "that uniform is a rather drab brown, and we all need some cheering up in these dreary times."

"It's the uniform of our infantry in the field!" Lilibet shot back. "The guards' ranks looked handsome and spiffy when I inspected their parade at Windsor."

Margot said, "I rather thought you preferred Royal Navy uniforms with that sharp black and white, especially on blond, Greek men—or man."

"Margot!" Elizabeth protested. "Daddy wears his dress Navy sometimes. At least I intend to wear mine when we visit the airfield near Sandringham. You are just wishing you had—"

"Enough!" I cut into their chatter.

They had been together entirely too much lately in these tense, terrible times. The tedious waiting for the continued Allied buildup of the invasion forces, which went under the still-covert names Operation Neptune and Operation Overlord, had made even them overwrought. Sometimes I thought the girls were affected by my nervousness and malaise too.

But they knew not to argue or even chatter when we left

behind the seemingly endless, windswept fens and motored through the gates of the Windsor family estate. Bertie loved it here however rough his father had been on him and David. His beloved, retired nanny, Charlotte Bill, still lived on the vast grounds in a grace-and-favor apartment he had arranged for her. Croplands and forests surrounded the central area of nearly five thousand acres, which were home to a village, a church, a railway station, and the royal mansion that the family called the Big House. Bertie and his siblings had been reared in a smaller home, the modest York Cottage, which our driver took us past.

Beside me on the seat, Bertie heaved a huge sigh, and his eyes misted. I reached over to take his hand as we left York Cottage behind and passed the Big House. The sprawling three-hundred-room Victorian mansion was now surrounded by barbed wire and had been closed for wartime. The skeleton staff living in the village had moved some of the furnishings to the smaller building where we stayed, so Appleton House seemed a suitable escape—and another effort to cut back on royal luxuries during the war.

Our abode here was charming, and we made do. Appleton had once been a farmhouse surrounded by large fields, but Queen Victoria's wayward son Edward VII—so unlike my own Bertie—had insisted that hares and his precious pheasant and partridge, which he loved to kill with huge hunting parties, be given free rein in this area. That drove out the would-be farmer at Appleton. At least my Bertie used high-shooting skill to bring down game birds for our table instead of enclosing them and picking them off like . . . like Luftwaffe bombers had done to our dear people.

Bertie was looking a bit gaunt and had an annoying cough, but I knew he would want to be out and about despite the cold and even the snow on the ground. I too would venture out, riding with the girls, hiking a bit.

"Here we are!" I announced the obvious, trying to gild over Bertie's sad nostalgia and the girls' testiness. "No one is to look at what's in the boot because surprises are afoot!"

I had no idea as we climbed out, stretched, and went into Appleton House what this visit would bring, but I was hoping for the best here at dear old Sandringham.

* * *

We played board games with the girls the next windy afternoon, but left them both reading while Bertie and I walked to the area that housed the grace-and-favor flats of retired staff. He always popped in on his old nanny when we were here, and I had come to see how very much she had filled in emotionally for his rather distant mother, the opposite of mine.

We had telephoned to say we would drop by and Bertie had a wrapped package for her, some chocolates that were so hard to buy these days. I was hoping he had also bought a box of those truffles for me to be opened under our candlelit tree tomorrow eve.

He did not have to lift the knocker. She was watching from her window and opened the door wide, beaming. She curtsied to both of us. "What a blessing to see you, Your Majesties!" she cried—and did cry, blinking back tears.

"Now, don't you 'Your Majesty' me, Lala, or I shall call you Charlotte Bill," Bertie teased, his voice already much lighter.

She gestured us in, and we entered the small sitting room, so cozy and warm with its fire on the grated hearth. Her silver hair seemed to gleam, and I thought she looked good for her sixty-nine years.

"You do know, my boy," she said with a little laugh, taking our coats and wraps, "that you were the one who named me Lala because you could not say Charlotte."

She sat in a rocking chair while we took the sofa. I saw she had teacups and little cakes out for us. I was glad Bertie always gave her a ten-pound note for the holidays and her birthday. How lovely, and yet how sad that these women were sometimes more dearly beloved than the women who had borne Victorian and Edwardian children. I knew Winston had supported his dear nanny for years and had said he had her photograph by his bedside.

The two of them were off to the races with their memories and laughs. At least they could joke over how strict the boys' father had been.

"He was forever haranguing you and David to keep your hands out of your pockets," Charlotte said. "He told me once I was to sew your pockets shut if I saw one more hand thrust in, but I dared to disobey him on that one. Ah, memories past, just like Christmases past in the Charles Dickens story I was recently rereading, as I used to read it to all of you."

I entered the conversation, but it mostly belonged to them. Ah, memories. I believe one time I was with my birth mother

Marguerite at our Walden Bury home when she plied me with candy and other sweets. Could that be why I loved them so?

"I pray for you both daily," Charlotte was saying. "I am so very proud of our Bertie and his loving and strong rule during these war times. Bless you both."

She poured us tea and poured her love over us. I could see why Bertie had turned out as he did with her on his side. Too bad that Bertie and David had suffered through a sadistic governess before Charlotte had "rescued" them. That cruel first nanny had seemed to dote on David, but had punished him overmuch, Bertie had said. Sad to think David had later found a woman to wed who was like that abusive, dreadful governess.

So, I thought, as the two of them darted off on another chain of memories, here was a woman of the servant class who had been the second mother to Bertie. If given the chance would the French cook Marguerite have been a second mother to me too?

* * *

The cook at Appleton House mostly kept within the boundaries of rationed food for our Christmas Eve dinner that difficult year. We had saved some ration tickets for this special meal, and Bertie's shooting foray with some local friends would give us stuffed partridge and roast pheasant instead of the traditional Christmas goose.

Midafternoon, we four sang Christmas songs round the piano while Lilibet and Margot took turns playing and hardly argued about what to sing next. Later, under a much smaller tree than the ones we'd had in the Big House, we exchanged our gifts: some photographs, two board games, gramophone records, warm sweaters, new bright yellow Wellies for me to walk the grounds here, and chocolates—not at all the grand gifts we would have had before the war.

The meal was leisurely and delicious. And then the traditional fruitcake and . . . and, I could not believe my eyes: a Yule log, the kind I had not seen since my early childhood days, a sponge cake frosted with chocolate icing and decorated with chestnuts to look like tree bark. That cake, I knew, had been one of the specialties of our French cook, Marguerite, who had called it *la bûche de Noël*.

Strange, but the view of that, even the rich smell, hit me hard. I was back again at my girlhood country house of St. Paul's Walden Bury, before I knew Marguerite had borne me. She had told the server that cake was for me to make a New Year's wish on.

The memories poured back to heat and crush me like a sparkling incendiary bomb: Mother there, Father, my brothers and sisters—and Marguerite standing in the door to the kitchen with her hands clasped and her eyes shining on my dear brother David and me.

I think everyone wondered why I cried now. Why I could barely choke down a bite of the special and delicious confection.

"A French tradition, Your Majesties," said our only footman, who had served it. "The Big House cook, who lives in the village now the place is closed, came in to bake it for you. Seems she had a French master chef teacher, even one from Paris, she did."

"Please thank her for us" was all I could manage. "I'll be right back," I told Bertie and the girls. "The cake is lovely, and please thank the cook. I hope I'm not coming down with something."

I went upstairs to the small sitting room between Bertie's and my bedrooms. I hoped he would stay with our daughters and not see me like this, but he came in from his door and sat down next to me on the old horsehair settee. Trying to regain control, I sniffled to silence and dabbed at my eyes.

"My dearest, are you not well?" he asked, leaning closer and taking my hand.

Tell him! my inner voice screamed. *Tell him now.*

"You and your memories of Lala," I said, my voice rough. "Oh, I had a sweet nanny too, but my mother was the dearest—"

"Yes. Yes, I know. Some sort of sad memory about losing your mother?"

I nodded fiercely. "But not what you think," I choked out.

"A bad one? But I know full well what a happy childhood you had. You are worried for your father's health, still mourning your mother?"

I nodded, tugged my hand from his so I could blow my nose. Now was the perfect time to tell him about my real mother, maybe tell him my other secrets too.

"Yes, I loved my parents so much. But once, when they thought I was old enough, they told me a family secret, and I vowed then to keep it a secret, but . . . but I suppose I should have told you years ago—before we were even wed."

"Something upsetting or even scandalous?" he asked, his voice a whisper. "All families have something in the closet.

But you can tell me—anything, my darling. Not to sound trite but . . . b-but we are all in this together. You have supported me and I you. So, is this secret why you turned me down twice when I proposed, because you were worried what I or others would say if they found out?"

"Papa and Mama said never to tell anyone, but it . . . it has bothered me, haunted me. That Yule log cake tonight— our French cook Marguerite Rodiere—at St. Paul's Walden Bury . . ."

"Yes. She made cakes like that?"

I nodded fiercely. "Yes. She favored me—little David too. Then my parents explained how much they loved children."

"What? But your parents were my ideal for rearing Lilibet and Margot."

"But they—wanted more children and couldn't. So—it was a done thing—Father went into her—Marguerite—and she had two more children for them, and Mother loved us all the same—more, she said."

He had gone silent. My stomach, full of holiday dinner as it was, flip-flopped. I was afraid to look up.

Bertie's voice was so quiet I could barely hear. "The Earl of Strathmore is your father, but this Marguerite is your physical mother?"

I nodded again wildly. Waited. Barely breathed. If this was so hard, no way in all creation could I tell him about my relationship with his horrible brother. Never.

"Then," he said, "you had t-two fine mothers who loved you dearly, and you earned and deserved that love. And have given that back to me in good times and bad. I don't know what I would have done without you in the past or now, especially since I seem to have lost my relationship with David, who has betrayed me and us all."

I wiped my swollen eyes and looked sideways at him.

"You should have told me before," he said and pulled me to him. "Long before. It would not have changed how much I love you, need you—how much you mean to me. Now we share your secret, now we still go on together, for that was nothing you did, nothing you could control or caused."

His arms went strong around my shoulders; my hips slid against his on the horsehair. I pressed my face into the side of his warm neck and held him tight. That last thing he said showed me that, even though he was down on David now, my other secrets must stay buried.

Buried deep.

CHAPTER TWENTY-EIGHT

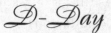 D-Day

So," Winston told us, solemn-faced and still standing, though our weekly luncheon table awaited, "here we are on the sixth day of the sixth month, the year of our Lord 1944, and I have come to let you know how the invasion has gone thus far, Your Majesties. On the sixth hour this morning, Operation Overlord commenced, and I can report that Generals Montgomery and Eisenhower have sent thousands of men, ships, and planes to overrun five key Normandy beaches. The cost will be great, but the result—I am yet waiting to hear more updates—but we have a beachhead!"

Bertie clapped him on the shoulder, then gripped that shoulder. "Monty and Ike aside, it never would have happened without you, Winston!"

"And you, sir! And behind all of us men stand our Valkyries like the queen and my Clementine," he added with a nod at me. "By the way, our breaking the code has given us perhaps the best hurrah of the day from that damned fox, Hitler's

General Rommel. We intercepted that he has said—privately, he thinks—that the invasion must be repelled on the beaches, for if they are lost, the Allies would win the battle of France, and then, the war. And I swear to you we are going to win on the beaches and then beyond!"

Bertie said, "It was brilliant of Eisenhower." He pulled out my chair at the table, and the three of us sat. "He raised the air support from three to five divisions and insisted on getting that pipeline laid from here to there for oil to keep our tanks going once they breach the German defenses."

"And how clever," I put in, "to install those artificial quays to make harbors off the five target beaches. Mulberry harbors, I believe the general said they are called."

"Ma'am," Winston said, turning to me, "if I still had my hat on my head, I would doff it to you." He looked at Bertie. "My best counsel and advice today, sir, is to stay on the right side of this formidable warrior woman and queen."

"None like her," Bertie said with a warm, proud glance at me.

I breathed a double sigh of hope and relief. That the forces of good would prevail against the damned Nazis. And that what I had told Bertie of my mixed British–French heritage had not shaken his devotion. Yet would he stay steady if I finally unburdened myself with the worst of my secrets?

* * *

The king gave a D-Day speech to the nation. I kept up my visits to our bases—much depleted now by the forces fighting on the Continent. But our hospitals were full, so I went there too, sometimes with Lilibet. That is, until she convinced her father that she should join the Auxiliary Territorial Service, called the ATS, as a mechanic and ambulance driver. Even though she would not be a full-fledged member of the ATS for months, she was proud to begin training and show us how that was going.

Both of us found time to visit what would be her section to see how she was faring. So there was Princess Elizabeth of England, heir to the throne, in oil-and-dirt-stained baggy overalls, on her knees by a lorry demonstrating how to change a tire.

I felt entirely overdressed in my usual suit and hat, but I still believed in keeping up appearances, however many of our troops were slogging through the mud and hedgerows.

Her father, smiling proudly, said, "I won't worry one whit now if I have a tire go bad. Just call Lilibet."

"This is entirely serious, Papa," she said under her breath. Two movie cameras were rolling, and I had asked Rowena to come along to take some still photos for us. Several newspapermen hovered. "If I'm going to drive an ambulance or even a lorry," she went on, turning a large wrench at the hub of the tire, "I must know how to tend to everything."

In a quiet voice, he leaned down and told her, "We are proud of you, and Philip will be too."

Bertie had been entirely more in favor of their long-distance, budding romance, and I had accepted she should at least stay friends with him. He had sent the king and me a handwritten note of gratitude for "allowing him to enjoy the warmth of our family."

I hated to say it, but he was somewhat winning me over,

though I did not want her to set her heart on him, or even trust him in some sort of intimate situation. No, I had seen a passionate young woman make that beastly mistake and come out feeling bruised and beaten. I had learned that D-Day merely meant *the* day of attack, but in a way that dreadful day with David years ago had been my D-Day, my day of disaster. Damn him, he had ruined my marriage bed and made me hate him and his vicious, chosen woman.

Bertie and I both gave our best waves and smiles to the newsreel cameras and Rowena's single-strobe one. Our Lilibet did not look up, but pulled the replacement tire closer, rolling it toward the propped-up axle.

I could not quite see myself doing that. I hoped she was different from me in some ways, at least in some important ways early in her life. I must admit, I had never been more impressed or proud of her.

* * *

Exactly one week later, 13 June, I made a visit to several local hospitals where our wounded men were being brought back from the Continent. It was the least I could do to try to keep spirits up, though the invasion—taking Europe back, as one newspaper had said—was going apace, despite dreadful casualties.

I was thankful that both Winston and Bertie had seen the wisdom of not going over yet, even to bolster morale. Let the generals do that for now, they had said, but they both wanted to visit soon. Winston had showed us a short letter of resignation

General Eisenhower had written in case his D-Day invasion went all wrong: *If there is any blame or fault, it is mine alone.*

Well, that hit me hard. More than once, I composed in my head a letter to Bertie with similar wording for when I might tell my shameful truth. I must clear my conscience and explain why I hated his brother whom he still cared for deeply despite his perfidy. But, like Lilibet, I did find some solace in helping by visiting the sick and wounded, of which there were many despite the turning of the tide across the Channel.

"This is Eddie, Your Majesty," the nurse who was guiding me through a hospital on the southern fringe of London told me. The young man was dressed, sitting quietly on the very edge of his cot, crowded in with the others. He looked like he might jump up and flee.

The nurse was very kind to escort me from ward to ward and bed to bed of our wounded. This entire room was filled with British boys we called "shell-shocked." Often, they had no visible wounds, but were so very damaged and haunted-looking.

"Hello, Eddie," I said in a quiet voice and stooped to take his hand in my gloved one. I turned back a moment to shake my head, so Rowena would know not to frighten him with the pop of the flashbulb on her camera.

I doubted if Eddie was yet twenty. He was blond and blue-eyed. His hand trembled. He shifted his wide, vacant stare to our hands and did not look at my face.

The nurse whispered, "That's what we call the thousand-yard stare, Your Majesty. He can't shake it off yet—what he's seen or had to do. Don't know if he ever will."

"I understand," I said, more to him than to her. "Eddie, I am glad to see you and I thank you for all you have done. You must rest and not be afraid of anything anymore.

"What do you know of his family?" I asked her, turning slightly away. "Have they been to see him?"

"Lost their home in an early bombing, ma'am, and the railway tracks still not repaired where they live, but they hitch a ride in now and then, his mother and sister. His father—missing in action."

"I see. Eddie, it has been an honor to meet you and hold your hand. You get better now so you can go back to your mother and sister. They need you and they love you."

His distant gaze focused and moved to my face. "Mother," he said matter-of-factly, not as a question, not in any sort of false recognition. Just "Mother."

Though I never did such a thing, I leaned forward and lightly kissed his cheek.

"Mother," he said again, looking through me, past me.

The thousand-yard stare, the nurse had said. It wasn't just a shell-shocked soldier who wore that look these days. I swear, I had seen it in my own looking glass.

*   *   *

After making more rounds, I was thanking the hospital staff—and asking them to let me know Eddie's progress—when we heard a strange whistling sound, almost like a shriek. It cut out, but was soon followed by a *boom-kerboom* that blew in the reception room windows and shook the very foundation of the building.

I was thrown backward to the floor in a heap of bodies. Both the doctor and my nurse guide partly covered me, then helped me scramble up as we heard more distant blasts.

"What in bloody hell?" a man shouted. "Thought we were done with that!"

I recalled Winston had mentioned Hitler was so furious at how the tide of the war was turning that he might try to bomb us again. But I had heard no approaching aircraft.

The nurse helped me brush plaster dust off my suit, then gave up. "Forgive me, ma'am, but I have to see to the patients. Things like this set them off."

I rose to go help her. I swear, I had to see to Eddie as if he were my own. But my driver and detective appeared, both covered with plaster dust.

"Your Majesty, some sort of weird bomb," Percy, my driver, gasped out. "No plane, no pilot. Engine just cut out and down it came. We must get you back now."

"But is there not a shelter here?" I asked the doctor. "You need to get these men into a shelter, especially if they panic because of what they've seen and heard in combat."

Detective Ransley took my arm and began to hustle me out. "The other robotic bombs seem to be falling to the west," he told me, or else he was talking to Percy, who raced along beside him. "We must head back, ma'am—now."

Squeezing me between the two of them, they gave me no choice, and they were right. At least the bomb had hit somewhere outside, not on this facility. As we rushed to the motorcar, another of those horrid things flew over, screaming like a banshee.

Silence again when its motor cut out.

Then the blast. My ears popped, my head hurt.

"Hitler's pretty upset about us getting a land hold and heading for him," Detective Ransley said, still holding my arm to hustle me into the motorcar. "Best get down, Your Majesty, lower than these windows, even if they are thick glass."

And so the queen of England, whose country was on the attack in Europe, had to put her head down, sprawl on the floor, and be covered with a blanket from the boot as if that damned Hitler could again bomb her and poor London to bits.

CHAPTER TWENTY-NINE

Information Fakery

I went straight into Bertie's arms when my driver and detective delivered me safely back to Buck House. He was waiting for me at the door, as if he were any husband worried that his wife may have had an accident.

"Darling, I cannot believe you had such a close call," he told me as he hugged me, then led me inward and up the stairs to my suite. "You look as if you've rolled in sifted flour."

"Plaster dust. I—we were all—thrown to the floor. Bertie, there were so many shell-shocked men at that facility, and I'm sure they are even more panicked—or nearly comatose—from that blast. It was eerie, I heard no plane or pilot, so what was it?"

"They've examined one that failed to detonate on the East End—"

"Not the East End again!"

"—and several other places in London. Since Winston cannot leave the war room right now, he's sending Brendan Bracken over to bring us up to snuff. We've had hints in reading the

German coded messages that they were planning to launch some so-called wonder weapons from bases in northern France, so maybe our forces will get there soon and destroy them—and the bloody Nazi dream of world domination."

"I'd best change my clothes then. I'll call for help to be quick." I pulled out my hatpins and sailed my hat onto the chaise longue.

"Let me help you. Brendan will be here soon, and we don't need others about. Here, let me take that coat. Oh, your hair is whitish too."

"Even without that, I'm finding silver strands from worry and fear for us—for all."

He helped me remove my coat and unfastened my pearls. As he unbuttoned the back of my dress quickly and deftly, I had two thoughts. First, where did he learn to free those little buttons so easily? And second—what a strange thought for such a terrible day—I had not been undressed by him ever. On our honeymoon, I was in a nightgown when he came in, and since then, with my servants and my own reluctance and request for . . . for bedroom privacy, for celibacy . . .

I stood before him in my slip and kicked off my shoes. I felt strangely vulnerable and almost naked. "Goodness," I said, moving away, "I shall have to find my own dress in my vast closet. But in all things, my dear, we can make do."

To my surprise and unease, he followed me into my dressing room with all its doors, shoes, and hat racks, my drawers of scant jewelry, for most of it had been secured or hidden in these terrible times.

I quickly jammed my feet in a pair of heels and shuffled through hanging dresses. I snatched one out, navy with a

pleated skirt and padded shoulders. Its silk hanger went spin-
ning away. I shimmied the lined garment over my head and
shook it a bit until it settled.

"Turn around," he whispered, looking me over and coming
closer. "I'll fasten it for you."

Feeling warm and not from rushing, I did as he said and
found I was staring at him and myself in one of the full-length
looking glasses. We both froze for a moment, though I felt
heated even more. From my close call today? From fear and
anger that this war we should be winning raged on?

No, it was the heat of need and even desire, the desire to be
protected and loved. It was regret that I had not told this dear
man why I held back, why I had asked for a marriage without
the marriage act and for the cold process of conceiving our
children without sexual intercourse. But my silence had been
not only for my shame, but for my desire to protect his feelings
for his hateful brother. And what would Bertie have done if I
had told? Called David out to some sort of modern duel? Cut
him off forever?

As if he'd read my panic, his arms came hard round my waist
from behind, and he bent to kiss the nape of my neck, then slid
the tip of his tongue down my backbone to the top of my slip.
Though still feeling flushed, I shivered. Now? Now in the rush
of preparing for a visit from Winston's war information chair-
man? Now, when I could have been killed this morning?

"I could not bear to lose you," Bertie whispered against my
skin and tightened his arms, moving them up to just under
my breasts, then gently cupping my left breast through my
garments.

"Or I you. That's why it frightens me so that you still say you are going over to visit the forces in France. Your visit to Italy was different, because it seemed farther from the heat of . . . of the action."

"But I will be back. I will be back, and we will go on, as a family with our dear girls—and together, my love. But for now this war must come first. We'll go to my office to wait for Bracken and his bad news as soon as I button you up."

Button you up, his words snagged in my brain as he let me go and went about his task. My breast, my entire body tingled. Surely, he thought I had been too buttoned up in our marriage, certainly in our lovemaking or lack of it, and that was entirely my fault. Yet he had put up with it, honored me, needed me, and cherished me. I still wasn't certain when—or if—I would tell him about his dear David's cruel attack years ago, but for the first time in years, since life in these times could be so short, I longed to atone for his empty bed.

*   *   *

"The war room generals have already dubbed the new rockets 'doodlebugs,'" Brendan Bracken told us as we sat in Bertie's office a quarter hour later. "Actually, they are a form of buzz bombs called V-1 rockets, pilotless, that get over the Channel in record time and can obviously be controlled, we think, at least approximately, for targeting."

With a shudder, I put in, "The whine or scream before the sound cuts out is as horrifying as the blast."

"The prime minister calls them terror weapons. The numbers

of dead are not in yet, but there will be high casualties. We can only pray our bombers or the advancing Allied forces soon get to the bases from which they are being sent. Then, sadly, though this is top secret from the public too, we have picked up some information there will soon be mobile launch bases for such hellish rockets in The Hague, the Netherlands, for an even more advanced rocket that can clear the Channel in something like four minutes."

"Too fast to be intercepted or shot down?" Bertie demanded.

"We will try, of course, sir. They are working on that straightaway."

"But," I put in, "you said some of this is top secret too. You didn't mean secret from our citizens? How could something this beastly and obvious be kept from our poor people who finally had hope we were winning since the D-Day invasion?"

"I need to explain that too, ma'am. Astute of you to pick up on that. Until we can promise to intercept at least some of them, we feel we must keep the public in the dark about the news of these Wunderwaffen, these wonder weapons. We will claim that there were gas line explosions that created the noise and destruction."

"Ridiculous!" Bertie said, rising from his desk chair. "They arrived in daylight. They have been seen!"

I should have kept silent and let him handle this, but I could not. "I agree!" I insisted. "Shall we start lying to our dear citizens who have already given and suffered so much? And then tell the truth later—or they will surely find it out and recognize it themselves—that they have not been trusted to take the truth?"

"The point is, Your Majesties," Brendan said, tugging at his tie as if he might hang himself, "they have been through so much and these are diabolical and deadly. Just for a few days until—"

"I repeat," Bertie said, "nonsense! Rumors and the truth will spread. I counsel against this and will phone Winston at once."

"Brendan," I said, my voice more quiet now, "I speak my mind here, which the prime minister has encouraged me to do. I lived through a close call today from one of these deadly doodlebugs, if that must be their cute name. It shrieked unlike any plane or bomb I have heard, and I have heard plenty of them. It then cut to a deadly silence followed by a dreadful blast. It was unlike the bombs the Luftwaffe rained on us before, for I have heard them too. So have our dear, beleaguered people who have been through the Blitz, and they will know their government is lying to them and that may break the bond of unity."

"Well said," Bertie put in. "Brendan, tell whichever general came up with this idea—for I cannot believe it was the prime minister—that the queen's close call will be reported to the newspapers with her impressions of this so-called wonder weapon, and we hope that official news releases will not be filled with fakery. The signs and mottoes have boasted 'England can take it,' and she—we—can."

"I'll head back immediately with that advice, Your Majesties," Brendan said and, looking abashed, quickly bowed his way out.

We collapsed into each other's arms. "These new weapons are terrible news but for one thing," Bertie whispered. "They show Hitler is panicked. He sees the handwriting of the Allied victory on his bloodstained, European wall and fears he cannot stop our forces there—so he does this here."

I nodded and held him closer, proud we had stood together on this. Advise and consent was really the duty of kings and queens, but we had come out stronger than that. I felt too that I must do something special before Bertie risked himself by going to France to support our fighting troops.

Sadly, we must both make out wills, which we had been hesitant to do, as if it would be bad luck. And I must somehow make my way to Bertie's bed and blast apart my too-long celibacy before something happened to one or both of us.

* * *

We both finally faced the possibility of our deaths, more than we had let ourselves do before. We made out our wills, and I made a separate one about the division of my personal jewelry. Someday, our dear and dutiful daughter Elizabeth would inherit all the royal tiaras, the diamond bracelets, and the ropes of pearls stretching far back to the first Queen Elizabeth. So I made certain that Margot, our spirited, go-getter Margaret Rose, had a good share of personal family items.

Lilibet was not happy to hear what we were doing, but she was old enough to understand. I promised her that she could go with me to see her father off at the airfield tomorrow evening when he went on an inspection tour of our forces in France.

That last night before the day he would leave was torment.

I wanted to say so much to him, so over a late private meal after the girls were in bed, I did.

"Bertie, you are not going for long, but I shall miss you. I cherish our time together, the family we have made."

We were in my sitting room, both tired, both distraught that the attack of the V-1s had continued, taking lives, destroying property and hope that our island was now safe since our soldiers were attacking the European mainland. At least Winston had agreed with us, insisting on a turnabout of plans to tell our citizenry the truth about the so-called wonder weapons.

As ever, I deeply regretted that the war had taken such a toll on Bertie. He looked thinner, so tired, and his persistent cough sometimes wracked him.

Yet I talked on, holding his hand, sitting close to him, while he listened raptly, looking almost dazed. His eyes seemed to glow with warmth and love.

"My beloved," he whispered, "tell me the truth. Do you have some sort of premonition about these coming days we are apart? That I might not return, that another robot rocket might strike near you?"

"No, I . . . I have no premonition but a hope about these hours we have left before we part. That you might hold me, that I might love you—as I have not for far too long."

His eyes widened, and his lower lip dropped.

"I will lock the door," I rushed on, "if you can help me to undress. You did a fine job with my clothing earlier today. And since we both convinced the powers-that-be we are against fakery, let me say, I love you and want you—want you to love me, really, man and woman, husband and wife."

He nodded and blinked back a tear. He pulled me to my feet and into his hard embrace. We walked, almost danced toward the door to my bedroom, before he remembered to run back to the hall door and lock it firmly.

"If I don't call for Bessie, I think they won't come," I told him as we walked together into my bedroom and he locked that door too.

"I hope this night lasts for a long time," he whispered, tugging my hand as we walked toward the bed with its sheets turned down.

I trembled in his arms and my voice shook when I whispered, "And after you come home, I hope that our love lasts for our forever."

CHAPTER THIRTY

Warrior Queen

Late afternoon the next day, Lilibet and I accompanied Bertie to see him off on his trip to Normandy. He had promised he would not be on the battle line but would meet with the generals and encourage the men, especially those wounded. Our destination was the RAF Northolt aerodrome in Ealing, so we only had just a tad over ten miles to drive. Despite our nervous chatter, I could hear a ticking clock in my head. God forgive me, and I had told no one, but this looming separation weighed heavily upon me, though last night had eased my guilt somewhat.

"Mummy, did you hear that the American magazine called *Time* has written that my uniform marks the first warlike garment to be worn by an English queen since the days of Boadicea? It sounds as if they know a bit of English history, doesn't it?"

Bertie blew out a puff of smoke. "Ancient history, perhaps," he answered for me. "Yet it rather sounds as if they don't know a fig about current affairs, as you are not quite queen yet."

"I didn't mean that part of it, and pray I will not be for many, many years. Remember when Margot finally realized I was next in line, she said, 'Poor you.' I'll bet that was because she saw how hard it is to be king or queen too. I am just glad to serve until that sad day, and—oh, sorry, Mummy, because I know you are on edge about Papa going over to France with all that fighting."

Although she sat between us, Bertie reached across her to squeeze my hand. "Talk about warrior queens," he said. "Your mother defends and protects me, you know. She's the warrior here."

We smiled at each other across Lilibet as she glanced from one of us to the other. I thought of a line from his D-Day speech to the nation and Empire: *The queen joins me in sending you this message. She well understands anxieties and cares . . .*

How true those words, truer than he knew, for although I had unburdened my secret about my birth mother to him, and although we had truly slept together for the first time in years, I still had not told him how David had abused me. But was that attack my fault? I had pursued the dashing Prince of Wales as had so many others, and so was I to blame as much as—

"Almost there," Lilibet said. Bertie squeezed my hand again and let go as we motored through the guarded gates. I noted a great deal of runway and very few aeroplanes, but then, no doubt they were in battle.

We were driven out to the waiting Lancaster bomber that had been redone inside from a fighter to a carrier. "Come in with me," Bertie said before he stepped outside the motorcar. "Let's all take a look at what they have done to the interior for my tour."

Bows and salutes, officers' names, meeting the pilot and co-pilot followed. Such brave, fine young men, and so many like them in the air fighting for us even now.

In the cabin of the aeroplane, Lilibet tried out the seat Bertie would use while I looked around at the décor. They had laid a carpet in the aisle and had arranged a desk for him and a nice galley. Ashtrays, so they knew him well.

I went forward into the cockpit, gazing at a maze of equipment and dials, then glanced out the window to try to get an idea of what the view would be.

And . . . and, coming straight for us, downward in a slight arc with its shriek muted, was one of those damned V-1 rockets I'd seen in photographs since my own close encounter. How could they know we were here? Would they try to kill the king before he could fly over to France?

I screamed and pointed. Bertie bent to look, his chin on my shoulder as our pilot guide squinted out into the setting sun.

"Down!" he shouted. "Both of you, down!"

"Lilibet," I screamed, "get on the floor!"

Bertie shoved me down and dove back into the cabin, yelling, "Get down. A rocket coming straight for—"

The rest of his words were drowned by the screech I had hoped never to hear again. But it veered over us, silent now, and then came the blast and shudder of the plane, of my very soul.

Bertie came back to help me get up. "Lilibet's all right. Are you? And don't think this is some sort of sign. I will be all right. And," he whispered, "the vows we made to each other for truth and unity and love last night—not even war or death can ever change that."

Those last words paraded back and forth through my brain as we bid him farewell and waited by our motorcar—with one eye to the sky for more screaming rockets—as the Lancaster carrying Bertie took off into the evening sky. Unity, yes, we had both promised as we joined our bodies for the first time since our honeymoon, when I had claimed—Lord forgive me—that I was ill. But I had vowed the truth to him, and now here he went off to war. I had not told him all the truth, not one word about David and me.

"Mummy," Lilibet's voice broke into my agonizing, and she reached over to take my arm. "You're biting your lip until it is almost white. Time will pass fast. Especially since you, but I too, will be busy filling in for him as Counsellor of State, and doing all those visits. He'll be all right, you know he will, however tired and even ill he seems sometimes. I rather thought he was a bit jolly and jaunty today and you too before that beastly bomb. I know how that feels, really I do, for when I receive a letter from Philip . . . well."

Well, indeed, I thought. This perceptive young woman had picked up on our sudden shift to a special joy from our new-found intimacy. What would I do without her, and Margot too?

I waved, although the aeroplane was a mere dot swallowed by the grey eastern sky.

* * *

One of the most rewarding and exciting events I attended while Bertie was in France—from which he wired me encouraging notes—was visiting the Second Battalion of the Home Guard under the command of my dear brother, that is, half brother, Mike. It had to be the Home Guards for him since he had been wounded in the Great War, which burdened him with physical disabilities and caused him to be rejected by the Army for medical reasons. I greatly liked his wife, Betty, so I promised I would write a report to her of how things were going under his command.

Just like poor, dear lost Fergus, Mike was a favorite to me of my five older brothers. Before he suffered from shell shock and a head wound and was a prisoner of war, he had been a tease and a great deal of fun. He was a bit solemn now, but then the formal occasion demanded it. Despite how bravely and loyally he had served Britannia before, I knew he longed to be with our fighting forces.

I had seen him so seldom lately that I did not care how formal this occasion was. As we walked together toward his assembled Home Guard volunteers I was to inspect, I took his arm.

"Is it true the king is over there?" he asked without turning his head, so only I could hear.

"He's in his element when he is with our men. General Eisenhower always says the same and calls the American soldiers and airmen his 'boys.'"

"Father's not well."

"I know. He's never gotten over losing Mother."

"Life's losses . . . Yes, but we go on. We Bowes Lyons have backbones of steel—from Mother, though she knew how to bend, have fun, and enjoy life. We carry on, no matter what, you especially with all your challenges and burdens, my dear-sister-Majesty," he added and squeezed my arm against his uniform before I gently, regretfully pulled it back.

Ah, a little hint of the old joking Mike, from before our family's losses, before that first war they dared to call "great," though that just meant "large." So, I decided then and there, this was great war the second, an even larger, horrid, hellish war.

* * *

As busy as I kept, I missed and feared for Bertie terribly. In a way, I felt I had only begun to make amends. Perhaps it was because I had not completely cleared my conscience yet, or perhaps it was because I had recently been to a spate of funerals of friends.

One of the V-1s—for I refused to call them by their doodlebug nickname—had hit between the palace and Parliament during a Sunday-morning service and had obliterated the Guards Chapel and some of our friends. Others in attendance were people we knew and had entertained in better days.

I was told the nave of the venerable chapel had been demolished but the altar was so completely untouched that several candles still burned to light the carnage as the rescue workers swept in. Sixty-three servicemen and -women and fifty-eight other worshippers were killed and scores more injured. I had not sent a message to Bertie on that, for he was seeing enough Nazi slaughter on his own. But to be in church, praying for victory and peace, and then to be obliterated seemed especially wrong.

And here I sat in church this morning at St. George's Chapel at Windsor with Margot and Lilibet while the bishop prayed for those lost souls, our servicemen and -women and the nation. As I peeked down at the order of service on my lap, the words blurred. As stoic as I strove to be, especially in public or with my girls, a tear slipped out and then another to wet my lashes. If I blinked, I would give myself away with slick cheeks.

But was it always right to wave and smile these days? Was I propping up my people or deceiving them? Was I guilty of information fakery?

To my surprise, Margot must have noticed, though Lilibet on my other side had her eyes closed. My youngest surprised me by slipping her hand in mine and giving it a little squeeze without turning her head my way or whispering something too loudly as she was often wont to do.

I squeezed her hand back and blotted under my eyes with the fingertip of my glove. It was a great comfort to know Margot had this tender and protective side. It reminded me of how I had consoled my mother at Fergus's funeral during that first grueling war. And now, who did my ailing father have to comfort him, remembering her too, facing eternity?

I must go to Glamis to see him again soon. I must call my dear younger brother who was still assigned in Washington, D.C., as a liaison to President Roosevelt. I longed to see that David, perhaps to convince him to come home to see Father again. Loving my younger brother as I did, I had once thought it a great sign of good luck that I had fallen in love with David Windsor, Prince of Wales.

"Mummy, we're going to sing," Margot prompted, pointing at the place in the program.

"Yes. Thank you, dear girl," I told her as Lilibet on the other side quickly turned to the correct hymn and traded me books as we all stood.

I nearly broke into sobs again, but of gratitude this time. For my very different but lovely daughters. And that Bertie would be home soon.

CHAPTER THIRTY-ONE

Reunions

Bertie was coming back from France on 25 August 1944—a belated birthday gift for me. It was a special day in so many ways!

"There he is, Mummy!" Margot shouted as if I were both deaf and blind, for she thought forty-four years sounded very old. "I'll run to get him! Be back with him straightaway!"

As if she were five instead of almost fourteen, she darted away. Lilibet went down the corridor too, but at a more measured pace. I took a last quick sip of my cocktail and hurried myself down the corridor too. Although it was early August and a hot, humid day, the stone walls and windy halls of Windsor kept the rooms quite cool. I did think, though, that my drinks not only calmed me but heated me up a bit, yet nothing could match the relief and joy of actually having Bertie home again. Even better, we were heading for Balmoral soon, and how I had missed Scotland.

I watched as Margot barreled into the king and Lilibet

hugged him next. I strode to him, embraced him, and we shared a quick kiss. To my surprise, my always-shaved husband had beard stubble, which made him look a bit like a ruffian, but then he had been living with the troops.

"You all look wonderful!" he said as if to counter my surprised expression.

I wanted so to say the same, but he looked pale and gaunt. No doubt, he had been burning the candle at both ends. Ah, I thought as I hugged him again then released him, at least London was not burning anymore, for the V-1 rocket attacks seemed to have lessened.

We walked back to our private quarters, arm in arm. "So much to tell," Bertie said. "But I am so exhausted—though not too much to celebrate a birthday with my three girls!"

Yes, he smelled of tobacco and exhaustion and did not look well. What would our lives have been like if David had not abandoned his duties as king and Bertie had only captained a warship at sea as Duke of York and not had to bear the yoke of kingship through this great, hard slog of a war? As much as I knew England and the Empire had been better off with Bertie as king, I blamed David for thrusting all this duty upon my beloved—and making him ill.

He went to freshen up while the three of us waited. I had sent for partridge from Sandringham, a luxury I hoped he would not resent, as a welcome-home dinner and my birthday meal. At his place on the table, the girls had put cards they had made, and my little stack of gifts awaited on the sideboard. But where was he?

"I'll go see how he's coming along," I told them. "Be right

back, and if the footman asks when to bring in the meal or the cake, tell him not yet."

I passed my rooms and knocked on his bedroom door. Nothing. No sound. Was his valet at least not with him?

I knocked again, but my heart knocked louder. I turned the handle and went in, only to find him with shaving cream on his face like a white beard while he sat up against a pillow and the headboard of his bed, as still as can be.

I gasped. It could not be that . . .

"Bertie?" I said and ran over to touch his shoulder.

His eyes flew open. My pounding heart slowed.

"Oh, darling, sorry," he said, looking startled, as if he were shocked to be here, to see me. "Total fatigue, that's all. I've seen so much. I don't want to talk of war at the table, but it's been so—sobering. Eight thousand Allied soldiers died in the first month since D-Day, more than half of them American, but our men too. Thank God the American general Mark Clark marched victorious for all of us into Rome in June, and our forces are close to taking Paris the same way. Winston said he'd phone if he had news of that."

"Let me shave you. I have shaved my papa a few times, wounded or paralyzed soldiers too back at Glamis in the other awful war."

I took the razor from his hand and gently skimmed it along his neck and chin, then wiped it off on the towel over his shoulder. He watched me through slitted eyelids.

"Will we pick up where we were?" he asked. "Between the two of us, I mean. Time moves on, war or not. Why, you are another year older."

"Dare you remind me of that when I have a razor to your throat?"

"I dare much. And I suppose I smell of tobacco, but you, my darling, smell of whatever pre-dinner drink you have had without me."

My face heated as I finished cleaning his face off with the towel. I had upped my liquor intake a bit lately, just to take the edge off, just to smooth things over and calm myself— not when I was going out for duties, of course. But I had been worried about Bertie, my father was even more ill—and I still could not rid myself of anger and guilt that the former Prince of Wales had treated me so brutally and cruelly. While Bertie had been gone, I had told Winston in no uncertain terms that I could not abide having that man back in England, whether or not he was with his wife.

"But," Winston had said, "he ruins everything he touches elsewhere. He can't even sit out this bloody war in paradise without getting into trouble. If he were here, I could keep an eye on him, distract him with minor duties."

"Winston, he would try to take over, undercut Bertie. You know his, well, his allure, though he is a hollow man. You championed him for a while."

He had leaned closer to me across our Tuesday luncheon table. "And did you never feel that allure, as you call it? I swear, Brendan Bracken could use him in the Ministry of Information, which, I admit, dispenses our propaganda too, in bolstering our beaten down populace. The king cares for his big brother, always will, so he would be amenable."

"But I am not. He and that woman would make a mockery—

a . . . a shambles of things. I have been on your side, Winston, but I ask you not to so much as bring this up to the king."

I stared him down, wondering if he would try to use old information he had about me to keep me quiet. That dossier on David's paramour. Could Winston know about my birth mother? At least I had told Bertie that. Surely, surely, he could not have in his armory that I had pursued the Prince of Wales, nearly thrown myself at him—and worse than that.

He had nodded and rapped his knuckles on the table as if rendering a verdict in court.

"You have been more than a wife and helpmeet to the king," he said, his face and voice serious. "You have been his advisor, his strength, his courage, his brain at times, and I know that full well. So I shall agree with you on this matter—at least for now—and not mention the wild thought to His Majesty, and I trust you will not either."

I gave a little, inelegant snort.

"Darling?" Bertie's voice broke in, dragging me back to reality. "I almost thought you had nodded off along with me. I am eager to resume the way we were the night we parted, but I have a feeling it will not be tonight. Let's celebrate your special day with our girls, just we four, before I fall face-first in your cake."

"We have a great deal to celebrate." I helped him don the jacket of his uniform again. "We are back together, we are going for a rest to Scotland and onward and upward in this war."

The moment we joined the girls, Alan Lascelles popped in the door without so much as a knock.

"Excuse me, Your Majesties, but the prime minister is on the phone, and he's humming that French cancan dance music. It reminds me of the night he sang 'Roll Out the Barrel' when Eleanor Roosevelt was with us."

"I'll be right back," Bertie said and rushed out.

"It better be good news," Margot said with a huge sigh. "We're never going to have this party."

He was back in a flash with a smile on his wan, thin face. "Paris had been liberated just today!" he cried—and I did cry.

"Rome, now Paris!" he went on. "Next—somehow—the dragon's lair of Berlin!"

He hugged me and swung me around once while the girls whooped and clapped. I must admit, it was a marvelous birthday gift.

"If only," Lilibet's calm voice put in when we finally sat at the table again and clinked together our wine or juice glasses, "London could be liberated. You know what I mean, no more V-1 rocket bombs and people huddled in the Underground stations again. During the Blitz they seemed defiant, but now they are depressed."

That threw a little pall on our double celebration, but she was right. The bombs, the deaths, the deprivations had gone on far too long, as Winston had put it once, like "great black oxen" dragging us along but slowing us down.

"Mummy, open your gifts before we have the cake," Margot prompted, and Lilibet nodded.

"Would you believe I have brought you a German Luger to continue your shooting lessons with?" Bertie said.

"Not, I hope, with that horrid swastika on it."

"Those things look like ugly spiders!" Margot said with a shudder, though that thought didn't keep her from popping more blackberries through her already dark-stained lips.

"No swastikas," Bertie assured us. "We shall destroy those as we would a poison spider."

We raised our glasses again, though I was wishing for something a bit stronger than my wine. I was just ready to cut the lovely iced cake when Alan popped back in.

"Regretfully, another telephone call. For the queen. From Glamis."

I stood and said, "I'll wager my father is calling to wish me a happy birthday. How I wish I could talk to my brother David today too."

"I too—mine," I heard Bertie whisper as I put my napkin down, rose, and went out.

But it was my father's longtime physician.

"I regret to tell you that the earl's condition has weakened even more, Your Majesty," he informed me. "Several of your family have been in to see him, but he is asking for you and David."

"He knows David is in Washington, D.C., in the British embassy."

"His mind is . . . is wandering, ma'am, and I thought it best to see if you can come. He seems very set that he must speak to you, rambling as he is about the old days. I do think he knows deep down that it is your birthday, for he keeps going back to when you were born, as best I can tell."

"Yes. Yes, I see. I'll come as soon as I can, as we were going to Balmoral anyway on the morrow."

I went back in to our now strangely muted celebration and sat, staring at my piece of birthday cake. "Grandpapa has taken a turn for the worse and is asking to see me. His mind is wandering . . ." I began. "Well, let me open these lovely presents, and we'll be off for Scotland early tomorrow, and I to see Grandpapa."

"I hope his mind doesn't wander to that ghost," Margot said, gripping her hands by her dessert plate. "You know, that monster of Glamis people always ask about. Mummy, you said it is just a frightening fairy tale, but I think some people believe it can still sneak up, scream, and scare people and ruin things."

"That," Lilibet said, with her fork and cake halfway to her mouth, "sounds as if you are describing one of those horrid V-1 rockets."

Or, I thought, as I reached for a birthday gift to unwrap, it sounded like my private life navigating minefields set one way or the other by family, friends, and foes.

CHAPTER THIRTY-TWO

Past and Present

*A*s we rushed to Balmoral and I was motored on to Glamis to see my failing father, a line from Bertie's D-Day speech kept revolving through my head: *We are not unmindful of our own shortcomings, past and present. Now one more supreme test has to be faced.*

I had been over that speech so much with him, nearly had it memorized after listening to him practice it. He was proud he did not need Lionel Logue to help him, that he could stand and deliver it himself.

And now I had one more supreme test of the several I yet faced. I feared I must bid farewell to my father and calm his ravings about past sins, if that's what he was tormented by. And when I came to die, what regrets would torment me, and would I blurt out my shortcomings?

For once, I did not look at the outer façade of the castle where the monster had supposedly been imprisoned. Papa's rooms—Mother's too—were on the other side. Despite having separate suites, de rigueur for the times, they had almost always shared the same sitting room and bedroom. Ah, such a love story.

As my driver opened the door, the house butler came out to greet me. I hurried inside, up the familiar stairs where David and I had played. I planned to telephone my dear brother after I saw Father, not just send a telegram this time. How I missed him, two peas in a pod Mother had said once, but now I knew the pod had been the womb of a rural French cook.

The doctor met me in the hall, so someone must have told him I had arrived. "Your Majesty, some good news," he said with a bow. "The earl is a bit stronger today, but still talking a blue streak. Perhaps you can calm him. The nurse has stepped out too. Shall I go in with you or come back later?"

"I thank you for your care of him, and please take a bit of a rest until I send for you."

He bowed again, backed away, then came back to open the door for me. The room was in semidarkness and smelled of salves and bedpans.

"Papa, it's Elizabeth," I said, putting my purse and hat down on the end of the big canopied bed. I sat on the side of it and took his hand.

He felt cold, his skin papery, and I saw purple bruises there.

"My dear girl! Is that imp David with you? You two are the last, you know, but that does not mean you are not our dearest."

I was not sure whether to try to tell him David and I were

in our forties now, or just play along. Couldn't he see I was full grown and leave the past behind?

"Yes, we are the youngest of your brood. I loved having a big family growing up."

"Quite right. And now that you are old enough, your mother and I need to tell you and David something about your beginning, so to speak."

I hoped he had not been telling the doctors and the servants what it sounded as if he would say. Could he be so demented that he was going back that far?

"It's all right," I said, trying comfort mixed with a dose of reality, because I could not bear to hear all that again. "David and I know about the arrangement."

"Whoever told you? Did your mother tell you on the sly?"

"It's all water over the milldam, Papa. And Mama has loved us like her own, so it's all right."

"It wasn't all right, really. I was not always faithful to her. I told her everything, that's what a good, strong, and true marriage needs, to share everything."

It was as if he were telling me—without knowing so—that I must tell Bertie about what the Prince of Wales had done to me, however I had pursued him, pushed myself on him. But Bertie was so weak, exhausted—oh, bloody damn, was I just looking for reasons to keep quiet on all that?

"You know, my dear," Papa broke into my agonizing, "I feel better already now that you are here and understand about the situation. She was a wonderful person, beautiful and bright, like you."

"I miss Mama too."

"I mean Marguerite. One of your middle names is from her, you know. I just wanted to tell you about her and, as soon as David gets here, I shall tell him too."

* * *

Papa had rallied so strongly, at least physically, that I soon returned to Balmoral. I shared with Bertie what had been said, but went no further with my own confessions. Would I ever share them, even on my deathbed? Besides, Bertie needed his rest and slowly began to rally too.

That night I used the telephone cable line we had at Balmoral to call David at the British embassy in Washington, D.C.

"Dearest, so good to hear from you!" his voice came strong and sure. "I got your message you were going to see Father, but when I didn't hear right away, I thought he might be better."

"Indeed he is, in body if not in mind. His thoughts wander terribly. He seemed obsessed with wanting to tell us about our real mother, and I am afraid he has probably babbled about it to the doctor and staff."

"Then I pray they consider his state of mind and are all loyal to the Strathmores—and their queen. I've told no one about all that but my wife."

"I finally told Bertie, and he took it very well. Let's face it, everyone has some sort of secrets in the closet."

"Like me, you mean?"

"No, I wasn't thinking of you, dear. Do the people you work with there know you—that but for your wife, I mean—favor men?"

"They may suspect, but my ties to you and my lovely conventional family keep my preference private and protected. Listen, Elizabeth, I agree with you that everyone has their secrets and peccadillos."

"Or sins."

"Have you turned fanatically religious?"

"When one sees people whose lives are suddenly shattered—and ended—from these new, hellish V-2s the Nazis are sending from the Netherlands, one does think of death. David, nearly three thousand more people are dead or are burying their loved ones because of those deadly, pilotless rockets."

"All right. Sorry. I suppose it seems a bit distant, sitting it out here and dealing with FDR, as they call the president, where bombs are not dropping. But as I said, everyone has their secrets."

I had never told David about my attack by the Prince of Wales, and I wasn't about to now. I would not have, even if Bertie had not come into his office, smiled and nodded at me, whispered, "Give him my best," and gone back out.

Of course, nor had David ever told me outright that he preferred men romantically to women.

"Would you believe," he went on, "that most of the U.S. citizens don't even know their president had polio and is a cripple in a wheelchair? Their press keeps that under wraps, makes sure he's seated or circumspectly hanging on to someone in photographs. And no one says one word in public or the press about the mistress he's had for years."

I gasped and nearly dropped the phone receiver. A public

man in a wheelchair had a mistress—had for years? "But you obviously know of it," I told David.

"Just as Winston wanted, I work closely with FDR."

"Does the First Lady know?"

"I take it she's known for years and gave him the chance for a divorce, which he did not take. See, secrets in the closet, even great big, public ones."

I thought of stoic, capable, and brave Eleanor. I knew she had been a soldier for her causes, but to bear all that too . . . And I thought of my own secrets in my royal closet.

"Elizabeth, are you there?"

"Yes. I wanted to say I will telephone you if Papa takes a turn for the worse."

"I will telegraph him immediately, but will he realize I'm not just away at school? I don't mean to joke, but we need to keep our chins up now, just as we did in the past—when we two first realized we were different from the others, and look at you now. I'm glad the king knows and took it well. He loves you, and I do too. Kiss the girls for me and keep your royal chin up despite the past or the present."

* * *

Dear Papa died in his sleep, two months later on 7 November 1944. Since we needed to return to London, we buried him rather quickly. David did not come for the funeral, and I missed him—with the lost members of my family—all over again. I spent three difficult days at Glamis, preparing for and attending

Papa's funeral. Of course, the king came and my girls too, but it was still difficult for me to say goodbye.

People were so kind. The local farmers and tenants turned out to stand in a bitter wind as the coffin, covered with the Union Jack, was pulled on a wooden cart by two of Papa's favorite horses while male members of the family—the king of England too—walked behind to the nearby cemetery where he was buried next to Mama.

Winston sent a lovely, heartfelt note. We were inundated with bereavement messages from far and wide. I even took bags of them back to London and eventually went through each one.

And so, nearly a fortnight later, I came to one postmarked from France, as mail had finally begun to sift through, since the Allies had pushed the Germans back toward the north.

The note was in French and signed only, *A Friend and Well-Wisher to the Queen and David.* The handwriting was a bit unsteady, and a single silver hair had snagged in the envelope with no return address. It was postmarked CALAIS.

The message translated to read, *The Earl of Strathmore was kind and generous, his Countess too. God rest their souls.*

That was all. I stared at it, sniffed the plain, white stationery and wondered: Was I looking at my birth mother's handwriting? After all, the anonymous signature referenced only me and David.

I told no one, not even Bertie, and put the note and the single silver hair for safekeeping in the bottom of my jewelry box under my signature strands of pearls.

CHAPTER THIRTY-THREE

Fairy Tale

𝒥 could not believe I was being honored in this way. Of
course, as queen, I was used to being the center of attention,
often looked up to, appreciated, yes, even honored. That was
because of my position, not for myself. Somehow, this felt different, felt like more, for they could have selected the king
instead. This gave my spirits a tremendous boost. And though,
unlike Bertie and Lilibet, I had not worn a uniform, this robe,
identical to the ones the members here wore, made me feel a
part of it all.

"We are proud to be breaking with centuries of tradition,"
the bewigged governor of the Middle Temple Inn of Law announced to the assembled guest and journalists. "For the first
time since the Inns of Court were established in the heart
of London to train barristers and lawyers during the age of
the first Queen Elizabeth, we have unanimously elected a
woman to join us as a bencher. This appointment is for life,

and we pray our new fellow—that is, lady—will have a long and fruitful one!"

Much nodding and *here-here*-ing followed. A few applauded. Flashbulbs popped. Bewigged heads turned my way. Standing erect along the back wall as if to hold it up, young students applauded. They were no doubt happy to be away from their grueling schedule of classes for this ceremony.

And Bertie beamed.

I gave a short speech of acceptance and gratitude: "I consider this day, 12 December 1944, a special and historic day. Though I am the first of my sex to become a bencher of this Inn, I like to feel that I am continuing a tradition rather than creating a precedent, for it is, after all, but a few paces from here that another Queen Elizabeth visited this society in the hall that was built with her permission centuries ago."

Nods all around. Public speaking was not yet my forte as it was for Winston, and, increasingly, for Bertie. He was looking at me with glowing eyes, so proud—so dear. I cleared my throat and went on.

"However, in this most challenging and difficult time for our beloved nation, we must remember that one woman stepping forward into a new realm is something many British women have also done in their own lives and their own ways, especially during these long and grueling years of war. They have become office workers, factory workers, security workers—even military officers and code breakers.

"Although the sanctity of family must always be first on the minds of women, all of us must step forward, queen to mechanic. Our daughter Elizabeth has become the latter, by helping our noble cause through repairing and driving ambulances and lorries. We women and men too must accept, welcome, and walk boldly through new doors to the future, a future, I pray, that will bring us peace.

"I am honored today and thank you for standing steady amidst terrible times. Traditions shall always be important to us English, but so shall striding out on new paths. Again, I thank you for this honor."

Applause. More *here-here*s. Some stamping on the floor with feet or wooden staffs of office. Of all my honorary titles, somehow this one, in such a man's world of hidebound, historic precedent, meant a great deal.

* * *

"We now present for your enjoyment and entertainment," our dear Margot announced to the audience, "our annual Christmas pantomime, this year *Old Mother Red Riding Boots*."

Gentle, somewhat muted laughter rustled through the crowd. Pantomimes were more like music hall fare or farce, a pastiche of jokes with a touch of slapstick, fairy-tale scenes, and music, not silent pantomimes.

Looking much older than her years with her formal gown and cosmetics, Margot, who loved being the center of attention, went on, "We welcome all four hundred of our honored guests and want you to know that the cost of your tickets will support the Royal Household Friend Fund to provide special comfort for our brave fighting troops. We are very happy and excited to be joined by the orchestra of the Royal Horse Guards this year for our three performances."

After the applause, she went offstage. During the musical prelude, Bertie reached over and squeezed my hand. We were so proud of our girls, who had taken lead roles in the traditional pageant. They had done *Cinderella* and *Aladdin* in the past. They seemed not children anymore, but young ladies. It was the first time Lilibet would appear as a woman instead of as a prince in these productions, since she was taller than Margot, who had snagged the princess roles before.

But that reminded me of the argument Lilibet and I had recently had. I hated that, felt a bit guilty, yet I was only trying to protect her from being overly emotional about Philip again.

Just two weeks ago, I had learned that his father, Prince Andrea of Greece, had died in exile in Monte Carlo on the third of December. She yearned so for Philip that I did not want to add to her volatile emotions over a man she did not know, one who had hardly acted as a father to his son for years. But I should have known one of Philip's often-delayed letters to her would mention the death.

"Mummy," she had said, nearly assaulting me when I had visited here last weekend. She waved an envelope at me. "Did you know Philip's father had died, and quite young, in his early sixties? Poor man, to not have his wife and son there, his daughters to comfort him at the end."

I thought of bluffing it through, saying the war kept a lid on information about other royals from other countries, but

I was trying very hard to buck myself up for truth telling lately—even planning to share my shocking, personal secret with Bertie soon.

"I didn't want to distress you with all that was going on," I told her. "I thought it best Philip tell you in his own words and own time, because I wasn't certain of his relationship to his father—emotionally, I mean."

"Well!" she declared, sounding a bit more like petulant Margot and not steady-as-she-goes Lilibet. "If you had told me, I could have written him in timely fashion—sent him my condolences. Surely you can grasp his feelings! After all, you just lost your father, and I know it pained you sorely. I thought you had changed your mind about Philip, his suitability or whatever we must call it. I thought he was winning you over."

"My dearest," I had said, taking her wrist and tugging her into the chair next to me where I was eating solo at the breakfast table, "I know he has already won you over. And yes, me too, but I just don't want you to fall for the first man who shows you interest and—"

"It is entirely mutual, Mum!"

I startled. Never had she called me the more formal, mature Mum rather than Mummy.

She scooted to the edge of the chair as if she would flee. "Here I am, starting to assemble my household now," she went on. "At your behest, I have my first lady-in-waiting, one from a list you approved. I have been here and there as Counsellor of State with you. I am taking on more duties for the crown. Surely, I can be permitted to think—and love—for myself!"

"It is just that I cannot bear for you to set your heart on one man when you have given mere passing nods to others. I want you to be very sure, not live with later regrets."

"So," she said, leaning closer and gently tugging her wrist from my hand, "did you make some sort of dreadful mistake? Surely not with Papa. Before Papa? He loved you from the first, he says, and that's the way for me with Philip. I am going now to write him a condolence letter and hope the last, cheery one I posted to him won't make him think I do not care one bit about his father. I know you had the most wonderful, trusting relationship with your parents and I want that too, so please tell me straightaway if you hear anything else about his family or even about him. Even if it is . . . is bad news in this horrid, blasted war!"

Her words echoed in my head even now amidst the silly plot of the play and sporadic laughter. I had let her down. I had tried to make it up to her, even attending two rehearsals for this pantomime, letting her show me the makeshift scenery she and Margot had mostly scared up from storerooms here in the castle.

I forced my mind back to the here and now in this draughty Waterloo chamber, where people laughed and applauded. I did appreciate how the place was decked out with an elaborate set, curtains, and furniture. The orchestra, men in their traditional blue uniforms, sat on the floor level with the stage just above, so it really was reminiscent of the West End theatres. I would tell Lilibet that, tell her how well she did in this and her many endeavors.

Other young people took minor parts, including Lilibet's first appointed lady-in-waiting, Mary Palmer, and yes, I had screened her well. In the pantomime, Lilibet was called Lady Christina Sherwood and Margot the Honorable Lucinda Fairfax.

Margot sneezed more than once at the powder in her curled wig. People had laughed nervously, not certain if that was part of the pantomime or not.

For this first of three performances, things went quite well, despite the silly plot, an amalgam of well-known fairy tales, all jammed together to make a laugh-out-loud, sometimes-slapstick story interspersed with songs and jokes. Margot acquitted herself well with her vocal solo, and both girls danced gracefully—that is, until they pretended to slip or bump into each other, then scramble back in place.

Lilibet ended the performance with the words, "We hope, in these challenging times, you have had your heart lifted a bit tonight. Our lives have been anything but a fairy tale lately, so now back to business, and we hope and pray you will all have a Happy Christmas and—from all of us—a peaceful New Year of 1945."

Yes, I yearned for peace. Even peace with my daughters. For easing my conscience with Bertie. And most of all, as that weak Neville Chamberlain had once claimed, I longed for *peace for our time.* He had been so wrong in what lay beyond the horizon. I prayed I was not wrong too.

More applause startled me, and I joined in. That, at least, reminded me of my proud investiture as a Middle Temple bencher. And a fairy tale—had my life been that but for the initial shocking setbacks of knowing my beloved mother was not truly my mother and then the shame with that damned David, Prince of . . . of deceit.

It annoyed me greatly that I overheard Bertie's private secretary, our friend Alan Lascelles, behind us, tell his wife, "That was a bit long and not very funny, but maybe it's just my mood in this drawn-out war, war, war."

I shot him a narrow-eyed look, which they did not see. How dare he throw a damper on things when we all needed to keep our chins up, no matter what secrets and sadness we held inside, whether it was past pain or current regrets that would not let go.

* * *

It seemed my time for making speeches. I had agreed to broadcast a radio talk in January of the new year, 1945, the year we hoped and prayed that victory would be complete with the taking of Berlin. That had been Winston's fervent prayer, before he traveled here and there, sometimes abroad to meet with Franklin Roosevelt, even Stalin of Russia. But today, I was going to broadcast in French to thank the children of Belgium for toys they had sent to Britain after their liberation by the Allies.

Again my voice quavered as I rehearsed. What if my French mother were listening? Would she be hanging on my spoken words, as I did her written ones hidden beneath my pearl necklace in my jewelry box? I was strangely certain that her hand had written those few words, words of encouragement to and pride in me. Oh, how much I read into that short note, how I skimmed my finger across the paper where her hand must have been. In a way, I had never been hers, and yet I was. What sort of a sad fairy tale was that?

"Blood, thicker than water," I must have said aloud, for Bertie looked up from frowning over the lines on a map showing the Allied advances.

"What's that, my love? I thought you were practicing in French. You must get the girls to listen to you practice, though they are hardly girls anymore, young women for certain."

"The war has made them grow up even faster."

"As the last war did us."

He sighed heavily but smiled at me across his desk. I had just popped in for a moment, but it felt good to be with him, alone, during his busy day. He looked peaked and wan, too thin. An unruly bit of hair fell beguilingly over his furrowed forehead. Once we got through this war, I would feed him Scottish food, drag him up to Glamis, and sleep all night with him again, make him stay in bed late and—

"Winston called," he interrupted my thoughts. "He is planning for the Yalta conference in the Crimea next month, anxious to see FDR as he calls him now—not to his face, I surmise. Winston was so joyous to see the Americans come into the war after Pearl Harbor but he has a fit now when the two of them don't see eye to eye. And then there is Stalin," he added with another sigh.

"But Winston's dealt with Stalin at a conference before."

"If anyone can really 'deal' with him. The man is a necessary evil. I say, just let the bad as well as the good speak their piece, get it all out, so at least there are no secrets. By the way, when Winston comes for lunch with us tomorrow, I shall tell him that. Let the dogmatic, modern czar of Russia speak his peace! Get it out, then deal with it, and go on!"

I nodded. Not today, but after sitting in on that volatile luncheon, I was certain would be the time to tell Bertie about the huge mistake I—and his horrid brother—had made. I vowed silently that I would get it out, then deal with it, and go on.

CHAPTER THIRTY-FOUR

Battle Plans

"Winston," I said after he steamed into the room and bowed through his greetings to us, "please help yourself to the food as usual."

I indicated the sideboard with the cold and covered dishes I knew he liked. I had ordered rather mildly seasoned food, for he'd come back from the February Yalta Conference in the Crimea with worsening stomach problems that were being treated.

I had recognized immediately and nudged Bertie that our P.M. was in some sort of a foul mood. Surely, the fact that the horrible V-2 rockets based in the Netherlands had finally been halted by the Allies taking over their launching sites would put him in a better mood, yet he looked livid. But with Winston, it was always best to let him explain things in his own way and time.

"I thank you for the offer to 'please help yourself,' ma'am, but I'm not sure I can do that anymore, and I don't mean lift a ladle or serving fork. With the turn of things, I'm not even sure I can finally lift us out of war to a complete victory anymore."

Bertie snapped to attention. "Something dreadful has happened? We've lost Monty or Eisenhower or they have lost a battle?"

Winston shook his head. "Monty's so furious that he should be locked up for his own good. But in a way we've lost Eisenhower, because our favorite American general has lost his mind! Lost his mind!"

"Winston," I repeated, indicating the table with a sweep of my arm, "please sit down here with the king, and I will serve all of us today. We will eat in civil fashion, and you can tell us what has happened."

The two men did not sit across from each other as usual but huddled at the corner of the table with their shoulders almost touching, like two boys who had been scolded for bad manners.

"It's the battle for Berlin, isn't it?" Bertie asked Winston as I dished out shepherd's pie on their plates. "Or has Stalin done something again and—"

"Yes, sir. Yes and yes," Winston huffed.

After serving them, I filled my own plate and sat across the table in Bertie's usual chair. Winston's eyes watered. Bertie looked intense, yet so much whiter than Winston's ruddy hue.

Bertie glanced at me, then darted his eyes toward the sideboard and made a gesture with one hand as if he had a glass and were drinking. I went back and poured both of them a whiskey and water. I went heavier on the water than they might have wanted. Some sort of dreadful revelation was coming, and I wanted both of them to be rock steady.

Though it wasn't to my taste, I poured myself a whiskey and water too, then sat again across from them, with my hands gripped in my lap, also ignoring my food.

Winston cleared his throat, downed half of his drink in one gulp, and said, "We have needed Joseph Stalin, but we know we can't trust him. But it's something else. Eisenhower has let me—let us—down. He refuses to push ahead to take Berlin from the west, so the Russians will do that from the east, take prisoners, take the glory, probably take Hitler and try him in some sort of a look-what-we-did show trial when it's been years of our British blood, sweat, and tears that fought and died for this."

I put in, "Those Russian rebels killed Czar Nicholas and his family, and now they have this new communist czar, I don't care what Stalin calls himself."

Winston nodded, picking up his knife as if it were a weapon but still ignoring his food. "Exactly. Quite right, ma'am."

"But why," Bertie said, "will the Americans not push ahead to take B-Berlin after all they've been through, after leading the charge through France, through G-Germany?"

Ignoring Bertie's sudden stuttering, Winston sighed and fumbled in his pocket to produce a cigar when I was expecting a map. Bertie reached for the pack of cigarettes lying on the tablecloth. Sometimes they almost made me wish I smoked, but I had never had that vice at least. Smelly and expensive. I supposed I smoked in a way, breathing in all their puffs of wispy clouds. I took a sip of my whiskey and water and waited for what else Winston would say.

"I admit," he went on, "I can't fault Eisenhower's motives, but he knows full well that war means sacrifice. God knows, we British have paid the price as far as we have come to stop Hitler's tyranny—Mussolini's too, though we haven't dispensed with him permanently either."

"We will," Bertie vowed. "Someday soon, we—the Allies—will."

"As for Hitler," Winston went on, "I've described for you the Nazi-run Jewish prisons or so-called internment camps that have been liberated so far, and no doubt we'll find more. They are indeed death camps, inhumane, unspeakably brutal. You were right to warn us early of what you learned about Jewish oppression when you were in France before the war, ma'am. Hitler's final solution for the Jews is to wipe them out—and wipe us out too, so we need to be certain he is eliminated from the face of this earth!"

Bertie said, "I agree wholeheartedly, the bloody bastard!"

"But to your question, sir," Winston went on with a decisive nod, stabbing at the air with his cigar. "Why has Eisenhower—with FDR's agreement and blessing, of course—halted the surge toward Berlin and why has he left the taking of it and capturing of Hitler to the Russians? I'll tell you why. Because he knows there would be mass American, Canadian, Australian, and British casualties in taking the city—one hundred thousand more, he estimates. Thanks to British and American bombing raids—those big Flying Fortress B-17s—Berlin is a pile of rubble already, but they are dug in deep like rats and may well fight to the death—and so take our brave Allied soldiers and officers with them."

"And," Bertie put in, "the Russians do not value the life of the common man, as we do. Without a second thought, they may mow down thousands for their own glory, their own people or their enemies. I regret that through my great-grandmother Queen Victoria, we have blood ties to them, to their previous czars. My father and Czar Nicholas were cousins but almost looked like twins."

Winston sighed so hard that his big body seemed to deflate. "All that aside, sir, Montgomery is raving mad that Eisenhower will not just plunge on heedless of the human and financial cost. Oh, yes, I see the value of winning without hurting more people if it is possible. But war goes by its own rules, and I longed to—I dreamed of—I needed to take Berlin."

I thought of my brothers Fergus, dead in battle, and Mike, never quite right after the Great War. I would still always call it that, though several years ago, the American magazine called *Time* had declared that we were fighting World War II after surviving World War I. But what if Fergus had not been lost and Mike not damaged in a final push, because someone else was hell-bent on taking one more town? Shouldn't Winston be relieved instead of furious?

Surely Bertie also saw the value in winning without hurting more of our people. True, then we could not say we had seen it through, that we were total victors, that we had eased our guilt and cleared Europe of its evil past without the Russians.

The three of us sat silent at that table for a while over our meals gone cold. The two men were stronger for facing the truth, for accepting that they would not ride into Berlin as heroic victors, that they must face disappointment at the end of this war after all.

And I thought again of my past pain and struggles. I longed to clear my conscience about David with Bertie. He would hate his brother then, the way these two hated their so-called ally Stalin. But would the cost of that—Bertie's being let down by his brother and even by his wife—be too much for him to bear?

* * *

"May I come in, dearest?" Bertie called out as he opened my bedroom door that night and popped his head in.

"Of course, and you do not need to ask," I told him. I was propped up in bed with a book I was not reading.

"Somehow, that is one of the blessings to come out of this damn, bloody war." He came in and closed the door—even clicking the lock behind him. Since I had opened my bed and body to him, we had been even closer. I suppose I had done that partly out of duty, partly out of guilt, especially when he had been so supportive when he learned about my French mother. *It was nothing you did, no blame on you*, he had said, and how I treasured those words.

Yet, to truly clear my conscience—and to show him what a wretched man his beloved brother was—I would be revealing something I did share the blame for. I should never have set my cap for the Prince of Wales, never fallen for him, never have gone back into the party room when everyone else had gone to bed. It pained me to think how well Bertie had taken my desire to have a sexless marriage, not that he didn't have a friend on the side in the beginning. But he did not demand, he did not act the way David did that night when he thought he had the right to shame and hurt me. For certain and forever I had the better deal of the brothers.

"Such a long day, such a long war," he said, sitting on my side of the bed so that it—and I—sagged toward him. He put his arms around me, and I held tight too. We both needed comforting after Winston's visit today, but surely he wasn't in the mood for a bout in bed, only affection. He looked and sounded so tired, almost beaten. He wore a silk robe over his pajamas and had his feet stuck in his favorite worn leather slippers, so homey—so newly normal for us.

"Do you want to talk about what Winston shared today?" I asked.

"What will be will be. We needed the Americans to win the war. The ultimate decision not to go bombing and stomping into Berlin is theirs. So we shall get through this wretched war. We shall rebuild—just as you and I have managed to already. We can even allow David to come home."

I stiffened in his embrace. "For a visit. Not to live?"

"Dearest, so many families are broken, shattered with lost members. I believe the first family of the land, we royals, must set the pattern for reunions, for a return to unity. I know you do not like the duchess, and, God knows, I do not either, but—"

"Bertie, why don't you go round and get in bed? As usual, this lovely Buck House of ours is cold and draughty, and we have to keep you healthy."

"Yes, yes, all right. We shall rebuild this palace and we shall rebuild London and our lives," he declared decisively again as if he were giving a speech. He went to the other side of the bed, kicked off his slippers, pulled off his robe, and got in.

Still shaken from his idea of bringing his brother—and his wife—home, I shoved my book aside, pushed my pillow down and burrowed under the covers to face him.

If I told him about David's attack on me years ago, I would have to admit my foolish pursuit of him when I had played hard-to-get with Bertie. He had not been well lately, did not look well now. But I could not bear it if David and that woman came back here where they would try to horn in, take over, advise us. We might look dowdy and old-fashioned next to their international flair and panache, but hadn't they made a mess of everywhere—even little Nassau—they had gone?

To my surprise, Bertie turned me so my back was to him, then drew me close against him into his arms again, as if I were sitting in his lap.

"You know how I feel about them, especially her," I whispered, deciding to take the soft approach and not rant like a fishwife.

"But you understand about loving a brother. He was my comrade and comfort when early life was hard. You love your brother David and miss him sorely. He'll be coming back to England soon, as he has done his duty there, near FDR, who they say is ailing too."

"Too? Meaning as Winston had been ill? Or are you feeling especially weak again?"

"Are my arms around you weak?"

"You know what I mean. You have lost weight and color. Your legs bother you, and your cough—"

"I will see this all through," he said, nuzzling the nape of my neck. "With your help and support—and our Lilibet's strength and maturity—I will see this all through."

I decided then that I would fight the battle over David and his wife another day. This moment was precious, important. I must build Bertie up, not tear him down.

And then I realized he had instantly fallen asleep.

But I vowed that somehow, some way, I would keep the Windsors from coming back and trying to take over, making Bertie less important, less attractive to his people, for I knew that would happen. And I must admit that almost the last thing on earth I would like to do is vie with that skinny, smart-mouthed woman for fashion and popularity. Never. I had waged a silent war against her for years and I would not let up now. Like the strong but caring American general from Kansas, I would pick my battles and somehow win my secret war.

CHAPTER THIRTY-FIVE

Spring Passing

Spring seems more beautiful this year," Bertie said as we walked the sunny gardens behind the palace. I had my arm through his, tight against his ribs. We had made love last night. Perhaps the winter of war was gone and lovely days like this were really here to stay. "It always passes too fast, you know," he added.

"The gardeners have begun to repair things beautifully," I said. "You can't keep flowers down here, even after bombs hit."

"Can't keep Britain and the Empire down," he said with a little smile. "Or the king and queen. We shall—we have—almost—come through. And though Winston and I were upset that Eisenhower did not push on toward Berlin ahead of the Russians, I still like the man's style. Ike Eisenhower is such an honest man to be bold enough to tell us straightaway that he must let us down on that, yet he loves deception and deviousness in battle."

"Mmm. All is fair in love and war?"

He turned quickly to look at me. "At least with us, they are never one and the same."

I nodded and smiled, but I knew my lips quivered.

"Do you know, my love," he went on, in expansive lecture mode now, "Eisenhower went so far as to have phony maps and attack site orders planted on a dead body he knew the Germans would find? He sent someone disguised as Monty into an area where we were *not* going to attack and ordered bombing at some sites where we had no intention of going in.

"So see," he said with a chuckle, "there can be good to come out of deception and lies."

I dearly hoped so. I was still at sixes and sevens about when and even whether to tell him about his brother's attack on me. He would then hate David, maybe blame him for my squeamishness over the years in our love life, for my wanting our children to be created through artificial insemination. I feared it would infuriate dear Bertie, maybe crush him. But would it turn him against me too? So I hesitated, but I must risk all since David was still lobbying to come back to live in England, to simply buy a country estate, he had written Bertie, to help in any way he could. And, of course, Queen Mary was pushing for all that. She missed the son, her firstborn, who I knew was her favorite, especially now that George was gone.

As we made a turn and headed back toward the palace, I said, "Won't it be wonderful to begin to have lovely garden parties out here? Lilibet is angling for one when Philip comes home—comes back from duty, I mean."

"You've settled things with her about their courtship? I know you were dead set against him at first."

"I am still dead set against his adopted father, Dickie Mount-batten, pulling Philip's strings and then Philip trying to control Lilibet. Now that Philip's father is dead, it seems he heeds Mountbatten above all others. Bertie, I heard scuttlebutt the other day that Dickie even boasted that through Philip, the Mountbatten dynasty would mount the throne someday, that the name of Windsor would not be used for future heirs if Lilibet wed Philip!"

"Damn bloody treason!" he whispered. He nearly crushed my arm against his ribs and ground out his half-smoked cigarette on the path with a fierce twist of his foot. "You'd think," he went on, propelling me along a bit faster back toward the palace, "Mountbatten would not keep landing on his feet after his various military follies. He tries something like that with Philip, he'll land on his bum—in exile. He can just trade places with David!"

"Now you sound like the one who doesn't want our eldest and heir to choose Philip."

"No stopping that—Lilibet's decision, I mean. At least she has a backbone of steel, because someday, she is going to need it. But I believe, as over the moon as she is about Philip, she has courage too. She's proved herself in this war, my love. But I am glad you told me what you heard about Mountbatten and his damned designs on our girl and our good name."

Bertie's usual pallor had gone red. I had not seen such a fierce reaction from him over something not war-related for years, but Lilibet and the family were not only dear but sacrosanct to him, as was the royal line. Again, I realized I would be risking much to tell him about his brother and me, but I could not have him and his duchess in this country! How I had prayed there was another way to stop that.

As we headed back, the mid-April sun seemed not so warm. Looking ahead, I saw Alan Lascelles rushing toward us, nearly at a run.

"Good news or bad?" I asked Bertie.

"Your Majesty," Alan said when he reached us, looking at me, not the king. He made a hasty bow and out of breath told me, "Ma'am, Your brother David Bowes Lyon is calling from Washington and insists on my holding the line open until you can come to speak with him. He has some important news for you and will not say what, only that he will tell you and you can tell the king."

Bertie was quickly out of breath as we went back toward the palace at quite a jog. He went with me into his office where the priority call with its private connection had been taken by Alan at Bertie's desk.

Out of breath myself, I picked up the phone. "David dear, are you calling to say you are coming home?" I asked as Bertie sat in his desk chair and Alan left us alone, closing the door behind him.

"Yes, I will be now. You will hear all this from the prime minister soon, I'm sure, as he's been notified. I thought it best I tell you and for you to pass it on to the king. Elizabeth, FDR has suffered a cerebral hemorrhage at his Warm Springs, Georgia, retreat."

"And Eleanor is with him or has gone to him?"

"Ah—he's coming to her—here in Washington."

I realized now that David was terribly distressed. Bertie was leaning forward, trying to hear. Had David been crying?

He went on, "He was with his . . . his mistress when he simply blacked out, but that's been hushed up, of course, though Eleanor knows. Things are all topsy-turvy here, for Eleanor has a special lady friend, and, God knows, I understand that, but—"

He was crying. I knew he admired Roosevelt and would now have to deal with his vice president until the president recovered, if he did. And whatever was the name of their vice president?

"What?" Bertie asked, reaching out to grip my arm. "Roosevelt's pulling out of the war early?"

"He's very ill," I told him, then turned back to the phone receiver. "David, what—?" I demanded even as our connection began to fade a bit.

"I admired him so," he choked out. "We needed him to finish the war, reparations, loans . . . Elizabeth, please break the news to the king before Churchill does, so he won't fall apart like I have. President Roosevelt is dead!"

* * *

The king urged Winston that we not fly to America for the president's funeral but instead have a memorial service for him here. Franklin Roosevelt, at age sixty-three, had died on 12 April, and we planned the service for 17 April in St. Paul's Cathedral. Though that great building had been damaged, it still stood strong.

European royalty representing the Netherlands, even Yugo-slavia, as well as other countries attended. Of course, there was a large American diplomatic contingent, here to help orches-trate the war, some in uniform, some in dark suits. Meanwhile, a memorial mass was also being held in Notre Dame Cathedral in liberated Paris. Of course, Winston had already paid tribute to his friend and fellow soldier in the war during a speech be-fore the House of Commons.

And the greatest honor of all, I thought, as Bertie, Lilibet, and I emerged from our motorcar to enter St. Paul's, the streets were awash with Londoners, standing silently in mourning. I wore black, the king his Navy uniform, and Lilibet her Aux-iliary Territorial Service skirt and jacket. And so many in the crowd wore black or grey.

The prime minister greeted us at the top of the steps. He scanned the huge crowd below and took off his top hat, blink-ing back tears before we went in. I said a grateful prayer that the war must surely be coming to an end. Winston would now have to work with the new president, a man named Harry Tru-man whom we had met briefly, and I had even forgotten his name at first in my shock and grief.

The long nave of St. Paul's was filled with black-clad mourn-ers, most there by invitation, others having queued up for hours. So solemn, so sad.

During the service, the elaborately robed archbishop asked for prayers for the new president and spoke of Roosevelt's long struggle with infantile paralysis, for which he was being treated at Warm Springs when he died so suddenly.

The band played "The Star-Spangled Banner." Winston's

shoulders shook as he cried through that, wiping his face and nose with his handkerchief. Ah, he had not learned to be a royal, to hold back one's emotions, but he was royalty to me.

The archbishop's voice droned on. I noted Lilibet—Princess Elizabeth I must call her today—sat ramrod straight, her expression set but impassive. A monarch's stance and look, I thought before my memory flew back to the days before the war when we had first met the Roosevelts. The ticker-tape parade in the New York City heat with the skyscrapers towering over us as the columns and walls of St. Paul's did now. The visit in the cooler weather to their private home at Hyde Park. Eating with plates on our laps—hot dogs, of all things—and chatting with Franklin's elderly mother, Sara.

She has been a real mother to me all these years, and I love her dearly, Franklin had said in his informal remarks that day. Yes, I shared that with him, that both of my mothers were real mothers to me all these years.

And Eleanor, capable, take-charge Eleanor with her own agenda. With her own person to love, David had said, a woman—and David would pick up on that. Did Eleanor care about Franklin's mistress of long years or had she simply moved on? Should I just move on from the only way I could see to keep the Duke of Windsor and his mistress-wife away, live with that and not tell Bertie, even if his horrid brother returned? No, I could not abide that, nor, I believed, could our king and country survive it.

I jolted back to reality as we stood to sing a hymn, a favorite funeral song for us royals, and Franklin was American royalty. The organ seemed to shake the very stone walls and floor as we sang, *I am weak, but Thou art mighty. . . . Bid my anxious fear subside. . . .*

When it was over, and we went back outside, I nodded to the crowds but did not smile or wave. Sitting in the middle, I held to Bertie's arm as we drove away. Lilibet waved out her window, her face solemn. I was so proud of her. And nervous too, for her dear Philip was coming home for a visit soon. Ah, to be so excited to see someone . . . I had been that way once years ago, so foolish. But I recalled how happy I was when Bertie came home from France safe and sound this last time. Surely, that was a real and lasting love.

CHAPTER THIRTY-SIX

Victories

$\mathcal{I}$ could tell Winston had been crying, but evidently—with the news he had to tell us that last day in April—with relief.

"The war is as good as over, for our enemies are gone!" he told us the moment he came in the door to the private room where we met for lunch.

"Mussolini and Hitler?" Bertie asked as I clasped my hands and pressed them to my breasts in anticipation.

"Mussolini's death has been confirmed. When he tried to flee Milan where he's been holed up, he was captured in a small village and shot to death—with his mistress. But worse, their bodies were displayed in a public square, hung upside down, and abused, to say the least. Your Majesty," he added, turning to me, "I shall not go into more detail in front of you, but you both have been my bulwark of strength, and I wanted you to know about him first."

"First before Hitler?" I asked when I saw Bertie was so happy he could hardly speak. "Did the Russians find him? He might have dubbed me 'the most dangerous woman in Europe,' but I call him 'the most deadly dangerous and ungodly man'!"

Despite my relief and bravado, my emotions had been pent up today, and not only because I was anxious to learn the fate of our enemies. I believed David, Duke of Windsor, was also a dangerous and ungodly man. Bertie had decided he would invite the Duke and Duchess of Windsor to come home when hostilities were ended. Was I dangerous to my marriage if I told him what I had bottled up inside me for so long? A danger to my family? But I had to risk all to keep that damned David from returning and undermining Bertie.

We still stood at the door, though Winston finally reached back to close it behind him. "It seems our enemies all had their mistresses, not true wives, like you have been a help and strength to the king these long years, ma'am. As for Adolf Hitler, he committed suicide in his bunker with his—well, I believe he finally did marry her—Eva Braun. The Russians were denied their final prize for a show trial. Evidently Hitler ordered his body to be burned when he heard what the Italians had done to their Il Duce. *Sic semper tyrannis!*"

"Yes," Bertie said. "Thus always to tyrants."

"And thus," I put in, "never take on the British Empire and the Americans!"

Bertie and I heaved huge sighs of relief, though Winston still seemed a bit subdued, even gloomy, as we sat down at our usual places at the table.

"Even if it is noon," I said, "let's have a toast. The end is in sight and happier days are here again, as the song says."

"There is something else," Winston said. "If we could just

get to that too—before our well-deserved celebrations. As I explain this, let's remember the big picture here, finally, as poor Neville Chamberlain read so wrong, that we will now have peace in our time."

"Whatever is it?" Bertie asked, leaning forward with his elbows on the table. "What is left undone? I realized we cannot declare total victory to the public yet."

Winston, his expression still so serious, said, "We must remember that sacrifices have been made and are yet to be made as we rebuild our cities, our country, and our lives. Sir, I have it on the best authority that the former king, your brother, and his wife do not have the best of intentions for their long-range plans once they return to England."

"David?" Bertie said, seeming to bristle. "He has assured me he wants to be a country squire, quite retired from affairs of state unless I ask him for advice or a particular service."

"And I assured you," I could not help but put in as my heart started to pound, "that is not the life for him, and he knows it. It hasn't been ever and won't remain so."

Bertie actually glared at me. My insides flip-flopped.

"Hear me out, please, sir," Winston said.

My hands were shaking, but I saw that his were too. He knew well the bond between the two royal brothers, stretched thin now but never broken.

Bertie nodded and lit a cigarette. For once, Winston did not reach for his cigar.

"The former king of England, Edward VIII, now Duke of Windsor, is not only keen to return here after the war, but to become a close advisor to you. You see, someone I greatly trust has come across correspondence with a friend of the duke's in which he admits that he hopes to become a 'caretaker king' should anything happen to Your Majesty. The war has taken its toll on you and the princess Elizabeth is young, he says, and he would be best to counsel her should she come to the throne. And, at one spot in this rather lengthy correspondence, the former king intimates he would even consider pushing the young Elizabeth aside so that a man could rule in these trying times."

Bertie's eyes were huge. I was so frightened and furious that for once I could not speak.

But Winston could. Winston always could.

"It smacks of family concern, I suppose, sir, but it also smacks of more than tampering with the kingdom and the Empire. It smacks of treason, and I have not a doubt the Duchess of Windsor is complicit and perhaps controlling on this. That is her character, I believe we all know."

My pulse pounded even harder. I wanted to say "Here, here!" but I sat stock-still and silent.

"She—that she-wolf," Bertie choked out, then paused. "She p-put him up t-to this."

"I know you have, at least informally, invited him back, sir, but I believe we have just spoken about two vultures circling above your head and that of your rightful heir."

I found my voice. "Is the person he is corresponding with Dickie Mountbatten?"

"It is not, ma'am. I guessed that too at first, but it is a friend of his whose name I did not know, and we are just plain lucky to have come upon that correspondence."

Turning to my husband and laying a hand on his arm, I said, "I'm sorry, Bertie, but he always was indiscreet at best. But this—"

Bertie interrupted and exploded, "The princess Elizabeth's dear uncle David shall not advise her from there, from here, or from exile, which is where he should remain! I shall tell him that I have been advised to rescind my offer. I shall have to deal with my mother, of course—"

"I will help you," I said, thinking this was going to be a double victory day indeed. Without my having to risk any sort of rift, David's treachery—his treason—had finally done him in with Bertie, I could tell. It was one thing to hope my telling him of David's treatment of me years ago would alienate them, but to have even the merest hint of danger to our beloved daughter had settled the matter.

"Thank you, Winston, for delivering that difficult news," I said.

Bertie reached to squeeze my hands gripped together on the table. "It is as if," he told Winston and me, looking dazed now again, blinking back tears, "David believes he would be more than a caretaker monarch. He must not trust us or wish me well to hope I would not be on the throne after he insinuates himself with our next monarch. And if that is true, as you intimate, Winston, he must not really want Elizabeth to rule at all."

"After all, sir, people tried to horn in with undue influence on young Queen Victoria. Excuse me, ma'am, but even her own mother did not have her best interests at heart."

I simply nodded, and Bertie gave out a huge sniff. We were both so stunned that it was still sinking in.

"Your Majesties, I believe you will understand today that I must not linger with you as I so often have during these precious times we have shared food, information, and thoughts." He rose slowly, amazingly looking for the first time like an old man. "There is much to do. Sir, I would advise telling your brother through a liaison—perhaps through Her Majesty's brother David—that you have reconsidered the invitation he should come back and feel it best if he stay away and enjoy his friends in Paris, New York, and Palm Beach. Best perhaps not to deal with him directly, at least for a time."

"Yes," Bertie said. "Yes. And thank you for the g-good news about our enemies—all of them."

I walked Winston out into the hall and down the corridor a ways.

"You did not trust the Windsors either, ma'am. Am I reading that right?" he asked, looking like an innocent cherub, but how much did he really know?

"Why do I think you know the answer to that already, Winston?"

"There are some things I do not know. Reading old dossiers is one way to stay informed, but some things are best not put in writing, and your brother-in-law should ponder that in his coming years of exile, in his continued party-boy days with his very ambitious wife."

"I never say her name," I blurted, as if this were confession time all round.

As his aide, who apparently was surprised to see him emerge so soon, came hurrying down the corridor, Winston whispered, "I don't know what I, the king, or this country would have done without you, ma'am. Victory in every quarter. And, Your Majesty, please remember I owe you a great debt. We all do, and I am ever your liege man."

He bowed, backed up a few steps, and turned away. I was deeply touched. Now I would never have to tell Bertie what David had done to me, for the mere hint of his hoping for Bertie's demise and his plans to control Lilibet or set her aside had damned him as surely as if he were Hitler or Mussolini.

I rushed back in to comfort Bertie. He cried in my arms, even on this international, if as yet informal, day of victory.

Epilogue

Seeing It Through

Victory in Europe Day was declared on 8 May, though the day before the formal announcement had simply read, *The mission of the Allied forces was fulfilled May 7, 1945.* Bertie was planning an address to Parliament next week, but today was just for rejoicing.

"Mummy, can we both go out into the crowd?" Margot pleaded for the fourth time. "We will wear hats. They won't even know it's us. Everyone is just screaming and dancing with joy!"

Finally, I gave in. "If you take some security with you."

"Well," Margot went on, "no one will be angry today, except they might kiss us! Everyone is simply kissing everyone! I won't mind, but if it isn't Philip's sweet lips, then Lilibet will—"

"Stop your teasing," her older sister ordered. "He isn't back yet, Mummy said we can go, so let's go!"

"Be back in an hour!" I called after them. "Papa says if they keep shouting, 'We want the king!' we must all go out, at least when the prime minister gets here through that press of people."

Out they went by a side door, and I could not spot them in the cavorting crowd. Everyone was waving and jumping about. Dancing, shouting, singing. It seemed all of London had pushed toward the gates of the palace, expecting us to make a victory appearance. I had dressed for that, plumed hat and all, but still Winston hadn't made it here yet and now the girls were gone.

Bertie, nattily attired in his Navy admiral's uniform awash with medals and gold buttons, joined me at the window. "I hear Trafalgar Square is packed, but they all seem to be heading this way," he told me. "We must go out. Winston has already made a victory statement from loudspeakers he ordered set up near Parliament Square. He phoned to say that, when he was done speaking, the crowd sang 'God Save the King.'"

"God *has* saved the king," I told him, putting my arm round his waist as we stood there looking down at the packed Mall. I did not say the rest of what I was thinking—that his brother's not returning to England was the ultimate godsend.

And God has saved the queen, I told myself. Saved me from having to deal with that treacherous Duke and Duchess of Windsor. Saved me from having to risk hurting myself as well as the duke by having to tell Bertie what had happened so terribly long ago. Besides, my dear brother David was home safely. Lilibet was elated that Philip would be back soon, and then we would see about that—and find a way to keep Dickie Mountbatten at bay.

It was only Bertie's health that worried me, but Winston had been ailing too, and somehow, I would manage to bolster both.

When he finally arrived and the girls returned, so excited, Winston was actually hesitant about stepping out onto the crimson-and-gold-swagged palace balcony with us, but we convinced him and put him in the very middle of the four of us. Lilibet and Bertie looked splendid in their uniforms. Margot and I wore light-hued spring suits. We could not have stayed inside if we had wanted to, for the deafening crowd cries of "We want the king! We want the queen!" had not ceased. Yet it was music to our ears, ears that would not have to hear the roar of bombers nor the screech of deadly rockets anymore.

Winston smiled, and the four of us waved our upright, stiff-armed gestures to our beloved countrymen and -women. The oversized Union Jack shifted in the breeze and then lifted to flap like cannon. Still, we smiled and waved.

Waved, just as I had that day in the New York City ticker-tape parade. As we had waved to bombed-out East Enders, trying to lift their spirits. As, I prayed, we would wave to our workers in the future as we rebuilt London, England, and Europe together.

I glanced sideways. Winston beamed with pride and nodded but did not wave. Bertie looked serious and exhausted yet elated. Lilibet smiled with excitement and expectation in her eyes, and Margot grinned at the roar of cheers and shouts.

After waving, waving, we stepped back inside together. Whatever the future held, we—I—would see it through.

About the author

About the book

Insights,
Interviews
& More . . .

Meet Karen Harper

Jeffrey A. Rycus

New York Times and *USA Today* bestselling author KAREN HARPER is a former Ohio State University instructor and high school English teacher. Published since 1982, she writes contemporary suspense and historical novels about real British women. Two of her recent Tudor-era books were bestsellers in the United Kingdom and in Russia. Harper won the Mary Higgins Clark Award for *Dark Angel*, and her novel *Shattered Secrets* was judged one of the best books of the year by *Suspense Magazine*. ∾

Behind the Book

Writing this novel was especially exciting for me because I had actually seen in person several of the important characters. From a historical novel, no less! Hm, am I getting older?

In 1986, on one of my husband's and my numerous trips to England, we came upon Elizabeth, the Queen Mother, posing for photos on the steps of St. Paul's Cathedral. We couldn't speak to her, of course, but stayed in the small, admiring crowd. It was before I had a smartphone with a camera and I was so gobsmacked (as the Brits like to say) that I just stared. Then, with a wave and a smile, up she went into the cathedral. Since she was born in 1900, she was either eighty-five or -six then and looked great.

However, I have actually met former general and president Dwight Eisenhower at Ohio University in Athens, Ohio, where I did my undergrad work. He came to speak at a convocation, and I was one of the student ushers. I had a moment where he spoke to me, but all I can remember from that very brief conversation was that his eyes were an intense light blue, and that he said I reminded him of his granddaughter. ▶

Behind the Book *(continued)*

I assumed later he meant Susan Eisenhower. Since my father had been a B-17 pilot, dropping bombs on Germany, he was even more impressed that I had met Eisenhower than I was at the time. (Can you find the brief mention of how the big Flying Fortress B-17 bombers helped defeat Germany? I had to work that into the story somewhere.)

I admit to being a rabid Anglophile. Or, in my case with all the novels I've written about real British women of importance, a better term might be Angloholic or Anglomaniac. On our trips to the UK, we have seen in person Queen Elizabeth and Prince Philip (obviously two other characters in this story), and Prince Charles, and we joined in a walkabout with Princess Anne at Leeds Castle in Kent when we just happened to be there on the same day she was promoting her Save the Children charity. I have yet to "run into" the younger generation of royals.

When I began to research the woman I knew as "the Queen Mum," I found that she was more than the smiling matriarch and granny who doted on Prince Charles and remained very close to her daughter Elizabeth, though

Princess Margaret's antics drove her to distraction. If you'd like a look at how the younger daughter turned out, one recent nonfiction book is *Ma'am Darling: 99 Glimpses of Princess Margaret* by Craig Brown (HarperCollins, London, 2017), which has recently been released in the States.

I used two books as my primary references in writing about the life of George VI's consort, Elizabeth Bowes Lyon. One was William Shawcross's *The Queen Mother: The Official Biography* (Vintage Books, New York, 2009). This is a huge volume. Since it is a book the queen approved, of course what is there and what isn't needs to be taken with a grain of salt. I think very few of us would give the nod to an "official biography" that is a tell-all.

Although one of the other books I consulted was what I would call a tell-all, its author did move in the same social circles as the royals. This is Lady Colin Campbell's *The Queen Mother: The Untold Story of Elizabeth Bowes Lyon, Who Became Queen Elizabeth the Queen Mother* (St. Martin's Press, New York, 2012).

I also consulted various books on King George, Winston Churchill, and ▶

Dwight Eisenhower. *Churchill and the King* by Kenneth Weisbrode (Viking, New York, 2013) was excellent. Churchill is a key character in my recent novel *American Duchess,* so I had previously read a great deal about him. We have visited numerous Churchillian sites in England including his underground war room, his birthplace, and his grave. Other references and personal visits gave me background for places like Buckingham Palace, which I have toured, and numerous other British and Scottish sites.

I also researched the dark days of the Blitz in London in such books as *London Was Ours: Diaries and Memoirs of the London Blitz* by Amy Helen Bell (I.B. Tauris, London, 2008) and *The Longest Night: The Bombing of London on May 10, 1941* by Gavin Mortimer (Berkley Calibre, New York, 2005).

There are numerous videos on YouTube and other sites where the royal Windsors of this era come to life, including the king's and queen's speeches to their nation in wartime. Googling Elizabeth's 1939 wartime speech to women of the Empire (eight minutes long) lets you hear her voice. Speeches by the king and Churchill can be Googled as can so much about the war.

A couple of random facts I found interesting: In 2011, with the help of Prince Charles, the body of the queen's lost brother Fergus was located in a mass grave in a quarry from the days of WWI. A memorial stone was placed there, though the queen never knew it, since she died on March 30, 2002, at the age of a hundred and one. "Lilibet" was at her bedside when she died. Sadly, Princess Margaret had died only the month before, on February 9, 2002, at age seventy-one. Of course, "Bertie" had died in 1952 at age fifty-six, so the Queen Mum lived many years beyond him, making new friends and a new/old life for herself.

Those closest to King Edward VIII, later Duke of Windsor, saw the man for the self-centered, shallow, callous person he was. Alan Lascelles once confided to Prime Minster Stanley Baldwin that he thought it best for the country if Edward would fall off his horse and break his neck. "God forgive me," said Baldwin, "so do I." During the war, the Duke of Windsor was heard to say that a heavy bombardment of England would make it ready for peace with Hitler.

The damning evidence about his hoping to return to England after the ▶

war and play an important part as "caretaker king" or advisor to Elizabeth has been recently revealed in royal biographer Christopher Wilson's articles in London newspapers. Wilson names Kenneth de Courcy as the duke's confidant who revealed the Windsors' letters and scheme.

The duke did return briefly to London in 1952 for Bertie's funeral. Elizabeth blamed him for helping to bring on her husband's early death and barely looked his way. The duke returned for two other royal funerals, but was never received by Bertie's widow. However, his niece Elizabeth ordered a royal funeral in England when he died, and he and his wife are buried in the royal grounds at Frogmore, Windsor.

I must admit, though I have always seen David/King Edward VIII/the Duke of Windsor as a bit of a villain, I do recognize that he, like Bertie, and their brother George, Duke of Kent, had a difficult upbringing. I have studied that in great detail and presented it as part of the plot in my earlier historical novel *The Royal Nanny.* So I could not resist having that nanny, Charlotte Bill (Lala), in her retirement in a scene in this novel.

There is an unusual paranormal point of interest, besides the monster of

Glamis. There have been reports of strange scratching sounds in the area of Buckingham Palace near where P.C. Stephen Robertson was buried under rubble and died during the bombing of the grounds. One report of a ghostly figure of a policeman in a wartime uniform has been seen, but it "dissolved before the onlooker" (from *The Queen's House* by Edna Healey).

By the way, if you saw the excellent movie *The Darkest Hour* about Churchill, it had one flaw. It left out that Queen Elizabeth was present at the P.M. and king's weekly meetings, and, if the king was absent, the P.M. met with the queen. She helped Bertie to make important decisions and often bolstered him, something perhaps not a popular fact with the men who then ran and recorded wartime history in the kingdom.

Prince Charles was very close to his grandmother. There is a YouTube video dated July 21, 2015, that you can see by Googling "Prince Charles speaks about the death of his grandmother." He loved her dearly, and she had a huge effect on him. Here are a few of the thoughts with which he eulogized her: "She meant everything to me." She was fun, full of laughter and affection. She wrote ▶

Behind the Book *(continued)*

wonderful letters full of wisdom from her experiences. She was a magical grandmother.

And, I add to that, she was a strong queen too, when that was sorely needed. The facts of history are important— to know what happened, even how it happened. But I love historical fiction because it gets inside history and the lives of those for whom it was the day-to-day present. Historical fiction not only lets the reader know what happened to people, but gives a glimpse into how they thought and felt.

Karen Harper
February 2019

Reading Group Guide

1. The Queen Elizabeth of this novel
   is not just the smiling, waving figure
   many of us recall. When she was
   Duchess of York and then queen
   during WWII, what were her good
   and bad characteristics?

2. The "surrogate" mother solution
   was not unknown among British
   aristocrats who were childless
   or needed "heirs and spares,"
   although it would have been
   nearly impossible for royals to
   pull that off. (There was a huge
   scandal in 1688 when Queen Mary
   of Modena was accused of sneaking
   a baby into her birthing room in a
   warming pan.) But how would you
   feel if you received such news that
   your "mother" was not your birth
   mother? Is it understandable that
   Elizabeth would hide the news?
   Be haunted by it? Why did she
   finally tell Bertie about that but
   not tell him her secret about David?

3. Does Elizabeth's hatred of Wallis Simpson stem only from the fact that Wallis was a rival whom David preferred? Was it because Elizabeth caught Wallis making fun of the "dowdy duchess"? Or was it more?

4. Why do you think Bertie fell so hard for Elizabeth Bowes Lyon? It is most unusual and almost scandalous for a member of the royal family to have a proposal of marriage rebuffed not once, but twice. Why did he persist, and why did she finally accept?

5. Is the queen good at assessing the loyalty and character of other people such as Winston? Brendan Bracken? David, Prince of Wales and later king?

6. It is unusual for me to write a main female royal protagonist who is overweight, drinks, and keeps huge secrets. Do you see her as sympathetic or do these traits weaken her in your eyes?

7. How are the personalities of the two princesses different? And, as far as you can tell, why? Do you recall Princess Margaret in her heyday?

If so, does this childhood portrait of her ring true? Have you seen such differences in sisters close in age?

8. Since there are so many historical characters in this novel, it could have been written without the minor fictional characters of Bessie Miller and Rowena Fitzgerald. But how do they contribute to this portrait of the queen and London at war?

9. On top of the war and her other problems, the queen has a "mother-in-law" challenge. Does she handle this well? Is she especially burdened by her mother-in-law being a former queen? How have you or others you know dealt with a mother-in-law situation?

10. During the war and the necessary American "invasion of England," what were some of the differences between the Americans and the Brits? Would that still be true today?

11. The king and queen were very wary of Winston Churchill in the beginning of the story. How and why do their attitudes change? Have you had such a relationship that went up or down over time? ▶

About the book

12. Does Bertie and Elizabeth's visit to his former nanny throw light on the characters of Bertie and David? I was amazed when I wrote *The Royal Nanny* about Charlotte Bill's life that the children's early years so impacted their adulthoods. Have you found this to be true in your life or the lives of others? ∿

Discover great authors, exclusive offers, and more at hc.com.